P9-DBP-682

Hilary Norman is the author of eleven internationally bestselling novels written under her own name and translated into seventeen languages, including *The Pact* and *Susanna,* and of *If I Should Die,* a thriller published under the pseudonym Alexandra Henry. Her previous novels, *Too Close, Mind Games* and *Blind Fear* are also published by Piatkus.

Deadly Games

Hilary Norman

PIATKUS

❃ Visit the Piatkus website! ❃

Piatkus publishes a wide range of exciting fiction and non-fictio
including books on health, mind body & spirit, sex, self-help,
cookery, biography and the paranormal. If you want to:

- read descriptions of our popular titles
- buy our books over the internet
- take advantage of our special offers
- enter our monthly competition
- learn more about your favourite Piatkus authors

visit our website at:
www.piatkus.co.uk

Note: This is a work of fiction.
Any resemblance to actual events, locales organisations, or persons,
living or dead is entirely coincidental and beyond the intent of either the
author or the publisher.

Copyright © 2001 by Hilary Norman

First published in Great Britain in 2001 by
Judy Piatkus (Publishers) Ltd of
5 Windmill Street, London W1T 2JA
email: Info@piatkus.co.uk

This edition published in 2001.

The moral right of the author has been asserted

A catalogue record for this book is available from the British Library

ISBN 0 7499 3265 1

Set in Times by
Phoenix Photosetting, Chatham, Kent

Ptinted and bound in Great Britain by
Mackays of Chatham Ltd, Chatham, Kent

For Jonathan,
with love

Grateful thanks to: Officer Sherman Ackerson; Howard Barmad; Jennifer Bloch; Christina Carroll of Naturally Books and Coffee in Chester, Connecticut; Rachel Connolly; Sara Fisher; Gillian Green; Clara Harmon, Sandy Abbagnaro and Dr Mario T. Gaboury, all of University of New Haven; Herta Norman; Hans Persson and his Adventureland website; Judy Piatkus; Helen Rose; Dr Jonathan Tarlow.

ONE

Chapter 1

He had heard it said that killing got easier the more one did it.

Not true.

Killing was hard. It was ugly and painful.

He had, to date, ended the lives of five people, and each time, while he was *doing* it, while he was actually snuffing out their last breath, he had screamed out in pain. And then, when it was done with, he had got sick to his stomach.

He had been so afraid of the act before the first time, that only his absolute conviction that it *had* to be done had helped him endure it. He knew he wasn't a born killer, could never be a *real* murderer. He did it – had done it each time – because he had no choice. Because he could not allow those people to go on living. Because it was either them or him, and he was not ready to die, not by a long chalk.

Fact was, he liked life most of the time these days, liked it more than he'd ever thought possible when he was younger.

Except for the killing.

Chapter 2

My name is Jake Woods and I'm a teacher.

Sounds like one of those first stand-up confessions at an AA meeting. Maybe that's because, to some, my decision to go back to school seemed like such a cop-out – literally, since that's what I used to be: a cop. Actually, I was only a cop en route to becoming what I *thought* I wanted to be at the time: a general investigator in the State Attorney's office. Before I changed my mind.

I'd gone the whole nine yards, slaved my way through five years at John Jay College, got myself a law enforcement internship with the NYPD and finally found the job I'd been striving for up in Albany. And then one morning I looked at myself in the mirror and faced up to what I'd known for a while. I did not, after all, want to spend my life investigating public corruption or narcotics or organized crime or white collar criminals. Fact is, I may be big on justice, but I don't enjoy prying. I am, by nature, a private man, who likes, where possible, to respect the privacy of others. Of course I still accepted that the investigating needed to be done, but I didn't want to be the one doing it. What I *did* want to do, I suddenly realized, was help train those more suited to do the job as well as possible.

No one gave me a harder time about the decision than I gave myself. I felt I was a flake, felt I was letting people down, had wasted their time and energy.

Simone told me I was wrong to feel that way.

My wife.

4

She helped me to understand what I guess I already knew, deep down. That the time of my life I had loved most had been my school and college days. That while I had the utmost respect for most of my law enforcement colleagues, the men and women I had felt most at home with, had most in *common* with, had been my teachers. As a student, I'd thrived on what the best of my professors had given me, and so *that*, Simone said, was what I now had to aim for, even if others saw it as failure.

'You'll only fail if you don't have the guts to turn around.'

She also told me that she'd always had a thing for professors.

I told her that's what finally clinched it for me.

We both knew it was only half a lie.

So I resigned from the Attorney General's office, went back to school, back to hunched shoulders and sore eyes and a neck that yelled out for Simone's soothing fingers, and about five hundred back-rubs later I became a criminal justice professor at the University of New Haven in Connecticut. The '*other* place', some call it, because Yale also happens to be located in Greater New Haven. And sure, it's no more possible for me than anyone else to overlook the beauty of that great campus, or to fail to relish the minds that enter and emerge from it, and frankly it's a pleasure to live so close to the Gothic façades and the buzz, but so far as I'm concerned there's a greater – albeit humbler – *reality* about 'our place', and I'm proud to be a faculty member.

I hope I make a reasonably good professor.

I *know* that I became a completely happy man when I began teaching.

And Simone was proud of me.

That was the icing on the cake.

At least, it used to be.

Chapter 3

He had to go.

Had to.

The very thought of taking care of that made him shudder, but there was no avoiding it.

He'd thought he was so right when he took him, thought that finally he'd found *the* one. Young, gorgeous, healthy, athletic, pulsing with vitality and hormones, ready for just about anything.

It was his own fault, he knew that. He ought to have known better than to pick a runner. Runners needed space, went nuts without it. Kept here any longer, this young man would lose it altogether, get sick in mind and body.

At least this way he'd be spared that.

He'd thought and rethought his method, agonized long and hard about the kindest, swiftest way. The bullet won every time. On death rows they seemed to feel lethal injections were the most humane way to go, but compared to *what*? Getting strapped down and fried?

He could, of course, use *Dim Mak* – death touch – lethal and swift if he got it right; and he was gifted enough, sufficiently highly trained, but the young man might fight back, might struggle, and then it would all get so *ugly*, and he didn't want that. That was the *last* thing he wanted.

He'd drugged the kid's food before now, put him out when he needed to, but with his appetite so erratic there was no

6

certainty he'd get enough sedative into his system to finish him, and anyway, he wasn't a damned pharmacist, so he might make all kinds of mistakes . . .

So when all was said and done, it *had* to be the gunshot.

In the dark, so he wouldn't see it coming, and ideally – for both of them – while he was sleeping. He'd use a silencer, just in case, though of course that was unnecessary.

No one would hear.

Chapter 4

On Saturday, May 13, a week before graduation and the end of the spring semester, I was feeling good, thinking about fixing lunch for when my daughters came home from their busy mornings, when the phone rang.

'Jake, it's Stu Cooper.'

The tension in his voice hit me right away. I've known Stu since Fran Gottlieb, an old school pal from way back in New Jersey, married him sixteen or so years ago. Stu's a happy-go-lucky kind of a guy, crazy about Fran and their son, Michael.

This was a bad news call.

Believe me, I know about bad news calls.

'Mikey's missing, Jake,' Stu said.

'How long?' I asked, hoping to hear just a handful of hours.

'A month.'

A *month*? How the hell long had it been since we'd spoken, for Christ's sake?

'What happened, Stu?' I shook the guilt out of my head.

'He disappeared April fourteenth,' Stu told me, and his voice started shaking. 'And no one's doing anything about it.'

'What do you mean?' I was bewildered.

'I mean exactly *that*.' The guy was close to tears.

'Is Fran there?'

'You think I'm bad, you can't imagine the shape she's in.' Stu took a second, cleared his throat, dragged himself together. 'That's why we're calling you, Jake. We need help. We need someone to *help* us.'

I shut my eyes, trying to figure the rest of the weekend, knew that today was a hopeless case, but the next . . .

'Tomorrow soon enough?' I asked.

I left early Sunday morning, headed north-east out of the city towards Hartford and picked up the Mass Turnpike to Boston. There are prettier routes, but I was in no mood for them. The fifteen-year-old son of friends was missing. My older daughter, Rianna, is fifteen, her sister, Ella, just nine. I worry about them all the time. What parent doesn't?

At least when Simone was still here, we could share the load – not that *sharing* actually diminished the fears. I remember nights early in both girls' lives when I'd wake with a jolt of panic and go flying into the nursery to check that the baby was breathing, only to find that Simone had beaten me to it. I remember we'd stand vigil over the crib, watching, listening, giving silent thanks, holding each other.

I remember it all so vividly.

We lived in a lovely old clapboard house near the seashore back then, at Madison. We'd found it together one weekend soon after I learned I had the New Haven job. Simone was as easy-going about the move from Albany to Connecticut as she had been about the earlier upheaval when my work had dragged us upstate to the State Attorney's office from New York City. Proximity to the ocean would be wonderful, she said, for Rianna, then six, and for the new baby when it came. And she was right, it *was* wonderful, for them and for us, and it was there that Simone – whose big thing was cooking – started up the local party catering business that brought her success and many new friends.

It also brought about her death in a car smash three years later while she was rushing a part pre-cooked dinner for six to its destination in a rainstorm.

That was when I learned about bad news phone calls.

The Coopers lived out of town, in Brookline. Busy with work and kids the way we all seem to be these swift-flowing days, I'd

9

only seen them five-or-so times in the years since Simone's death, usually for catch-up lunches or dinners in either New Haven or Boston, but I'd met Michael twice since he hit his teens and found him a warm-hearted, delightful, good-looking boy. Only a matter of time, Fran and I agreed, till he started breaking some hearts and having his own torn up a little.

This wasn't the kind of heartbreak we'd had in mind.

The house was good, solid, comfortable, a family home. I remembered one time when we'd all visited and barbecued in the back yard, the kids having a ball, grown-ups ensuring they stayed away from the burning charcoal but otherwise completely content with our food and a few beers and good company. Fran was a redhead with laughing hazel eyes, and Stu made her laugh a lot.

No one was laughing now.

'Tell me,' I said, after Stu and I had clasped in a brief man-hug and I'd held Fran in my arms, feeling how thin she'd become, feeling her shake with sobs.

We were in the den, family pictures and mementos everywhere, along with Stu's golfing cups and Michael's own trophies – the kid was running almost as soon as he was walking, Fran used to say.

Stu did the telling. On Friday, April 14, Mikey had packed a bag for the weekend because he was going to stay with his best friend, Steve Chaplin. He'd never made it there.

'And because he packed a bag,' Stu said, 'the cops figured he was leaving home – running away.'

'Juveniles do run away all the time.' I knew as I said the words, they weren't what they needed to hear. Which didn't make it any less true; Michael Cooper was a juvenile, and though he had seemed an easy, happy kid when I'd last seen him, that didn't mean he mightn't have changed. Those damned early testosterone surges do it to a lot of us, after all; turn sweet-natured boys into tearaways with short fuses, making parents lose patience . . .

'Not Michael,' Stu said. 'The police kept asking if we'd had problems, and we made the big mistake of telling them the truth, that sure, we argued about things – what family doesn't?'

'Did you argue about something that day?' I had to ask.

'*No*,' Stu answered frustratedly. 'Nothing major, not even the kind of thing that might get blown out of proportion by a teenage mind.'

'That's what the police wanted to believe,' Fran told me. 'What they *still* seem to think, even after four weeks.' Her eyes were moist, reddened. 'Mikey was going to stay with the Chaplins – *that's* why he packed his bag, not because he was running away. He would *never* do something so cruel to us.'

I agreed it seemed unlikely.

'No one's listening to us properly,' Fran said. 'They say there's no evidence of anything bad happening to Mikey, but that's not true.'

Stu leaned forward, brown eyes intense, couched in pain. 'Something weird happened a couple of weeks before he went missing. Someone sent him a gift, anonymously.'

'What kind of a gift?'

'One of those horrible computer games the kids love.' Fran screwed up her nose. 'This was one Mikey already had.'

'Though it was some kind of special edition,' Stu added.

'Which game was it?' I asked, since with my own fifteen-year-old, I knew a little – as little as possible, I have to say – about the genre.

'*Limbo*,' Fran answered, with more distaste.

'I've heard of it,' I said, 'though I don't think it's one I've seen Rianna play.' She seemed to favour the sport-related games, at least at home, though I had an idea she sometimes played other kinds with friends.

'There was a note with it.' Stu brought me back to the point. 'Unsigned. It said that the sender knew Michael was already logged as a *Limbo* master, but thought he might enjoy owning the special deluxe edition.'

'Master?' I queried.

'Some kind of ranking of expertise,' Stu explained. 'The note also said the sender had been watching Mikey on the track—'

'You remember what a good runner he is,' Fran interrupted.

'Sure.' I nodded towards the trophies.

'He'd been *watching*,' Stu continued, 'and said he felt Michael had great promise, that one of these days he might reap rewards more amazing than he could imagine.'

'Does *Limbo* have anything to do with athletics?' I asked.

'Not really,' Stu answered, 'except the two heroes are these plastic-type moronically all-round gifted physical specimens, able to fight, scale tall buildings – you know the kind of thing, Jake.'

'And kill,' Fran added softly.

I looked at her, saw the dark terror behind the eyes. 'Still just a game,' I said gently, then looked back at Stu. 'It's the note that's more troubling, of course, in the circumstances. Could I see it?'

'We don't *have* it,' Stu said, his frustration terribly clear. 'If we'd had it, we could have given it to the cops, and then they might be taking us more seriously.'

'We think maybe Mikey kept it on him,' Fran told me, 'because it seemed so important to him.'

That was what had caused the arguments Stu had mentioned, she went on to explain. Michael had been galvanized by the message in the note, wanted to believe it might have been sent by some track talent scout, had refused to see the creepiness in it – and in a way, Stu and Fran had been glad about that, glad their child hadn't been too scared.

'Though of course,' Stu said, 'a little scared might have ...' He trailed off.

'His school work went on the back burner.' For a few moments, Fran was the stronger. 'Suddenly all Mikey wanted to do was train.'

'So we argued with him,' Stu said, 'and after he disappeared, we told the police about that and the gift and the note, but they said since we didn't *have* the note for them to check out, there was nothing they could do about it.'

'And since then,' Fran added, 'all they've done is focus on the fact that we argued with Mikey.'

'For a while,' Stu said, quietly, 'they even acted as if I might have done something to him.' He paused, swallowed hard, went on. 'They asked me if I ever hit him. I told them I didn't. "Not *ever*?" they asked, like that was impossible.'

'We never even had to contemplate smacking Mikey.' Fran's eyes were filling again. 'We really never had to – he was always such an easy boy.'

'You know how he is,' Stu said.

'Sure,' I said, and paused. 'How was the gift sent?'

'By regular mail,' Fran said.

'And no' – Stu's jaw was set hard – 'we didn't keep the packaging because we didn't know our son was going to disappear off the face of the earth.'

We all quit talking for several seconds after that. In my case, I was still taking it in, absorbing the horror and the possible ramifications. For Fran and Stu, I knew full well, the dreads had to be rolling around and around for the thousandth time. Unstoppable thoughts of the worst kind.

'What can I do?' I asked them, finally.

'Talk to the police,' Fran said. 'Make them believe Mikey's no runaway, make them realize that something very bad must have happened to him, that . . .'

'That someone's taken him,' Stu stepped in, eyes burning.

'Problem is,' I said, slowly, thinking, 'I don't know anyone on the Brookline force – nor in Boston.'

'But you must have contacts who do,' Stu said.

'Not really.' I felt bad. 'You remember how quickly I resigned from my job in Albany, Fran.' I winced a little. 'So far as my personal law enforcement record goes, they probably stamped a big F for flake beside my name – which means I'm not in a prime position to call in favours, especially with people who don't know me.'

Stu stood up, walked across to the open glass doors that led out onto the back yard. A tabby cat I didn't remember seeing before sat on its haunches, washing. Stu's back was to me. I was glad I couldn't see his face.

'But you teach criminal justice.' Fran wasn't giving up

so easily. 'That has to give you credibility with the police.'

I shook my head. 'I'm not so sure, Fran.' I tried to explain. 'It's true that in my line of work we have to keep up-to-date with methods and new developments, but to the police that often means we're getting in their way. *And* they tend to favour those who served their time, ideally till retirement.'

Stu's back was still turned.

I took a breath. 'But I'd be glad to ask some questions, confirm they're treating Michael's disappearance seriously.'

Stu turned around. 'That's all we're asking, Jake.'

Fran stood up. 'Can we go now?'

'Sure.' I hesitated. 'Though I think maybe I should go in alone.'

They both got the point.

'I'll drive him over,' Stu said to Fran, who nodded. 'We like one of us to be here to answer the phone, in case.'

Fran came across, put her arms around me. 'Thank you, Jake.'

I felt that awful fragility again, felt her quivering, wondered if it ever let up these days, wondered how much she managed to sleep at night, if at all.

'I wish there were something I could really do for you guys.'

I could hear Stu already out at the front door, keys rattling in his hand.

Fran drew back. 'You're going to try. That's something.'

With all my heart, I hoped so.

Chapter 5

The teenager was sleeping when he entered the darkened room.

A blessing for them both.

He trained the infrared beam from his night glasses, took a long, last, regretful look, then focused hard on the head. Right temple, glowing green in his light.

He raised the gun, safety already off because he *truly* did not want the boy to know, didn't want it to be any tougher than it already was.

The boy stirred. Woke. The light was invisible to him but he knew someone was there, knew something was wrong, *worse* than wrong, and terror flew into his eyes.

Oh shit, oh Christ, oh God, how I hate this.

He squeezed the trigger.

Two screams rose into the dark along with the thud of the muffled bullet. Followed by moaning, writhing.

Not dead. Go again.

He moved in tighter. His hands were shaking, gripping the gun. The wriggling and sounds of pain had ceased, but the kid was unconscious, not dead.

Don't be such a fucking coward.

He trained the beam and the gun's barrel right between the eyes. Easier now there was no more movement.

Another bullet.

Only one scream this time.

15

Chapter 6

I emerged from the police building and walked towards Stu, who was pacing alongside his car, eyebrows raised in query. I shook my head, not wishing to prolong yet another stage of his pain a second more than necessary.

'Sons of bitches,' he said when I got up close. Almost snarling.

'No, Stu.' I patted his arm.

'You shook your head.'

'Only because I don't think I made much difference.' I looked at him. 'How about we go someplace, get a cup of coffee while I fill you in?'

'On what?' The aggression was still there. 'On how they're doing all they can? I heard that tune already.'

'Stu.' I stepped past him, opened the passenger door.

'Okay,' he said, walked around, got in, slammed his door. 'Tell me.'

I told him. That I'd been careful not to push too hard or offend, lest it backfire on us. That the good news was I hadn't gotten the slightest sense of apathy. The police were deeply concerned about Michael, particularly in light of the gift and reported note, had done what they could on that score, checked with the post office and private firms in case the delivery had been recorded in any way.

'They do seem to think' – I chose my words carefully – 'that the gift and note could point to Mikey having gone off with someone of his own free will.'

16

'No way,' Stu said, emphatically. 'No *way* would he ever go with a stranger.'

I looked at him. 'Not even if the stranger said he was a talent scout? Wasn't that what Michael hoped the note meant?'

'Not even then,' Stu said, then shrugged. 'Well ... maybe.' Some of the tautness in his face slipped away, and his features seemed to droop. 'What difference, Jake? What the hell *difference* if Mikey believed the bastard thought he was a great runner? Isn't that just as much of an abduction as if he hit him on the head or ...?' He shook his head and closed his eyes.

'I don't know. *They* don't know. Yet.' I forced myself to go on. 'They're doing all the right things, so far as I can tell. No one suspects you of anything, Stu, and they've also ruled out any custody element. They always consider custody issues, because they're the most common motive for juvenile abductions, not always because of divorce – sometimes it's grandparents or other relatives who snatch kids – though Michael's a little old for something like that, of course.'

Stu opened his eyes and stared out through the windshield.

'I'm sorry, Stu. I guess you've heard all that before.'

He nodded, said nothing.

'Did they tell you they scanned Mikey's photograph into the TRAK system?'

Another nod.

'Which means that law enforcement offices all over the country now have it.'

'I *know*.' The slackness went from Stu's face, the jaw tightened again.

I persevered. 'They've spoken to all Michael's teachers and fellow students. His friend Steve told them they'd talked about the arguments over school work versus training, said it was bugging Mikey some.'

The chin pointed sharply my way. 'The arguments weren't that heavy – we told you.'

'I know.' I made my voice more positive. 'Bottom line, Stu, is that the gift and note aside, there's been nothing – thank God – to indicate abduction.'

17

'So where *is* he?' Stu's Adam's apple worked. 'Where's my *son*, Jake?'

'Kids his age go missing all the time.' I could hear myself treading the party line, not much liking myself for it. 'Sometimes they just go off on their own, especially after a bust-up with their parents – which the cops *don't* feel is the case here. Sometimes, they get persuaded to do things they know their parents might not approve of.'

For the first time, Stu showed a flicker of something like hope. 'You mean, like some kind of training thing? You actually think Mikey could have been talked into going off with this person because he thought they could help him become some kind of track star?'

'It's not impossible.'

'Doesn't sound like Mikey,' Stu said.

I didn't respond to that, didn't know the young man well enough. 'Most times, the cops said, they come home when they're ready.'

'It's been a month, Jake.'

'I know.' I fought for something else to say. 'At least he's on the missing juveniles list and in the TRAK system.'

'Along with Christ knows how many others.' Stu shook his head. 'You may only have been a cop for a short time, Jake, but half an hour in there and you sound just like one of them.'

I absorbed his bitterness, could not blame him for it.

We drove slowly back to the house. I watched Fran's face as she looked at Stu and saw that my session had made no difference, and I saw his face as he realized that nothing had changed here either. No one had phoned with news of their son. No kidnapper had called asking for a ransom. And Michael had not called to tell them he was coming home.

Fran put a sandwich in front of me, and I think I ate it, though I can't recall what was in it. I remember that she didn't eat anything, and that Stu chewed his way through his food like an automaton.

I suggested they get in touch with the National Center for

Missing and Exploited Children, and Stu told me, almost curtly, that Fran had already done that. I mentioned the Polly Klaas Foundation, and saw Fran nod, manage a semblance of a smile in my direction, trying, I knew, to make up for Stu's anger.

I told them, as I was leaving, that I would talk to some colleagues, find out if there was anything more that could be done in the absence of evidence.

'Thank you,' Fran said, and gave me a hug.

'Goes for me, too,' Stu managed.

We shook hands. I saw the desolation in his expression, and had to struggle to stop myself from looking away.

I knew no one I spoke to would have anything useful to say.

Chapter 7

The body had been taken care of.

Same hideous process as before.

First, the covering up, so he didn't have to look at it a moment longer than necessary. Looking always reminded him. Always would.

That wasn't your fault.

Sure it was your fault. That's the whole thing, isn't it?

Then the clean-up. So much blood, he felt like Lady-fucking-Macbeth. Then the tarpaulin. The kid was heavier than he looked, muscle weighing more than fat, of course. Then the shrink-wrap covering. Nauseating, loathsome, but effective. And finally, thank Jesus, into the cold room.

Gone.

Except in his mind.

The blood was still seeping in there.

One day, he suspected, it might drown him.

Chapter 8

Home.

Later than I meant to be, but the girls were both there, safe and sound, with Kim.

No worries there, thank the Lord.

I had the magnificent good fortune to find Kim Ryan within a week of moving to New Haven, back in '95. She read my ad on a bulletin board at the university where she was studying that summer, and after I met with her, I knew I didn't need to see anyone else. Kim's twenty-eight, with short fair hair, eyes sharp enough to take in danger to my children at three hundred yards, and a brain acute enough to know *exactly* how to deal with it. She's slim and petite-looking but physically tough and, most of all, she's kind and loving. She knows how and when to give my daughters a cuddle, knows how to keep them in order, too. She knows she is not their mother. She is their very good friend, and mine. As is Tom, her husband, a computer analyst with one of our city's multitudinous electronics firms.

The Ryans have been trying for their own family for several years, but there's no bitterness or hopelessness in them on that score. I know they both derive honest pleasure from Rianna and Ella. Sometimes, if I have to attend some UNH function or maybe go out socially (I was talked into my first post-Simone date five years after losing her, and I've had some pleasant times with a handful of nice women since then, but nothing more serious), both the Ryans come to the apartment, and sometimes, Kim tells me, they fool around on our couch like overgrown teenagers – though never, she adds, until both girls are asleep. Like she has to *tell* me that. I trust Kim and Tom implicitly, would never have dreamed of leaving Rianna or Ella with anyone I did not trust one thousand per cent.

I owe Kim so much. She's not the world's greatest cook, and when I get home after work the apartment often still looks like a tornado just hit, but those things don't seem important to me. Kim knows how to distract Ella when she's approaching tantrum mode, how to calm her down when a crying jag's already underway. It was Kim who made sure that the girls knew the serious stuff about New Haven, such as the city having been the first place in the US where both hamburgers and pizzas had been served and where the Frisbee had been invented by Yale students. It was Kim who first took them for rides on the antique carousel at Lighthouse Point Park, and who told me about the potential for hiking, picnicking and fishing at Sleeping Giant State Park close by. And it was Kim, too, who recognized that despite Rianna's natural emotional calm, she also had unusually abundant physical energy that needed a regular outlet. Which was how come Rianna came to take up and love gymnastics. And needless to say, it was Kim who found and checked out the High Fliers Club, and then discreetly told me about it so I could decide for myself before we took Rianna there for the first time.

Hard to be sure, sometimes, if there's a role left for me.

Hell, that's not true.

I am their father.

Ella was in bed, and Kim had already made spaghetti for her and Rianna when I reached home – more than enough pasta to stretch to three.

'I'm going to leave you guys to it,' she said, after I'd finished hugging Rianna.

'You can't go now,' I said.

'Sure I can.'

'You cooked dinner.'

'Doesn't mean I have to eat it.' Kim grimaced, and Rianna

grinned. Actually, Kim's meat sauce is one of her finer culinary accomplishments. 'If I go now, I'll be in time for a take-out with Tom.'

'Pizza?' Rianna asked her.

'Sushi.'

'No contest,' Rianna said.

'How rude,' I remarked.

'Just honest,' Kim said.

'Seriously,' I said, 'I wish you'd stay.'

'No, you don't.'

The ability to read my moods is yet another of Kim's qualities, so I guess she could tell I'd had a bitch of a day and figured a cosy family evening was what I needed more than anything. So she left, and I went upstairs to kiss Ella goodnight, and she woke up and then created about joining me and her sister at the kitchen table, and for once I gave in because did it really *matter* if she was a little tired at school next day?

'Has something happened to Mikey?'

Rianna threw me that curve about five minutes into dessert. She knew where I'd gone that morning, had not known why, but then I'd hesitated over answering a couple of her questions about the Coopers, so being Rianna she'd guessed that something was up. (Either my life's jammed with mind-readers or I'm too damned transparent for my own good.)

Now I had to decide, fast, on truth versus my children's peace of mind.

Truth, maybe – but only after Ella was back in bed.

'Mikey wasn't there,' I evaded.

'But he's okay?'

I looked into Rianna's calm grey eyes – her mother's eyes. 'Fine,' I lied, and glanced at Ella, who was eating ice cream but fading fast. 'Bed soon, sweetheart,' I told her.

'After my ice cream,' she said.

'But of course,' I said.

Ella's eyes are a fascinating kind of slate-blue, neither Simone's nor mine – my eyes are plain old brown – and they

23

can blank you out if she chooses, or nail you, if that's her intention, or they can melt your heart, especially when she's smiling. I received one of those natural, no-strings smiles of hers at that moment and knew it was thanks because I'd relaxed the rules for once, and there was something almost mature about that which surprised me. Rianna's the mature one in our family, fifteen going on twenty it sometimes seems to me, though it has nothing much to do with age. Simone spotted it when she was just three years old.

'Our daughter has wisdom,' she told me.

We were on the beach at the time, with friends on Long Island, and our firstborn was playing in the sand. I looked at Rianna and saw healthy, sun-warmed, tender-soft arms and sand-splodged legs and one of those delightfully earnest expressions that she wore when she was fully focused on something – but I couldn't see anything approaching *wisdom*. Yet I've come to see that Simone was absolutely right.

My wife was right about many things, so I guess she had wisdom too.

Rianna waited till Ella was tucked up in bed and she and I were washing the dishes before she returned to the question of Michael Cooper.

'Something's happened to him, hasn't it?'

'I'm afraid so.' No hesitation this time. No point. 'He went to stay at a friend's house a while ago, and never showed up.'

Rianna had been drying a plate. Now she set it down, carefully, and looked at me, a frown puckering her forehead. 'How long ago?'

'A month,' I answered quietly.

'Wow,' she said. 'Do they think he ran away?'

'The police think he may have. Fran and Stu don't believe that.'

'But if he didn't . . .' The grey eyes were appalled.

I stopped washing up, reached out my left hand, still soapy, touched her arm. 'I know, sweetheart.'

'Is there anything we can do?' Rianna asked.

24

'I don't think so,' I told her. 'I talked to the police who've been looking for Mikey. They're doing all they can.'

I remembered the game with the ugly name – *Limbo* – and considered asking Rianna about it, but then I figured that the sweet evening had already been tainted enough.

'Try not to worry too much, baby,' I said.

Rianna nodded.

'You, too,' she told me.

Chapter 9

Later, when he felt sufficiently recovered, he checked out the young woman, hoping she might make him feel better. Cheerier.

At least she was still holding her own.

Females are tougher, they say. He had never doubted that, and this one, with her Tae Kwon Do skills and her perfect sixteen-year-old hard-soft body, had not disappointed him yet.

But then, of course, she had not yet faced her ultimate challenge. And now that would have to wait awhile. Until her new companion had been found, brought in, tamed.

That part was fascinating. They were always frightened, which upset him, but he was learning to cope with that. Fear was his speciality. He knew all about it, understood it, realized what these teenagers were too young to accept.

That fear itself is the great enemy, the true destroyer; that there is *nothing* more satisfying in life than its conquest.

He realized that he was going to have to put as much of his life as possible on hold for a while now – not an easy proposition, but necessary. His priority *had* to be finding another young male. The utterly-and-completely perfect complement to his female.

He didn't want to keep her waiting too long. Different for her than for him. He had anticipation on his side. The thrill of the hunt – something it had taken him a long time to comprehend. She had only darkness and fear while he sought her companion. If she had to wait too long, her own perfection would suffer, she would grow lacklustre and dispirited, perhaps even sickly, like the others.

Oh Lord, not again.

He pushed that negative thought right out of his mind.

No more replacements. Never again, not once he'd found the next young man. It would all work out after that, he would make sure it did.

Start looking.

Chapter 10

I was lying in bed, thinking about Michael Cooper and my daughters, and every damned time I shut my eyes, I saw either Mikey as I'd last seen him, a strong, healthy, happy young man, or I saw Fran's terrified eyes or Stu's fiercely set jaw.

At three a.m. I gave up on sleep, got up, pulled on a robe, had a quiet check on both girls, then padded softly, avoiding the familiar creaking boards, into my study and switched on my PC.

I find my computer quite comforting when I have insomnia, its glow in the dark welcoming, all of its not-quite-real world awake with me. I've taken to e-mail, but have never entered a chat room, though I guess I can begin to comprehend their attraction for some. Sometimes, at night, I work, sometimes I browse, visit libraries, catch up on correspondence.

Tonight, though, I had a mission, and as soon as the machine had completed its start-up, I went on-line, found a gaming website and typed LIMBO into the search box. No problem, except there was so *much*, and I hadn't realized there was a sequel on the market: *Limbo II*.

I saw the word *Review* and clicked onto it.

On the face of it, the first **Limbo** looked like any number of other survivalist-based games, but as it began to suck us in we soon realized it was one of the sleeker, deadlier varieties. Still and all, we said – at least, those of us who get paid to analyze such things – there were a lot of great games out there, so what exactly *was* the magic ingredient that was making this one such a mega-seller? Some felt it was Ghoulo, the mutated half-wolverine, half-human monster creep who survived in the post-apocalypse Manhattan underworld by munching on just about anything or any*one* he could gouge his fangs into.

But most of us knew that **Limbo**'s real appeal was generated by Steel and Dakota, the last surviving teenagers in New York City. Two nice teenagers from nice, happy homes, trapped in a terrifying underground hell. Both of them gorgeous, natch, but still normal, despite their amazing bodies and abilities. Dakota and Steel weren't afraid to *admit* they were scared as hell. Cyber-heroes they might be, but beneath those untouchable bodies, they were *human*, like the rest of us, and maybe, just maybe, if we – even the less-fit, sponge-muscled mortals – were faced with evil gangs, cave-ins, floods, starving packs of canines turned ravening beasts, not to mention Ghoulo himself, maybe even *we* might find strength we never dreamed of . . .

I could see there was an awful lot more, mostly about how the second game differed from the original, that and a whole bunch of incomprehensible stuff about FMVs and RPGs, but I stopped actually reading right there, logged off, turned off, made my way to the kitchen and lit the gas beneath the kettle.

I like this kitchen. It's a far cry from the handsome, homey one we had in the house at Madison, but then that was Simone's territory, the place where she practised her art, the room everyone gravitated to whenever possible.

It was also the room that became the most unbearable after we lost her. For eighteen months, it remained, of course, our kitchen, the room in which we prepared the food we needed to eat in order to stay alive; but whereas before it had been the heart and soul of the house, after Simone's death it seemed achingly empty and desolate, the place in which I think maybe I missed her most.

Except for our bed.

I fought so hard to settle our lives back into some semblance of normality. Not so much for myself as for Rianna – nine when her mother died – and for little Ella. But for all its loveliness and familiarity, the whole house seemed to die along with Simone. Not instantly; it was more of a long drawn-out decaying process, as if while the woman who'd nurtured it had died in the blink of an eye, the house had crumbled into grief more slowly, had only gradually come to realize – as we all had to – that she was never coming back.

That was when I decided to move my fragile little family into the city for a fresh start in a home that wasn't going to twist my heart every time I turned around. Rianna – ten and a half by then – came with me to New Haven to check out the apartment the realtor had found for us – a handsome brownstone walk-up in Wooster Square – and I remember holding my breath as she walked around, slowly and silently, taking in every room, every nook and cranny, before returning to my side in the living room, taking hold of my hand and saying: 'It's good, Daddy.'

'Really?' I stooped so I could look straight into her eyes. 'I don't want you agreeing to something just because you think it's going to be easier for me. I want you and Ella to be happy about what we decide.'

'I know that.' She wore her earnest expression. 'I really do like it. I can see our things here – like the rocker in that corner over there . . .'

I looked across and found that I could picture it there too.

'And you could do your work in that little room and look out at the trees.'

The square was almost surrounded by cherry trees, not in blossom at that time, but still pretty, and I hadn't gotten anywhere near as far as planning my study at that point, yet I could see that Rianna was absolutely right about it.

'And . . .' She hesitated.

'And what, honey?'

Her hand was still in mine. 'Maybe it won't be so hard any more.'

This kitchen is different. It's a lot smaller, and it never looks or smells as good as the old place did, and things are seldom where they're supposed to be, but it has come to feel like home, and as in most homes, I guess, it's where people come to when they can't sleep at night.

Fran was right about *Limbo* being horrible, I decided, as I poured boiled water onto a tea bag, though I didn't suppose it was as grotesque as many on the market. More to the point, however, I'd seen nothing in that description that was going to help bring Michael back home. Certainly no more obvious link to him than to any other American teenager, particularly as he lived in Brookline, Massachusetts, rather than in New York City.

Just a weird choice of gift and a disturbing, perhaps sinister, note.

I sat at the table and stirred a spoonful of honey into my tea.

My kids weren't the only ones who had school to go to in just a few hours. Less than a week to graduation and then the summer would expand before me, together with my famous (only to those who knew me well) to-be-written novel, the one I was positively, finally, going to actually get to write this long vacation.

Energy would be needed, along with motivation and self-discipline. Not to mention inspiration. And plenty of sleep.

No way Professor Jacob Woods was going to get back to sleep *that* night.

Chapter 11

It was Friday before Kim called me at UNH to say that Stu Cooper had telephoned again. I'm ashamed to say I caught myself out in a sigh, then guiltily snatched up my office phone to return his call. Thing is, I'd talked to Fran twice since Sunday – I *knew* she was dying by inches, that each day that passed without news of Michael, *good* news, plunged that white-hot dagger deeper through both his parents' hearts. I just didn't know what the hell I could *do* about it.

But I called anyway.

'We've been thinking,' Stu said, without preamble, 'that maybe we should hire a private investigator.' He went on fast, before I could say a word. 'The police have advised against it – but they would, wouldn't they. And whatever you told us, we just don't feel they're doing enough, and frankly, Jake, even if all it's going to achieve is us feeling that at least we're doing something other than just sitting and waiting, maybe that's better than nothing.'

He stopped talking, waited for me to say something, but I was chasing words around my head, hoping to find the right ones.

'We thought you might be able to recommend someone,' Stu prompted.

'Problem is,' I began, slowly, 'I honestly can't see what a PI could successfully accomplish with so little to go on.'

'We know all that, Jake.'

'I'm not saying I won't help you find one,' I went on. 'I just want to make sure you realize there's not much they'd be able to do.'

'Still,' Stu said, 'Fran really wants to try, so if you don't mind, we'd like to know who's the best – and we know it's going to cost, and we don't care.'

I bit back my natural resistance to the idea. 'I can't tell you off-hand, but I'll check a couple out, see who comes out tops.'

Least I could do, I figured, was make sure they didn't get ripped off.

Chapter 12

A whole damned week had passed, flashed by like the blink of the proverbial eye.

He'd been searching when and where he was able, mindful not to arouse suspicion. He knew how to make himself inconspicuous, a useful talent for hunting. He had never minded this part, the tracking, the marking, the waiting. It was just the killing he couldn't stomach.

Plus ça change.

He wished he had more time. Another cliché – so much to do, so little time – but how true. Work, home, the regular patterns of life, taking care of *her* needs. Finding *him*.

Young men with potential *everywhere*. Tennis courts, playgrounds, pools. The gym at the Y. The parks, watching them skim by on their blades, young masters of all they flew past. Some loving to be watched, some oblivious.

The runners, at least, he now ruled out. He still found his eyes tracking, appreciating, but forced himself to look away. Once bitten . . . He had to focus on those who could achieve their physical release in a limited space.

School would be out soon and then they really *would* be everywhere. On the beaches, going to camp, even vanishing into offices and stores, taking vacation jobs.

He really could not wait much longer.

She needed company.

Chapter 13

I'd found a private investigator for the Coopers. Guy named Norman Baum.

It was Baum's partner, Thea Lomax, who ran their office on George Street in New Haven, who was initially recommended by Sigmund Green, a criminologist acquaintance. But then it turned out they'd recently opened a new branch in Boston, with Baum in charge, which meant that he would be better placed for the Coopers, provided we got along.

'He's very experienced,' Green confirmed after Lomax had suggested I go see her partner, 'and he gives a shit.'

I knew that was true within twenty minutes of meeting him at Lomax & Baum. The offices were on the second floor of an old building in Boston's Leather District; two freshly-painted rooms, furnished with second-hand desks, chairs and cabinets, though the computer and peripherals looked sharp and efficient.

The man himself was unspectacular to look at: average height, a little overweight, skimpy greying hair, brown, myopic, intelligent, *kind* eyes; his suit, a greyish tweed, had probably been elegant once-upon-a-time (maybe on someone else), and his shoes were clean but scuffed. Like I said, nothing special. But he virtually *flinched* when he heard about the Coopers' plight, went very quiet while studying Michael's photograph, and after that there seemed to be real anger burning in him, perhaps because he knew something bad had probably happened to the kid – or perhaps because, like me, he feared there was all too little he could do about it.

He said as much.

'I wish I could say I felt optimistic.' His voice was soft, saddened.

'Tell me about it,' I said.

'It's up to you – or rather, to the parents. If you want me, I'll do everything – and I mean *everything* – I can to find the boy.'

'We want you,' I told him.

'But I won't be making any promises I can't keep, and I won't let the Coopers waste one cent more of their hard-earned money than I think they're wise to spend.'

'I'm grateful to you for saying that,' I said. 'I'm a little concerned that Stu and Fran may have reached a point where they think pouring cash into the pot is better than doing nothing.'

'Not into Lomax & Baum's pot,' the PI said.

I felt he meant it. And who could say that Baum might not even surprise himself and learn something useful that the cops had missed?

Just so long as it wasn't something really shitty.

I sensed from those sad, angry eyes that Norman Baum's heart wasn't above breaking a little, even over a total stranger.

TWO

Chapter 14

He saw him.

Freezing fingers on the back of the neck. Clutching at his heart. Clichés again, but true just the same. Oh, yes.

Oh, yes.

Just a regular public basketball court on Manhattan's West Side on a Sunday afternoon – Sunday, May 28, 2000. Just a few young guys playing an informal game, fooling around but pretty skilful at the same time. So many courts, playing fields, gyms – three cities in just a week. More good-looking, physically-gifted teenagers than he could easily count . . .

Yet this one young man shone. *Shone.*

He was fifteen, sixteen tops, and he was a natural, not one of those weird-looking beanpoles who looked as if they'd been genetically modified to flick balls easily into baskets – though it did look effortless to *him*. He was beautiful to watch. Wearing shorts and a grey sweat top, sleeves cut off at the shoulders – powerful shoulders, yet not too muscled, the whole package lean, slender and oh-so-relaxed as he ran around the court.

Oh Christ, not another runner.

He took a deep breath, turned away from the court with an effort, but the sound of laughter, breathless and filled with youth, with *joie de vivre*, forced him to look again. The laughter was *his*, as he'd known it would be, the handsome face filled with it, a smile created to finger right through the chest and grab the heart.

He probably worked out at a gym. Runners didn't play ball, they *ran*, for fuck's sake, didn't they? *Didn't they?*

He'd be okay. He had to be.

The ball was his ... he was being challenged ... he went with it, kept it, played boldly, took chances, leapt high, shot the basket, came down on an uneven piece of ground, fell—

Oh dear God ...

He was already on his feet, laughing again.

He was courageous, too.

The one.

Chapter 15

'Coming for a sandwich, man?'

Robbie Johanssen checked his watch. 'Can't.'

'Got a date?' Carl Smith, one of the guys, asked him.

He shook his head. 'It's my mom's birthday. We're throwing a surprise party for her, and the deal is I get home in time to make sure she goes out so we can get the place ready.' He looked at the others, already halfway down the block. 'Tell the guys I'll see them next week, okay?'

'Sure, man.'

Robbie watched Carl catch up with the others, then turned for home, figuring he'd have to move some or catch a cab – but it was less than twenty blocks and he was a fast walker, and at least that way he could work out as he went exactly how to persuade his mom that he really *didn't* mind if she went out to the concert that Mark and Anna Franklin had invited her to as part of the plan.

He turned north onto Amsterdam, thinking about her whole attitude to birthdays – though only her *own*, no one else's, definitely not his. She believed, he knew, that the Franklins had forgotten it was her birthday, and that suited her because she didn't *want* them to remember, hated what she called a 'big fuss', so the concert was okay from that perspective. The thing was, Robbie didn't think she really *wanted* to go out at all, because what she truly wanted to do was have a quiet dinner with him, but she wouldn't tell him that because she felt that

41

sixteen-year-olds ought not to have their widowed mothers' birthdays inflicted upon them . . .

'Goddamn politics,' he muttered, passing a pair of seriously pretty girls walking arm-in-arm, one of whom, a blonde with a real sexy mouth, grinned right at him. *No time*, he told himself, resisting a glance back over his shoulder; not if he was going to make sure Lydia went with the Franklins *and* get the place set up for the party.

That, of course, was another problem. His mom hated surprise parties, had once told him he was never, ever to organize such a thing for her.

He turned left onto Eighty-seventh, shaking his head.

For an easy-going mother, Lydia Johanssen laid down a lot of rules.

Robbie grinned.

Made to be broken.

He entered the beige stone building on West Seventy-third – identical in almost every way to its twin next door, and linked by a common back garden – waved hi to Solomon, one of the doormen, took one of the two elevators up to the top floor and used his key to open the front door of 15C.

'Mom?'

Lydia Johanssen came from the rear of the apartment, smiling. 'Hi there.'

Robbie gave her a hug, then stepped back and gave her a swift *sotto voce* burst of 'Happy Birthday', and Lydia laughed and joined in, singing to herself in a sweet, low harmony. Her contralto voice had been admired by many in its time, though it had been a good long while since she'd sung on stage; nowadays, she was a well-respected coach, her clients men and women of all ages and talents, more than a few coming to Lydia simply because they found their sessions with her an enjoyable physical and emotional release.

'Looking good, Mom,' Robbie said, and headed for the kitchen.

She did look good in simple linen slacks topped with a crisp white cotton man-style shirt, long straight dark hair tied back in a ponytail. Some people said Lydia and Robbie looked alike, but they both thought that was just because their hair colour was the same and they had a tendency to similar gestures. Lydia's eyes were honey-brown, however, while Robbie had his father's clear blue eyes and his slightly cleft chin, though Aaron Johanssen had been shorter, stockier than his son. Anna Franklin had once told Robbie he had Aaron's smile, too, and Robbie had liked that idea because it had made him feel as if, when he was smiling, he was carrying around a little of his father inside him.

'Good game?' Lydia came in to the kitchen as he was pouring some juice.

'Not bad.' Robbie held up the Tropicana carton in a query, but she shook her head and he put it back in the refrigerator. 'Not getting changed yet?'

'No rush,' she said, and sat down at the table. 'You made plans for tonight, kiddo?'

'Not yet.' He downed half the glass. 'Looking forward to your *Lieder*?'

'I guess,' she said, and wrinkled her nose. 'Not sure I'm quite in the mood for Schubert, though.' She grinned. 'I think I'd rather we were going to Birdland or the Blue Note – then maybe you could have joined us.'

There it was – no element of nag or reproach; that had never been her style. She encouraged his independence, always had, he was thankful to say. But he *knew* she didn't want to go to the concert this evening – hell, they *all* knew, Anna and Mark Franklin most of all. And later on, when – and if – the party ever got underway, they'd all laugh about it, at least, he *hoped* his mother would laugh about it with them, though it was hard to be sure about that.

'Too late now,' Robbie told her brightly. 'The Franklins have the tickets, and it isn't their fault you didn't remind them it's your birthday.'

'I'm thankful for that, at least.' Lydia shook her head. 'And I wouldn't dream of letting them down now.' She hesitated.

43

'Though I wish you weren't going to spend the evening alone. Maybe Josh could come up.'

'I'll ask him,' he said.

'You could order pizza.'

'Sure, Mom.'

'Maybe get a movie?'

Robbie went across to her, bent, planted a kiss on the top of her head. 'Quit worrying about me, would you, please, and go get ready for your evening. Run one of those nice long baths you like.'

Lydia glanced up. 'You trying to get rid of me?'

'Finally,' Robbie said, 'you got it.'

Lydia lay back in the big bathtub originally installed by the first owner of the twin buildings, who had used their apartment – and the two others on the top floor, prior to their subdivision – as his Manhattan home base. She wasn't sure when he'd moved out, when 15C had actually been turned into a self-contained residence, but she and Aaron had moved in seventeen years ago.

A lifetime.

Made languid by the warmth and the scent of her bath oil, Lydia allowed her mind to wander back. So many special moments over those years ... major landmarks among them, some joyful, some dreadful; the best, perhaps, conceiving Robbie on the December night after Aaron had played at the Alice Tully Hall to a standing ovation, making them both euphoric. Aaron, so seldom egotistical, had confessed to Lydia a fleeting but extraordinary sense of immortality during his bows, and a moment after that disclosure they'd both torn the clothes off one another and hurried to their bed, and had, almost certainly, created their son.

Seventeen years ago.

And today she was thirty-five, and a widow, trying to avoid looking at what she thought might be the beginnings of cellulite on her thighs, and marking off time.

Five years, exactly, since Aaron's first heart attack in the midst of the huge party he'd arranged for her thirtieth. They'd so nearly lost him right there and then, and if it hadn't been for Daniel Asher's medical training they would not have had their last three months together. Before the second, massive attack felled him in his Carnegie Hall dressing room moments before he was due onstage for Rachmaninov ...

Lydia sat up sharply, sending a swell of water up and down the tub. *Stay on the good times.* More than enough of those to dwell on, even after Aaron; unthinkable back then, but true nonetheless. Work, her continuing saviour, her ability to share her own, albeit limited, talents with others. The added good fortune of having neighbours who didn't object to music, so that when the weather was too fine for Lydia and her client to want to be shut in the sound-insulated music room, they could escape up to the roof garden and sing out to their hearts' content.

Her friends, too, were a blessing, had helped drag her up out of the darkness: Mark and Anna, of course, and the Ashers, and the Steinmans – Josh's parents, just two floors down – and Carla Radici, and all her music-related acquaintances.

Mostly, though, it had been Robbie who'd helped her survive. Robbie, who had adored his father, who'd never seemed to much mind being an only child, partly, Lydia believed, because Aaron had been such a great friend to him. They had grieved together, then simply gone on together, sharing the past and their loss but managing to move forward.

She was so lucky to have Robbie, so blessed, could not imagine being prouder of the son she was still privileged to be living with.

Not for much longer, she thought now, standing up and shaking water from her right foot before stepping out of the bath. Soon enough Robbie would be ready to head off to university – though he was not, never had been, any great shakes as a student, had been reproached more than once by both his academic and sports teachers at Ethical Culture School, for his butterfly disposition.

And it was true, Lydia reflected, drying herself, that he did have a tendency to become fascinated by a new subject or sport or hobby, rise to the challenge of conquering whatever it was, then move just as swiftly on to the next.

'At least he'll be a good all-rounder,' she'd remarked to one of his critics.

'But don't you want him to *excel*?' the critic had asked her.

Lydia had thought about her son, about his vital mind and body, his love of life in general, his liking for so many kinds of people, and the fact that so many of them seemed to like him in return.

'I think he does,' she'd answered.

Chapter 16

Oh, how he loved computers, had from the very beginning.

Love at first sight and touch. The world opening up to him for the first time. Machines with brains but no hearts or souls, no capacity or will to taunt or wound. Brains able, less than twenty-four hours after seeing the young basketball player for the first time, to tell him pretty much all he needed to know about Robert David Johanssen and his widowed mother, Lydia.

Nice family. Intelligent mind to match the body. Top-notch liberal school. Fine all-round sportsman, if a touch fickle. Mother apparently decent, 'normal', a gifted singing teacher with plentiful friends. No politicians or law enforcement types in the family, the pianist husband Aaron Johanssen – nationally renowned, though not a world-class figure – already fading from public memory. No one, so far as he could tell, significant enough to arouse *special* interest from the police. Affluent enough to live in a good building, but not especially wealthy, so no bodyguards or abnormal security precautions to worry about, and no hang-ups about allowing Robert – Robbie, to most people – out alone or with his pals.

All criteria met.

All gratitude to Lydia and Aaron Johanssen for making him so well.

For giving him to me.

Chapter 17

Oh, what a lovely evening she'd had – *everyone* had had – Lydia reflected happily over her late – *very* late – Monday morning breakfast.

It had all been so sweetly thought out, so considerately, carefully different from that other event five years ago, yet still, deliberately, pointedly, a *party*. Not a big bash, just a dozen friends, cosy and fun, with the players among them taking turns at Aaron's Bechstein, and Lydia singing jazz with Mook Swanson and David Steinman, Josh's dad, and Robbie looking so *relieved* that it was all okay and that she hadn't minded and was, in fact, having the best of times.

Not like old times.

Now times.

That afternoon, coming in after school, Robbie wandered through the lobby, asked Anthony, the on-duty doorman, how his head cold was doing, and spent three full minutes hearing about the condition of the guy's sinuses. Escaping into the mail room to open 15C's box, he found amongst the bills and junk mail addressed to his mother, a note telling him to check the package box.

He unearthed a brown padded envelope with a typed label addressed to Robert D. Johanssen, tucked it with his mom's stuff under his left arm and walked back through the hall to the elevators, musing about who'd sent him what. He couldn't remember ordering anything lately via the Net, except a

Shania Twain CD, and Amazon had gotten that to him last week . . .

Letting himself into the apartment, registering the silence, he recalled his mother telling him she had a dentist appointment this afternoon. Lydia hated going to see Dr Schreiner, but this morning, tired as she'd been, she'd mentioned the visit almost blithely. That was when Robbie had known for absolutely certain that she'd had just as fine a time the night before as she'd seemed to be having, which meant that he and the Franklins had done good.

He off-loaded Lydia's letters onto the hall table, went into his bedroom to dump his school stuff, then carried the package into the kitchen and put it on the table while he went to the refrigerator and grabbed himself a can of Dr Pepper.

'Okay.'

He sat down, turned the envelope over. It was one of those efficiently sealed, easy-to-open jobs where you just pulled a tab and slit it end to end, and if you weren't too impatient or rough, it usually worked.

Like this time.

Robbie withdrew the contents, and frowned. It was a computer game, but it was one he already had. In fact, he had *Limbo* and *Limbo II*, which meant this was some kind of foul-up, which meant the hassle of sending it back.

'Bummer,' he said, and drank some soda, then noticed that the game was not exactly like the *Limbo* he had on his stack, but some kind of special deluxe edition – though aside from the fancier package, he didn't know how the game itself was different.

Setting down the can again, he delved back inside the envelope, found a folded piece of white paper, unfolded it and saw it was printed with one of those fancy computer fonts.

Fancy, and weird.

A small gift for you, young man — a collector's item you may not already have. If you don't, being a Limbo master, you should.

I've been keeping an eye on your sporting achievements, Robert Johanssen, and I feel you should know that I think you're a gifted enough all-rounder to consider formal pentathlon training. Or at least you could be gifted enough if you quit chopping and changing.

Maybe you need a little time out to consider that.

With the right attitude, and some particularly good fortune, you might find that life could offer you some amazing rewards.

No signature. No return address. Robbie looked over the note for another moment, then shrugged. It made no sense. Either it was from some fruitcake, or maybe it was someone's idea of a gag. Pricey gag, though.

He stood up, drained the Dr Pepper and binned it, picked up the note and the game and took them into his bedroom, where he tossed them on the floor beside his bed, then elbowed his school work over the edge to join them, so he could lie down and have a snooze. His mother wouldn't be back for a while, and he was dog-tired after last night *and* a hard day at Ethical.

Man, he was tired.

It was not until next morning, just as he was finishing his cereal and his mom was pouring her first cup of coffee of the day, that Robbie remembered the package.

'Why didn't you tell me about it yesterday?' Lydia was jarred out of her early morning tranquillity.

'I forgot.'

'How could you forget something like that?' She didn't wait for an answer. 'Where is it?'

'In my room.' He got to his feet, carried his bowl to the sink, put out his right hand to turn the tap.

'Leave that,' Lydia told him. 'I'd like to see it, if you don't mind.'

Robbie turned around. 'Why would I mind?'

'It might be private.'

Robbie laughed. 'Hardly. It has nothing to do with me.' He left the kitchen and came back a moment later, school bag in one hand, the game and note in the other. 'I figure it's some kind of mistake.' He handed them to her.

50

She read in silence, her brow furrowing. 'Doesn't seem like a mistake to me.'

'A joke, maybe?'

'Maybe.' She was unconvinced.

Robbie dumped his bag on the floor and sat down again. 'Don't look so worried, Mom. It's nothing.'

Lydia shook her head. 'Someone's been watching you. I don't like the idea of that too much.'

'I thought it was kind of creepy too when I first read it, like maybe some perv had been checking me out, but then I figured it might just be one of the guys kidding around.'

'Who?' Lydia was disbelieving. 'None of your friends would do something like this.' She looked closely at her son. 'Has there been some trouble I don't know about? At school, or—'

'No trouble.' Robbie grinned and stood up again. 'Honestly, Mom, don't freak yourself out. Maybe it's just what it says – maybe someone thinks I'm really good at sports.'

Lydia glanced up at him sharply. 'I hope you're not kidding yourself that this is someone talent spotting for Team USA or something like that?'

'I wish.' He shook his head. 'It's bull and I know it.' He paused. 'And by the way, whoever wrote it was wrong about calling me a '*Limbo* master'. I play the game, but you know me, I don't have the patience to stick with any of these things long enough to get to be any kind of master.'

Lydia looked back down at the note, said nothing.

'What, Mom?'

'I wonder if we should report this?'

'To who?'

'Whom,' she said automatically. 'The police, I guess.'

'What for?' Robbie asked. 'It's just a gift and a note, and I can't see what the cops could do about it even if it is a little weird. This is New York City, after all – weirdos' world.' He retrieved his bag. 'I gotta go.'

'Where's the packaging it came in?' Lydia wasn't ready to let it go yet.

51

Robbie thought. 'I left it in here, I think. It was just a padded envelope.'

'Which I threw down the chute last night with the rest of the trash.' Lydia pulled a face. 'Damn.'

'See?' Robbie grinned again. 'You should be more of a slob, like your son.'

Lydia smiled back at him. 'Time to go to school, slob.'

He bent down to kiss her, saw she was still anxious. 'I'm sure it's nothing to get worked up about, Mom.'

'I know,' she said.

Robbie strolled over to the door. 'I promise not to talk to strangers.'

'Don't be a smart-ass,' she told him. 'Just be careful.'

'I will,' he said, 'if you promise to forget about it.'

'About what?' Lydia said.

She heard him leave, looked down at the computer game on the table, felt an urge to take it quickly to the garbage chute outside and get rid of it, together with the note. Then again, maybe it might be better to hold on to them, in case Robbie noticed someone hanging around him, or anything like that.

Anyway, it wasn't hers to throw away.

She took a swallow of coffee, but it had gone cold, so she picked up the cup, took it over to the sink, then quickly turned back, picked up the offending items and put them in the bottom drawer of the kitchen dresser.

'Out of sight,' she said aloud.

If not quite out of mind.

Chapter 18

He'd asked himself a couple of times why he had sent the game again, why he'd gone out of his way to risk putting them on their guard. He knew it was wiser to avoid rituals of any kind in what was bound, one day, to become the subject of an investigation. Serial criminals, he'd read, could be compulsive about that type of thing. And it wasn't as if there had been any *need* to send Robert Johanssen the game.

Superstition. He'd never been afraid to walk under ladders, had never been troubled about spilling salt or putting keys on tables. But when it came to *this*, he had to admit to having become almost superstitious about certain things. He had used the gift and note with all of them, and even if he had not yet achieved his ultimate goal, at least no one had begun to link the missing kids. So no point, he'd decided, in breaking the pattern now, or it might all get spoiled, and he couldn't *bear* that.

Not before he'd gotten them both together.

So they could play the game.

The real game.

Chapter 19

Robbie went to school that day, stayed late with Phil Breckenridge, Candice Clarke, Larry Jackson and some of the others to write Amnesty International letters, and then came home, relieved to find his mother almost back to her normal self. Her questions about his day were somewhat loaded; for the time being she clearly cared a heck of a lot less about math or science than about whether he'd noticed anyone out of the ordinary watching him at any point during the day. But at least she didn't come out and use the word '*suspicious*', and appeared to accept his judgement that things were fine and normal.

'Your mom's so much cooler than mine would be,' Josh said when Robbie went down to 13B, the Steinmans' apartment, after dinner. 'If someone had sent that loony-tunes gift to me, I don't think Mel would let me out of her sight for a second.'

'Sure she would,' Robbie said lightly, wishing Josh would quit talking about it.

They were in Josh's bedroom, surrounded from every conceivable angle by posters of his current passion, Britney Spears.

'You kidding?' Josh – who wore tinted spectacles and frequently, during school vacations, dyed his mousy hair rainbow colours, and whose parents were, in Robbie's opinion, *incredibly* cool about their son's fads as well as the fact that he sometimes used their first names – shook his head. 'If I'd 'gotten that note, my mom would have made my dad hire a bodyguard by now.'

'Shut up about the note, Josh,' Robbie said good-humouredly.

'Not that anyone's going to send me a note like *that*,' Josh went on with a grimace of self-deprecation, always the first to concede to his total lack of sporting prowess.

'Shut up about the frigging *note*.'

'What's eating you?' Josh was genuinely baffled.

'Nothing.' Robbie paused. 'I'm just bored with it.'

'How could you be bored with something like that?'

'Because it's *nothing*.'

Josh peered over his spectacles. 'Are you freaked out about this, Rob?'

'Of course not.' Robbie knew he sounded unconvincing.

'You sure?'

There was no mockery. Josh and Robbie were best friends, and not just because location had thrown them together. Josh had always teased his mother and, to a lesser extent, his father, but it was just a superficial kind of fooling around, and when the chips were down all the Steinmans were crazy about each other. Which was why Josh had found the premature death of Aaron Johanssen almost unbearably affecting. Robbie would never forget the way Josh had spent time with him, sitting, walking, doing things, doing *nothing*, talking, being silent, whatever he'd needed whenever he'd needed it.

'I mean' – Josh still wasn't quite done – 'maybe your mom was right about calling the cops.'

'Josh, for fuck's sake!' Robbie said.

'You *are* freaked out.'

'Maybe I am – was – just a little.'

'But not any more, huh?'

Robbie shook his head. 'Just some wise guy's idea of a gag.'

'Pretty dumb,' Josh said.

'Yeah.'

They were both quiet for a moment.

'Candice's birthday tomorrow,' Josh said.

'Uh-huh.' Robbie nodded.

'You got a present yet?'

'A book. You?'

Josh shook his head. 'Not yet.' His brown eyes glinted. 'Think she already has *Limbo*?'

'Enough, man,' Robbie said firmly.

Candice's birthday dinner was held at Eden, down in the East Village, an attractive enough cliché of a restaurant, with a *trompe l'oeil* exotic garden sprawling over the two side walls and behind the bar, serpents peeking malevolently out of bougainvillea, ready to pounce.

Candice and James Dickson had said they wanted to go dancing after dinner, and Josh was all for that, but when Angie Molina had pointed out it was a school night and her parents would kill her, Robbie had agreed with her. Josh and Suzie McLean had jumped all over him, telling him not to be such a wuss, but as it happened, no one could agree on exactly where they wanted to go, and the fact was, the places they all really wanted to go to were heavily into ID checking *or* heavily into members only, so for the time being Angie and Robbie were off the hook, wusses or not.

'Can you believe this?' Candice said while their entrées were being cleared from the table. 'My mother told us last night she wants us all to get out of the city this summer in case the West Nile mosquitoes come back – talk about *neurotic*!'

'Who says the West Nile thing's going to come back?' Robbie asked.

'I do.' Josh, returning from the rest room and picking up the tail-end of the conversation, slipped back into his seat. 'I think there's going to be a mega-plague some time in the next few years.'

'Steinman's talking bull again,' Suzie said.

The waitress returned to take their dessert order: chocolate mousse cake for James and Angie; pistachio ice cream for Candice; cheese cake for Robbie and Josh; cinnamon and apple crêpes for Suzie.

Robbie stood up.

'I used the last of the paper,' Josh told him.

'What paper?' Candice asked.

Josh smiled at her. 'Poop paper.'

Robbie smacked him gently on the back of his head. 'Don't be gross, man.'

'Are we going dancing or not?' Candice asked.

Robbie headed for the staircase.

Chapter 20

Finally.

He'd been watching from out in the alley behind the restaurant, squinting through the panel of glass in the back door that gave him a view of the men's room door for so long that his eyes had begun to burn. He'd spotted Steinman going in twice, the black guy from the kids' table once, and he'd caught a glimpse of the cute blonde and the girl with short red hair going into the powder room; he'd *almost* lost track of how many other diners and members of staff, but only almost, because he knew he *had* to count people in and, most significantly, *out*, so that if Johanssen did come on down, he'd know who else was in there with him.

He found it surprising that no one had challenged him, asked him what he was doing sitting out back of a restaurant in a van, watching the door, but no one had so much as glanced at him, let alone told him to move on. Even when a bus boy had brought out some garbage a while back, and he'd waited for just the right second, just before the door closed behind him, and used a matchbook to wedge it open – even then, no one had been around to notice.

Going his way now.

He saw Robert – Robbie – go into the men's room.

Saw the young waiter who'd gone in two minutes earlier come out.

He got out of the van, walked briskly to the back door, opened it, pushed open the door marked 'Men'.

The young man was at the urinal. No one else there or in the stalls.

He went over to the washbasins, looked at himself in the mirror.

Saw calm, cool confidence in his eyes.

Johanssen finished, came across, turned on the hot water tap at his basin, picked up the bar of soap, did not look at him.

Now. Fast.

He needed a sure thing.

Dim Mak. Death touch. Potentially dangerous.

Not with *his* skill, his knowledge of the seventy-four chi cavities in the human body that could be hit or pressed to cause unconsciousness (thirty-six to cause death).

The teenager went down like a stone.

He caught him easily, *tenderly.*

If anyone saw them now, he'd say the kid was drunk.

Out the door.

Into the van.

No one saw them.

Chapter 21

Lydia was at her desk in her study writing a long overdue letter to her old friend Cynthia Gregory in San Francisco, when the front door bell rang.

She got up and went to the door.

Josh was out on the mat, looking uneasy.

'Is Robbie here?'

Panic hit instantly, dagger-sharp, somewhere around her solar plexus.

'What happened?'

'Nothing happened.' Josh shifted weight from left to right foot.

Lydia took a deep breath. 'Come in, Josh.'

He came through the door, closed it behind him.

'What's the story?' She tried to sound light.

'I don't know exactly.' Josh gave a small shrug and shook his head. 'Rob left the restaurant without telling anyone – said he was going to the bathroom, and never came back.' He paused, trying to avoid Lydia's eyes. 'Only that's not the kind of stunt he plays, so I guess I'm kind of worried.'

Lydia felt the panic rise higher, shoved it back down. 'When?'

'I'm not sure.' Josh chewed his lower lip. 'Maybe an hour ago, maybe a little longer.'

'How much longer?' She heard her tone sharpen, couldn't help herself.

'Maybe two hours.' He met her eyes. 'I'm sorry, Mrs

Johanssen. I just figured – for a while we all figured – he just went out for some air or something.'

'Didn't you go to the bathroom to check on him?'

'Of course,' Josh said. 'I did that after he'd been gone, I don't know, about fifteen minutes.' He met her gaze. 'I mean, I didn't think to go sooner – I mean, you don't, do you?'

'No,' Lydia said, managing a touch of kindness. 'I suppose not.' She knew she should ask the teenager into the living room, sit him down, could see he was upset, but she felt oddly rooted to the spot, wanted this to begin and *end* right here and now, wanted Robbie to walk through that door and find them standing here in the hallway . . .

'So when I saw he wasn't down there,' Josh went on, 'wasn't sick or anything, that's when I thought he must have gone for a walk or maybe run into someone and gone to talk to them.'

'You looked around the whole restaurant?'

'Sure.' Josh looked uneasy again. 'Well, not right away. I mean, I *kind* of looked around as I was going back to the other guys, and we talked about it, where Rob might have gone.'

'And then you checked all the tables?'

He nodded. 'Sure. And we asked the *maître d'* if he'd seen him, and our waitress, and we went out front, but he wasn't there.'

'Is there a back exit?'

'We checked that too,' Josh said. 'There's an alleyway behind the restaurant, but there was no sign.'

'And you're sure he actually *went* to the rest room?'

'Yes.' Josh shook his head, confused. 'No, not really sure. I mean, I guess I wasn't facing that way, and the place was pretty jammed, and then they brought our dessert, so . . .' He trailed off.

'Okay,' Lydia said. 'Okay.' *Stay calm*, she told herself.

'I'm sorry.' Josh took off his tinted spectacles, wiped them, put them back on.

Lydia thought, for a moment, that he was going to cry. 'Not your fault.'

61

'It's just not like Rob to do something like that. It's more the kind of thing maybe I might pull, but not Rob.'

'No,' Lydia said.

'So what should we do?' Josh asked her, needing guidance. 'I mean, do we call the cops or something?'

She shook her head. That *was* what she wanted to do, more than anything, to call them right this instant, not waste one more second, but she knew there was no point. 'I don't want to overreact,' she said. 'If we call the police now, when it isn't even—' She glanced at her wristwatch, saw that it wasn't yet eleven-thirty. 'It's too soon to start panicking, Josh. All they'll do is tell me to wait.'

That's exactly what they would say, she knew that. *Wait for him to come home.* They'd assure her that sixteen-year-old guys were, by definition, unreliable. And, of course, they were right.

Except that Robbie *was* reliable. Considerate.

'Mrs Johanssen?'

She looked at Josh, saw he was waiting to be told what to do, his usual bravado shrivelling by the minute.

'Go home, Josh.'

'But what about—'

'It's late, Josh, and it's a school night. Your parents will start worrying.'

'Okay.' He didn't move.

'I'll be fine,' Lydia told him. 'I'm sure Robbie will be home soon.'

Josh started towards the front door, then turned back. 'Will you call me? When he comes in.'

'I don't want to wake your parents.'

'They won't mind.' Josh was firm, more like his usual self. 'I'll explain. They'll want to know Rob's safe.'

Lydia nodded. 'I'll call.'

One second after the door closed, her legs went to jelly. She leaned against the wall, gazing unseeingly at *Dog Hill*, the Pat Singer Central Park painting that was one of Robbie's favourites.

Considerate. But not a saint, thank goodness. He *might* have

62

seen someone else, gone off with them, someone, maybe, the others didn't know about or maybe didn't like. But that didn't ring true. Josh was right – with a table of friends waiting for him, there was no way Robbie would simply go off without saying anything.

He might, though, have felt suddenly unwell, decided he had to get out, and if the place was as busy as Josh had described, he might not have been able to face returning to the table to let them know. *That* was feasible, surely.

Except if that were the case, he would have come home.

If he could.

Lydia got to her feet, went over to the telephone, picked up the Yellow Pages, and started calling hospitals.

At two a.m., having long since lost the temporary relief she'd gained from establishing that Robbie had at least not been admitted to any Manhattan emergency room, she called the police.

The officer she spoke to at the 20th Precinct was kind and not at all dismissive, but, just as she'd known he would, he suggested Lydia stay home, try to get some rest or maybe ask someone to come sit with her while she waited for her son to come home. Which he almost certainly would.

Almost.

'From what you tell me,' the officer said, 'your son's bound to come back or call to let you know what's happened.'

Bound to.

The man was right. Robbie being Robbie, he would not let her go through the night in this kind of uncertainty.

If he could help it.

She was still sleepless at seven-thirty a.m. when Melanie Steinman telephoned.

'I told Joshua it was too early to call,' she said in her soft voice, 'but frankly he's been fit to be tied.'

'Robbie hasn't come home yet.' Lydia didn't wait for the question.

'And he hasn't called?' Melanie's disbelief was palpable.

'No.' Lydia felt suddenly close to tears. 'Give Josh my love and tell him not to worry too much.'

She put down the phone, swallowed the urge to howl, then picked it up again and called the 20th Precinct, where a female officer suggested that if she was really worried, she should come by and file a report, maybe ask someone else to man the phone for her. Melanie was, of course, the obvious choice, but well-meaning as she was, Josh's mother irritated Lydia at the best of times, and this was definitely not one of those.

She called the Franklins.

Anna answered, plainly wide awake. 'What's happened?'

'Robbie didn't come home last night.'

'Oh my God.' A brief pause. 'What do you need?'

Lydia told her. Anna said that was fine.

'Are you sure? Don't you have something on this morning?'

'Only my aerobics class,' Anna said. 'I'd do anything to get out of that.'

'Thank you, Anna,' Lydia said, and put down the phone again.

Robbie, where are you?

Chapter 22

Robbie came to in the middle of a nightmare.

His head was aching, felt heavy, *real* heavy, like there was something strapped to it, which made no sense at all.

He groaned, a hollow, not-quite-normal sound. His feet were cold, his hands warm, encased in something ... gloves?

He opened his eyes, blinked hard.

Nothing but pale blue light.

Robbie jolted in panic, thrashed his arms around in space, couldn't *see* his own arms, tried touching his head, but the gloves were so thick, cumbersome ...

'Don't panic.'

He heard the voice, turned his head, trying to find the speaker.

'Keep calm.'

A male voice, a little distorted, but low and soothing, like a doctor's, maybe.

'Where am I?' He remembered where he *had* been. The restaurant, with Josh and Candice and the others. The men's room, taking a piss, going to wash his hands ... *pain*. Nothing more.

'Where *am* I?'

'It's okay,' the voice told him. 'You're okay, you're perfectly safe.'

'Am I in the hospital?' Maybe he'd been in some kind of accident – maybe this was the ICU.

'Not in the hospital,' the voice said. 'But quite safe.'

Robbie tried turning his head again – still the weird heaviness. 'My head,' he said.

'Your head is fine.'

'Why's the light so *blue*?'

'You'll understand soon,' the voice told him. 'When you're ready.'

'What's going on?' Robbie asked. 'What *is* this place?'

'Do you think you're ready to see?' the voice asked.

'See what? I don't *understand*.'

'If you're ready to take a look at where you are, I think you'll like it.'

Okay. Suddenly Robbie realized what was going on. This was just a *dream*, that's all. So he might as well give in, roll with it. His head still hurt, and he felt kind of sick, but it was just a dream . . .

'I guess I'm ready,' he told the dream-maker.

The blue light went out, leaving him in pitch darkness.

'*Hey*!'

No answer.

About to yell again, Robbie realized that his eyes were growing used to the dark, that he could make out a shape, right ahead of him. A shape that looked like a high, curved ceiling, arching down on both sides into walls, stone walls . . . more darkness beyond the arch, slipping away, far away, down a . . . *tunnel* . . .

That's *it*? He was starting to feel better, more confident, about ready to scoff at the dream-maker. *I've had better nightmares than this, I can tell you.*

Then he heard it. *Something coming.* A weird kind of tread, not footsteps exactly, squishier sounding, *stranger*, like a big animal moving through mud, but not four-legged or fast. Slow, deliberate. Oddly familiar.

Breathing, too. Unhealthy. Wheezy, nasal, like an old man with a lousy head cold and even worse habits.

Robbie grinned in the semi-dark. He knew now what it sounded like. Like Ghoulo, the flesh-eater. *Not too original, man.* The blue light on its own had been creepier, more effective. Any *Limbo* freak could dream *this* up, though he guessed now that it was likely to get scarier any second, if Ghoulo shambled any closer and tried to take a chunk out of him, but still . . .

The tunnel vanished into blackness.

Shit.

The blue light was back.

Time to wake up, Rob.

'So, young man', the voice said, 'do you know where you are now?'

'Sure I know,' Robbie answered. He was getting uncomfortable again; the dream was going on too long, and he didn't feel so good.

'Somewhere under the city,' the voice said.

'Yeah, yeah,' Robbie answered back. 'Like in *Limbo*. So I've worked it out, and now I'm ready to wake up.'

'You're not asleep,' the voice said.

'Yeah, yeah,' Robbie said again.

'This is just the start of it, Steel,' the voice said.

Steel. Now Robbie understood why he was dreaming this. It was because of that weirdo gift and the note, which made it a perfectly logical bad dream to be having.

'You're not asleep,' the voice said again. 'This is not a dream. This is real, Steel. This is happening.'

'Yeah, sure,' Robbie said in his muffled voice. 'I'm Steel, and Dakota's in the next tunnel, and Santa Claus is coming in on the next train.'

'Something like that,' the voice said benevolently.

Robbie stopped listening to the voice. The thing on his head was starting to stifle him, give him a headache.

'Would you like to see Dakota now, Steel?'

'What?' Robbie said, irritably.

'I asked if you would like to see Dakota?'

Intrigue pushed away the feeling of irritation. 'Why not?'

The blue light went out. Darkness startled him again, then turned into something else.

A small room, dimly lit, with damp-looking stone walls.

Like a cell. Robbie had to strain his eyes to see. There was someone in the room, lying on a mattress on the floor. A *girl*. She was lying on her side, sleeping, Robbie thought, peering at her, trying to get a better look. Long legs, bare feet, the soles grimy . . . wearing that skimpy leather get-up that Dakota wore in the game. Her right arm was flung up, half-covering her face, but her hair was long and dark, like . . .

'That's neat,' he had to admit.

'Dakota.'

'Okay,' Robbie said, on the edge of admiration.

'*Dakota*.'

Robbie realized that the male voice wasn't talking to him now, but to the girl in the cell.

'Wake up, Dakota.'

The girl groaned a little, covered her face more.

'*Dakota!*' Sharper now.

She gave a whimper. Her arm moved, exposing her face.

She was beautiful, Robbie saw. *She'd make a good Dakota*.

The dream had taken a freaky kind of sideways step, he realized. He'd have thought that if he were going to dream *Limbo*, he'd dream the real thing, but this was a living, *human* girl, not a cyber-heroine. Just a girl.

'She's just a girl,' he told the dream-maker.

'Wrong,' the voice answered. 'She's Dakota. Just as you're Steel.'

Uh-huh, Robbie thought, but didn't say.

'She had another name outside,' the voice told him, 'just as you had. But now she's Dakota. You *were* Robert David Johanssen. Now you're not.'

Definitely time to wake up.

'I know it's hard to take in,' the voice said gently.

'I'm going to wake up now,' Robbie said.

'I brought you a gift, Dakota.' The voice addressed the girl again. 'Put on your headset so you can see.'

Robbie was hardly listening. He was staring at the girl again. She had blue eyes, he could see now, with deep shadows beneath them, and she was thin. Too thin. She was fumbling around for something on the mattress beside her, then picked it up. Some kind of contraption. A *headset*, the voice had said. Robbie heard her sigh, saw her pull the thing over her head. Down over her ears, over her eyes. *Goggles*. Ugly. Covering her lovely face, turning her into a kind of half-monster.

'Shit.' She spoke for the first time. Softly, huskily.

She looked down for something else; apparently she could see clearly now that she was wearing the *thing*.

Gloves. Big, clumsy-looking gloves. She pulled them on.

'Oh my *God*.' Her voice cracked a little.

She was looking straight at Robbie.

'Steel,' she said.

'That's right,' the voice said. 'I told you I'd bring you another, and here he is. Isn't he just *perfect*?'

Robbie knew now why his head felt so heavy, why his voice was muffled, why his hands were so unwieldy. He put them together, felt strange, leathery thickness, then put his right hand up to his face, felt for the goggles, found them.

'Leave it,' the voice told him sharply. 'You won't like it if you take it off.'

'I don't like it *now*.'

Robbie struggled against panic. He hated panicking, hated feeling out of control, always had. He tried to calm down by telling himself that the dream-maker was doing a heck of a job, after all. *Nightmare-maker*.

More than anything in the world, he wanted to wake up.

'Get used to it, Steel,' the voice said.

THREE

Chapter 23

Kim spotted it first, not me.

The piece in the *New York Times* about a sixteen-year-old boy, son of a late, lamented concert pianist, who'd gone missing not long after the arrival of a mystery gift.

I was cleaning out my underwear drawer, tossing out old jockeys and trying to marry off odd socks. What I was *really* doing, of course, was procrastinating. Now on my summer break, I had already made the girls breakfast, and Kim had taken Ella to school (Rianna took herself these days). I'd collected and opened the mail and sorted out which bills needed paying promptly and which junk could be thrown out. And then Kim had come back, so I'd skulked off to my bedroom and hit the Y-front drawer.

In other words, *anything* rather than what I was meant to be doing, i.e. writing my novel, which was, by the way, a ghost story set around the Yale campus. I had no commission, of course, and no real belief that I'd find a publisher if it ever did get written, but it was an old idea that stemmed from way back before Simone's death, and when, at the start of 2000, the urge to write it had at last returned, like an old, deep itch, I had welcomed it as a sign of healing and better mental health. The plan was that I would use my summer recess – at least in the quiet days until the girls began their own vacation – to write full time, researching as and when necessary either in the UNH library, which remained open through the summer, or at Yale itself.

That was the plan, anyway . . .

Kim knocked on the door. 'Jake, can I come in?'

'Sure.'

She glanced at the pile of underwear on my bed. 'More writer's block?'

I didn't answer.

'They do say,' Kim ventured, 'that the only way over that is to actually *write*, even if it's not very good.'

'They say all kinds of things,' I said. 'Most of them useless.'

Kim held out the *Times*. 'Something here I thought you should see.'

I took it from her, saw the piece she'd marked with a small, neat X, saw the photograph of a missing boy named Robert Johanssen, read just a few lines, glanced up at Kim, then took the paper over to the phone on my bedside table and sat down.

'Damn,' I said.

'Think there's a connection?' Kim asked.

'I certainly think we should find out.'

I called the Boston office of Lomax & Baum, and was glad to hear Norman Baum's own gentle voice as he picked up. We'd talked several times during the past two and a half weeks since I'd arranged for the Coopers to hire him; often enough to know that Baum had been trying hard to find out something helpful about Michael for them but failing every step of the way.

'You've seen the *Times*,' Baum said promptly.

'Just this minute.'

'And you think we should contact the mother.'

'I think we should find out about the mystery gift,' I said.

'I agree,' Baum said. 'I was going to call you anyway. I'd call the lady myself, but I figure she might not want to talk to a PI.'

'You think I should call her?' I found I wanted Baum's approval.

'You or one of the Coopers,' he said. 'Though just in case they haven't picked up on the story yet, I'd rather not get them all worked up.'

My sentiments exactly.

*

I found a listing for Lydia Johanssen, wondered if I should plan my call more thoroughly, script my approach a little, since I was clearly pushing myself slap bang into a desperate and delicate situation. Then again, maybe that was all the more reason for simple directness. Maybe I wouldn't even get to speak to the lady herself, or maybe she would refuse to talk to me.

While Kim went out again to fetch some groceries, I made the call. The number rang twice and was answered by a female voice, low and tentative.

'Is that Mrs Johanssen?'

'It is.'

'My name is Jake Woods, calling from New Haven, Connecticut.'

'Yes?'

She was giving nothing away, and I didn't blame her. I took the no-prevarication route, painful but best in the circumstances. I explained that I'd seen the *Times* piece, that friends of mine were in a similar position and that I had an idea that the mystery gift referred to might mean there was a link between both disappearances.

'How old is your friends' son?' Mrs Johanssen asked, still quiet but urgent now.

'Michael's fifteen,' I told her.

'How long has he been missing?'

I hesitated, realizing that my answer would cause her only more dismay. But then, maybe we were going to find that the gift was a red herring and that there was actually no connection. On the other hand, if there was, the sooner the poor woman found out, the better for her son.

'Almost two months,' I answered. We were now seven days into June.

For a long moment, she said nothing.

'I realize there's probably no link at all, Mrs Johanssen.'

She gathered herself together. 'What kind of gift was Michael sent?'

'A computer game,' I told her, all tensed up, hoping like hell I was wrong.

'Oh.'

Just that one word, probably all she could manage at that instant. Already, I felt sick at heart, for her and for what this might mean for Fran and Stu.

'It was a game called *Limbo*,' I expanded.

'Yes,' she said. 'You said there was a note?'

'Yes. Unsigned.'

'Like Robbie's,' she said.

Christ.

'Mr Woods . . .' she began, then stopped.

'Yes?' I tried to help her along.

'Could we meet?'

That threw me. 'Of course,' I said. 'If you think it would help. Or I could just pass the information to the police – if they don't already have it.'

'I'd like to have it first hand,' Lydia Johanssen said. 'Maybe I could meet your friends, too?'

I hesitated, thinking about what that might do to the Coopers. Would it help Fran to have another mother in the same position to talk to, or would it simply destroy any lingering hopes that Mikey might be a runaway or amnesiac somewhere, perhaps still on the way home to them?

'Let me come to you,' I said, abruptly. 'If you wouldn't mind that.'

'Of course I wouldn't mind.' She sounded surprised. 'But I thought you said you're in New Haven?'

'It's just a train ride,' I said, 'and I'm guessing you'd rather stay close to home. You and I could talk first, and then maybe you'd like me to talk to someone at the NYPD about my friends' son.'

'That would be very kind.' She paused. 'Don't you have to work?'

I liked her straightforwardness. 'I'm on vacation,' I told her. 'I teach at the University of New Haven – you might want to check me out – Professor Jacob Woods – make sure I'm who I say I am.' I paused.

'When can you come?'

76

I thought about the girls, knew that Kim was going to be around today after school. 'I need to wait for someone to come back here, confirm it's okay for me to leave, and then—'

'I can't expect you to drop everything,' Lydia Johanssen said.

'It's okay,' I reassured her. 'There's nothing to drop. Unless I hit a snag, I'll catch the next train out and see you later.'

When Amtrak's doing its thing properly, I usually enjoy the train ride into Manhattan, get a corny kick out of the first sighting, even after all these years. I don't even mind Penn Station, so long as it isn't rush hour or a Friday afternoon. Today, the twelve-twenty ran on time, getting me into the city at two p.m., and the line for cabs wasn't too long, *and* the traffic going uptown wasn't too bad – but still, despite those small boons I felt taut as a violin string by the time I paid the driver and got out of the cab on Columbus Avenue, not far from the corner of West Seventy-third.

It's a part of town I've always liked, blessed with a variety of decent restaurants, close to the park and walking distance from Lincoln Center. A nice place to live, I imagined, for the widow of a pianist and her son. Decent, clean, attractive, populated by an interesting cross-section.

Safe.

Lydia Johanssen was waiting as I came out of the elevator, standing just inside the open front door of Apartment 15C. She was younger than I'd anticipated. And frankly, though it maybe wasn't the kind of thing I ought to have been noticing right then and there – not the kind of thing I'd noticed too often since Simone, as a matter of fact – she was lovely to look at.

'Professor Woods,' she said, stretching out her hand.

'Jake, please.'

'I'm Lydia Johanssen.'

I shook the firm, cool hand, looked into tense, large amber-brown eyes set in a pale oval face framed by dark, straight, long hair. The eyes were scanning my face, searching, checking me

77

out, I guess, wanting to be sure I'd really come to help and that my motives were honest. Intelligent eyes.

'Please come in,' she said.

I stepped into the Johanssen hallway, saw one of my favourite Pat Singer paintings and a delicate, air-brushed landscape. It was an attractive, homely hallway.

'I can't thank you enough for coming all this way.' Lydia Johanssen walked ahead of me into her living room. She wore beige slacks and a long-sleeved creamy cotton top that looked way too warm for the weather; but then again, I'd seen what grief or deep fear could do to people's bodies as well as their minds, and I remembered suddenly that after Simone's death I'd felt cold for weeks . . .

'I'd say I felt bad, dragging you here,' she said, 'but the truth is I don't, not really. I'm too grateful for that.'

'There's really no need,' I told her, meaning it, especially as I felt so damned sure that all I was bringing her was *more* fear.

'It's all right,' she said. 'I'm not expecting miracles from you. Just share what you know, please – *all* of it, nothing edited.'

She had to look up a little to talk to me. In flat, neat shoes, Lydia Johanssen was not short by any means, but I'm on the tall side, six feet two inches, broad-shouldered *and* – according to Rianna, who likes to take care of my health – developing the beginnings of a paunch.

She told me to make myself comfortable, asked me to call her Lydia, bade me sit down in a big old armchair covered in soft ivory-coloured fabric while she went to make some coffee. I took the opportunity to look around the room. That same feeling of home. A lot of photographs. A few of the lady herself and, I presumed, her late husband, Aaron; nice-looking man, though not the way I imagined a concert pianist to look, however *that* was . . . A bunch of photos of the boy whose picture I'd seen in the *Times*. Robert Johanssen, seriously good-looking, dark-haired like his mom, with laughing blue eyes and a cleft chin like his father's.

I felt anger hit me hard, the way it had at the Coopers' that Sunday.

Two great kids – young men from solid, safe environments. Plucked out of their everyday lives, out of loving homes. *Taken*. Abducted. I wanted so badly to be wrong about that, but the games link made it painfully probable.

It also made me wonder exactly why we were wasting time brewing coffee when surely we ought to be talking to the police and the FBI, who were probably aware, by now, of the connection. Lydia had told me on the phone that she wanted to hear about the other case first hand, and maybe, I thought, remembering Stu and Fran, this woman wanted to feel she had a tiny measure of control, wanted the facts before the big machine gulped it down and ground into all kinds of action she might never get to hear about. Already I could see that this was going to be a very different scene than the one I'd played with the Coopers, both so distraught because they'd felt no one was taking Michael's absence seriously enough.

If the cops and the FBI knew about *Limbo* and the notes in both cases, they'd be taking it very seriously indeed.

I wouldn't say that, on the whole, I'm an ostrich-type person, but I found myself wishing just then that Kim had never seen the damned *Times* article. Norman Baum had made the connection, after all, and even if no one in the Brookline Police Department happened to have read that paper yet, it had to be just a matter of time before everyone knew.

And I could have been home with my disorderly sock drawer and writer's block. Selfishly detached from this mother's pain.

We drank our coffee and talked about Robert – Lydia called him Robbie – for a while, and I filled her in a little about myself, my past, the reason the Coopers had come to me, about Norman Baum's attempts, and about the Coopers themselves; and there were more parallels with Mikey, outside their interest in computer games and their apparently stable backgrounds. They looked reasonably alike, both dark-haired, tall, naturally athletic, both good-looking kids. They were popular, had good friends. Neither was heavily into academic work; both were easy-going, sports-loving boys – though it sounded to me as if

Michael was more intense about his running than Robbie was about any one sport. Both just regular guys. Good, happy, healthy, *normal* teenage males. Like countless others.

That thought chilled me, too.

'One thing,' Lydia said, 'was that the note said Robbie was a *Limbo* "master", but Robbie told me that wasn't true. He said he already had the game and was quite good at it, but hadn't had the patience to stay with it long enough to be outstanding.' Her mouth twisted a little. 'Apparently, real "masters" have to be pretty obsessed.'

I tried to recall whether the Coopers had mentioned if Mikey had been obsessed by *Limbo*, but mostly I remembered Fran's distaste when she'd talked about the game.

'Have you ever played?' I asked Lydia.

She shook her head. 'Not my idea of fun.' She paused, clearly filled with dreadful tension. 'Did the Brookline police learn anything from Michael's note?'

'The Coopers couldn't find the note after he vanished – they think Michael might have had it with him.'

'I had Robbie's,' Lydia said, 'gave it to the NYPD along with the game. They agreed there might be a connection with his disappearance, but evidence-wise it doesn't seem to have been worth much.' She listed their non-findings, her face stiff with what I thought might be anger. 'No fingerprints; the paper's one of the most commonly used brands in the country; and the font's standard with most PCs.'

She stopped talking, looked down into her lap. I saw her lips compress, her chin set tight, knew she was fighting hard to stay composed.

'Okay,' I said after what I hoped was a decent break. 'So what do we do now? Make a call or two, see if Missing Persons knows about the Coopers?' I paused. 'Or is there someone else you'd like to call first?' I wanted her to make this decision, figured it was part of that scrap of control she needed.

Her chin tilted up and her eyes met mine again. Back on form.

'No one else,' she said, and there was a semblance of a

smile in the warm-coloured but desolate eyes. 'Let's make the call.'

They came swiftly. Detectives Mary Calhoun – thin, wiry with short fair hair and keen blue-grey eyes – and Marcus Hobbs – tall African-American with a gentle, empathetic face. I took a back seat while Lydia filled them in, then told them all I knew about the Michael Cooper case. Whether or not the Brookline police had learned about Robbie Johanssen, word had not yet reached these two detectives. They listened attentively, made notes, wasted no time, thanked us both, assured Lydia they'd be acting on the new information without delay, and left.

It was a little before five. The whole meeting had taken less than forty minutes.

There was no more reason for me to stay.

'I guess I should be going,' I said when Lydia came back into the living room, having seen the detectives to the door.

'Yes,' she said. 'Of course.'

She glanced at her wristwatch, seemed startled by the time. She looked pale and drained, which was hardly surprising.

'I could stay a little longer,' I told her. 'If there's something I could do.'

Lydia shook her head. 'No,' she said. 'You've done more than enough.' A thought struck her. 'I could make you something to eat. You must be hungry.'

'Not really,' I said. 'I'll get something on the train, be back home for dinner.'

'With your children,' she said softly. 'Of course.'

I stood up. Suddenly, I felt awkward, displaced. It had been such an unnatural first encounter, easy in a curious way because circumstances had overridden convention. But now I'd accomplished what I'd come for, done what little I could. It was time to go.

Fact was, though, I didn't really *want* to.

Good manners drove me out to the front door, nevertheless.

'You've been so kind.' Lydia's voice was suddenly as fatigued as her face. 'I truly don't know how to thank you.'

'There's no need,' I told her again. 'I just hope it helped a little.'

'It did,' she said.

'I guess you won't hear anything for a while,' I said.

She shook her head.

'They'll be linking up with Brookline, maybe talking to the FBI.'

'Yes.' Getting close to the edge again.

Time to leave, Jake. Give the lady some space, peace and quiet.

To hell with peace and quiet. What she needed – *all* she needed – was one noisy, normal, dark-haired, blue-eyed sixteen-year-old back in her home, in her arms.

'If there's anything else I can do,' I said, 'please call me.'

'I will,' she said.

On the train, on the way back home to my daughters – thank God, thank *Christ* – I found it impossible to stop thinking about Lydia Johanssen and how she had to be feeling right now. I hoped she'd gone directly to bed, fallen asleep, but I doubted that, doubted if she'd gotten much sleep at all since Robbie had gone.

I felt suddenly angry with myself, unsure if I'd handled this the right way. Maybe I ought to have simply called the information in to the cops, either in Brookline or New York, left it to them to work it out between themselves; and then maybe Lydia wouldn't have needed to know just yet – or at all – about the possible link with the Coopers.

I mean, what had I left her with? The awful added burden of knowing that someone else's son had gone missing in frighteningly similar, sinister circumstances, almost two whole *months* ago, and had not been heard of since. Lydia Johanssen had been grateful, courteous and incredibly brave in my presence, but surely all I'd actually achieved was to multiply her terrors by five thousand per cent.

Good one, Jake.

Good one.

Chapter 24

Robbie was *not* getting used to it, as the voice had told him to.

The only thing he was getting to understand about this whole *nightmare* was that if he ripped the headset off, detaching the goggles and earphones, and took off the gloves, without having been *told* to do so, he found himself plunged into pitch darkness and absolute silence – into something, he supposed with awful, sick terror, like live burial.

That, to date, seemed to be the only form of punishment for disobedience. Disconnection from life, from even these *morsels* of the world; his senses still alive and buzzing, flailing around in the dark.

So every time he took off the headset because he felt he had to, he found himself having to put it back on after just a few minutes. To get reconnected.

The big problem was what he was connected *to*.

Chapter 25

Lydia called me two days after my trip to New York. I was alone in the apartment in the early afternoon, actually sitting at my computer in my study; I'd written two pages that morning, two lines since lunch. The gardens of Wooster Square were tempting me to wander on out and stroll in them. In other words, words were not exactly *flowing*.

'There've been some developments.' Lydia's voice sounded desperately strained. 'I wasn't sure if you might have heard, via your friends, but I thought maybe you'd want to know.'

'I've heard nothing,' I said tensely. I'd talked to Norman Baum on my return from New York, and we'd both agreed that telling Fran and Stu before they had to know would only salt their wounds the way I had Lydia Johanssen's.

'Detective Calhoun came to see me this morning to tell me that the missing persons' database has found three more similar cases.'

Jesus. 'Where?'

'One, a boy of fifteen, from Harrisburg, Pennsylvania, and two girls – one aged sixteen from Providence, Rhode Island, the other from Atlantic City, just fourteen years old.' Lydia cleared her throat and went on. 'They've all gone missing during the past four months, Jake, and they've all been sent the game.'

I didn't know what to say. I was stunned.

'I know,' Lydia said. 'It's too horrible to take in.'

I made myself get a grip. After all, *she* was handling it.

'Did Calhoun say anything else?'

'Mostly that the FBI is setting up a task force to deal with it. A *major* task force was what she said.'

'That's good,' I said.

'I guess so,' she said.

Yeah, sure, it's terrific. Now she knew her son was just one of five abducted children. *Abductions.* That, at least, was no longer in question.

'How're you holding up, Lydia?'

'I don't know,' she answered, honestly. 'I'm here. Getting up in the mornings, getting through the days, going to bed at night, then starting over again.'

'Getting any sleep?'

'Not much.'

Stupid questions.

'Do you have people around you?' At last, something halfway intelligent. 'Taking care of you?'

'I have some good friends,' Lydia said.

'Thank God for good friends,' I said.

'Yes.' She paused. 'I just wanted to let you know what had happened, Jake. Thanks to you, at least a lot more people are going to be working on finding Robbie and the others.'

'They would have made the connections anyhow,' I said.

'But you saved some time, and I'm very grateful for that.'

'Anything else I can do for you?' I paused. 'Anything at all.'

'No, I don't think so.'

Why should she need a stranger when she has friends?

'Thank you for bringing me up to speed, Lydia,' I said.

'Least I could do, Jake.'

I wished her luck and we said our goodbyes.

I put down the phone and stared back out onto the square, irritated by myself for being so damned polite and unnatural. The woman had such dignity and courage, and I was filled with admiration that she could convey such strength when she had to be falling apart inside. Yet all I'd done was thank her for the information, as if she'd just called from some store to tell me an order had come in.

Shit, Jake.

I stood up and paced the small room. I was giving myself a hard time for no good reason. There *was* nothing that I could do for Lydia Johanssen. Only one thing would comfort her, and that was Robbie's safe return, and the FBI was the organization best equipped to achieve that, God willing, not Jake Woods, professor of criminal justice and once-upon-a-time investigator. The lady had called me out of courtesy, nothing more. What I needed to do now was to get on with my big summer plans, write some semblance of a first draft of the damned book, and then, when the girls got out of school, maybe take them away somewhere, either to the ocean or upstate someplace into the countryside, and have some good old-fashioned fun with them before we all forgot how.

Easier said than done.

I went to visit Fran and Stu the day after I heard about the other cases. In most respects I found them in worse shape than before; hardly surprising, given that another month had gone by without word of Mikey. In one way, though, Stu, if not Fran, seemed a little more positive.

'At least now we know everything really *is* being done,' he told me, when his wife was in the kitchen. 'I mean, I feel terrible for the other parents, but at least now they know we were telling the truth.'

'They knew that anyway, Stu,' I told him. 'They just needed more facts.'

His face got all twisted up then. 'We told them our facts, Jake.' He glanced towards the kitchen, barely managing to keep his voice down. 'They thought we were bad parents – they thought Mikey had run away from us. They didn't *listen* when we told them about the note.'

I told Stu that so far as I knew, the NYPD's preliminary examination of the note sent to Robbie Johanssen had yielded nothing to date.

'At least they *believed* her.' He was very bitter.

I started trying to tell him again that I thought he was wrong about the local police, but then Fran came into the room and Stu changed the subject, but Fran said she knew pretty much exactly what he'd been saying to me, and she was afraid he was becoming obsessed, and that wasn't going to help bring their son back home.

Yet again, I knew there was nothing I could do to help, except maybe get out of their faces. Which I did, feeling worse than ever.

I did what I could to put it all out of my mind, but I just could not settle. Whether I was writing, reading, shopping, cooking, playing with my kids, talking to Kim and Tom, or working in the library at UNH, my mind kept straying back to the Coopers and to Lydia Johanssen.

Especially to Lydia.

Rianna nailed me late one Saturday evening when, unable to sleep, she came to find me in my study and looked over my shoulder at my computer screen.

'You're on the same page you were working on this morning.'

'Thank you, child.' I swivelled around in my chair and looked up at my beautiful older daughter. 'Have you been growing again?' It seemed only yesterday she'd still been small enough to fit snugly on my lap, and now here she was in her baggy *High Fliers* T-shirt, a gorgeous grey-eyed girl with marvellous winged eyebrows, endless legs and strong bare feet.

'What's up, Daddy?' Rianna was not to be diverted.

'Nothing's up with me. How come you can't sleep?'

She shrugged. 'I was sleeping, but I woke up.'

'Bad dream?'

'Nope. Just not tired any more.' She looked pointedly past me back at the computer. 'Is it really tough?'

'Oh, yeah.'

'Poor you.' She looked sympathetic, then wandered across to the table that supported my big old globe, which had always fascinated her. She spun it now, then stopped it with one hand and fingered South America. 'It's not just the book that's bugging you, though, is it?'

'Isn't it?'

'You've been off someplace ever since you went to New York to see Robbie Johanssen's mother.'

'Have I?' I'd told the girls just as much and as little as I'd felt I could get away with, given that they already knew about Michael's disappearance. The thought that I'd let my personal reactions to outside horrors affect me sufficiently for Rianna – and perhaps Ella, too – to notice, dismayed me. 'I'm sorry, sweetheart. I haven't meant to be that way.'

Rianna turned to look back at me. 'It's okay, Daddy. I know you've been upset because of Mikey and the others.'

'Others?' The links found via the missing kids' database had not yet made the papers or the TV, and since I'd heard the news I definitely hadn't told either Rianna or Ella. *Last* thing I wanted was to give my own children nightmares.

She looked a little abashed. 'I heard you talking to Kim and Tom.'

That had been two evenings ago, when I'd believed her to be in her room.

'I wasn't eavesdropping,' she said quickly.

'Really?' I was a touch dry.

'I just heard you.' She shrugged. 'I couldn't *un*-hear what you'd said just because I wasn't meant to hear it.'

I smiled. 'I guess not.'

'I didn't tell Ella,' she reassured me.

'I'm glad,' I said.

We looked each other in the eye for a moment or two, and I knew she was searching for something. And damn it, but where – or rather, *who*? – did my mind beat an instant path to? Lydia Johanssen.

And not *just* because of her monstrous predicament.

Damn it.

Chapter 26

I phoned her Monday morning, after the girls had gone to school.

Lydia picked up quickly, sounded distracted, preoccupied, claimed to be glad to hear from me, told me there was no news, thanked me for calling. Polite but awkward. I had clearly been spot-on when I figured that Lydia Johanssen needed no back-up from me. I wished her well – from the bottom of my heart – and said goodbye.

Better this way, I decided. For me, anyway. At least now I'd be able to put her out of my mind and concentrate on my own world.

I'd actually written five pages when she called me back.

'I'm so sorry, Jake.'

'What for?'

'There were people with me when you called this morning, and it was very difficult to talk. I was actually so glad to hear from you, but you must have thought me very rude.'

'I never thought that,' I said. 'I assumed you were pre-occupied.'

Lydia laughed wryly. 'I've forgotten what it feels like *not* to be preoccupied.'

'I wasn't sure if I should call you or not,' I confessed.

'Why not?'

'I don't want to impose on you. This is a very private time for you.'

'You're not imposing, Jake, believe me.'

I believed her. I asked her to hold for one moment while I saved my puny efforts to disk, so I could pick up the cordless phone and abandon my desk.

'I'm back,' I told her.

'I've disturbed your work,' she said.

Now I laughed. 'The kindest thing anyone can do for me these days is disturb my so-called work.'

'I thought you said you loved teaching.'

'I do. This is not teaching.'

I told her a very little about my so-called ghost story novel. She said she was impressed. I told her not to be. She said it was probably far better than I was making out, that she had me pegged as overly modest. I liked her more by the second.

'May I explain something to you, Jake?'

'Of course.'

'When you came to see me, although we were strangers, I had a feeling that you understood, *really* understood, something about this black pit I've fallen into.'

I didn't speak, had no wish to interrupt.

'You didn't say much. You didn't try too hard. I felt that was because you understood.'

'I can't begin to know what you're going through, Lydia.'

'I didn't say you *knew*. Just that you seemed to understand.' She paused, then went on quickly. 'My friends are being wonderful. I know I'm lucky to have them, and I'm probably being very ungrateful, but the truth is that when they're with me right now, I feel so hemmed in.'

Her pause seemed deliberate to me, as if she was giving me a chance to stop her, but I didn't want to. Lydia was talking to me, *really* talking, and I guess that was what I'd been waiting for.

'I feel I have to behave so well when people are around,' she went on, 'which isn't their fault at all. My dear friend, Anna Franklin, for instance, wouldn't care if I ripped off all my clothes and started screaming – well, I guess she'd call the doctor, but that's not the point.' She paused again, for breath. 'The point is I don't *want* to behave right now. I don't really want to have to do anything, *be* anything. I'm in limbo – just like the title of that terrible game. But my friends keep trying to drag me up out of my pit. They bring me food, they try to make me more comfortable – as if I *could* be comfortable, as if I could *eat*, as if I could care *less* about anything while Robbie's wherever he is, maybe going through hell, maybe going through nothing at all.' She stopped abruptly.

One thought too far, I was aware.

'Damn,' she said. '*Damn*.'

'Don't,' I said. 'It's okay.'

'See?' Lydia said. 'That's exactly why I wanted to call you back. You're easy to talk to – to be hysterical with. You have no expectations as to how I should be; mostly, I suppose, because you don't know me.'

'Maybe I just know when to shut the hell up,' I said.

She laughed. I liked the sound.

'There's something else, too,' she went on in an abrupt switch of mood. 'About the FBI investigation.'

'Problem?'

'I think so,' she answered. 'From my point of view.' And paused again. 'Could you possibly spare some more time, Jake? I know it's an imposition.'

'Hey,' I said. 'I thought we'd covered impositions.' I was filled with pleasure, intense and rather complicated. 'Are you free for lunch tomorrow?'

'Of course,' Lydia said.

'I'd invite you to New Haven, but I know you'd sooner stay put, so if Kim – she helps take care of my daughters – if she's free, I could catch a morning train.' I paused. 'If you'd like.'

Lydia said she would.

We'd arranged for me to catch a cab from Penn Station directly to the Ocean Grill on Columbus Avenue, just a few blocks from the street where the Johanssens lived. Lydia was waiting for me at one of the outdoor tables, shaded by a parasol, a glass of cold white wine in front of her. We shook hands and I sat down, facing her.

'This is nice,' I said, thinking again, with something like a rush, how good she looked in her simple, beautifully-cut beige linen shift dress. Her bare arms were smooth, well-shaped. I wondered if she worked out, thought again of my own waistline, not that bad whatever Rianna might say, but definitely not as lean as it had been. Maybe, I thought, I should start going to the gym with my daughter.

Lydia smiled at me. 'You look good,' she said. 'More relaxed.'

'I feel it.' I looked around. 'The weather helps.' It was a gorgeous New York City day, blue sky, warm, fresh-feeling air, passers-by in good spirits.

'You know,' Lydia said, 'for a moment or two, sitting here, waiting, sipping a little wine, I felt I was back in the real world.' She shook her head. 'A delusion, of course.'

'Would you rather skip lunch, go back home to talk?'

'No,' she answered firmly. 'Not at all.'

I tried to gauge her expression, but she was wearing dark glasses, which made it tough. 'If you're being polite because I've come into the city again and you think I'm expecting lunch, you don't have to worry about me.'

'I'm not,' Lydia said. 'Though the fact is, you *have* come a long way. But I've been spending far too much time cooped up, so I've organized the next two hours. Sally – my part-time housekeeper – is going to take any calls, and if anything important happens, she's going to call me on my cell phone.' She leaned sideways, pulled a small flip-phone out of her bag and put it on the table. 'So we might as well order, and I intend to at least *try* to relax.'

'Good.' I ordered myself a glass of Chardonnay.

We managed to keep off horrors right through our first course and part-way into our crab cakes and roasted corn salsa. It *was* an effort – we both knew we were masking, she far more than I, of course – but it was nice, too. Lydia actually managed to eat something and I learned a little more about her singing career and work as a teacher, and then she shared a few anecdotes about her late husband. I told her some things about

Simone and the car crash and our move into New Haven, and about Rianna and Ella – though not too much about them, because it seemed so damned unfair for me to be talking about my children, who were safe and sound – *please God* – at school.

I figured it was time to get down to business, that Lydia was probably just holding back so I could enjoy my lunch.

'You said you had a problem with the FBI.'

Lydia laid down her fork, took off her glasses. 'More a concern than a problem.' Her eyes seemed to darken. 'I talked with Roger Kline two days ago – he's the special agent in charge of the task force, you know?'

'Yes.' Baum had told me, said Kline had a good record for results.

'I asked if they were working with the designers of the game, thinking it might give them some more insight into the kind of person they should be looking for.'

'Good idea.' Sounded like a route the FBI would automatically take.

'He fobbed me off,' Lydia said. 'Kline said he'd talked to the partners of the software corporation behind *Limbo* – Eryx Software – said they were shocked anyone could use their game this way, but that seemed to be the extent of his interest in them.'

'I doubt that.' I regarded her dubious expression for a moment. 'What's your concern? Are you suggesting someone there might be involved?'

'No, of course not,' Lydia said. 'Though I guess nothing's impossible.' She paused. 'I just feel that for some reason the game is important to whoever's taken Robbie and the others, and it seems logical to me that the people at Eryx must know more about *Limbo* than anyone else.'

'Very logical,' I said.

She leaned forward just as our waiter approached to see if we'd finished. Seeing the intensity on Lydia's face, I abandoned the remainder of my last crab cake and our dishes were cleared away.

'I've decided to go and talk to them myself,' Lydia said quietly. 'To the directors of the corporation. That's what I really wanted to run by you, Jake.'

'You want to go to Eryx?'

'Why not?' Her chin tilted defiantly.

'Have you run the idea past Special Agent Kline?'

'Not yet.'

'I think you should, if only because I'd guess his people are taking a much harder look at Eryx than you think.' I paused. 'On the other hand,' I went on slowly, 'if you have questions to ask, I guess no one has a better right to ask them.'

'Thank you.' The defiance retreated a little.

'But I would caution you against doing anything without consulting Kline.'

Lydia sat back again, reached out to pick up her dark glasses, put them back on. I could no longer see into her eyes, but I was starting to know the lady well enough to have an idea that she was not easily put off.

'Don't dismiss the FBI too lightly.' I guess I'm not that easy to put off either when I have something to say. 'I know enough about the way they operate when it comes to crimes involving young people to know that right now you can be damned sure they're pulling out all the stops.'

'You think so?' Still dubious.

'They may not let you *know* what they're doing, Lydia,' I said, 'but I can promise you there are men and women out there tearing their hair out, working all hours, getting next to no rest, spending no time with their own families.' Now I was intense. 'Take the note, for example. It may not have given much away at first sight, but the FBI has amazing means at its disposal, and they're going to be using all of them, you can bet on it – and not just on the note, on every tiny *crumb* of information.'

The waiter came back, offering dessert menus. We both ordered coffee and then I kept right on going, hoping to make her feel just a little better.

'Kline will probably run the investigation from DC, but he'll have agents out in the field wherever they're needed.

Depending on exactly where the other kids were when they were taken, there may be mobile command posts set up. Kline may be talking to Eryx, or he may already be way ahead of us, maybe have some target pinned down, someone maybe with a game-related prior.'

'You think so?'

I didn't want to paint *too* rosy a picture. 'I'm not saying he has, Lydia, just that he *may* have. You may not like the fact that Kline's keeping his cards close to his chest, but it's probably because he believes the investigation's going to run more smoothly that way, on a need-to-know basis.'

'But *I* need to know,' Lydia said, so passionately that the people at the next table glanced towards us in brief interest.

'Not necessarily about the whole operation.' I leaned in closer so she could hear me even if I lowered my voice. 'Kline doesn't know you well, Lydia. He doesn't know what you might do with any information he might share with you. He can't be sure you might not get it in your head to go on some TV show.' I saw her face. '*I* know you wouldn't do anything like that.'

'Do you?'

'Yes, I think so. I think – I *know* – you have too much commonsense to do something like that, and I'm sure Kline respects you too, but with something as big as this, with five separate families involved, he has to run the tightest ship he can.' I stopped, grinned wryly at myself. 'I guess I'm sounding like an ad campaign for the Bureau.'

'Something like that,' Lydia said.

'I just wanted to reassure you in some small way.'

'Fine,' she said. 'Thank you. I'm reassured.'

'But you still want to go talk to the people at Eryx.'

'I do,' she said.

Chapter 27

There was only one good point about the *thing* that Robbie was connected to by his headset and gloves: it made it hard for him to keep thinking about the terrifying fact that he was a prisoner in a small, cell-like room that he'd only been allowed to see for an hour or so at any one time.

A room with one dim, caged-in lightbulb, a mattress on a concrete floor, a door without a handle, some kind of weird electronic apparatus he'd been keeping right away from, and – behind a screen – a lavatory and washbasin, with paper and soap and a single, almost blunt, plastic Bic razor. If it weren't for the fact that the darkness was so much *worse*, the sealed up room would probably be driving him right over the edge.

The other halfway bearable aspect of the *thing* was its bizarre familiarity. It had taken some time to sink in at the outset. But at around the time he stopped crying like a damned baby, Robbie had turned his head to the right and seen a sign that read 34th Street Station. It had looked just like a subway station sign, only it had been hanging haphazardly and there had been no people and no proper lights, and the platform had been broken and piled up in several places like jagged rock formations. And then he'd heard something, and it hadn't been the sound of a train approaching through the tunnel – it had been something horribly like the sound of wild dogs growling . . .

And that was when Robbie had known for sure that what he had at first believed to be part of a dream was quite real. That he had somehow crash-landed smack bang in the heart of what *looked* like a life-sized game of *Limbo*.

He'd looked down at himself at that moment, and had realized for the first time that he was no longer wearing the jeans and new shirt that his mom had bought him the day of Candice's birthday dinner. He was wearing *leather*, his feet were bare, and he had what looked like a big hunting knife strapped to his waist.

Just like the knife that Steel carried, the one with the ugly serrated edge.

His killing knife.

He'd almost passed out then.

Which was when the voice – the *man* – had spoken to him again.

'From now on,' the man had told him, 'you *are* Steel. And for as long as you keep your headset and gloves on, you will stay – as you have obviously now come to understand – in *Limbo*. And as uncomfortable as that may seem to you right now, your only alternative is darkness and silence, which I *strongly* recommend to you as being useful only for sleeping.'

Robbie had laughed then; a high-pitched, brittle, hysterical kind of a laugh. It *was*, after all, still a dream, he had decided. Just one long fucking *nightmare*.

He must have said that out loud – or maybe the dream-maker was a goddamn mind-reader, which would not have surprised Robbie too much – because the voice told him that he was wrong.

'This is not a bad dream, Steel. I told you that before.'

'It has to be a dream,' Robbie had argued.

'No, it does not. This is *real*, Steel. And what's more, this is an honour.'

That was what he'd said, the fruitcake dream-making shithead.

'An *honour*.'

Chapter 28

Lydia called me the morning after our lunch.

'I'm going to visit the software corporation the day after tomorrow,' she said without any preamble, 'and I wondered if you might like to come along?'

I had been sitting on the couch paying monthly bills with an ancient *Lassie* movie playing on cable. (What can I tell you, I was raised on the good old dog, and yes, my eyes still do moisten just a little when she gets hopelessly lost. But isn't that what cable's for – helping to deaden your brain for tasks like paying bills?)

Lydia's invitation threw me.

'I *did* hear you yesterday,' she went on, almost briskly, 'and I know it's almost certainly a fool's errand, but I just can't stand this waiting around doing nothing.'

I'd found the remote and turned off the collie. 'That's what Fran and Stu have been finding the hardest part, too.'

Not quite the hardest, I guess we were both probably thinking.

'Maybe they'd like to come with us,' Lydia suggested without conviction.

I didn't think that was such a hot idea. 'If we want to get these guys on side,' I said, realizing I'd said *we* only after I'd said it, 'maybe learn something about the psychology behind the game or whatever else you have in mind, I'd say the less people the better.' I paused. 'Have you planned your approach?'

'Not really,' she admitted. 'I did talk to Agent Kline.'

'And he okayed this?' I was surprised.

'Not exactly. In fact, he was distinctly unenthusiastic about it, but he didn't *forbid* me to go.' Lydia swept straight on before I could get a word in. 'But then I called Eryx and asked to be put through to the president of the company, whose name is Scott Korda, by the way.'

'And?'

'And he was in a meeting, *but*' – there was a small air of triumph in the word – 'he called me back almost immediately. He knew who I was, told me he's deeply concerned about Robbie. But the main thing was he said he's keen to help any way he can.'

'That's good.' I guessed it *was* good, despite my reservations.

'So, Jake, would you like to come?' She made it sound like a challenge. 'It just so happens they're located in Connecticut.'

'I know,' I told her. 'I looked up their website last night.'

'You did?' Lydia sounded pleased. 'Does that mean you will come? I'd be so grateful for the moral support *and*, of course, for the benefit of your experience.' She paused. 'And frankly, I'd appreciate the company.'

Chapter 29

Robbie had figured out a couple of things.

First, the headset and other paraphernalia were part of some kind of virtual reality simulator. He'd learned a little about that stuff over the years, had seen a few of the movies, from *The Matrix* down, knew that the military used real sophisticated versions for training soldiers and pilots.

Second, the crazy bastard holding him prisoner was using it to make him think he was playing a mega-hi-tech game of *Limbo*.

An *honour*, he'd called it.

And he'd called *him* Steel.

He hadn't actually played the game here, not yet. The guy had just been running it past him, like something that seemed close enough to touch – but not quite. *Thank Christ*. Robbie knew all too well the bad stuff that happened to Steel in the computer game, had never had the slightest desire to get sucked into his PlayStation like some character in a Stephen King story and face those perils for *real*.

But he had a bad, bad feeling it was only a matter of time before that happened.

There was a kind of routine down here. Whenever the equipment was turned off by his invisible gaoler, when he'd been given permission to take off the damned headset, the *real* light was switched on for a while so that Robbie could eat and use the john and wash his face and hands and rinse his mouth and even shave, after a fashion, with the almost blunt disposable razor; it was lucky, he guessed, that he didn't have much of a beard. He hadn't managed to figure out how the food came in. It was sandwiches, mostly, and he *thought* the guy brought them in either when he was sleeping or trapped in his VR world and couldn't see or hear what was actually happening around him.

It gave Robbie the heebie-jeebies to think of the dirt-bag creeping in and out, but then, just about *everything* about this gave him the heebie-jeebies. The good news, he supposed, was that he was being given food, which meant he was being kept alive, which meant *hope*, didn't it? And the sandwiches weren't too bad; he'd been too upset at first and way too suspicious to eat anything, but then hunger had gotten the better of him, and already the food and drink cartons were becoming the highlights of his day. *Day or night?* Impossible to tell.

Whenever the light went out he escaped into sleep for a while, woke back to the ongoing nightmare, panicked all over again, decided he couldn't take any more, then managed to get himself back under control and forced himself to use the darkness to think. It was important, he had decided, to keep trying to work out this craziness, to fight against becoming totally passive – at least in his mind – so that when his chance came to get out of this fucking hole, he'd be ready.

Mom will get me out before that.

He held onto that hope above all else.

His mother would have the cops working on this, and maybe his kidnapper wasn't *just* a fruitcake, maybe he'd asked for a ransom or something else, something crazy and impossible, like the release of all the inmates of Riker's Island or something. If it was just cash, he'd be okay; they weren't rich or anything, but his mother would find a way to raise whatever his kidnapper asked for, even if the cops didn't want her to, because she would not, would *never* let anything bad happen to him if she had any control over it. He might not be sure of anything much down here in the dark, but he was certain of that.

The sooner the better.

Please, Mom.

He thought about the girl a lot, too, the one the voice had called Dakota but who was, of course, just a *girl*; pretty, but messed-up and scared as a cornered animal. He thought she'd probably been down here a lot longer than he had, though he didn't want to know how long. He hadn't seen her since that first time. He'd asked about her, but most of the time, when he asked questions, he received no answers.

Robbie thought that maybe a lot of the time the man wasn't down here at all, that maybe he just came to check on him and the girl now and again, to bring them food, make sure they were alive, mess with their heads a little.

What if he stops coming?

That was the kind of thought Robbie couldn't take for too long. That was when he grabbed for the headset and gloves for another non-interactive session with the *Limbo* underworld – anything to take his mind off that kind of terror.

There was only one thought he did like to keep running, like a prayer, a mantra.

Please, Mom, find me soon.

Chapter 30

Of course I went with Lydia. Number one, I wanted to help if I could, and not just her and Robbie, but Mikey and the Coopers and the other families. Number two, I was so damned glad she wanted me along that it surprised me.

There'd been no one since Simone who'd made me feel that way.

I kept having to remind myself that there was a time and a place, and that this was neither. And then I got mad at myself in case I was, in some way, taking advantage of Lydia at a time of great vulnerability.

I don't really think that's the way I operate though.

I certainly *hope* not.

I had another reason for going along. I was still not at all sure that the visit to Eryx was a good idea, and smart as I thought Lydia was, her emotions had to be so inflamed that I feared her diplomacy skills might go out the window. Kline and his team were right, I was sure, to want to keep those people on side for the kids' sakes.

Still, Lydia Johanssen *was* a smart woman.

On their website, Eryx subtitled themselves 'the fathers of *Limbo*', and the corporation described itself as being dedicated to providing the highest quality products and entertainment possible for today's game-saturated industry. The two founders, Scott Korda and Hal Hawthorne, had launched the company a decade ago, designing puzzle games for their bread and butter, but with aspirations to bigger things. At the outset, Korda and Hawthorne, both graphic artists, both computer-obsessed, had done most of the writing and game design themselves, but then they'd been joined by William Fitzgerald, also a graphic artist and, according to his partners, a programming genius. They were all game compulsives, but – so Korda said on the website – Fitzgerald was the one who'd enabled them to shoot for the higher plane they'd dreamed of. They'd produced a half-dozen adventure games before *Limbo* had shunted them high onto the bestseller lists. These days there was a large enough team of designers, programmers and artists to allow Korda, Hawthorne and Fitzgerald to sit back, if they so desired, and play games to their hearts' content, but all three had chosen to stay heavily involved at Eryx's creative heart.

I'd printed out a copy of all that self-trumpeting stuff and handed it over to Lydia when I met her at New Haven train station, so she could read as I drove my old Cherokee.

'Eryx Software,' I told her as we headed onto the turnpike towards Old Saybrook, 'is just one arm of a bigger corporation. The games, including *Limbo*, are published by Zeus Interactive, also headed by the same guys and based in Hartford.'

I took a swift sideways glance at her. She looked good, a little different again, businesslike this time in a navy suit with crisp white shirt, hair pinned up.

'On reflection,' I went on, 'I guess I am pretty impressed that Korda should have taken the time to call you *and* agree to this meeting.'

'I don't know,' Lydia said. 'Given what's happened, I suppose he had to.'

'*Someone* had to call and to see you, but Korda could easily have handed this over to his PR chief, or maybe even his lawyer.'

'You're more cynical than I am,' Lydia said.

'I guess I am,' I agreed. 'Sometimes.'

She read for a while and gave a faint snort of what sounded like derision.

'What?' I asked.

'This stuff about no prospective employee being allowed over the Eryx threshold unless they're just as game-enslaved as the partners,' Lydia said. 'It makes them sound like wide-eyed innocents, not the multi-millionaires I'm sure they must be.'

I smiled. 'The kids they employ probably *are* pretty innocent.'

'Probably kept in some dark hole, like creative mushrooms,' Lydia said.

Both as cynical as each other, it seemed.

No dark holes anyplace *we* could see at the Eryx HQ. The offices were frankly lovely, in a beautifully maintained nineteenth-century white clapboard house surrounded by gardens and woodland.

The boss himself was waiting for us when we arrived in the entrance hall.

'Mrs Johanssen, I'm Scott Korda.' Clipped Massachusetts accent, stockily-built, smooth-skinned, hair as golden as his spectacle rims, wearing a fawn-coloured linen suit with a no-collar cool white shirt, he was elegant and just formal enough for the occasion. He nodded at me, then gave his full attention to Lydia. 'I'm sorrier than I can say about your son.'

I flinched inwardly. He made it sound as if Robbie was dead.

'But we're all going to do whatever we can to make sure you get him home, safe and sound.' Korda added an upbeat spin, an instant fix.

'Thank you for seeing us.' Lydia turned to include me. 'This is my friend, Professor Woods.'

'Jake.' I shook Korda's hand. 'Hope you don't mind my coming along.'

'On the contrary.' Korda smiled at me. 'I'm glad Mrs Johanssen didn't have to make the journey alone.'

'That goes for us too.'

We turned around. Two men were approaching through an off-white door with stained glass panels. One, tall and whippet-thin, with pale skin, red hair and a razor-sharp nose; the other about five-eleven, slim too, with a pleasant, easy-going expression and short brown hair edging back from his line-free forehead. They were both wearing suits, the red-haired man's slightly crumpled, the other's sharper, with a beautiful cornflower-blue silk tie.

'My partners,' Korda said, and made the introductions. The whippet was Fitzgerald, the one with the receding hairline Hawthorne. Their colouring might be different, I noticed, but all three men – who I figured to be around my age, maybe a little younger – looked fit as fleas and all had startlingly clear blue eyes. If Lydia and I had been expecting tired, slouch-shouldered computer slaves, we'd been mistaken. Korda and his partners veritably sparked with energy, their message – the antithesis of a Surgeon-General's warning – crystal clear: *Limbo is good for your health.*

We shook hands all round, Hawthorne and Fitzgerald echoing Korda's sympathy, and adjourned to the president's office, a joy of a room with more stained glass in the windows and doors that opened out onto a quiet garden. On the whole, I tend not to recognize flowers and plants, but I knew enough to appreciate the careful blending of wild with cultivated – *and*, to top off all that perfection, there was a black retriever dog, lying just outside the open doors, chewing on some kind of store-bought fake bone, tail thumping.

'Nice dog,' I said.

'That's Donald,' Korda told us. 'My son's an old-fashioned boy, very keen on Donald Duck.' He grinned. 'Loves Disney, no aptitude for computer-generated anything, even games.'

'Which puts *us* in our place,' Hawthorne said.

At the mention of his son, the smile in Korda's eyes had seemed to me to become very genuine. Hawthorne's humour, though of the wryer, slightly self-deprecating variety, seemed okay too, at first glance.

Lydia, who hadn't said more than a few words since we'd entered the president's office, shifted slightly in the armchair she'd been invited to sit in, a few feet from where Korda sat on a settee. She looked edgy. I felt much the same way.

106

'Jake' – Korda addressed me – 'I gather from the FBI that it was you who picked up on the link between Robbie and Michael Cooper.'

No one had indicated before this instant that they'd known about me.

'Actually, it was my housekeeper who spotted it,' I told him. 'Though in any event, since it was in the *New York Times*, it was only a question of time.' I didn't bother to add that Norman Baum had also noticed it, decided that mention of a private investigator would only add to the tension.

'It's certainly turned our world upside down,' Fitzgerald said, a touch grimly. 'We created *Limbo* much as we've devised all our games – for fun, for pleasure, and to a limited extent for the advancement of skills in children and young people.'

'That's what we like to think, anyhow,' Hawthorne said, affably wry again.

'What we *do* all think,' Korda came in swiftly, 'is that we owe Jake a big debt of gratitude for getting us all on the case that little bit faster, so we can work together to nail whoever's behind this terrible crime.'

'So,' Fitzgerald said, 'how do you feel we can help you, Mrs Johanssen?'

At last. I looked at Lydia, saw her draw a quick breath, composed again.

'First,' she answered Fitzgerald, 'we'd like to learn more about *Limbo*. Clearly it's significant somehow to the person who's taken my son and the others, which makes me interested in finding out about the types of people who like your game.'

'Makes sense,' Korda said.

'You think a gamer has the kids?' Hawthorne asked.

'I don't have the first inkling who has them,' Lydia said.

'But our game has the dubious honour of being the common link,' Korda said, growing a touch brisker, matching her manner. 'So let's make a start on trying to give you what you need, Mrs Johanssen.' He looked at Fitzgerald. 'Bill, where do you think we should begin?'

'Introduce the team?' Fitzgerald looked at Lydia. 'The people who create the games.'

'I thought the three of you created *Limbo*,' I said.

'The original,' Korda agreed. 'The prototype, if you like.'

'But there's a larger group you need to meet,' Hawthorne said, 'without whose contributions the game would never have gotten off the ground.'

Sounded like an awards ceremony to me.

'Fine,' Lydia said, and got to her feet.

I stood too, and the others followed suit.

Out in the garden, glossy black Donald glanced up, thumped his tail again, and then returned to his bone.

The rest of the team, a fairly compact group, seemed almost as happy as the retriever. However much Eryx's success had grown in the marketplace, Korda told us, he and his partners had remained determined to keep the creative side as neat, tightly-focused and committed as possible.

I wasn't surprised the young people in that group were happy. Their working environment was amazing. No partitions, no vending machines, no fluorescent lights, nothing so ugly or utilitarian as a carpet tile in sight; these employees enjoyed stripped wood floors, working fireplaces, chairs that were probably ergonomically designed but actually looked comfortable, pottery coffee pots and mugs, a kitchen even Simone might have liked, and those gorgeous stained glass windows everywhere.

If I hadn't known they were in the business of making computer games, I think I might have felt almost envious. Take my word for it, the working environment of a non-Ivy League university professor is not quite as benevolently landscaped.

Ah me.

'Meet the gang,' Korda said, and after that it was all systems go.

We met head programmer Ellen Zito, in her end-twenties, a seriously pale young woman from Brooklyn via MIT, with fair hair so short it was almost crew-cut, clad in baggy pants, an

108

Eryx T-shirt and boots. She was just finishing a Japanese take-out lunch and reading *Wired*, but looked sleep-starved, and Bill Fitzgerald confirmed that Zito was probably *the* most obsessed of the whole team, but that she was also possibly more talented than the three partners rolled into one.

We also met Meg Binder – the only other female – a fresh-faced Texan with a nose ring that sent shudders down my spine because I'm horribly aware that in the fullness of time my own two girls may do much the same or worse. Meg was introduced to us as a level designer.

'Like a set designer?' I asked, thinking of the theatre or movies.

'In a way,' Meg answered, 'though levels are also the different stages through which players have to progress to achieve their ultimate aim.'

In *Limbo*, for example – so a guy called Lars Hendrick, with red apple cheeks and a ponytail, told us – level one was a Manhattan subway station post-apocalypse, where Dakota and Steel, the two teen survivors, wake up after the catastrophe and encounter Ghoulo for the first time. I noticed just then that Lars's necktie had tiny hairy monsters all over it, as did the twisted fabric belt around the waistband of Meg's combat pants. *Cute*, I guess, if you were the kind of person to find flesh-eating mutated wolverines cute.

They were a friendly bunch. We met an earnest young man responsible for sound effects called Anton Gluckman; another level designer, borderline emaciated, named Jazz Brown, and a sleepy-eyed character named Dave Kaminski, whose role at Eryx seemed hazy, but who appeared, we both agreed later, to be crazy about Meg.

I guessed that somewhere on the premises – or maybe at the Hartford offices – there had to be accountant types and legal eagles and PR and publicity people, the kind who were surely needed to keep the colder financial heart of the corporation pounding healthily along. But if they were here, in the Connecticut countryside, Lydia and I did not meet them. We, I'm sure we both realized, were being charmed by this troop of eager beavers, seduced by the relaxed bustle of the place, by the ease of the atmosphere, and I have to say, I think that ease was pretty real.

We listened and tried to learn as Ellen Zito told us a little about the extended team needed these days to create an even halfway ambitious computer game – not just the gaggle of artists and programmers, but the musicians, animation experts, the actors for voice-overs and, sometimes, for action. We watched and tried to concentrate as Meg and Lars gave us a demonstration of the game, and glancing at Lydia from time to time, I could tell that despite her natural repugnance, she too was impressed by their exuberant intensity as they faced and overcame obstacles and horrors.

We came away after more than three hours, drained, and started back in virtual silence. We were passing through a part of the state I'd always found less lovely than the rest, east of the river having been dedicated to industry rather than farming, though today, after all the contrived attractiveness of Eryx Software, I think I was finding the drabness something of a relief.

'You okay?' I asked Lydia after a while.

'Mm-hmm.'

'So what did you think?' I gave her the ball. It was, after all, her show.

'They couldn't have been more helpful.'

'True,' I said, and waited.

'They were so helpful, I kept wanting to run screaming out of the building.' She took a short, sharp breath. 'And, oh God, that *building*.'

'You didn't like it?'

'*Like* it? It was so perfect I couldn't stand it!' She paused. 'You know what it reminded me of? That book by Ira Levin about the men who turned their wives into perfect robots.'

'*Stepford Wives*.' I smiled, driving on.

'It wasn't the kids,' Lydia said. 'They were terrific, I thought, didn't you?'

'Uh-huh.'

'I can't even really say it was Korda or the partners.' She was searching. 'It's hard to say exactly *what* it was.'

'Maybe just a few too many positive vibes?' I suggested.

'All that *optimism*,' she agreed.

'They were a very cheery bunch,' I said.

Lydia laughed, a pure release of tension. 'Listen to us,' she said. 'Talk about a couple of old cynics.'

'Less of the old.'

'Compared to *them*?'

'Okay.' I shrugged. 'Compared to them, I guess we're about ready to go pick up our wheelchairs.'

We crossed the Connecticut River at East Haddam, by the Goodspeed Opera House, which diverted our conversation for a little while to musicals and singing in general, and how Lydia's students were faring without her. I asked if she thought it might not help her as well as them to give maybe a couple of classes each week, but she said she couldn't think of doing that, so I didn't push. It wasn't my place, and anyhow, I understood that right now Lydia needed to put every ounce of her energies into her fight to get her son back – even if all she could actually *do* was will the FBI to move heaven and earth.

'Are you hungry?' I asked her when we were back on Route 9. We'd been offered lunch and snacks back at Eryx, but neither of us had wanted anything but coffee, and suddenly it was almost evening and I felt starved.

Lydia nodded. 'I guess I could eat something now.'

'You sound surprised.'

'Actually, I'm not really. I think I'm hungry, properly hungry, for the first time, because I've been involved, because I've tried to *do* something, or at least learn something.'

We'd missed the turn-off for Chester, so we headed on towards Old Saybrook and stopped at Dock and Dine on Saybrook Point, where I thought that the river views might be what we needed. Lydia ordered chicken, I was in a steak mood, and we just sat for a while with a glass of wine each and mulled over our thoughts.

'I've been unfair.' She started talking first. 'On Eryx, I mean.'

'You expressed your feelings.'

'If I'm honest,' Lydia said, thoughtfully, 'I think I could *almost* see why they love it all so much. From their standpoints.'

We both paused to eat a little.

'The game's fairly brutal stuff,' I said.

'And they call it entertainment.' Lydia shuddered and put down her fork.

'I'm sorry. Don't stop eating.' It had been good to see her relax for a while. 'Let's not talk about it till we've finished.'

'I can talk now,' Lydia said. 'I don't think I can eat any more anyhow.'

A big wave of pity rocked me. She was so amazingly brave ninety per cent of the time that I tended to forget her agony – no, not really to *forget* it, not for a second, but maybe to try and push it away for a while.

'I wish Meg and Lars hadn't been so good at that demonstration.' She shook her head. 'Not that I took in all that much.' She hesitated. 'Brutal really is the word, isn't it? All those horrors.'

I thought about the twisted, pulverized subway stations, and about the dark tunnels and sewers and rats and the flesh eater – and put down my own knife and fork. 'Enough to give anyone nightmares.'

Lydia nodded. I realized suddenly that she was wrestling with something.

'What's bothering you? Is it the game, or Eryx in general?'

'Neither, exactly,' she said.

I waited.

'I think I'm quite a down-to-earth person, on the whole,' she said. 'I guess I'm intuitive, sometimes, with others, but I've never claimed for one second to be in any way psychic or, heaven forbid, clairvoyant.'

'But?' I was intrigued.

'It was while we were sitting in Scott Korda's office with Hawthorne and Fitzgerald,' she said. 'In that perfectly lovely

112

room, with the garden and Donald the dog outside.' She paused again. 'I *felt* something.'

I remembered seeing her shifting uncomfortably a couple of times, recalled assuming she was just keen to move things forward. 'Can you be more specific?'

'I told myself it was my imagination. And once we got *on* with things, I did put it out of my mind, but now . . .'

'Now?' I tried to be gentle, but I was very curious.

Lydia shook her head. A few strands had come away from her tidy, pinned up hairstyle, and with the early evening sun behind her they formed a soft frame around her tired face. 'I don't know, Jake,' she said. 'It's absurd.'

'Try me.'

'You know how the place felt, overall,' she went on. 'Like a kind of beehive, all those young workers cross-pollinating away, sparking with creativity. It was all so *warm*, don't you think?'

'I guess.'

'And yet, at that one point, in Korda's office I felt so *cold* I can hardly describe it.' She shook her head again in her effort to explain. 'But it was nothing to do with air-conditioning, or any breeze from the garden. And I could swear it had nothing to do with anxiety – I *do* seem to feel colder these days, but that's a very different sensation.'

'And this was what, exactly?' I was fascinated. 'If you can explain it.'

'I guess it was something else *beside* the cold,' she said. 'Or maybe something within it, a part of it, if that makes any sense at all.'

'You're a rational, very lucid person, Lydia,' I told her. 'Doesn't mean you can't experience *irrational* feelings from time to time. I know I do. If that helps.'

She smiled at me. 'Okay,' she said. 'Here it is.'

'Okay.'

'Malevolence.'

She looked at me intensely as she said the word, and I could tell she was using me as some kind of sounding board, waiting to see how I'd react.

113

'So do you send for the men in white coats now, or do you just put me back on the train?' She managed another smile.

'Do you know,' I asked, slowly, 'if the feeling came from any one of the three partners? Or was it more general than that?'

'I have no idea,' she answered honestly.

'And it only happened the once, just in that room?'

'Yes,' she said.

Our food was cleared away. We both turned down dessert and settled for coffee, and the instant our waitress was gone, I returned to the subject.

'Do you think,' I asked as straightforwardly as possible, 'that maybe you *wanted* to feel something?'

'A kind of wishful thinking, you mean?' Lydia nodded. 'Of course, it could have been something like that, but on the other hand, I've never experienced anything like it before.' She paused. 'Though obviously my son's never been abducted before either.'

I saw sudden hot tears spring into her eyes, had to curb an impulse to get up and put my arms around her.

'I'm sorry.' She got herself back under control.

'Don't you even *think* about apologizing,' I said softly.

The coffee came, saving us both, I guess. She took hers black, and so did I, but whereas she took no sugar, I poured in a whole sachet, more than I usually used, maybe because I felt I needed a hit of energy.

'You know,' I said, taking it slowly, thoughtfully, 'I guess I've come away with a kind of a feeling about Eryx, too – though nothing as forceful as yours. I feel that, in all fairness to those three men, I ought to be impressed by the care and concern they showed.'

'But you're not?' Lydia's eyes were intensely interested.

'Not really, no.'

'Is it just the product, do you think? The fact that we both find *Limbo* so repugnant, and they clearly love it so damned much?'

'Maybe,' I said, 'but I don't think that quite covers it.' I gave a small shrug. 'Maybe it was because they so badly want the abductions not to be in any way their fault.'

'They're hardly to be blamed for wanting that,' Lydia said.

'No,' I said.

I knew that neither of us was quite convinced.

Chapter 31

It gave him no pleasure at all to observe Steel's distress – for pity's sake, he was no *barbarian*; he wasn't doing this to torture the young man. On the contrary – as he'd been trying to impress upon him – he was bestowing a great honour on him.

Dakota and Steel had become two of the biggest cyber stars of the past few years, right up there with the likes of Lara Croft or Leisure Suit Larry or any of the other greats. Steel and Dakota, stars of *Limbo*. All the kids wanted to role-play them, probably all the biggest-name teen actors were already preening in readiness to nab the leads in the movie whenever that came to pass. And here *he* was, offering real kids, *ordinary* kids, the biggest chance of all – in the real thing. Which had, it so happened, cost him sums of money that would send their tiny minds reeling.

Still, it was tough on the young man, he could appreciate that. Getting used to the VR environment and, of course, the captive conditions. Better for Steel when he began playing the game. Better too, of course, when the time was right, for him to see Dakota again. He'd asked to see her a few times, which was, he felt, a normal, healthy response, and one that bode well for the *real* game.

His game.

Not the one he'd first intended. He had trouble, sometimes, even remembering just what that had been, though maybe his interest had simply waned a while back. After it had changed, mutated, he supposed, a little like Ghoulo (though the nasty and rather *cheap* Ghoulo had never been to his personal taste) into something far more interesting. Something much more compelling.

Something no one else would ever see.

Which was a pity, he thought.

But they wouldn't understand, he knew that, was crystal clear about that.

He was still clear about quite a lot of things.

Like, for instance, his new concern about Dakota, who seemed to have lost her own curiosity about Steel, who had begun to lose energy along with her weight. These young people didn't seem to understand that they had to eat to keep healthy, to stay strong. Basic logic, for Christ's sake. Didn't their parents teach them *anything*?

Parents. He knew all about parents.

If Dakota didn't perk up again soon . . .

Don't think about that.

At least Steel was eating, and his asking for Dakota had cheered him up, proving his theory that initial loneliness increased their longing for companionship. It was vital that Steel start yearning for Dakota, just as it was vital that he get to grips with his large-as-life *Limbo* world. The kids had to settle down. If they didn't, they wouldn't be able to perform properly, wouldn't be able to do Steel and Dakota justice, to do *him* and all his efforts justice.

After all he had done, all he was giving up, he was entitled to quality.

He knew that, ultimately, he was going to have to give up everything.

Even his life.

Which entitled him to the very best game anyone had ever experienced.

Didn't it?

Didn't it?

117

Chapter 32

Rianna was in the gymnasium at the High Fliers Club, working the uneven bars. She moved from the low to the high bar, released her grip, then regrasped, moved into a handstand and on from there into a big circular swing and dismount.

Okay.

Her breathing was laboured, her cheeks flushed with heat, forehead damp with perspiration, and she knew Coach Carlin was going to tell her she'd wrecked a series of pretty neat moves with that lousy landing. But the truth was, she didn't really care as much as she was supposed to, because it had *felt* so great, the final swing and taking off from the bars, almost like flying, and she'd felt at that instant that she hadn't *wanted* to land, had just wanted to go on soaring through the air . . .

Marsha Carlin was smiling as she came across the gym, picking up Rianna's towel and jacket along the way, tossing the towel to the teenager as she got close enough.

'How'd that feel to you?'

'Fantastic.' Rianna wiped her face and arms and took the jacket from the coach. 'I know the dismount was pretty terrible, and the landing . . .'

'Terrible might be overstating it.' Coach Carlin smiled. 'But the rest was so good, such an improvement, Rianna. I'm very pleased.'

The tawny-haired, middle-aged woman moved on, still smiling at the fifteen-year-old's manifest pleasure. Carlin knew that with another gymnast she would have belaboured the negative points, but she'd learned a long time ago that Rianna's talents far outstripped her ambitions, and if at first she'd felt disappointed by that, she'd gotten over it. Frankly, these days, she was delighted to have a young woman who came here for her work-outs just because she loved the sport, *needed* it for its own sake rather than for what she – or her family – could get out of it. What counted with Jake Woods, Carlin knew by now, was his daughter's safety and happiness, pure and simple. The professor had spoken to her a few times about the potential dangers of the gym environment, and she hoped she'd laid most of his fears to rest. Though Woods was not the kind of father, Carlin realized, who was *ever* going to quit worrying about his children, whatever their age.

'I'm surprised you let Rianna keep on coming,' she'd said to him once.

'I don't see I have much choice,' Woods had said. 'I know what it means to her.' He'd smiled at her. 'And I do get a real kick out of watching her in action.'

'Must be tough, sometimes,' Carlin had said, 'being a parent.'

'It is,' he'd agreed, 'but worth every ounce of anguish.'

Marsha Carlin thought that Rianna and her sister were lucky girls.

Rianna did some stretches while she cooled down, her mind already switching away from the gym. That was one of the big differences between herself and the serious gymnasts at High Fliers, she realized: her inability to reflect endlessly on an exercise, to replay her last move over and over so as to analyze flaws.

Now, picking up her gym bag and heading for the door, Rianna was thinking about what was going on with her father these days. He was definitely distracted, not getting on with writing his book, which was almost all he'd talked about for weeks before spring semester had ended. He was just as warm and loving as ever with both her and Ella – maybe even a little more so, his hugs fiercer than usual – but Rianna had learned to read their father pretty well over the years, and right now, no matter how much he tried to cover, something was really bugging him.

She knew, of course, that it was partly Michael Cooper. Rianna didn't even want to *think* about what might have happened to him and Robbie Johanssen. She'd asked her dad about what *he* thought, but though he was pretty straight with her about most things, he'd been reluctant to talk about this.

Trying to protect me, Rianna told herself, standing beneath the hot shower, washing her hair. Which was why she hadn't hassled him; she didn't want him to know she was upset. *Like father, like daughter.*

It wasn't stopping the bad dreams, though.

But something else was going on with her dad, she thought, turning off the water, grabbing a towel and stepping out of the stall. Something had changed. Something, perhaps, to do with Mrs Johanssen. She'd mentioned her thoughts to Shannon Gates, her closest friend, and Shannon had suggested that her father and Lydia Johanssen were having an affair.

'I don't believe that,' Rianna had said, unequivocally.

'Why not?' Shannon had asked. 'I told you I heard my mom say your dad's a very sexy guy. If *she* thinks so, why wouldn't Lydia what's-her-name?'

'No reason,' Rianna had answered, 'except I'm pretty sure he'd tell me if something like that was going on.'

She still felt that. After all, he'd talked to her even before he'd gone out on his first date five years after her mother had died, so why wouldn't he talk to her about this? Unless maybe he felt bad because of the awful circumstances . . .

If there *was* something going on, Rianna decided, pulling on her jeans, she wouldn't give him a hard time the way some kids did with their divorced parents. After all, she couldn't expect him to be a monk.

But sexy? Rianna still couldn't quite see that. He was the best, the absolute *best*, and any woman would be lucky to have him. But *sexy*? Come on – he was just her father.

Chapter 33

Robbie knew he was going to play the game.

The man had told him so a little while back, and that had pushed his fear levels up to boiling point, because up to now nothing too bad had actually happened to him – nothing bad, that was, unless you counted being frigging *kidnapped* and shut up in a black hole and being force-fed weird VR sessions by some invisible freak. And who knew what playing *Limbo* down here was going to mean?

Well, not actually playing. The man had called it an *exercise*. Something about *initiation*, he'd said, but when Robbie had asked what that meant, he hadn't answered, and Robbie had had the unnerving sense that maybe he wasn't really there at all, maybe his voice was on tape, set to a timer, and that terrified him more than anything, the idea that he might have been abandoned, so that no one would ever find him . . .

'Okay, Steel, get ready.'

Robbie almost jumped out of his skin.

'Put on your headset.'

Blue light again.

'Stand up.'

Robbie stood. His legs felt gelatinous.

'Now move to your right,' the voice told him. 'Three paces sideways.'

Robbie knew now that he was going to use the big gizmo that he'd seen in the *real* light from the bulb, which meant it was part of the whole simulator thing.

'It's going to feel different under your feet, Steel.'

It did. Softer than the concrete, and squishy, which made him cringe for a second in case it sucked him down – that was the weird way his mind was working these days: *fifty thousand ways to get crazy without really trying*. But nothing bad happened, though his heart was thumping so hard he was sure the man could hear it.

'All right, Steel, raise your arms and take hold of the bar – you've seen the bar, remember? Just get hold of it and wait.'

Robbie gripped the bar through his gloves.

And it *began*.

Darkness first, but not ebony, just the darkness of the tunnel again.

He heard them coming before he saw them, heard a scraping, scratching sound from way off, then panting, a *lot* of panting, and then he did see them, saw the red gleam of their eyes as they came through the tunnel towards him, and it was almost a low rumble because there were so *many* of them, coming, coming, just the way the rabid dog pack came at Steel in level one . . .

You're just role-playing, man, they're not real.

But it was getting louder, and oh Christ, oh Jesus, there they were, they were coming right at him, he could see their fangs now, gleaming sick white in a glint of light from somewhere . . .

Robbie's right hand let go of the bar, instinct taking over, reached down for the knife at his waist – *Steel's knife*. His move was clumsy, almost tipped him over, but then he had it in his hand, though it felt too light to be a real knife – for Christ's sake, why would a kidnapper give his prisoner a fucking *knife*? And anyway, the dogs were getting closer, and there were too many to fight, so the knife was no damned *use*. And at the very last minute Robbie turned and threw himself against the wall of the tunnel, or tried to, but though he could *see* the wall, he couldn't *feel* it, and he was falling, crashing to the ground – and he felt *that* okay, bruising pain along his side, his legs – and the pack of animals thundered by, snarling, growling . . .

And was gone.

Not real. Just virtual reality.

Of course.

That's why you couldn't feel the wall, Robbie, because it's all VR and the sensors are in your gloves, not on your body.

Learning curve. His first 'exercise'.

Bastard.

Nothing unreal about his pounding heart or dizziness.

'How was that for you, Steel?' the voice asked.

Fuck you, he thought, but didn't dare say.

'Fun, wasn't it?'

'If you like that sort of thing,' Robbie said, anger emboldening him.

'You didn't like it?'

'Not a hell of a lot.'

'Never mind,' the voice said. 'It'll get better.' He paused. 'You can take off the headset and gloves now. It'll be light for a while.'

And that was the end of that conversation.

With no more feedback, no more questions or answers, Robbie went on trying to rationalize as far as was possible. If this was supposed to be practice for some kind of game of *Limbo*, and if he was supposed to be playing Steel, then he figured he hadn't done too well just now. Robbie might not have played the game – the *normal* game – well enough to become a master, but he could remember Steel dealing with the rabid dogs by killing as many of them as possible, slashing at them, blood spraying. He'd started out okay, he guessed, by grabbing for the knife, but that had just been instinct, a defence mechanism, and after that he'd been just plain Robbie Johanssen, not Steel, too scared to do anything more than jam himself up against the tunnel wall till they'd thundered by.

But it worked, didn't it?

This was all about survival. Until they came to get him out of here. Survival. Not letting it make him crazy. Eating, drinking, trying to rest. Letting the game, in whichever form, keep him occupied, keep him *sane*. Computer games were good for you, some people claimed up there in the real world; good for reflexes, good exercise for your brain – not replacement for physical exercise, but still *good* for you.

They didn't know about this version though, did they?

Chapter 34

Scott Korda, Hal Hawthorne and Bill Fitzgerald were having their regular Monday morning meeting in Korda's office at Eryx Software. It was an informal affair, sitting around on the sofa and armchairs rather than around the granite-topped table at the other end of the room, Hawthorne and Korda in jeans and T-shirts, only Fitzgerald looking more businesslike, almost preppie, in navy blazer and beige trousers.

The atmosphere in the room was glum.

'I talked with Kline yesterday,' Korda said, 'asked what we could be doing to help with this thing, and he told me nothing, but that he'll be in touch.'

'What does *that* mean?' Fitzgerald was already feeling irritable, and the week had barely begun. 'Are we involved or aren't we?'

'Of course we're involved,' Hawthorne said. 'Our biggest-selling product has become linked to a serious crime against young people. For all we know we could be suspects.'

'Along with everyone else who ever had anything to do with *Limbo*.' Korda shook his head in dismay. 'This is all so *ugly*. That poor woman coming here, trying to understand the game, as if that was going to help find her son.'

'I didn't mind her coming,' Fitzgerald said, 'but I wasn't so sure about Woods. He's not a relative, doesn't *seem* to be her boyfriend, though I could be wrong about that.' His pale brow furrowed. 'I don't care too much for the notion of a criminal justice teacher using Eryx as training fodder for next semester's students.'

'I got the impression,' Hawthorne said, 'that he was just being a friend.'

'And don't forget,' Korda added, 'he's also friendly with the Cooper family. Seems reasonable to me that he came along.'

'All the same,' Fitzgerald persisted, 'it wouldn't hurt to have someone keep half an eye on him, just in case he turns out to be the type to shoot his mouth off. If the news people really start making something of the *Limbo* connection, parents are going to get scared and Lord knows what that could do to sales.'

'Could just as well boost them,' Korda commented dryly.

'Not if our competitors decide to use it against us,' Fitzgerald said, then shrugged. 'Maybe Kline should consider all of them suspects. Maybe the whole thing's just been set up to discredit *Limbo*.'

'Sounds like an old *Columbo* plot,' Hawthorne said.

'I think Bill's kidding,' Korda said.

'Not entirely.' Fitzgerald shrugged again. 'Maybe you should mention it to Tillman.' Alan Tillman was the Eryx lawyer.

'Want me to ask Nick to do a little checking into Jake Woods?' Korda asked. Nick Ford was their security consultant.

'Seems paranoid to me,' Hawthorne said.

'Wouldn't hurt,' Fitzgerald said again.

Chapter 35

Lydia had never appreciated feeling she was being patronized. She *had* felt it, though, when she'd finally met with Special Agent Roger Kline earlier that morning – a meeting she'd been pushing for since returning home from Eryx.

Kline had arrived at her apartment shortly after eight-thirty accompanied by a female agent named Angela Moran. Kline was average height, trim figure, though Lydia noted that his waist was rather firmly cinched in by his belt; vanity, she decided in an instant judgement, might be no bad thing in the task force leader if it translated into a passion for positive results. The woman with him was a gently rounded type with a surprisingly sweet face; somehow Lydia had never associated the FBI with sweetness.

Kline's face certainly had sharpness, a small, beaky nose, straight tight mouth, angular cheek bones, and small eyes so dark she wondered if he wore tinted lenses. *More vanity*?

Lydia had welcomed them both, brewed the coffee that Melanie Steinman had brought her on Sunday morning from Sensuous Bean, offered them the Danish pastries that Sally had brought in the same afternoon (which Moran had accepted and Kline had turned down), and thanked them both for coming.

'We understand you have some concerns about Eryx Software.' Kline had got to the point swiftly after the niceties.

'*Possible* concerns.'

'Okay.' Kline had fixed her with his sharp eyes and waited.

Lydia was determined not to prevaricate. 'It's an intuition

127

thing, I'm afraid.' She'd smiled tensely. 'I imagine that word makes your hearts sink.'

'Not at all,' Agent Moran had told her, wiping her Danish-sticky fingers on her paper napkin. 'Hunches can be far too accurate, sometimes, to dismiss lightly.'

The agent in charge had said nothing.

'It was a feeling, I'd say,' Lydia had tried to explain, 'rather than a hunch.'

'Why don't you just tell us about it, Mrs Johanssen?' Kline had said.

Lydia thought, on reflection, that she'd done a pretty decent job of expressing the personal sense of disquiet she'd experienced in Korda's office, remembering to back it up with Jake's own dissatisfaction.

'You probably know Professor Woods used to be an investigator in the State Attorney's office in Albany.'

'Not for very long,' Kline had said.

She had gone on rapidly to say that both she and Jake hoped the FBI would be taking a good close look at Eryx and its directors.

'Already taken care of,' Kline had told her.

Smoothly, politely, swiftly. Sweeping her concerns neatly up in a pan and dumping them, Lydia had felt certain, in a trashcan marked something like *'Anxious mothers' neurotic intuitions'*.

They'd been helpful enough in other ways. Agent Moran had spent time making sure Lydia understood some of the enquiry tools she could regularly access via her own computer: the FBI's missing person pages, currently running photographs and details of Robbie, Michael and the other three; the National Center for Missing and Exploited Children, its own home page linked with the Bureau's . . .

And not long after that, they had left.

Lydia thought she ought to have felt grateful for their visit, but she did not. Instead, she felt irritated, frustrated and, indeed, patronized. And now she wanted to talk about her feelings with someone, but wasn't sure who.

Or rather, she *did* know who, she just wasn't certain it was the right thing to do.

Because the FBI visit was not the only reason she really wanted to speak to Jake Woods, was it?

He was a kind, decent man.

He also had warm, honest, gentle brown eyes. A long, straight nose, well-shaped mouth, strong jaw. Soft-looking, wavy hair.

Big, comforting shoulders.

What was she *doing*, thinking that way about a man at a time like this? She'd hardly found anyone remotely attractive since Aaron, so how could she possibly do that now, with Robbie still missing?

She could *not*. She could no more contemplate a relationship now than she could have sprouted wings and taken flight over Manhattan.

So why had she dreamed about him last night?

Chapter 36

Truths came to visit him at night, sometimes.

Dark, jagged things, stripping away the covers, tearing through the smooth, seamless womb of his fantasy world. Truths about himself. About what he had become. He faced them in the small hours, impaled himself on the spikes of those truths, writhed before them.

Kidnapper. Pervert. Sadist. Murderer.

Early dawn came to his aid, lifted him off the spikes, tended his wounds. Those words did not describe *him*, didn't ring true at all. They were not what he was, not deep inside. Certainly, they were not what he'd intended to be.

This was supposed to be a *game*. Just a game. The best ever, the most daring ever, but still just a game.

Full daylight banished the ugly words almost completely, turned truths into lies. The womb healed, sealed up again, enveloping words and deeds, making it possible to go on. For now.

One day – one night – he *knew* it would open irrevocably, rip apart so completely that he wouldn't be able to suture it together again. And then it would all spill out, would soil everything else in his life with its stench.

But then, at least, it would be over.

Sometimes – more and more often – he longed for that to happen.

Chapter 37

I had been having bad dreams about the abducted kids. I'd called Lydia on Saturday after our trip upstate, but her machine had picked up and I'd decided against leaving a message, decided suddenly that maybe it was time for me to back off, respect her privacy, get on with my own life, concentrate on my family.

The weekend over and the girls back in school, I'd really tried to get back to work on the novel, but it still wasn't working out for the same reasons as before. I just could not get Michael Cooper or Robbie Johanssen out of my mind. Or Lydia.

Mostly Lydia, darn it.

And the Eryx triad.

I called Norman Baum on Wednesday morning.

'Am I making any sense at all?' I asked him. 'These guys were impeccably mannered, well-educated – probably old money, all of them; three apparently decent men saying how much they wanted to help. Appropriate responses to everything.' I paused. 'They may be just what they appear to be.'

'But you don't think so.'

'I don't *know*. That's the thing.'

'Are you saying one of them might be involved with the abductions?'

'No, that's not what I'm saying at all.' I was still reaching for it. 'It was just this sense that everything was a little too perfect. Maybe I just don't trust perfection.'

'So where's this leading, Jake?' Baum was being patient with me.

'I'm concerned that the Bureau may feel they're squeaky clean and out of the frame.' I wanted to be honest. 'Or maybe it just bugs me that even if they do a real number on Eryx, neither Lydia nor I are going to hear about it.' I paused again. 'My problem is that if I try checking these men out myself, Agent Kline is going to object big time, and I don't want to piss him off, for everyone's sake. Besides which, my own skills are so damned rusty they'll probably hear me coming twenty miles off.'

'In other words,' Baum said, 'you want me to do this for you?'

'In other words.'

I liked the man more than ever.

Chapter 38

Lydia's need to call Jake was still there, had persisted for over a week.

It's just being alone, she had told herself repeatedly. Being in the apartment without Robbie, constantly fighting the impulse to think about him, about where he was, about what was happening to him, about how he felt, about how *scared* he had to be, about whether he was giving up hope that she would find him.

And yet, in the rare moments when she did manage to stop thinking about her son, she was assailed by dreadful guilt for doing so. The previous night she had even had a dream in which Aaron had arrived, without notice, had simply swept into the apartment wearing his tailcoat and a carnation button-hole, coming directly from the platform at Carnegie Hall. Only this time he hadn't come to see Lydia, as he had in countless dreams before; this time he'd come to harangue her for taking time out to write a grocery list instead of spending each waking second sending thoughts to their captive son.

In the dream, she'd been sitting at the kitchen table, pen and pad in hand, writing down *Tropicana Smooth* and *Organic honey*, when Aaron had strode into the kitchen.

'If you *have* to do that,' he'd told her, 'at least write down peanut butter. He'll want a good stock of that when he comes home.'

'Robbie doesn't like peanut butter any more,' Lydia had tried to tell him, but Aaron had swept out the way he'd entered,

133

and it had been too late for her to tell him anything else. She had put down her pen, laid her weary head on her arms on the table and had begun to weep, but then she'd felt arms wrapping around her, strong, comforting arms, and she had raised her face, and the arms hadn't belonged to Aaron, but to Jake Woods, and Lydia had found that she hadn't minded that at all, and that had started her crying again.

Then she'd woken up.

And now, this morning – Wednesday July 5, the day after the worst Independence Day she'd ever experienced, far worse even than the first Fourth of July after Aaron's death – she was finally making that call, half hoping he might be out so she could either leave a message or put down the receiver.

'Jake, it's Lydia.'

Lovely, low voice, a little tentative perhaps.

'Hey,' I said, 'I was just going to call you.'

'Really?' Calm sounding, unruffled.

I started by telling her about my conversation with Baum the previous Wednesday, asked her, somewhat belatedly, if she minded.

'Are you kidding me?' The warmth and relief in her voice was answer enough. 'It's *exactly* what I would have done if my mind wasn't almost completely mush.' Lydia paused. 'So why were you about to call me now, Jake?'

'Because I just got Baum's report.'

'And?'

So much *hope* in that voice it squeezed my heart. 'Nothing significant,' I told her quickly. 'Basic profiles of Korda, Fitzgerald and Hawthorne.' I paused. 'Shall I read it to you over the phone, or do you have a fax?'

'You know what?' She stopped. 'You're probably busy.'

'Not especially,' I said. 'The girls are on their school vacation now, but they have plans for the day, so I'm surplus to their requirements.'

'It's just that I was wondering' – Lydia sounded uncertain – 'if you'd mind my coming to visit you. I could take the train,

134

escape for a little while *and* see the report – so long as it isn't inconvenient—'

'It isn't,' I assured her. 'Not in the least.'

'Are you sure? Jake, you know you can tell me to take a hike.'

I laughed. 'You tell me which train, and I'll pick you up.'

I met her at the station, struck as always by her loveliness. Her long hair was loose today, and she was wearing chinos with a beautifully cut white shirt, carrying a rain jacket over one arm. Other faces were beginning to tan, but Lydia's face seemed to be growing progressively paler, yet she was no less attractive for that.

Friends, Jake, I told myself firmly. Nothing else.

She'd brought a bunch of flowers, pretty blues and violets, hesitated for a moment as she handed them to me, said she'd discovered a long time ago, to her surprise, that not all men liked being given flowers, though she didn't quite see why that should be. I assured her that I was the kind of man who *loved* being given flowers, and that since I couldn't remember the last time it had happened, this bunch was all the more welcome.

'If it's okay with you,' I said as we got into my car, 'I thought we might as well have tea at my place. Unless you'd be happier out somewhere – New Haven's full of good teashops and cafés.'

Lydia smiled at me. 'I'd like to see where you live. Will the girls be there?'

I shook my head. 'They're still with friends right now, then Rianna will go to her gym, and Kim and Tom have invited Ella to their place for a barbecue.' I glanced my watch. 'I don't have to pick them up for four or five hours.'

The topic of my daughters troubled me suddenly. Every mention of other people's children *had* to be twisting the knife in Lydia, and abruptly I started worrying about taking her to the apartment, with evidence of the girls all over. Mind, it wasn't the first concern I'd had in the past few hours about bringing Lydia into my home. Fact was, I was somewhat relieved that

Rianna and Ella weren't going to be there; partly for Lydia's sake, partly because of my younger child's tendency to be something of a loose cannon. Mostly, I think, because of Rianna's ability to read me so damned easily.

Nothing to read here except friendship – and new friendship at that.

Oh yeah?

In the time between our phone call and leaving for the train station, I'd baked a cake: a biscuit base with tart sliced apples, latticed over the fruit and dusted with sugar.

'This is wonderful,' Lydia said, after we'd sat down in the living room. 'Tastes homemade.'

'One of Simone's recipes.'

'I'm impressed.'

'Don't be,' I said. 'She taught it to Rianna when she was seven, which puts it just about in my realm of expertise.' I couldn't help noticing that Lydia seemed unable to manage more than that one small mouthful. Thinner as well as paler, I realized with a pang.

'Rianna sounds very capable,' she said.

'That she is,' I agreed, curbing the temptation to expand on the subject.

I'd set our tea tray on the low table before us, beside Lydia's flowers. The table was carved Mexican pine; the bookshelves along two walls were some kind of blond oak. Our furniture in general is a mixed affair, some transported from our old house, some already here when the girls and I moved in, some picked up by us in local stores and antique markets. We're probably an interior designer's nightmare, but from our perspective it all seems to mesh together. It's liveable, rather than splendid. It's home now.

Lydia told me she liked the apartment, said my personality was stamped all over it. Mixed up and chaotic, I said, smiling. Comfortable and easy-going, she said. Coming from some people, I might have regarded that as a back-handed compliment, but in Lydia's case I felt she meant it, which pleased me.

We talked very generally for a while: about those aspects of Manhattan that I missed and those I did not, about the merits of life in New Haven, about the weather, of course, about Hillary Clinton's senatorial bid, about my very limited knowledge of opera and about Lydia's love of jazz.

I knew we'd done with skirting around the real business of the afternoon when Lydia told me about Kline's visit and her reactions to it. I understood her feelings, thought she was probably correct in her assumptions.

And then I gave her Baum's report.

He'd come up, in less than a week, with three decent, if limited, profiles on the Eryx directors, and so far their histories seemed to bear out their appearances: Korda and Hawthorne both Harvard men, Fitzgerald a former Yalie, with more than their clear blue eyes, graphic art and computer backgrounds in common.

They were all men of property. Korda had a horse farm near Salisbury in the Berkshires, and a large house closer to Eryx Software outside South Glastonbury near the Meshomasic State Forest – a lonely situation, according to Baum. Fitzgerald had a small, also somewhat isolated estate east of Moodus near the Devils Hopyard State Park. Hawthorne lived near Chester in what Baum reported as by far the most obviously charming surroundings, closest to 'civilization'.

None of the men was presently married, though the circumstances of their single status were different. Korda, thirty-nine, the smooth, golden boy-type president, was divorced with two young children, both living with their mother, Pamela, in a town house near the UN in Manhattan. Fitzgerald, thirty-seven – the programming genius – had lost his pregnant wife in an accident three years ago. Hawthorne, a year younger, was a bachelor, and Baum had found no reference to any long-term relationship in his recent life. Though Korda was the majority shareholder, the other two were partners in Eryx and Zeus Interactive, and all three men appeared to have been in a solid financial position prior to setting up the corporations, their monetary stability stemming from wealthy family backgrounds.

That – Baum had added by hand in an informal postscript – *might just be the basis for the 'perfection' you mistrusted, Jake. Money, and a whole lot of it. But if you or Mrs Johanssen want me to dig a little deeper for you, I'm willing.*

Lydia was silent when she finished reading. I gave her a couple of minutes.

'Not much there,' I said, finally.

She shook her head, seemed to have a little trouble saying anything for another moment. 'I don't know what I was hoping for,' she said, with an attempt at self-mockery. 'A red arrow pointing over one of their heads.'

'One of them sounds like he might be worth a closer look,' I offered.

'Hawthorne?' Lydia shrugged. 'Because he's never married?'

'No long-term relationship.'

'No *recent* relationship that Baum could find out about. Hardly grounds for accusing a man of abducting five teenagers.'

It was my turn to take a second or two.

'Anything in there that meshes with that cold sensation you felt at our meeting?' *Malevolence* was the word she'd used then, but I didn't want to start putting thoughts in her mind – Lord knew there had to be enough crashing around in there already.

'Nothing.' Lydia looked right into my eyes. 'So maybe that *was* just an overreaction, my imagination working overtime.'

I said nothing.

'What are you thinking, Jake?'

'Nothing specific.' I shook my head. 'Just that I don't think we ought to dismiss your instincts too swiftly – and that for my money, Baum's opened up some avenues I think maybe we should follow through, even if we do end up duplicating FBI work.'

'Avenues such as?'

'We have three men close to forty apparently living alone, albeit for different reasons, two of them in fairly isolated surroundings.' I realized how this was sounding. 'I'm not suggesting anything sinister. Just that Baum's report makes me want to ask for just a little more before we turn away. I looked at her. 'What do you think?'

She lifted both hands from her lap in a small gesture of semi-defeat. 'Why not? Nothing to lose.' A thought struck her. 'Has Mr Baum sent you his account yet? Because if he has, I'd like you to give it to me now so I can settle it.'

'But you didn't hire him,' I pointed out.

'No, the Coopers hired him, but he's been working on my behalf, too.' Lydia was suddenly crisper. 'Jake, this is not open for debate. Robbie is my son. I'm paying Baum. Okay?'

'Okay.' I wasn't going to argue with her, all too aware that this was another of the few things she could actually feel she had some control over. 'But as it happens, Baum hasn't billed me yet, which makes him a very rare bird.'

'Don't private investigators usually ask for retainers?'

'Always, but as I said, Norman Baum's not your average PI. I asked him about his fee, and he told me he felt a little conflicted because of doing this job without consulting the Coopers, his primary clients. He also said he hates taking money for nothing, so why didn't we just wait and see? *His* words, not mine.'

'He must be paid,' Lydia said firmly. 'He's done this work for me.'

'I'll tell him.' I paused. 'Would you prefer it if he made his next report directly to you?'

She waited an instant before answering, looking at me quite hard, quite intently. I had this feeling she was reaching into me, gauging something, I'm not sure what exactly. It was a stirring kind of feeling, but then just about everything about Lydia Johanssen stirred me.

'If you don't mind staying involved,' she said quietly, 'I'd prefer things to go on as they are.'

'I don't mind that at all,' I said.

Chapter 39

Scott Korda was making himself an omelette in the kitchen of his house near South Glastonbury on Wednesday evening when Nick Ford telephoned.

'What's up?' Korda tucked the phone under his chin and flipped the omelette in his copper pan.

'Thought you should know that a PI out of Boston – outfit with a second office in New Haven, by the way—'

'Where the professor lives,' Korda interjected.

'In one,' Ford said. 'Anyhow, this PI – guy called Norman Baum – has been asking questions about you and your partners.'

'What kind of questions?' Korda sprinkled a little thyme over the omelette.

'Just basic fact-finding, background stuff: where you live, where you went to school, married, divorced, that kind of thing.'

'And you think Woods or one of his friends hired him?'

'Stands to reason.' Ford had a sandpaper-quality voice. 'And Mrs Johanssen was in New Haven this afternoon, visiting with the professor at his apartment.'

'I can't say I'm especially surprised they've been trying to find out more about us. Poor woman didn't seem the type to sit home and wring her hands.'

'So this doesn't concern you?'

'Why should it?' The omelette was ready. 'Nothing sinister that a PI – or the FBI, come to that – could discover about any of us, is there?'

'I'm not sure Bill's going to agree with you.'

Korda slid his supper smoothly and neatly onto a pre-warmed Rosenthal plate, put the copper pan into the sink for Roman, his housekeeper, to wash and put away, and tossed the green salad he'd prepared earlier. 'Does Bill have to know?'

'Wasn't it his idea to keep an eye on Woods?' Ford asked.

'I guess.' Korda wanted to eat. 'I'll mention it to him tomorrow, tell him you said it's no big deal. Goodnight, Nick.'

'Want me to go on keeping tabs on them?'

'I guess,' Korda said again.

'Have a nice dinner,' Ford said.

Chapter 40

Another exercise. More practice for the 'real thing'.

Except that today, the voice had just told Robbie, it was Dakota's turn.

'Your turn to relax and watch,' he said.

'I don't want to watch,' Robbie told the man. 'Those damned goggles weigh a ton on my nose and the whole thing puts pressure on my head and makes me nauseous. I don't want to put them on right now.'

'Fine,' the voice said, 'if that's the way you want it.'

'It is,' Robbie said.

'But the downside of that will be darkness and silence for the rest of the day – or perhaps longer.' He paused. 'You can't just pick and choose, Steel. This is not a Sunday afternoon stroll in the park, in case you hadn't noticed.'

Robbie put on the headset and gloves, misery engulfing him.

'Good boy,' the voice told him. 'It'll be worth it.'

Go screw yourself, Robbie said in his mind.

And then, suddenly, there she was again. The human Dakota. There, but not *really* there, which made him wonder for a moment if she was any more real than the rest of it, than the VR tunnels or the dogs or the subway station. After all, there she was before his eyes, yet he couldn't *touch* her. And yet, he did know, looking at the girl in her hideous goggles, so depleted-looking, diminished even since the last time he'd seen her, he *did* know that she was real, as real as he was.

And he could also see that, like last time, she was seeing *him*.

'Hey there,' he said, talking to her, his voice soft, careful in case he scared her.

Nothing.

'Dakota?'

Not hearing him, so maybe they weren't to be allowed to communicate. But if she could *see* him . . .

Robbie raised his right gloved hand in a salute.

No response to that either – but then again, she wasn't looking at him any more. Her head was turned to one side, looking at . . .

Whoa.

He'd been so busy staring at Dakota that he hadn't noticed where she was.

Not in her cell. Nor the subway station. Another *Limbo* virtual environment. A city sewer.

'Christ,' Robbie said.

His stomach lurched as he remembered the things that Steel and Dakota had encountered at that level of the game: roof falls, rats as big as beavers, a visit from Ghoulo, and *worse* . . .

He was glad he was only watching today. *Man*, was he glad.

Dakota was hunched over in her leather tunic, her body language at maximum tension, and suddenly, through his earphones, Robbie heard a high-pitched squealing, a kind of screeching, and it was hideous, grating up and down his spine. He was almost as tensed up as she looked, and he *knew* what was coming now, and he knew what Dakota was going to do, because he'd seen her do it before . . . Correction, he'd seen the *cyber*-Dakota do it, had seen her slice the head right off one of those fucking giant rats, had seen her leap, Tae Kwon Do-style or whatever, right over the top of those suckers . . .

God, no, please don't let them come.

He knew they *were* coming, though, was waiting for them to come seething, streaming through the sewer channel, waiting for Dakota to get the better of them, of the son-of-a-bitch who was putting her *through* this . . .

But there was nothing. *Nothing*. And Robbie stared at the girl's face below the grotesque headset, and he saw that her mouth was rigid, the lips so pale they were almost bleached, saw that she was trembling violently . . .

The sound cut off. *Silence*.

Then the image. First to blue. Now to black.

Robbie almost toppled back, jolted, shocked. 'What happened? What the hell *happened*?'

No one answered him.

If Steel thought *he* was upset, what about *him*?

Worse for him.

The girl was losing it, no doubt about that now. Not just her lustre, but her *courage* – the greatest calamity of all. Nothing to do with her *fear*. That was the whole point about courage, that not everyone understood. Nothing *to* courage unless the person was afraid to begin with. Any fool could be brave in the absence of fear. It took intelligence and sensitivity to realize danger and be frightened by it, and after that it took great courage to face it.

Steel had made a good start in his first exercise, even if he had tried to escape from the dog pack rather than stand and fight, but once again that had been a case of innate intelligence, of instinct. Steel would fight when he felt he had no choice, when he was *given* no choice.

Dakota had been like that in the beginning. If he closed his eyes, he could still hear her early screams reverberating in his memory, and oh, how they'd thrilled him with their promise of things to come. But today, there had been no screaming, not even any real horror. She had seemed beyond fear – worse, she'd seemed *beneath* fear. Dulled, submissive.

The way the last, not-quite Steel had been at the end.

Oh God, he could hardly *bear* it.

Not again.

Not another one.

Chapter 41

Rianna knew that Lydia Johanssen had been in their apartment for tea the previous day. In the first place, her dad had told her, and in the second, two-thirds of the apple cake he'd baked – *he'd* baked, not Kim – was still on a dish under a cover as evidence.

She'd asked him about it, and he'd told her that Lydia had come to talk some more about her son's disappearance. That, Rianna supposed, was why she hadn't eaten much cake. It had seemed, at first glance, almost a slight against her mother. Her father had baked a Simone Woods cake especially for this person, and she had rejected it. Reminded, though, of the woman's misery, Rianna had realized that was a churlish over-reaction. If she or Ella went missing, she doubted if their dad would be able to eat cake or much of anything till he got them home again.

She told Shannon about it next day on the phone.

'Come *on*, Ree,' her friend said right away. 'He's in *love* with her. *That's* why he baked the cake.'

'You think?'

'Do you know what she looks like?' Shannon asked.

'I still haven't seen her.'

'I thought maybe your dad had described her, told you how gorgeous she is.'

'Uh-uh.'

'Not a word?'

'Not one.' Rianna paused. 'I guess she has to be very vulnerable right now.'

'And men like vulnerable women,' Shannon said. '*Older* men, anyhow.'

Rianna thought about the vulnerability thing after the call, while she was making her bed. Her mother hadn't been that kind of person; she'd always been strong, ready for anything, always *doing* stuff, for them or other people. But then, Simone hadn't had to go through anything like Lydia Johanssen . . .

Rianna tossed down her quilt, smoothed it over, then sat on the bed.

She wondered what Lydia *did* look like.

Their dad had shown her and Ella another photograph of Robbie Johanssen the other day, and Rianna had to say she thought he looked like one of the cutest guys she'd ever seen. Seeing the picture had upset her though. It was one thing allowing herself to empathize with Robbie's mother, quite another to think about what might be happening to *him*.

Rianna definitely did not want to think about that.

Chapter 42

It took Norman Baum a week to compile his follow-up report. No great shakes, he told me on the phone, but probably worth looking at. Since he had a sick cousin to visit in New York City, and since Lydia was still clear about her preference that I stay involved, we agreed to meet at her place and, at her insistence, for lunch.

Baum and I drove into the city together, the PI getting hair-raising speeds out of his old VW, and arrived on the dot of noon with chocolates and the report.

'I am so glad to meet you, Mr Baum,' Lydia told him at the door.

'It's Norman,' Baum told her, 'and the pleasure's all mine.'

I glanced at him, and saw that my unprepossessing friend – we'd only actually met the one time, but I already considered him a friend I'd be glad to have – was actually blushing as he looked at our hostess.

'I must look a sight,' Lydia said, bringing us into the living room. 'It's the first time I've done any real cooking in a while, and I think I've gotten a little carried away.' She saw our side-long glances. 'And before you start telling me I shouldn't have gone to so much trouble, let me tell you it's been good therapy.'

'It smells too good to argue,' I said.

'And the only sight you look,' Baum added, 'is a beautiful one.'

Lydia smiled. 'I like this man, Jake.'

He was right, I thought, watching her go to fetch ice for our drinks. She'd tied her hair back in another ponytail, a few strands escaping again, her colour was heightened by cooking, and she looked almost relaxed. *Beautiful*, just as Baum had said, and I only wished I could click my fingers and magic away our reason for being here.

'We'll wait till after we've eaten to get to your report, Norman,' she said after she'd returned with the ice and was fixing our scotches. 'If you don't mind.'

'Not at all,' Baum said. 'I guess Jake's told you I haven't found anything too significant.'

'He told me,' Lydia said, and handed us our drinks.

A couple of hours of real pleasure followed. Baum asked if he might see the music room, and once inside the soundproofed walls, we persuaded her to play her late husband's piano for us. I don't know what she played – I'm not the world's most knowledgeable guy when it comes to things like that – but I know it was *lovely*. She told us, afterwards, with disarming modesty, that she wasn't much of a pianist, but you could have fooled us. We asked her to sing for us, too, but she declined, and we didn't press her.

Lunch was a treat. Dainty portions of angel hair pasta with a delicate clam sauce to start with; perfectly roasted lamb for the main course; and a steamed chocolate pudding with vanilla ice cream that had Baum almost moist-eyed with pleasure.

'You were right, Jake, about my needing to do things,' she said during the meal. 'I even gave one singing lesson this week – though it was only to Sally. I haven't really wanted her around here, working, since Robbie was taken, but part of our deal was always free lessons, so I was feeling guilty.'

At her insistence, we left the washing up, and Baum made his report.

Korda, he had established, was a collector. Of property mainly, with an apartment in Manhattan on the Upper East Side, a Beverly Hills house and a villa in Cap d'Antibes on the

French Riviera, as well as his farm and the house in Connecticut. He also made no secret of his collection of horses, motorbikes, old movies and antique jewellery. His New England home, though isolated, appeared as approachable as the farm, but it was rumoured to be a kind of homage to state-of-the-art technology on the inside, which Baum assumed included a high level of security.

'Korda has two sisters, a retired banker father and his mother writes coffee table books on beautiful homes,' Baum went on. 'Korda and Pamela divorced because of irreconcilable differences and he gave her pretty much what she asked for, including the UN town house. He sees their kids quite often, and even when he's in the city they stay over at his place, so presumably the wife has no problems with that.'

I had asked Baum to try and discover if all the anonymous notes had referred to athletic prowess. He'd used an FBI contact to do some nosing and the answer was yes, with one exception: the girl from Atlantic City, who was, it seemed, a cheerleader contest winner rather than an athlete.

'Does Korda have sporting connections?' Lydia asked.

Baum looked down at his report, flipped over a page. 'Fine high school gymnast, halted by injury.' He looked back up at her. 'Can't have been anything long-term, because these days he plays tennis and squash, and swims.'

'I understand Eryx sponsors some sporting trophies,' I said.

'And Korda always presents them.' Baum nodded. 'Usually says something about organizing the events to give something back to the young people who've made them so successful; says they choose sports to emphasize that they agree that it's unhealthy for kids to spend all their time hunched over PlayStations or Dreamcasts.'

'What guys,' I said.

'Want me to go on?' Baum asked Lydia over the top of his bifocals. 'Or take a break?'

'Go on, please, if you don't mind,' she told him.

'In case either of you was wondering, Hal is Hawthorne's given name, same as his late father's,' Baum continued. 'We already know about the home near Chester, but he also owns an upstate New York winery and a waterfront apartment in Boston.'

He told us he'd done some low-key checking around in Chester, cautious because it was probably the kind of town where too many questions about a local would bounce right back to the subject, and Baum figured we didn't want that to happen. According to those locals he had asked, Hawthorne led a comparatively simple life, frequently patronizing the town's establishments. His wealth traced back to a great-grandfather in publishing. His father had been a disabled war hero and benefactor who'd died young; his mother had remarried another rich man and was also charitably active.

'Still nothing at all on the relationship front, but he may just be the kind of guy to keep his personal life under wraps,' Baum told us. 'Sports-wise, back as far as high school, it seems Hawthorne tried hard but was unspectacular – more the cerebral type even then, gifted in math and science, and into computer technology early on, before he got to Harvard.'

He moved on to William Fitzgerald, the most work-obsessed of the partners. Word was he'd bought the house near Devils Hopyard State Park two years ago, installing his own production studio, in which he was rumoured to work several nights a week; and he also kept a place on Riverside Drive here in the city – seldom used, according to a doorman.

'What does he produce in his studio?' I asked.

'No one knows, and again, I didn't push too hard. I did establish that he's by far the most privacy-obsessed of the three, which is maybe why I had trouble learning much about his parents – father a lawyer, not much else.'

Though work seemed to take up most of Fitzgerald's life, he was also known to be Olympics-crazy, having attended every Games, summer and winter, since leaving Yale.

'Do we know if he's going to Sydney?' I asked.

'No bookings yet that I could trace,' Baum answered, 'but that doesn't mean much.'

At college, he said, Fitzgerald had been lionized as a runner.

He might be a loner now in his spare time, but his bereavement probably explained that. After all, Baum said, the man worked at something he patently enjoyed and excelled at, mixed with young, talented, energetic people all day long, so going to ground after hours didn't seem unnatural.

'I can understand a man keeping to himself after such tragedy,' Lydia said.

'Tragedy's been known to drive people nuts,' Baum pointed out.

'Do we know anything about the accident that killed his wife?' I asked.

'Car,' Baum said simply. 'She was driving.'

My heart went out to Fitzgerald. At least Simone had left me my girls.

'The Olympic passion sounds pretty healthy,' I said, moving along.

'Though working nights in his own studio when a guy's already made his pile and then some is definitely obsessive. Mind you,' Baum added, 'the industry seems to do that to a lot of them. I took a look at Ellen Zito and a few of her colleagues – Hendrick and Kaminski – still haven't been able to nail exactly what that guy does, by the way – but Zito works nights too, though in her case she stays at Eryx. Then again, she doesn't have a big house, just a small apartment in Hartford.'

'Anything on Meg Binder or the others?' I asked.

'Nothing of interest, but I was focusing on the partners.'

'So that's it?'

Baum nodded. 'Afraid so.'

'You've done a great job,' Lydia told him. 'I'm very grateful.'

'I'd like to have dug up something that said "come get me",' the PI said.

'I don't know.' I mused for a moment. 'I still say Hawthorne merits a closer look at by the Bureau. The absence of relationships is unusual.'

'Unusual equals aberrant?' Lydia raised an eyebrow.

'A lot of serial killers are loners,' Baum said, then halted abruptly, red-faced.

'It's all right, Norman.' Lydia was kind. 'You can't watch every word you say.' She shook her head. 'But even if they live alone, I don't think we can really call any of these men "loners"'.

I moved things along. 'What do you think about Korda? A collector, which makes it not *that* bizarre a leap to imagine him as a collector of physically gifted young people, maybe?' The notion made me shudder inwardly and I, too, was instantly regretful of having voiced it.

'Except' – Baum saved me – 'the man's life seems even more jammed full than the others, and the marriage hasn't thrown up any nasty traits, or else his ex probably wouldn't be letting the kids spend so much time with him.'

'And many wealthy people collect *something*,' Lydia added.

'I think we have to face some facts,' Baum said, starting to wind things up. 'Obviously we're in no position to conduct a real investigation into these men, and candidly' – he looked towards Lydia – 'I don't think we've found anything entitling us to demand the FBI take a more than routine look at three upstanding citizens, just because they run the corporation that created *Limbo*.'

'Especially because of that,' I agreed. 'They do, after all, have the most to lose if public opinion turns against the game.'

'Though surely,' Lydia added quietly, 'if a person were insane, they wouldn't care about their business one way or another.' She paused. 'Same thing if they're just plain wicked, and very rich into the bargain.'

'Anything's possible, Lydia,' Baum said, with a small, gentle shrug.

'Just not very likely,' I felt I had to add.

Baum left soon afterwards to see his cousin, having agreed earlier that I'd take the train back to New Haven when I was ready. Lydia and I washed the dishes together, saying little, and I could tell that the report and conversation had pretty much exhausted her.

'I should go,' I said when we'd put away the last dish. 'Let you get some rest.' It was almost five o'clock.

'Do you have to?' Lydia shook her head. 'I'm sorry, of course you have to.'

I thought there was a kind of plea behind the courage. 'Actually, I don't. Kim's with the girls, and she knows I might be late.'

'Won't her husband mind?'

'Tom? No, he's fine about things like that. If he misses Kim when she's sitting Rianna and Ella, he just comes over to join them.'

'You're lucky.'

'I know it,' I said.

We went back into the living room and sat down. The phone rang twice, and both times as Lydia went to answer I saw her knuckles whiten as she clenched the receiver, but each time it was just a friend calling to check on her.

If it were me, I decided, I thought I might start screaming.

Or maybe that wasn't how it was. Maybe it was the way it had been for me after Simone. I hadn't screamed then, except on the inside. I'd screamed *plenty* on the inside.

'I'm sorry,' she said after the second call. 'Sometimes I put the machine on when I can't take any more of that, but on the whole I try to answer myself, just in case.'

We sat quietly again for a few minutes, but I could see there was something going on in her head, something she wanted to say to me.

'Tell me,' I said, at last.

'I think I must be getting quite brazen,' she said.

'Brazen's not exactly a word I'd use to describe you.'

'I wouldn't be so sure. I have yet another favour to ask you. One you really must feel free to turn down.'

'Okay,' I said.

'I've been thinking about Hawthorne,' she said. 'I know what I said earlier about his single lifestyle not meaning anything, and I did listen to what Baum said at the end, but I still can't help feeling that maybe Kline should at least be *nudged* in that direction – in Eryx's direction in general. You said yourself that you thought the same at one point.'

'I did,' I admitted.

'So I'm going to call Kline tomorrow, ask if I can see him again.' she paused. 'And I would very much appreciate your support if I do get to see him.' She shook her head. 'Not just moral support, really. When he was here with Agent Moran and I mentioned you, Kline was so swift to dismiss you, but if you were actually *here* . . .'

'I think he'd be just as likely to dismiss me.'

She caught her lower lip between her teeth for just an instant, really just an *instant*, but the fragility behind that tiny gesture all but blew me away.

'I'm sorry, Jake.' She was already pulling herself together. 'I shouldn't have asked.' She started to stand up. 'You must get home.'

'Sit down.' I got to my feet. 'Please, Lydia, sit down. I'm going to call home, see how Kim's fixed tonight.' I saw her face. 'If it's a problem for her or Tom, I'll go back.'

'You promise?'

'I'd have no choice.'

I made the call, ascertained there was no difficulty and that Tom might come and share the spare bed with Kim.

'The girls want a word,' Kim said.

Ella came on the line first. I told her the truth, that the lady I'd been visiting needed me to stay over in New York so we could go to a meeting together, but that I'd be back next day.

'Okay, Daddy.' Clearly, Ella had no problem with me either. If she had, she'd have had no compunction about letting me know. I told her I loved her and she told me she loved me back, but I could tell she was keen to get back to whatever she'd been doing.

Rianna was next. I knew I had to be a little more precise with her.

'We're going to try to see the FBI agent in charge of the task force, honey.'

'That's Agent Kline, right?' she said.

'Right. But if he can't see us tomorrow, I'll come home anyway, okay?'

'Fine,' she said.

'Everything okay with you guys?'

'Fine,' she said again, then paused. 'Where are you going to sleep, Daddy?'

I realized I hadn't even thought about that. 'In a hotel,' I told her.

'Which one?'

'I don't know yet, but New York City has a zillion of them.'

A zillion of them, maybe, but every one I tried was fully booked.

As it happened, I didn't find that out till *after* I'd left Lydia's apartment at a quarter to six, having told her confidently about a couple of decent places that always had rooms free, which I knew because colleagues at UNH often came into Manhattan on last-minute trips.

I finally managed to scrounge up a lousy scrap of a room in a place on Broadway, called Lydia as promised, lied about being pleasantly ensconced, gave her the phone number and told her I'd call next morning, after which I went out for something to eat. Dog-tired and in no need of anything more than a sandwich, I went to a bar, downed a ham on rye with mustard, washed down by a beer and *three* whiskey chasers.

It's been a long while since I drank that much. *Long* while.

So when I wandered on back to my so-called hotel and found Lydia in the lobby waiting for me, I guess my defences were way down.

She'd changed into blue jeans, baggy white sweater and sneakers. She looked just plain *great*. 'I called you a while back,' she explained quietly, 'and realized exactly which "pleasant" hotel you were staying at.'

'You *know* this place?' I was surprised.

'A musician friend of mine stayed here once, so I know what a hole it is.'

'It's fine,' I said.

'It is not fine,' Lydia corrected, 'which is why you're coming back to my place and staying in our guest room.'

I was in no condition to argue.

Truth was, I didn't want to argue.

Chapter 43

Rianna lay awake for a while that night.

Her father hadn't called again, which she'd half expected him to, even though he hadn't *said* he would.

He'd told her he was going to a hotel, but she'd heard the tiny hesitation before he'd said that, which made her wonder . . .

Wonder what, Rianna?

Her father was nearly forty years old. He did not need permission from his fifteen-year-old daughter to stay in a hotel or *not* stay in a hotel, whatever the implications. Besides, Rianna wasn't sure that she'd especially mind if he was staying over with Lydia Johanssen – if he was, right this moment, in *bed* with Lydia Johanssen. After all, he had to have slept with women since her mother – that was normal, wasn't it?

Damn right it's normal, Shannon would have said if she were here.

Except those women – if they existed – probably hadn't been really important to her father.

And Rianna had the distinct impression that Lydia Johanssen *was*.

'Okay,' she said into the dark, and found she was smiling.

She didn't mind that too much. Didn't really mind that at all.

So long as Lydia didn't *hurt* him.

Chapter 44

A sound woke me.

I was instantly sober, knew exactly where I was. In the double bed of Lydia's guest room.

I thought I knew what the sound was, too.

Lydia was having a nightmare.

A bad, *bad* one.

I lay there, trying not to listen, unable *not* to, unsure of what to do. The glowing clock on the bedside table told me it was 3:53. I couldn't just go to her room – she was bound to feel embarrassed and that was the last thing I wanted . . .

She cried out. A keening sound, almost a wail.

I got up, put on the robe hanging on the back of the door, tied the cord and went out into the dark, strange corridor in search of the sound.

There.

I opened the door. It was dark in here, too, but I could see her shape in the bed in the middle of the room. She was hunched up under the covers, arms flailing, moaning more softly now, but still *moaning* . . .

I thought of turning on the light, but that seemed too harsh, so I padded over to the bed, looked down for a moment more.

Lovely hair in disarray, half covering her face.

I put out my right hand and gently touched her cheek.

She stirred, gave another of those awful moans.

'Lydia.' I stroked the soft skin lightly. 'It's okay.' I've never understood why we say such things, why we tell people things are okay when they're so patently anything but. Yet still, I said it again. 'It's okay, Lydia. Wake up.'

She woke up, saw me, and her own right hand flew up to cover mine. That was her immediate waking instinct, to keep my hand on her cheek, and the realization of that filled me with something dangerously close to joy.

Long, long time since I felt that.

'You've been having a nightmare,' I told her, the way I might have told one of the girls. 'Just a bad dream, that's all.'

She didn't speak, but my eyes were growing used to the darkness and I thought I saw tears on her cheeks. And then she let go of my hand and put out both her arms.

Don't misread, Jake.

No way I could go into those arms without getting onto her bed.

'Jake,' Lydia said urgently. 'Please, Jake.'

I got on the bed, felt her arms hold me tight, put mine around her.

The scent of her, the *feel* of her, was almost too much to bear. So soft, so warm, so incredibly *good*.

The greatest comfort in the world, yet not simply a comfort hug for either of us.

No *way*.

'Lydia, are you sure?' The age-old question, but I had to ask it, had to be certain this wasn't an extension of her dream, that she knew exactly what she was doing. I couldn't stand the idea that I might be taking advantage of her.

'Very sure,' she said.

No remnants of sleep in her voice now.

She knew exactly what she was doing, where we were going. Thank Christ. Oh, thank *Christ*.

I hardly remember getting undressed. One minute Lydia was wearing a silky-feeling pair of pyjamas and I was wearing that robe – then it was all *skin* and a jumble of sensations, wonderful, all-enveloping sensations and emotions; though the sweetest, the most miraculous of all, for me, were our kisses, our mouths coming together, and oh, dear Jesus, the intimacy, the warmth, the sheer *closeness* of those kisses . . .

I was inside her then, in that dark, sweet, black velvet place, and she was moaning again, but oh, such *different* sounds than before, thank God, and then I was crying out, too, and I don't know what I was saying, or even if there were real words coming out of my mouth, and it didn't matter, I didn't *care*.

Only about her. Only about Lydia. How much I needed her. How much we needed each other.

Too soon after, much too soon, that question of Rianna's snaked back into my head, the one about where I was going to sleep tonight. I wondered, suddenly, half guiltily, if I'd already had this in mind; thought not, *hoped* not . . .

'Don't start feeling guilty.'

Lydia's voice startled me. I turned my head, saw her watching me, gentle humour behind those lovely eyes.

'Not on my account, anyway,' she told me.

'Not guilty, exactly,' I said, feeling my way, trying to be honest. 'Maybe just afraid I might have taken advantage.'

Lydia's eyes held steady. 'Do you honestly believe I would have allowed you to do that, Jake?'

'No.' Truth.

'Well then,' she said.

And came into my arms, this time to sleep.

I woke up to a killer headache and an empty bed, struggled back into the robe, slouched into the bathroom to splash my face with cold water and steal some Listerine from the cabinet, and found my way to the kitchen.

Lydia was already dressed, in jeans again with a plain white T-shirt, and making breakfast. 'Good morning.'

I stood in the doorway for a moment, watching her, loving what I saw, then started to move towards her, already looking forward to holding her again.

'I figured you wouldn't want much more than toast and coffee.' She turned away from me to the stove. 'Coffee first.'

Her tone was warm but distinctly breezy, the manoeuvre deliberate.

A rebuff. Not imagined.

A cold, sad feeling clamped itself around my heart.

'Lydia?'

'Sit down, Jake.' She set the coffee pot on the table, then the cream jug.

'Thank you.' *Great speech, Jake.* Real eloquent.

I was already starting to wonder if I'd dreamed the night.

We both sat down.

'Let me go first,' Lydia said, her cheeks a little flushed. 'I feel I need to, before we get too uncomfortable.'

'Did something happen?' Maybe she'd had a call, maybe I hadn't heard the phone ringing.

'No.' She paused. 'I just think you must be wishing last night never happened.'

'No,' I told her, quickly, definitely. 'That's not true at all.'

'Then you're thinking maybe it *shouldn't* have happened.'

That was a little closer to the truth, close enough, at least, to keep me silent.

'I do understand how you must feel,' she went on swiftly. 'First I ask you to stay in the city, then I all but drag you from your hotel, and then, in the middle of the night, you're faced with me at my most vulnerable. And so of course, being the kind of man you are, you came to take care of me, and the fact is if anyone took advantage of the situation, it was *me*.'

'Are you kidding me?' I was staring at her.

'No, Jake, I'm not.' Lydia stood up, went to fetch the toast. 'Last night was truly wonderful' – she said with her back to me – 'the very best thing that's happened to me for a long time.' She turned to me again, face determinedly set, voice bright. 'But I'm not going to let you worry that we've started something you're not ready for, because it goes without saying that *I* certainly have other things on my mind.'

Robbie. Poor lost Robbie.

I have never been so thrown by any woman. Not even by Simone, who was always damned good at throwing me curves to keep me on my toes.

'Lydia,' I began, hardly knowing what to say, my head felt so messed up.

'Toast's ready,' she said.

Going downhill, man.

I stood up. 'Lydia, we have to talk about this.'

She smiled, held up the toast rack. The smile wasn't real, it was a kind of armour-thing, and I guess that made the toast rack a shield.

'Let's have some breakfast,' she said. 'Then, if it's still okay with you, we can try calling Kline.'

Down and *out*.

To cap it all, Kline wasn't available to take our call; neither was Agent Moran. Lydia was offered another alternative, but she held out for the man in charge. I heard the timbre in her voice during the brief conversation: mother in battle, not a trace of hysteria, just pure steely determination.

'What now?' I asked her afterwards.

'Do you think he was avoiding me?'

'I doubt it.' I paused. 'I think maybe you need to trust Kline a little more.'

'I'm not sure I trust anyone any more,' Lydia said, then flushed a little. 'That's not really true.' She shook her head. 'I know all the good things you've said about those people, how much they care, but I'm just finding it hard to believe that a man like that could care *enough* about my son.'

'Not the way you do, of course,' I said. 'But I'm sure he does care about Robbie and Michael and the others.'

'I hope you're right,' she said.

That was when I realized I'd been waiting, like some selfish kid, for her to bring *me* into the trust equation, to say she trusted *me*, whatever she felt about Kline. And of course she hadn't said that, because she hadn't needed to say it, because it went without saying, or ought to have.

And because right this minute, as she'd said so succinctly over the breakfast table, she had more important things on her mind.

Time to go home.

Again.

Chapter 45

He knew that this time, once the girl had gone, he'd have to act swiftly to find her replacement. He'd given Steel another solo exercise this morning, and the kid had seemed upset because there'd been no sign of Dakota, had seemed genuinely worried about her.

Sweet Steel.

Good, reassuring, to see that tender aspect. Sweet savage. Two of the characteristics he'd be hoping to see more of in time.

Steel had gotten mad, thrown a little tantrum, said he wouldn't play, then, later, that he wouldn't eat. He'd kept his cool, had made the usual threat about darkness and silence, and it had, of course, worked. It was always such an effective tool of persuasion, targeting, as it did, basic, primitive fears.

Still, it was yet another reminder that he must not make the same mistake as before. This Steel simply could not be allowed to deteriorate. He had to find another Dakota – the right one this time – to match him, be *worthy* of him.

And he had to find her quickly.

Chapter 46

Kline phoned me Saturday morning. He was brief and to the point, told me right off that it was a courtesy call.

'I've just talked with Mrs Johanssen, and now I'm telling you exactly what I told her. Okay, Professor?'

'Certainly.' I was pretty crisp, too.

'First, I want to remind you of something you certainly already know, and that is that I'm under no obligation to tell you anything about the FBI investigation.'

'Of course not,' I said.

'The fact is, we are still running checks on Eryx from the top all the way down. Candidly, I don't think that's where we're going to find the abductor – but we *are* looking closely at all those people, and that means that you, Mrs Johanssen and Mr Baum need to keep well away from the corporation from now on. Do you understand me, sir?'

'Of course,' I said. 'And I appreciate your calling me.' It was the truth and, frankly, a lot more than I'd anticipated.

'I'm not sure if Mrs Johanssen feels quite the same way,' Kline said. 'Maybe you could make sure she understands?'

'I'll do my best.'

He thanked me and we left it there. I could have tried pressing him – Lord knew there were enough questions running through my mind – but I knew Kline would not, perhaps could not, have answered them, so I gave the guy a break.

After all, his time was precious to Robbie and Mikey and the others.

This was the man with their lives in his hands.

I did not envy him that.

Hal Hawthorne more or less ruled himself out of the frame later that day – or at least he *began* the process an hour or so after Kline had made that call to me. So Norman Baum told me Sunday evening, after it was all over.

Hawthorne must have noticed – had probably been *meant* to notice – federal agents Fred Friedrich and Martha King sitting in their unmarked car, supposedly on their lunch break, eating hot dogs in a parking spot conveniently close to where Hawthorne was having his hair cut early Saturday afternoon in Chester. Waiting, Baum and I guessed later, to see what kind of an effect their presence might have on him. That was just our interpretation of why they were there. The significant part of the story was that when Hawthorne came out of the barber's shop, still brushing clippings from his shoulders, he walked up to the car, tapped lightly on King's window and told the agents that rather than see them wasting valuable time, he'd be perfectly glad to show them – and any team they chose to bring along – around his house.

'How'd you find this out?' I asked Baum when he called to fill me in.

'I know a guy who knows a guy who knows Friedrich,' Baum answered. 'And before you ask, Friedrich was only drafted in on Saturday because someone else got sick, so this doesn't mean we get regular access to the LIMBO task force.'

According to Baum's contact, Hawthorne had told them he'd feel a heck of a lot more comfortable going about his daily life after the Bureau had eliminated him from their investigation, had said he found the notion of being even a borderline suspect in this crime almost unendurable.

'Lawyers cleared the way for both sides,' Baum said, 'and Kline's team went in and searched the place.'

'Only chance they were likely to get, I guess,' I said.

'Exactly.'

The orders to the search team were that they should be

meticulously thorough *and* circumspect. Nothing was to be overlooked, neither was anything to be damaged, and permission was to be obtained prior to opening every closet or drawer, before even a glance into anything resembling a crawlspace, attic or basement . . .

'And?' I asked, though the answer was pretty much a foregone conclusion.

'Nothing.'

'And that's it? Just that house?'

'Word is Hawthorne volunteered the same thing for his winery and the Boston apartment, but my guy doesn't know whether those searches took place, because Friedrich went back to regular duties.'

We agreed I would tell Lydia. I wasn't looking forward to it. We'd spoken twice since I'd left New York, both awkward conversations, Lydia making it clear, without saying as much, that she felt it best we stay away from each other.

This time at least I had something to say, though nothing that was going to bring her fresh hopes of a breakthrough.

'So that's it?' she said when I'd finished. 'They search one man's house, after he invites them in, and that's *it*?' She sounded fit to be tied, like it was one of those days when she just couldn't take any more.

'Probably not,' I said. 'Kline isn't naïve. He knows suspects swing different ways under scrutiny: some become hostile, others try pretending it isn't happening; some do just open themselves right up to put an end to it.'

'Innocent people,' Lydia said dryly.

'Kline will know that Hawthorne may have seized a chance to rub their noses in his innocence – he'll also know it doesn't mean he *is* innocent. Doesn't make him guilty either.' I paused. 'I really do think that the main point here and now is that he *did* open himself right up to Kline's team – and Baum's pal said they asked a lot more questions around Chester than he'd been able to.'

'Do we know what they learned?'

'Nothing new. That he's a fairly sociable guy, uses his town, has a regular cup of coffee, for instance, with the owner of a bookstore – even throws occasional dinner parties for neighbourhood people.'

'Has he always done that, or is it a recent thing?'

'A cover-up tactic, you mean? Not so far as they could tell.' She sighed. 'What about Korda and Fitzgerald?'

'Nothing as satisfactory.' I'd made up my mind not to fudge. 'Baum's guess is that without good reason they won't risk turning Korda into an adversary. Seems he's a pretty big cheese with serious family connections—'

'What kind?' Lydia jumped right on that.

I smiled. 'Not *that* kind of family. Relatives in the legal profession, even a judge or two. Enough to make them wary of anything that might smack of harassment.'

'And Fitzgerald?' Lydia asked.

'Very litigious, apparently. If they are following up on him, they'll be a lot more subtle about it.'

'Do you think they are?'

'Probably,' I said. 'But I'd guess it's mostly elimination while they work on digging up possible suspects from the consumer end of the game link, or wherever else they're looking.' I wanted to give Lydia something halfway positive. 'For instance, I imagine they're looking at all the real *Limbo* "masters".'

She fell silent. I could almost feel her last hopes for a swift solution crumbling into dust, could only begin to imagine her desolation at the prospect of the vast ocean into which the Bureau was casting its nets.

'They know what they're doing.' Easy for me to say, with my children safe in their rooms. 'You need to believe that, Lydia.'

'I don't appear to have any choice,' she said.

Not a word, I was all-too aware after we'd said goodnight, not one single word to tell me that our night together hadn't been buried in an emotional filing cabinet under '*Shameful*', or worse, '*Never to be repeated*'. I knew it was unrealistic, even wrong to think of a deeply intimate relationship at this time in Lydia's life. But in those moments when I let myself reflect honestly, I knew that I had felt, that night, like a man who'd just emerged from seven years in the desert and been given his first drink of pure, cool water – forget water, I was talking *wine*, the kind that warmed you through to your toes. So try as I might, I just could not seem to stop myself from hoping that maybe when this was over, maybe, God willing, when Robbie was safely home again . . .

And there was that other thing. I had never met Robbie Johanssen, but I was beginning to care so intensely about his safe return that I couldn't even bear to imagine any other outcome. For Lydia's sake and his.

Maybe for mine, too.

Chapter 47

It was *done*.

Thank heaven.

Or hell.

Over with. Same as before, but more smoothly, no last-second horrors. Just the girl, sleeping in the dark, not waking when he'd entered, and he'd wondered at that moment if maybe she hadn't *wanted* to wake, had not wanted to go on at all, so that he was really doing her the greatest favour by putting her out of her misery.

One shot, perfectly placed despite his shaking hands – still shaking now, the whole awful sickening thing still anathema to him, as it was every time.

He thought he'd screamed again, but he couldn't quite remember.

Too much had happened since. First, the hideous business of covering, cleaning, wrapping, removing to the cold room. His own sickness.

And then, the revelation.

He had been keeping up with the FBI investigation as well as he could – not easy, given the lack of time – *always* tough on him, taking care of all he had to do, all his responsibilities, and he *was* a responsible man. But he was using his resources well now, all his skills and daring.

And today he had found out something remarkable, something *amazing*, and almost too wonderful to dare believe in.

The professor. The one Steel's mother seemed to have hooked up with, the one who'd been poking his long nose into things that didn't concern him, supposedly because he knew the Cooper family, though he hadn't fooled *him* for an instant; *he* knew it was just because the guy wanted to get into Steel's mom's panties, and wasn't *that* really sick?

That wasn't the point, though, not any more. That was not the amazing part of what he'd learned today. That piece of happenstance, of sheer, unarguable *destiny*, was the fact that Professor Jacob Woods had a daughter.

Not just any daughter.

He had seen photographs.

Rianna Woods was fifteen. And beautiful.

And a fine gymnast.

He'd almost stopped breathing when he'd seen those pictures.

He knew that cameras *did* sometimes lie, knew he had to go see for himself, check her out at close quarters, in the flesh. But already he was ninety-nine per cent sure, all his instincts telling him so, his pulses flying, his gut somersaulting, his whole body and mind *burning* with that almost certain knowledge.

The one in the cold room was already little more than a memory. A *thing* now, sad, but gone, finished.

He had something else to focus on now.

A true companion for Steel. A worthy playmate.

The real Dakota at last.

FOUR

Chapter 48

It was like a new lease of life.

A transfusion.

It was Thursday, July 20, 2000, and he had found Dakota.

He watched her playing Frisbee with her little sister and the Ryan woman in Wooster Square. Rianna threw carefully to Ella, who made the catch, cheered by Ryan, then attempted but failed to skim it back to Rianna, only just missing General Wooster's sculpted left shin.

He was watching from a car, holding a map of New Haven as a prop. No sign of the professor, but the fifteen-year-old was as securely taken care of as she had been every time he'd seen her over the past two days. Either she was home, or else she was accompanied by father, housekeeper or friends, and once inside the High Fliers Club, there was the vigilant Coach Carlin.

He was going to find this harder than most. But he would not give up.

This was *meant to be*.

Even were it not for the poetic justice of taking the daughter of the cop-turned-teacher who seemed to have forgotten he'd resigned from law enforcement over a decade ago ... Even were it not for that, he would have found himself unable to turn away from Rianna Woods.

She was a ravishing young woman. Child-woman in many ways, less sophisticated than some fifteen-year-olds these days, perhaps, but with a mature manner, nonetheless. Tall for her age, slender but not too thin, small breasts still developing. Still her *daddy's* girl. Beautiful face. Winged dark eyebrows over grey, thoughtful eyes. Wide, sensuous mouth with a full lower lip. Lovely in gravity and laughter.

He'd watched for a while yesterday when Woods had gone to meet first the younger girl – emerging from a friend's house in Milford – and then Rianna, coming out of the gym club. Their hugs had been so natural and loving they'd brought stinging tears to his eyes.

No hugs in *his* childhood from *his* father.

Only himself to blame for that, of course.

But it still hurt.

No time to think about that now.

He'd have to work out something a little special, *different*, for Rianna. And he'd have to be super-careful when he sent the game. Though of course this time he knew he'd have to wait until afterwards to send it, otherwise Daddy wouldn't let her out of his sight for so much as a second.

By the time the package arrived for Professor Woods, though, his tall child-woman would be gone. And *then* wouldn't he be sorry for interfering in things that didn't concern him?

No more Rianna.

Dakota.

Chapter 49

No matter how she tried, no matter how illogical she told herself she was being, Lydia just could not put Eryx out of her mind. She had spoken to Jake a couple of times since Sunday, and he had deliberately steered away from the subject of Korda, Fitzgerald and Hawthorne, and she knew he was probably right to do so. Just as she knew that the FBI was probably right to be turning the focus of its investigation away from the corporation.

But 'probably' was not a word that impressed Lydia right now. It was too much like saying that they would 'probably' find Robbie sometime soon. And that he would 'probably' still be alive. *Knock on wood.*

Not good enough. Nowhere near good enough.

She still could not forget the sensation that had assailed her in Korda's office. She had fought hard to dismiss it, or at least to make some sense of it, link it to someone or something in particular, but she had failed. Nothing so easy as that.

Easy. Why should anything be easy for her? It certainly wasn't easy for Robbie. Alone, terrified, facing Christ-only-knew what . . .

Stop that. Think practically.

It was time for her to *do* something.

Even if none of the Eryx partners or employees was directly involved, that didn't mean they mightn't be a link to whoever was. She had suggested to Jake once that maybe she should return to the corporation for another visit without him, that perhaps they might feel less on their guard with her on her own, but Jake had rejected that absolutely, especially after Kline's admonition to stay away.

But the fact was, she was growing more desperate every day, more than even perceptive, empathetic Jake realized.

She was alternating between trying *not* to think about their night together, and actively seeking out the memory to warm herself, remind herself what life could still feel like. Guilt was winning hands down though.

More important things than sex, or even comfort, to focus on.

Only one, really.

Getting Robbie home.

Chapter 50

The plan was all worked out. More complex than any he'd undertaken before, and much more open to last-minute impediments. Bolder, more audacious. Riskier.

Bold is good.

Father said so.

This girl was more sheltered than many teenagers these days.

Good fathers protected their children for as long as they could.

Even the best, though, could not take care of them every second of every day.

Especially when they had their mind on other things.

His mind was perfectly concentrated now.

He was concentrating on Rianna Woods. On Dakota.

Watching.

Waiting.

Chapter 51

On Saturday morning, Lydia was on the road.

In a rental car (living in Manhattan, she didn't keep a car of her own, but her licence was still current) en route to William Fitzgerald's house east of Moodus. She'd planned out the route, had taken first the Connecticut Turnpike, then Route 9, west of the river, by-passing Chester (and the probably, possibly, *maybe* innocent Hawthorne), crossing the river over the steel drawbridge near the Goodspeed Opera House, as she had with Jake what seemed like months ago, then taking 156 . . .

Then what?

She was in no doubt as to why she'd come back to this part of Connecticut. Because she was desperate and in despair. Because she couldn't be sure that anyone else *would* come. Because Fitzgerald was litigious and Korda was too important. Because Kline felt – possibly, maybe, *probably* – that sniffing around these people was a waste of time and resources. That was why she'd come here, all alone, because she felt she had to find a way to draw her own mental line beneath the names of all three Eryx men before *she* could move on.

There was the turn-off . . .

Her biggest problem right now was that she didn't have a real plan. What was she going to do when she found Fitzgerald's estate, if she got anywhere near his house without being stopped by some security guard? Look at it from a distance? Knock at the front door? And then what? Say she'd come for a cup of coffee while she waited to see if she experienced another manifestation, like some cheap clairvoyant? Fitzgerald would love that.

Dammit, Lydia.

The closer she got, the more uncertain she became. What if he *was* involved? What possible good could her blundering around do Robbie? What if she found something and in so doing warned Fitzgerald off?

There.

The word 'estate' was much too grandiose, she saw right away, because it was only a few acres of land, some of it grassland apparently just sitting there waiting for someone or something to use it – animals, maybe, or children. But there were no children here, of course, because the man's poor pregnant wife had died in an accident, which was why these days he spent all his time at Eryx or shut in his studio at home . . .

Guilt stabbed her hard. And a new sense of futility.

Yet still she drove on, through the broad open gateway, down the private road, tree-lined on both sides, towards the house at the end, and there were no security guards to stop her.

It looked rather charming, friendly, with Tudor-style beams, like a British house maybe . . .

No sign of Fitzgerald. No sign of anyone.

Smoke. A curl of it, coming from a stone chimney above the red-tiled roof. Which meant, presumably, that the house wasn't shut up, that someone was in there. Or around somewhere.

Maybe watching her.

Lydia stopped the car, turned off the engine, opened the door and got out.

Might as well go a little closer, take a look now she was here.

Though she didn't have a clue what she was looking *for* – other than to see, perhaps, if the house was capable of concealing five teenagers.

That's what the FBI's for.

Except that Kline wasn't going to look – whatever he'd told Jake – in case Fitzgerald sued. Well, let him sue *her*, for trespass or harassment, she didn't care, not if it helped her find Robbie.

The roadway beneath her feet was tarmac, her soft-soled loafers silent as she walked, and she was grateful for that, for the absence of crunching gravel to betray her. Though what if she was being observed already? What if the man himself was watching her, and what if he *was* the one who had the kids? What if he decided she'd made his hiding place unsafe and so he moved them?

For God's sake, Lydia.

Suppressing a sudden urge to bolt, she hastened her pace and walked all the way up to the house, summoned her courage, pushed the door bell and waited.

No one came. She rang again, then knocked in case the bell was broken, then stepped back a few feet, saw the smoke still wafting skywards.

Which didn't necessarily mean anyone was in the house at this moment. Which meant that maybe she could poke around a little outside without being seen or halted. Maybe look for low-level windows or a door that might lead to a cellar . . .

She walked along the left side of the house. The brickwork, she noticed, needed pointing, and though the huge oak trees towards the rear were beautiful, the gardens around the building were less lovely than they might have been.

Other things on his mind?

She continued around. Windows and doors all closed. No sign of a cellar, no sinister-looking outhouses or disused garages or . . .

Nothing.

She walked back around to the front, started towards her car, then stopped and turned back again.

There was something she suddenly felt she had to do.

Call his name.

'Robbie!'

Too soft, too hesitant.

She took a deep breath and gave it all she had.

'*Robbie!*'

Nothing.
She turned around.
Another car was entering the gateway into the private road.
A car with markings.
Connecticut State Police.

Chapter 52

'Dad, it's for you.'

Ella brought me the cordless phone. I took it from her and went on washing up our lunch dishes.

'Jake Woods,' I said.

'Jake, it's Lydia.'

Instant pleasure. I squeezed out my dishwashing sponge and dropped it into the sink. 'How are you?'

Ella was hovering near the refrigerator, her slate-blue eyes fixed on me with keen interest, while the fingers of one hand played with her new short haircut.

'Believe it or not' – Lydia's voice sounded strange – 'I'm at a police station in Moodus. I'm in custody, Jake, and I need your help.'

Scott Korda was in his car when Nick Ford called.

'Thought you should know that the cameras out at Bill's house recorded a visit a couple of hours back from Lydia Johanssen—'

'Alone?'

'Until the state police picked her up.'

'Nice to know the systems work.'

'Of course they work.' Ford had been responsible for their installation. 'The tape shows she had a pretty good snoop around the outside of the house before the cops arrived.'

'That it?' Korda asked.

'Bill's not home, and I guess no harm's been done, but I thought you'd want to know, maybe talk to Kline.'

'No sign of Woods?'

'Not today,' Ford answered. 'Not yet, anyhow.'

'Have you told Hal what's happened?'

'He's my next call. I think he's at the winery for the weekend.'

'Leave him be,' Korda instructed. 'Guy deserves a little peace and quiet. Which I plan to have, too. Leave the cops to handle Lydia Johanssen – they'll probably contact the FBI themselves once she tells them why she was there.'

'Maybe being arrested'll keep the lady out of our hair for a while.'

'I'd like it to keep her out of *Kline*'s hair,' Korda said. 'Then maybe the FBI can concentrate on finding the sonofabitch behind all this.'

'And the kids.'

'Amen,' Korda said.

Lydia had sounded deeply embarrassed, and I'd felt all kinds of things in the first few moments after her call. Mad at her for her recklessness, but also more than a little blown away by her courage. I didn't know exactly what she'd done, but it went without saying she'd acted foolishly – *crazily*. But she was the mother of a kidnapped son, and that, it seemed, flung normal rules out the window.

I'd asked if she needed a lawyer, but she told me that all she needed was someone to come and vouch for her, guarantee she'd stay away from Fitzgerald's property, and give her a ride home since they'd taken away her rental car. I'd organized things swiftly. Rianna was going to High Fliers, so all I had to do was get her there, but Ella had no plans, and the Ryans were out of town visiting Tom's family.

I had thought I'd have to find twenty different ways to keep my younger daughter sunny on the trip to Moodus, but as it turned out, Ella couldn't imagine anything more entertaining than going with her dad to a police station upstate to pick up a

185

woman who'd been *arrested* – though I got the impression she'd have preferred it if Lydia had busted into Fitzgerald's house rather than just walked around on his land. Ella said she couldn't quite see why the cops should arrest a person for walking around, so I had to deliver a swift lecture on private property and a person's right to peace and quiet in his home and back yard.

'Does that mean Mrs Johanssen's a bad person?' Ella asked along the way.

'No, Ella, it does not mean that at all.'

'But you said—'

'You asked why the police made the arrest. I'm explaining the law.'

'So that means she broke the law.'

'Yes, I guess it does.' I tried to concentrate on the road as well as my explanation. 'Mrs Johanssen's just been doing everything she can to try and find her son.'

'Robbie,' Ella said. 'The kidnapped one.'

'That's right.' I hated talking to her about the abductions.

Ella turned to me, reached out and touched my right forearm in a sweet gesture of comfort. 'Daddy, I know all about the case – *all* the kids do.' She paused. 'Do you think Robbie and Mikey are dead?'

I felt sick. 'No, sweetheart, I do not think that.' I took a sideways glance at her, wanting to check she wasn't too upset, but she looked fine. 'And please don't say anything like that in front of Mrs Johanssen.'

'I wouldn't be that dumb,' Ella said with dignity.

Even my baby's growing up.

Chapter 53

Thank you, Mrs Johanssen.

For being enough of a pain-in-the-ass, enough of a devoted, passionate, despairing mother to ignore whatever he was sure the FBI had told her. For having gone off on her own, chasing after what could surely be no more than shadows, on the grounds of the vaguest, maternal, unsubstantiated suspicions.

For getting arrested and, most crucial of all, for calling the professor.

Who had done *exactly* what was needed; who had taken his youngest chick with him in his car in order to drive up and rescue the attractive widow-mom from the clutches of the state police.

Leaving his older chick almost unprotected.

As unprotected as she was ever going to be.

Chapter 54

Rianna was taking a rest after a series of vaults when she noticed Alex Vecchio – the young guy with a limp who answered the phone and took care of maintenance at weekends – come into the gym to talk to Coach Carlin.

They both looked at her.

She saw the coach's face, and a bad feeling hit her.

The coach was coming across.

Rianna's feeling got worse, like a big fist clenching in her stomach.

'There's been a car accident . . .'

She heard Marsha Carlin's gentle words, was taking them in, but at a weird, detached level, someplace over her head, as if they were enclosed in one of those cartoon speech balloons, floating, not quite real, not quite connected to her . . .

'It isn't bad so there's no need to panic, but your father and sister have been taken to a hospital out of town, on the way to wherever they were heading.'

'Upstate,' Rianna said numbly. 'They were heading upstate.'

Coach Carlin picked up her jacket and put it around her shoulders, while Vecchio picked up her bag, and they began walking her towards the door. Rianna could feel other people watching, wondering . . .

'The man who called told me your father had booked a cab to take you there. It's already here, so you can leave right away.'

Rianna stopped. 'My dad's okay?'

'Okay enough to order you the cab.' Carlin smiled.

'What about Ella?' The bad feeling wasn't going away.

'So far as I know, neither of them was badly hurt.'

'But they must be hurt if they're in hospital – if they want me to go there.'

'Your father probably just wants you to go because he knows you'd be more anxious if you couldn't see them,' Carlin reasoned.

That made sense, Rianna supposed, and started walking again.

'I wish I could come with you,' the coach said, 'but I can't leave the club.'

'That's okay,' Rianna said mechanically. 'I'll be fine.'

They reached the door, stepped out into the hallway. Vecchio gave her bag to Carlin, mumbled something about hoping everything would be okay, and Rianna thanked him, was surprised by how normal she sounded.

'You go change,' the coach told her. 'I'll wait for you.'

'No,' Rianna said. 'I don't want to change. I don't want to waste any time.'

'I don't want you catching cold.'

'It's almost August,' Rianna said.

Carlin reached out, gently took hold of her arms. 'Rianna, the man who called really did make a point of saying neither of them is badly hurt.'

So why isn't Daddy on the phone, telling me that himself?

Memories of the night her mother died flashed vividly through her mind.

The coach saw her expression.

'Let's get you in the cab.'

She came outside with Rianna, checked with the driver to make sure he had the destination details right, checked his licence was up-to-date; opened the door, put the bag on the seat, kissed Rianna on the cheek, knew that the girl scarcely felt it as she got into the back beside her bag, staring ahead into space.

And watched the car drive her away.

Chapter 55

Getting Lydia out of the police station wasn't hard, but it took time.

She was still embarrassed and she looked angry, though that, I felt, was mostly directed at herself. Her cheeks were flushed, there was a stain – probably coffee – on her blouse, and her mascara was smudged. I wanted to kiss her or, at the very least, put my arms around her, but she was stiff with awkwardness and Ella was watching, so I settled for lightly placing my right hand at the small of her back as we left the scene of her humiliation.

'Did they put you in a cell?' Ella asked from the back, a few minutes after we'd gotten back in the Cherokee, Lydia sitting up front beside me.

'Ella,' I said warningly.

'I don't mind,' Lydia said, and answered: 'No, they didn't.'

'Did you see any *real* criminals?'

I glanced at my child in the rear view mirror, saw her eyes gleaming with curiosity. I guess I had to be grateful for the emphasis on '*real*'.

'I don't think so,' Lydia answered.

'What did the cops do to you? How did you *feel*?'

'*Ella*,' I said, more forcefully.

'Sorry.' Ella sat back in her seat.

'They didn't do anything to me,' Lydia said, 'and I felt foolish.'

'For doing it' – Ella leaned forward again – 'or for getting caught?'

I guess that's the kind of thing I say to her when she's in trouble at school, so I didn't rebuke her for it now, maybe because I was curious to hear Lydia's answer.

'For getting caught.' Lydia cast a quick, guilty glance my way. 'But that's only because of my particular circumstances, Ella. I'm not saying it's okay to trespass.'

'I know,' Ella said. 'Daddy already gave me that lecture.'

I couldn't help grinning, saw that Lydia was smiling too, and was suddenly hugely glad that I'd had to bring Ella along.

Lydia turned around in her seat. 'Great haircut.'

'Thank you,' Ella said, pleased.

We drove on a while, and I told Lydia that unless she was hungry or needed to stop, I ought to get back to New Haven so I could pick up Rianna, and she said she didn't need anything, and her guilt was back.

'One question?' I couldn't wait any longer.

'Of course.'

'What were you hoping to achieve?'

'She wanted to find Robbie, of course,' Ella said from the back.

I threw her another withering look via the mirror.

'Ella's right,' Lydia said. 'I know it was stupid, but the fact is, I would go anyplace, do anything, if I thought it would help find him. And if I upset people, or tread on Kline's corns, that's too bad.' She paused. 'I really am sorrier than I can say for dragging you both up here, but that's *all* I'm sorry for.'

'My dad would do the same thing,' Ella said, 'if I was missing.'

'*Were*,' I corrected.

'God forbid,' Lydia said.

I glanced back at Ella again, saw her smile of approval.

I was disproportionately happy that she liked Lydia.

Chapter 56

The cab was barely out of the city when the driver pulled off the road into the loading bay of a factory named SPARKELITE. Three parked trucks and a white panel van aside, the bay was empty. Late Saturday afternoon kind of empty.

'What's wrong?' It had taken Rianna a second to register, her mind way ahead, spinning ER nightmares.

'Something's up with the car,' the driver told her. 'I gotta take a look under the hood.'

'But I have to get to the hospital.' Rianna sat forward anxiously.

The driver opened his door. 'If it's what I think it is, it'll just take a few minutes to fix.'

The hood went up. Rianna sat and waited, wishing she had a cell phone like Shannon and half the kids at school, but her father thought there might be something in those health scares. If she had one now, she could call the hospital or maybe try and get hold of Kim and Tom – except they were out of town, and though Rianna knew Tom used a cellular for business, she didn't have his number, and anyway, she didn't have a damned phone either, and what use would calling Kim *be*, other than for comfort?

Comfort sounded good.

'Hey!' the driver called out from under the hood. 'I could use a hand here, if you don't mind.'

Rianna hesitated.

'It's going to go a whole lot faster with two pairs of hands,' he called.

She opened her door, got out, went to join him up front.

He was stooped over, pointing at something with his left hand. 'That's the problem – see it?'

'I don't know . . .'

'There. See?'

Rianna knew less than nothing about car engines, but if this was going to get her to the hospital sooner . . .

She leaned forward to try and look at what the driver was showing her.

And he hit her.

Chapter 57

Entering New Haven, I drove directly to the High Fliers Club to pick up Rianna, both passengers still on board. I'd been wondering if I should invite Lydia to stay for dinner, maybe for the night, or if I should find her a hotel room – no shortage of decent places in this city tonight, I imagined, so no cause for her to feel further embarrassed about *that* . . .

I asked them both to stay in the Cherokee while I went inside.

No sign of Rianna in the hall or by the drinks machine, so I went and peeked into the gym itself. A few youngsters were still working out, but it was mostly an adult crowd at this hour.

No Rianna there either.

Marsha Carlin was at the far end, taking a man in his mid-twenties through his paces on the big floor mat. She saw me, looked unusually pleased for just a moment, and then her face changed and she hurried across, wiping her palms on her hips.

'Hi there,' I said as she approached. 'Is Rianna in the changing room? I didn't see her out in the hall.'

The coach looked me up and down. 'You're okay,' she said.

'I'm fine,' I said.

'And Ella?'

'She's outside in the car, with a friend.'

'She's okay too?'

I looked at her face, saw she'd turned pale. 'What's wrong?'

For a moment she seemed almost frozen, as if she thought

that by just standing there, saying nothing, time might stand still and save her.

And then she told me.

We all went into automatic. I believe I was beyond panic, too afraid to do anything so *pointless* as panic. Carlin went to call the police, while I went outside to fetch Ella and Lydia.

'There's some confusion,' I told them both as calmly as I was able.

'Where's Rianna?' Ella asked.

'I'm not exactly certain, baby,' I answered. 'That's why we have to go inside and wait for a while, till we find out.'

I felt Lydia's eyes on me, knew she'd recognized my fear and that it was horribly familiar to her, knew she was saying nothing for Ella's sake.

I took my daughter's hand, and though ordinarily she hated that these days, she didn't pull away, gripped my fingers tightly till we'd passed through the front door and were in the hallway.

'What's happened to Rianna?' The question was stark, demanding a truthful answer.

Her hand felt cold in mine. I stooped just a little way. Ella's some way off her sister's height, but she's getting there fast. Her eyes were fixed on mine again, still demanding but afraid.

'We don't know what's happened,' I told her gently, every word breaking me apart. 'It's possible – only *possible*, mind – that someone's taken her.'

'Oh my God,' Lydia said, very quietly.

'You mean someone bad?' Ella's eyes were still unswerving.

'I hope not.'

For a moment or two, Ella seemed to struggle against tears, but then she won her battle. 'I'm okay,' she said. 'Go find Rianna.'

'We're just . . .' I choked up suddenly, swallowed hard and got on with it – after all, if my nine-year-old could do this, so could I. 'We're making a few calls, doing some checking.'

'I'll stay with Ella,' Lydia said, chalky white.

I nodded. 'Thank you.'

'Go *on*, Daddy,' Ella said.

I turned and ran towards Carlin's office.

To his credit, Agent Kline returned my call even before the New Haven police had arrived at High Fliers.

'Did Rianna receive a gift?'

'Of course not, or I would have called you.' Hope soared for just a second as I absorbed that – then crashed again. Even if this did turn out to be a coincidence – some *other* monster – there was nothing to say the outcome might not be just as bad.

Or even worse.

The cops arrived, then two federal agents. All the gymnasts still on the premises were spoken to, then sent home and the doors locked. Alex Vecchio was tracked down to a pizzeria in North Haven and brought back to give his version of events before being released. Vecchio had not seen the cab driver, but Marsha Carlin *had*.

She was beside herself. 'I should *never* have let her go with him. How could I have been so *stupid*?' She had been crying, her eyes red now, the lids puffing up.

'That's not going to help,' Sergeant Jim Connolly, a big, burly police detective told her firmly. 'What we need from you is a description.'

I was in Carlin's office with them, pacing while this was going on, and in a room as small as that, my pacing had to be driving them both nuts, but neither said anything to me, just let me pace. Mind, I think I could have yelled or let off fire crackers at that point and Marsha Carlin wouldn't have dared say a word. She'd hardly *looked* at me since first telling me that she'd let Rianna go off in a cab with a stranger. A small part of me had registered pity for her, even at that instant, but it was too small a part to allow me to say anything to comfort her.

'I told you, I hardly looked at him.'

'But you went outside and talked to him,' Connolly said.

'To check he had all the details—'

'You *said* that already,' I said loudly, still pacing.

196

Carlin went scarlet.

'Go on, Coach,' the policeman said, ignoring me.

'And to make sure his licence – his badge – was up-to-date.'

I'd heard her say that, too, at least three times, but I managed to hold onto myself and keep quiet.

'So I wasn't really looking *at* him.'

'But you did see him,' Connolly said patiently.

'Yes, but . . .' She looked about to bounce off the walls. 'I keep thinking I must have seen something useful, something different about him, but I *didn't*. He was just a *man*, wearing a baseball cap, like I said – a Ravens cap, I'm certain of that, with the new logo.'

'You're sure you didn't see his eyes?' Connolly asked.

Carlin shook her head. 'He was wearing sunglasses, I told you.'

'What kind?' I stopped pacing for a second, knew I ought to leave this to the cop, knew I was only being tolerated because I'd once been a cop too, so I was meant to know how to behave, but I just couldn't stay silent. 'What *kind* of sunglasses, Marsha? Designer? Wraparound? What colour lenses?'

'Dark,' she said helplessly. 'Just ordinary sunglasses, not wraparound, not designer, so far as I could see.' She had no option now but to look up at me, and I'd seldom seen anyone as wretched. 'Jake, I wasn't *looking* at his glasses – I wasn't looking at *him*, not that way, not the way I would have if I'd thought I was going to need to describe him.'

'What about his shirt?' I couldn't help myself. 'His watch? Was he wearing a watch? What were his hands like? Were they tan? Pale? Freckled? Was he wearing a ring? Was he wearing gloves? What kind of a voice did he have? You spoke to him, for Christ's sake, you must have heard his *voice*.'

'Professor,' Connolly said quietly, 'I think things might go better if you wait outside, go check on Rianna's sister.'

'How might they go better?'

'Maybe the coach might remember some details if we ease off a little.'

'Why don't we just let her *sleep* on it overnight?' I knew I was being a bastard, but I couldn't help that either. 'Every

197

minute that goes by, Connolly, my daughter could be further away.'

'Oh *God*.' Carlin buried her face in her hands.

'Professor.' Connolly's look told me to let him do his job.

'Okay.' My heart was going a mile a minute. 'I'm sorry.'

'There's an artist on the way,' Connolly said. 'She's terrific, knows just how to ease those little touches out of a person.'

'Good,' I said, opened the door and left the room.

An artistic rendering of a new-logo New Havens Ravens cap and a pair of nondescript sunglasses. Big help.

Lydia and Ella were sitting on a bench near the drinks machine, Lydia gripping a cup of coffee, barely touched and now cold, Ella with a can of Coke on the floor between her sneakered feet.

Lydia rose when she saw me. 'Anything?' she asked softly.

'Nothing.' I sat down on Ella's other side. 'How're you holding up?'

'Do they know who took Rianna?'

'We don't know for sure that anyone's taken her, honey. It might all be a mistake.'

'You think so?' Her eyes sought mine eagerly, then fell away, hope dashed.

'Would you like me to take Ella home?' Lydia offered. 'Stay with her there?'

I teetered between wanting my little girl away from here, and wanting her where I could see her, know she was safe.

'I want to stay here, Daddy.' Ella clinched it.

'Okay, baby.' I looked back at Lydia. 'You should go – you don't need this.'

'Of course I'm not going,' Lydia told me.

'I could call you a cab to take you to the station.'

'Jake, I don't want to go,' she said. 'Unless you want me to.'

'Up to you,' I said.

Information came in less than thirty minutes later of a cab that had been stolen a few hours earlier from a burger joint car park. The driver had been inside the restaurant, the place busy, the car park crowded; no witnesses, just the ever-growing likelihood that Rianna was in grave trouble.

Connolly advised me to take Ella home, wait there. I told him I wasn't going anyplace unless he swore to me on his three children's lives that I would be kept fully informed every inch of the way, not just left in a vacuum. He gave me his word and I chose to believe him.

We were getting into the Cherokee when I noticed Marsha Carlin was having trouble getting the motor of her Renault started. My first impulse was to let her stew, but then I asked Lydia and Ella to wait and went to see if I could help.

'I don't know what's wrong,' she said miserably.

'Is this a regular problem?'

'It's never happened before.'

'Want me to take a look?'

'It's okay, Jake, I'll manage.'

'Open the hood, Marsha.' I was starting to feel I'd been too hard on her. After all, I knew how much she cared about Rianna and all her young gymnasts.

Carlin reached for the lever and popped the hood.

I'm no mechanic, but it didn't take a genius to know that any number of motor parts – belts, pipes, wires, screws – were not where they were meant to be. Which meant, presumably, that whoever had Rianna had calculated that Carlin might have chosen to drive her to the hospital rather than letting her go in the cab.

We headed back inside and within minutes I'd been patched through to Roger Kline again. 'No coincidence,' I told him.

'Certainly seems less likely.' Kline paused. 'Is there anyone at home who could say if a package has arrived since you went out today?'

'No one.' My stomach felt like a submarine on dive.

'I think you should go home, Professor, don't you?'

'On my way,' I said.

No package. No note. No messages.

Connolly called less than an hour after we got back.

'They found the cab just north of Hamden, in a factory loading bay. Place was closed for the weekend – no one's been there since Friday afternoon.' He paused. 'It's being taken apart for evidence.'

'How long?'

'They're on it now,' Connolly said. 'It went right to the top of the queue. I don't know how long, but if there's anything there, they'll find it.'

'If you don't mind, Jake,' Lydia said some time later, 'I'd like to stay.'

'If you want,' I said, not really looking at her. I guess we were both aware that I hadn't looked her straight in the eye since that first moment outside the club.

An awful quiet hung over the apartment like invisible fog, dragging us down. Ella was being much too compliant, not her usual self at all. I couldn't count the times in the past when I'd wished for just a touch more submissiveness, but now I found myself almost wishing for a tantrum – anything to help me pretend things were normal.

Normal. *Christ.*

Lydia offered to make sandwiches and I let her, knowing she needed to do something. I didn't eat anything, nor did she. Ella took a bite or two, then stopped, looking very white, poor kid.

'Maybe you should go to bed, baby,' I suggested.

'Okay,' she said quietly.

'I'll come tuck you in.'

'I'm okay,' she said.

She came back less than ten minutes later wearing a night-dress with a teddy bear motif. She looked suddenly younger than her nine years, and impossibly fragile. Lydia and I were still sitting in the kitchen, not talking. Seeing Ella, I turned around in my chair and put out my arms. She came into them and I held her, not too tight, just close enough to feel her warmth, smell her hair.

Rianna, where are you?

*

We sat up all night, transferred to the living room, Ella and I huddling on the couch until she was sleepy enough for me to be able to get up and move around without disturbing her. I could tell that Lydia was feeling isolated, only a couple of feet away in an armchair, but alone, just the same, in a fast-growing sea of self-recrimination. I hadn't touched on that subject, and neither had she, but it hung in the air, in that fog, between us.

If I hadn't had to leave town for Lydia, this might not have happened.

Not exactly true, of course. Rianna would still have been at High Fliers that afternoon, so the abductor would simply have had to invent another way to get her to go with him – that was, if the driver had actually been the abductor and not just some hired man. Or maybe there was more than one kidnapper – maybe we weren't looking at one evil sonofabitch but a whole gang . . .

Meantime, Lydia was blaming herself, and if I'm perfectly honest about it, I think maybe I was doing the same.

The phone rang at 7.02 a.m.

Connolly again.

'They found a hair. Nothing else. Just one hair.'

Nausea hit me so hard I almost had to drop the phone.

'Rianna's hair is long and dark, isn't it, Professor?'

'Yes.' *Beautiful hair, like heavy silk.*

'Someone's going to be calling for a sample, maybe from her hairbrush, okay?'

'Okay,' I said, and swallowed hard. 'Nothing else at all?'

'The car was cleaned,' Connolly told me. 'The guy knew what he was doing.'

'So the hair could have been left deliberately?'

'Could have,' the detective said.

The street buzzer sounded as I was shaking cornflakes into a bowl for Ella. Lydia had offered to make breakfast, but I'd turned her down, and God knew she understood my need to be busy better than anyone else.

I buzzed the police officer into the building, went back into the kitchen to pick up Rianna's hairbrush from the counter – all ready for him in a sealed plastic sandwich bag – and went to open the front door. The guy was in plain clothes, his ID in his right hand identifying him as Detective Mark Olivier; a briefcase in his left hand.

He was looking down.

At a brown padded envelope lying on our doormat.

We looked at each other. Olivier was young, black, with glasses, wearing a light raincoat which appeared to be damp. I hadn't realized it was raining, wasn't sure I'd have noticed if a hurricane had blown in.

'It's addressed to you, sir,' he told me.

It was clear from the way he spoke and looked down at the package that he knew all about the background to Rianna's disappearance.

We both crouched down. There was no stamp or franking mark, and the white label was typed:

PROFESSOR JACOB WOODS

To me, not Rianna.

'Want me to pick it up, sir?' Detective Olivier asked.

I nodded.

He held it cautiously by one corner, almost like a suspect bomb, then straightened up and brought it into the kitchen, nodding at Lydia and Ella, both silent, then laid it on the table, well away from the coffee pot and milk jug.

'Does it look like Robbie's?' I asked Lydia quietly.

She was ashen-faced. 'I won't know till you open it. Don't forget I threw away the envelope before I knew what was in it. I never got a real look at it.'

'What is it, Daddy?' Ella looked like she might cry.

'Maybe nothing,' I said.

'Why don't we go into the living room?' Lydia asked her gently.

Ella went like a lamb. Maybe she was too tired to protest, or maybe she just didn't want to know what was in the envelope.

Olivier opened his case and took out fine rubber gloves.

I remembered the hairbrush in my own right hand. 'Shall I put this in your case, before we forget?'

'Thank you, sir,' he said.

I laid the brush gently down in the case beside a small leather zipped bag.

Olivier picked up the envelope, checked it over for the best way to open it, saw it was simply folded at the top edge and sealed with sticky tape, found it easy to peel away.

'Don't—' I started to say, then saw he was already placing the tape in a tiny evidence bag and putting it in his case. 'Okay,' I said. 'Thank you.'

'You're welcome, sir,' Olivier said.

It *was* the same, inasmuch as it contained the game, the same deluxe edition of *Limbo* that Robbie, Michael and the others had been sent.

The note was quite different.

Your very special girl has been given a VERY special opportunity.

Keep your nose out, and MAYBE you'll see her again. And try not to worry too much. She's in good hands. Well-loved, in fact. Because she really is THE one. At last.

I thank you for your great gift, Professor, and offer you this in return.

To help you try to understand at least a little more.

203

Chapter 58

Rianna awoke in a strange place with a bad, bad headache, the worst she'd ever had in her life, clamping like a vice around her head.

Something was on her face, covering her eyes, something heavy, smelling of leather, making her feel sick.

She put up her hands to pull it away, but they were covered too. With something thick, like the ski gloves she'd worn that time they'd all gone to Vermont years ago when her mom was still alive – except these were heavier than those gloves, thicker, clumsier.

'Daddy?' she said softly, in a whisper.

The thing covering her eyes was making the light in the room seem blue, a strange, unnatural kind of blue. The bed – floor? – she was lying on was hard and cold. *Oh my God, oh my God, where am I?*

She remembered the cab driver.

She remembered the message at the club, about her father and Ella and the car accident they'd been in.

She remembered Mrs Johanssen's son.

And instantly, icily, unbearably, Rianna knew, without a fragment of doubt, that whatever had happened to Robbie and Mikey had now happened to her.

She opened her mouth and began to scream.

Chapter 59

Half the LIMBO task force seemed to be moving in to our apartment, and I'd never imagined I could be so glad to have a bunch of grim-faced, resolute strangers in my home.

'Who are they all, Daddy?' Ella had looked a little scared.

'They're working to bring Rianna back to us, honey.'

'But what are they all *doing*? Why aren't they out looking for her?'

'There are other people out there doing that,' I told her, believing it was true. 'These people are here to get all the facts they can about Rianna, anything at all they think might help find her, so we need to help them. Okay?'

'Shall I ask them if they want something to drink?'

'That's a great idea, honey.'

The envelope, note and the game had already been taken away, either to be flown back to FBI headquarters in DC, or else to the closest facility capable of full and swift analysis. I knew, though, that someone who could clean a car so perfectly, leaving just one hair almost certainly to tantalize, taunt or confuse, was more than capable of leaving no useful clues with his package, or even of planting a false trail.

Of Kline himself, there was no sign, but I'd been talking with another agent by the name of Phil Rubik, a middle-aged man with crew-cut hair, a stout neck and a clear determination to get on with the job in hand *despite* me.

I was just the father now.

I'd thought I'd understood Lydia's feelings of frustration

before, but now I knew I'd never come close. I knew I ought to go sit with her for a while, tell her that, but I didn't. Christ knew how much I had longed to be with her since that night in New York, and now she was here with me at this most terrible of times, and I was doing pretty much what she had done: keeping her at arm's length.

'One thing's clear now,' I said to Rubik later.

'What is that, Professor?'

I used to like people calling me that. I don't think it was because I wanted or needed the kudos; there was just a nice sound to it, and I guess maybe I thought I'd earned it. But over the past few weeks, in conversations with Kline especially, I'd found myself starting to feel patronized by the use of the title. Kline – and Rubik, too – made '*Professor*' sound like an ego trip by a flunked-out investigator who'd made do with teaching.

Not that I gave a goddamn *what* they thought, so long as they found Rianna.

And brought her home safe and well.

'What thing's clear now, Professor?' Rubik asked again.

'That taking Rianna must mean the abductions are connected to Eryx in some way.' I watched his face, which stayed carefully blank. 'He wrote "*Keep your nose out*" in his note. He wouldn't say that if he weren't pissed at me for sticking my nose *in*, would he?'

'I don't think that's conclusive,' Rubik answered in a measured tone, like a nurse talking to a potentially hysterical patient. 'No one's saying your daughter's abduction's a *coincidence*, Professor—'

'Will you do me a favour, please?' I interrupted.

'If I can.'

'My name's Jake. I don't need you to use my title.'

'If you'd be more comfortable with that,' Rubik said, the nurse again.

'I'm glad no one's saying it's a coincidence.' I brought him back on track again, my tone not quite as hostile as I felt at that instant. 'It would be perfectly clear to a child of *five* that this could not be a coincidence, Agent Rubik. I'm referring to the perp's note to me.'

'The note would certainly seem to indicate that whoever abducted your daughter has clearly noted your friendship with both the Cooper family and with Mrs Johanssen.'

The man talked like he had his head up his *ass*.

'The Coopers and Mrs Johanssen' – I fought to hold my temper – 'are friends with a lot of people, but *their* children have not been kidnapped, thank God for them, because *they* haven't been asking too many questions about Eryx.'

Rubik did not like me. The narrowing of his already narrow eyes and the reddening of his fat neck told me that much. I guess from his point of view I'd given him no reason *to* like me.

Ask me if I gave a fuck if he liked me or not.

'The game connection still holds good, obviously,' Rubik said.

'Obviously,' I repeated.

'Which is why we're still following up on that, Jake.'

Now I hated him calling me *that*, too.

Rubik put out his pudgy right hand and touched my forearm in what was meant, I guess, to be a gesture of consolation. 'Trust me on this, Jake,' he said. 'And trust us to know what we're doing.'

I don't know how, but I managed not to punch him.

I did trust them, up to a point. They were certainly working a smooth, rapid-fire investigation, so far as I was being permitted to see. Interviews were happening all the time, so I was told – quietly and probably off the record – by Sergeant Connolly, himself now being steadily edged out of the picture as the Bureau took over.

The other residents in our building had all been quizzed about the delivery of the package, about how someone had got in and left it on our doorstep. No one knew, no one had seen anything or anyone, and our other neighbours all around Wooster Square said the same.

People living and working in the vicinity of High Fliers had all been spoken to. Nothing, no one.

The West Haven man whose cab had been stolen was still being interviewed, though no one was implying any involvement on his part and, *big* surprise, he'd seen nothing and no one either. The men and women who worked in the burger joint had nothing useful, though it was proving hard, Connolly said, to find all the customers who'd been eating there at the time the cab had been stolen. The dry cleaners to the left had been closed; the shop to the right had been empty for two months. If anyone living over those units had seen anything, they weren't talking.

'They're wasting *time*.' After listening to twenty minutes of negatives from the well-meaning Connolly, I was losing it.

'No one's wasting time, Professor,' he said gently.

'Why are they still talking to the damned cab driver? Do they think someone paid him to have his car stolen?'

Connolly shook his head. 'They think he's kosher. He's pissed as hell at being kept off the road, wants to know if the FBI's going to pay his rent.'

'So why don't they move *along*?'

We were in the small hallway, the investigators having taken over the living room and kitchen – and I wasn't letting anyone into the bedrooms unless they had a damn good reason.

'Maybe they think he saw something without realizing,' Lydia's voice said.

I turned around, hadn't realized that she had come out into the hall.

'That was why the New York police tried to find people who'd been in the restaurant the night Robbie disappeared. They said that a possible witness was better than no witness, and that one thing might lead to another.'

'We know all about that, don't we?' I knew I sounded aggressive, didn't like myself for it, but couldn't seem to stop. 'What led to *this* was me having to be out of town getting you out of trouble instead of being here taking care of my daughter.'

Lydia was ashen again. 'You're probably right.'

I didn't say anything. Out of the corner of my left eye, I saw Connolly walk away towards the kitchen, leaving us to it.

'And I know that telling you how bad I feel about that isn't going to help you or Rianna one bit,' Lydia said, 'so do you mind if I use the phone to call a cab to take me to the station so I can get out of your hair?'

'I didn't mean that,' I said.

'Of course you meant it, Jake. Why shouldn't you?' She spoke quietly but decisively, as if she'd thought about nothing else for the past several hours. 'Though if we're really honest about this, my blame goes back a lot further than yesterday. We both know that it's your helping me with Robbie that's led to this.'

'I contacted you,' I reminded her, and I guessed it mightn't hurt to remind myself of that the next time I was lashing out at the wrong person. 'I *chose* to get involved.'

'Because you're a kind man.' Lydia was still very pale.

I shook my head, suddenly unable to speak, everything welling up inside.

'I should get home anyway.' She touched my right hand, tentatively, as if afraid I might snatch it away. 'I heard one of the men say they're going to be leaving soon, and I think you need some quiet time alone with Ella.' She paused, searching my face. 'Any time you want to talk, Jake, *any* time at all, day or night, I'll be on the other end of the phone.'

'Thank you.' I almost asked her to stay – I *think* I wanted that – but I wasn't sure, wasn't sure about anything, just felt like lying down on the ground and letting it all roll over me like a big pounding wave.

'I'll come back any time, too, if you want me,' Lydia said.

I nodded. I wasn't capable of more than that, not just then.

Rubik came out of the living room. 'We're going to be pulling out any time now, Jake, so if I can answer any more questions before that . . .?'

Lydia let go of my hand. The loss of her touch left me feeling even colder, even more lost than I had before.

209

'I'll go make that call,' she said, and went into the kitchen.

'Nice woman,' Rubik said. 'Shame about her son.'

I had another, unreasonable urge to hit the man, but instead I turned to him, even managed a semblance of a smile, I think.

And let those waves keep on rolling over me.

Chapter 60

'Stop screaming.'

A male voice, loud and penetrating.

'Stop screaming, Dakota.'

Rianna's gloved hands moved to her ears, couldn't reach them because of the thing covering them.

But she stopped screaming.

'That's better,' the voice told her. 'You're okay. You're going to be just fine. There's no need to panic, no need for such a fuss.'

Fuss. Oh God, what was *happening*?

'Would you like to see where you are?'

Not sure, not *sure*.

'Yes.'

'Good girl.'

She thought, for a second, that the voice sounded familiar, but it was too strange, too distorted. The cab driver? No. *Maybe*? Impossible to tell.

Dakota? Was that what he'd called her?

The blue light went out, left her in pitch darkness.

Panic engulfed her. She was beyond screaming now, reduced to a kind of terrified whimpering. *Oh God, oh God, oh please . . .*

There was something . . . The darkness wasn't absolute, after all, or maybe her eyes were just growing accustomed to it. Shapes . . .

'Take a closer look,' the voice told her.

Rianna could hear something else now besides his voice.

Dripping?

Something else, too.

Another voice.

'Goddamnit,' it said softly.

She saw him.

He was sitting on a bench, in a small room with a low ceiling, one dim caged-in lightbulb high on a wall, and some kind of weird contraption on the floor.

He was young. Her age, maybe. Cute, if he weren't so scared looking, so drained and tired.

Rianna knew who he was.

'Recognize him?' the first voice asked her.

'Robbie,' she said.

'Wrong,' the voice said.

'He's Robbie Johanssen.' Rianna knew because of the photographs. And she'd known almost as soon as she'd woken up that she was probably in the same place as Lydia's son, so this maybe-cab-driver-kidnapper wasn't going to tell her she was wrong.

'Robbie!' she called to him.

'He can't hear you right now. And you are wrong about his name.'

She *wasn't* wrong.

'Don't you know who he is?' he asked her. 'Don't you know, Dakota?'

Dakota again.

Finally, it penetrated.

And the worst, the sickest, the most terrible fear Rianna had ever experienced came right along with it.

The voice said it for her.

'That's Steel,' he said. 'Your Steel.'

Robbie was tired of sitting in the dark, so he put the headset back on, and then the gloves. He didn't know why *he* insisted he put on the damned gloves before he'd agree to turn on the whole shebang, because unless he was actually doing an exercise the gloves weren't necessary, but it was just one of the stupid rules down here, and sometimes it beat just sitting in the dark. He hoped that starting things up now wasn't going to spark off an exercise because he didn't feel up to that – he just felt like hanging out someplace not quite so black, even if it was a frigging *Limbo* set.

That was how he'd begun thinking of it, like a movie set. It helped a little to do that, reminded him of when he'd first woken up down here and had thought he was dreaming, and it hadn't been so bad while he'd still believed that . . .

He saw her instantly, saw her long dark hair, felt pleased. *Dakota's back.*

'Take a closer look,' *he* said.

He did. She looked better, different, though it was hard to tell with those awful things covering her eyes. Headset apart, she looked pretty wonderful.

Gorgeous even.

Terrified.

Not her.

'It isn't her,' Robbie said.

'Better than her,' he said.

Oh Jesus. Another girl, which meant . . . He didn't want to think about what that meant.

'It's okay, Steel.' He sounded jubilant. 'No need to look so anxious. This is the real one. The real, the one and only – *Dakota.*'

Robbie could see that the new girl was younger than the last, even more vulnerable-looking, and he hated *him* more than he'd ever hated anyone in his life.

'Fuck you,' he said, his hatred stronger for a moment than his fear. '*Fuck* you, you bastard.'

'Now, now,' the voice rebuked him, though there was some amusement in it. 'That's no way to welcome the young lady, is it? I got her for *you*, Steel. Just for you.' He paused. 'Say hi to your Dakota.'

Robbie said nothing.

'Say hi to your mate, Steel.'

213

Chapter 61

At Eryx Software, the partners were having an after hours emergency meeting in Korda's office with lawyer Alan Tillman and Nick Ford.

'We should be doing something,' Korda said, the black retriever at his feet.

'Such as?' Hawthorne asked.

'I don't know,' Korda said. 'It just worries the hell out of me that it's *this* kid who's been taken.' He looked grim. 'I'm ashamed to be so self-interested, and I'm sorrier than I can say for Woods, but the fact is, if the new victim were a total stranger the FBI would probably have shifted its focus away from Eryx, but as it is . . .'

'Sales are down already,' Fitzgerald said. 'Any more searchlights on us and we'll have a full-scale disaster on our hands.'

'I just don't see how we can avoid it,' Korda said.

'Maybe,' Hawthorne suggested, 'you two should do what I did – invite them into your homes, encourage them to go over this place, too, and the Zeus buildings.'

'Not such a bad idea,' Ford said. 'Sooner they look, sooner they go away.'

'Not necessarily,' Tillman said. 'There could be legal complications.'

'Such as what?' Hawthorne said. 'We just play ball instead of this waiting game. It's not fun, but I don't foresee complications, not if we volunteer.' He paused. 'Could even be good PR.'

'Over my dead body,' Fitzgerald said. 'No one's setting foot over my threshold, not at home anyhow.'

'But think of the relief when it's over, Bill,' Hawthorne said.

'We're not talking about root canal,' Fitzgerald snapped.

'You value your privacy,' Korda soothed. 'We all do.' He paused. 'Maybe you could give this some thought, Alan,' he suggested to the attorney. 'See if this is something that might come back and bite us afterward . . .'

'I'll do that,' Tillman said.

'I meant that about turning it into a PR bonus,' Hawthorne said. 'We could hold a press conference, invite the parents of the missing children and the FBI, show the world we have nothing to hide.'

'I don't know,' Tillman said.

'It's a possibility,' Korda said doubtfully.

'*I* know,' Fitzgerald said flatly. 'Turn this awful thing into a media shindig and you can count me out.'

'Got something to hide, Bill?' Ford asked jokily.

'Not funny,' Hawthorne said.

'Don't be an ass, Nick,' Korda said.

Donald got up, stretched, then padded over to the far end of the room.

'I don't give a fuck what Nick or anyone else thinks,' Fitzgerald said. 'It was bad enough having the Johanssen woman snooping around my house. No one else is coming in without a *bona fide* warrant.'

Tillman looked at Korda, who looked at Hawthorne, who shrugged.

Donald yawned.

Chapter 62

Night two without Rianna.

I'd persuaded Ella to bed, finally.

No rest for me.

I'd talked to a few people on the second phone line that the FBI had installed for me for normal use, in case, *just* in case, the abductor called. I knew that was not anticipated, but they wanted to cover all possibilities, and I was grateful to them for that.

Not that I'd told them as much. I was the original bear with a sore head.

Father-bear in agony was more like it.

I called the Coopers, thought it best they learned the news from me, heard the awful fresh pain in their voices, for me and Rianna and Ella, but most of all for Mikey, slipping steadily further away from them. I heard guilt, too, in Fran's half-whispered tones, for involving me in the first place; told her, as convincingly as I could manage, that it was more likely my involvement with the Johanssens that had led to this, but that it was really no one's fault but the abductor's. I knew she didn't believe me, and in a way, of course, she was right not to.

Kim and Tom, back in New Haven from their trip, had been with us all afternoon and evening, almost too shocked to speak, doing things for me and Ella in a daze. They had both wanted, really wanted, to stay with us tonight. And Norman Baum, hearing the news from one of his FBI pals, had called and offered to come over, sit vigil with me. But I'd said no to them all.

I didn't want anyone. Just my daughters. *Both* my daughters.

The pain was literally unbearable. I could not believe I was going to survive it. It was there, in my head, my heart, my guts, burning me, knifing me, spreading like some raging cancer until I was fit to scream, then levelling out for a little while, then starting over again . . .

For the very first time, I was glad Simone was not here.

Some time during the endless night, a part of my mind crept out of our apartment, out of Wooster Square, out of New Haven and Connecticut, into New York, into Manhattan, over to the beige stone building on West Seventy-third Street, up to the fifteenth-storey apartment, and into the dark bedroom where Lydia and I . . .

I snatched it back. To where it belonged.

Here, alone, with thoughts that needed to be – that *had* to be – directed to Rianna, my lost child. Wherever she was, whatever she was going through – and that I could not think about or I knew I really would lose my mind, and I couldn't do that, not to her or to Ella – but wherever she was right now, she needed every particle of strength I could will her.

Rianna's strong, I told myself, knowing that, at least, to be true.

Please let her stay that way, I prayed. Prayed all kinds of things, made all the usual kinds of bargains that God, if He's listening, must hear millions of times every day in every language known to man.

Lydia had been going through this for much longer. And Fran and Stu. And the other parents I hadn't met, but felt suddenly connected to.

My mind slipped back to New York City again, slithered, for a few warming, guilt-wracked moments, back between the sheets to curl in Lydia's arms.

And again I dragged it back.

Oh God, Rianna, my baby, where are *you*?

*

Lydia lay in her bed, eyes open in the dark, gazing at nothing, thinking about heartbreak. She pictured her heart, fractured five years before after Aaron's death, healing slowly, painfully, but *healing*, thanks to Robbie, leaving only the scar, tucked inside where no one else could see it. Except that the scar had been ripped open again, bloodily, gaping, other kind people trying vainly to dab at it, stem the flow, failing.

Jake had managed it, for a while.

Just a patch job, of course.

And now, thanks to her – *and the monster, Lydia, don't forget the monster* – but decidedly thanks to her and her damned foolhardiness, her sheer *idiocy*, Jake's own private scar, the one left by the loss of his wife, had been opened up again too.

At least he has another child.

The thought was so unworthy, so *shameful*, that Lydia sat up in bed, gasping for air, feeling she deserved to be slapped.

She lay back again. She was so tired, so drained, yet she could not sleep.

She thought about Rianna, about the photographs in Jake's home of that lovely young woman. She wondered if Rianna was maybe with Robbie right this minute, if perhaps through this horrible development Jake's daughter might be bringing her son a little comfort, maybe even some *hope*, letting him know that his mother and her father and the FBI were going to find them, bring them home, no matter what. That it was just a matter of time.

What about the others?

Lydia couldn't think about the others. It wasn't that she couldn't picture them – she'd seen their photographs on the FBI website. But she couldn't seem to visualize them all *together*. In a way, she thought that might have been quite a comforting image, all those kids helping each other, looking out for one another. But somehow she just couldn't see that, and that scared her even more, because if the others were not with Robbie and Rianna, that might mean . . .

Don't go there.

Her mind returned to the image of Jake's heart breaking open.

She wanted so badly to pick up the phone and call him, but she knew he didn't want to talk to her.

Maybe, when the children were home . . .

That thought, the *neediness* of it, was so great, so overwhelming, that Lydia's hands, her fingers like claws, clutched at the sheet beneath her, and one of her fingernails pierced the cotton, made a small hole. She got out of the bed then, breathing hard, heart pounding crazily, perspiring, and she found the little hole, dug her middle right finger into it and made it bigger. And that felt good, felt like what she really wanted to do, what she *had* to do, so now she punched her entire hand into the hole and ripped at it, and she had the tear really going now, and she was crying out loud, yelling, wordlessly, just wailing rage and grief and frustration and shame, and she tore the sheet right off the bed and ripped it into as many shreds as her strength would allow . . .

Doing it to *him*.

Chapter 63

His nights had been getting worse prior to finding the new Dakota. Truths bearing down on him like burning coals being shovelled from some invisible furnace, hot coals searing him, sizzling as they hit the blood in his mind.

Time running out for his dream, for *him*, and he'd known he had to get it right before it was too late, before they stopped him. The FBI, the parents, all those people hunting him.

But he had her now, didn't he? Had them *both*.

So he was keeping the lights on tonight.

Because tonight was too special to destroy with waking nightmares and sneak previews of the abyss.

He knew exactly what he had done. Knew that by taking this particular Dakota, by acting in haste and, in part, out of resentment against the professor, he'd taken substantially greater risks than ever before.

So what?

A swifter end to everything. A faster track to hell.

So what?

So long as he had enough time, that was all he asked, just enough time.

Surely he deserved that much?

And risks aside, he had gone to great lengths to divert his hunters.

At least for a little while.

Chapter 64

Eric Stephen Barnes had had a bad shock.

It had come in the mail.

A big package. Barnes didn't get packages, not any more. Not for years. Once upon a time, packages had brought him a mix of pleasure and pain. Mostly, though, they'd brought him trouble. Big, unspeakable trouble.

He had run after the mailman soon as he'd opened it and seen the contents, had found him just leaving the building, had told him it was a mistake, had asked him to take it away. But the mailman had said it had his name and address so if there was a mistake, it wasn't *his*, and he couldn't take it away, it was his duty to deliver it, and anything else was Barnes's problem.

Oh Jesus.

He had read about the game in the newspaper just a few days ago. He allowed himself to read the newspapers sometimes, the decent papers, the *safe* ones. So he knew about the kids and the game.

He knew something else, too.

They'd be coming. Sure as his name was Eric Stephen Barnes.

Nothing he could do about it except wait. Sitting all alone in his one-room apartment in the 'city of brotherly love'; in his almost barren home, shelves without books, no TV, no magazines; only one photograph, of his mother, pictured with himself aged three. Better days, almost happy then. Almost normal.

He had been so careful. So scared, but so careful. Scared in case the thoughts got the better of him again. Scared in case the cops came again. He'd done everything, *everything*, to stop the thoughts; had got rid of the TV, had stopped reading almost anything in case he read a line or saw a picture that might spark them off . . .

He kept himself clean, too, went through more bars of Dove in a month than most people probably got through in a year – the checkout girl at the drugstore had told him that, laughing at him, so he'd had to stop going there. Anyway, too many of their products carried pictures of babies and children, and too many moms came in with their kids. The A&P was no better, but at least it was bigger and more anonymous, so he could scoot in, move around the aisles fast and scuttle back out again without anyone noticing him or getting familiar.

He still *felt* the dirt, though, because it was inside him. They'd told him a long time ago that he was filthy, and he'd known – still knew – that they were right. He'd tried swallowing soap once, but all that had done was make him puke, and he'd known he was no cleaner afterwards. He'd even bought bleach, but he was no fool, knew what that stuff would do to him, how agonizing it would be, and however much he knew he probably deserved it, he couldn't face that.

So they were going to come, and they wouldn't believe anything he told them. He could swear on his mother's life and on every Holy Bible from every church in the whole of Philadelphia, and they *still* wouldn't believe him.

He had the package ready and waiting for them, sitting on the floor in the corner of his room. The envelope was almost intact. He always opened mail carefully, didn't like mess, knew that a scrap of torn paper out of place was a mouse magnet, that they liked making their nests with fragments of paper, and maybe he mightn't have minded having a mouse around for the company, except they were dirty, and he had to do all he could to stay away from muck, or else it would all start again.

So the envelope was almost exactly the way it had been

when the mailman had delivered it to him, and maybe they'd find fingerprints on it.

Except his *own* prints would be on top of whoever else's, wouldn't they? And once they had him, they wouldn't be interested in anyone else. Even if the package had been mailed to him, they'd say, he might have mailed it to himself.

'Why would I do that?' he practised saying to them. 'Why on earth would I *do* such a thing?'

They wouldn't listen.

Why should they? All those missing kids. They needed someone to blame. Might as well be him. Eric Stephen Barnes. He could already hear the judge doling out each name like there was a stink under his nose.

Meantime, he was waiting for them to come.

Chapter 65

I'd been trying to play *Limbo* with Kim when the call came.

The FBI had taken the 'deluxe' version, so I'd asked Kim to buy a copy so we could try it on Rianna's PlayStation. I'd already forgotten most of what Binder and Hendrick had tried to teach us at Eryx, and their equipment had been infinitely more sophisticated than Rianna's, but Kim had seemed to know how to start out. Even so, we'd been getting nowhere fast, and if anything about this nasty piece of 'entertainment' was supposed to 'help me understand' why Rianna had been taken, I still didn't know what the hell it was.

Probably, I thought, the sonofabitch had been playing games of another kind with me when he'd written that. Trying to taunt me, torment me a little more, perhaps push me further off track.

The call pushed *all* games clean out of my head.

It was an aide of Kline's, calling from DC. Female, pleasant, with a twang in her voice, telling me that the boss had asked her to let me know that a suspect was currently being questioned.

The rush of blood to my head made me dizzy.

'Where?' I asked. 'Who is it?'

'I'm not able to give you that information.' Still agreeable.

'I'm not asking for details. Just tell me where – tell me *something*.'

'I'm sorry, Professor, I can't tell you any more than I have.'

Instant, pounding headache.

'You mean Kline said not to tell me where in case I get it in

224

my head to go there, right? I wouldn't do that – I just want to *know*.'

Nothing doing. Kline had wanted me to have that news a.s.a.p., but nothing more than that. Special treatment for the *professor*.

I thanked her, then spoiled the moment by asking her to tell Kline that if he was planning on keeping silent from here on, I'd come to headquarters and sit outside his office until I got chapter and verse.

'Agent Kline isn't at headquarters today, Professor,' she told me.

'Just *tell* him, okay?'

'I'll relay your message, Professor.'

Yes, sir, no, sir, three bags full of nothing, *Professor*.

Chapter 66

Lydia was in the bath when the phone rang.

'Damn,' she said, because she'd forgotten to switch on the machine – then decided it might be about Robbie and leapt out of the tub so crazily that water cascaded over the side onto the floor.

She grabbed her towel and reached the phone in her bedroom on the fourth ring. 'Yes?'

'It's Jake.'

She was so glad to hear his voice that it took a second or two for his next words to penetrate. '*Suspect*,' she heard, *thought* she heard.

'What did you say?'

'I said they're questioning a suspect, but that's all they'd tell me.'

'Kline called you?'

'One of his aides.'

For one ugly moment, Lydia felt a surge of anger because no one at the FBI had called *her*, and that was probably because Robbie was further down the list of abductees now, not *freshly* kidnapped like Rianna . . . Then she slapped the thought down, dragged her towel more tightly around herself, sat down on the side of the bed and listened to what Jake was telling her.

Chapter 67

Ford brought the news to Korda, together with his opinion that they should just sit tight now, hold off announcing any press conference.

'This may be nothing,' he said, 'just some poor patsy being brought in for questioning. On the other hand, it may be the break we need to let us off the hook for keeps.'

'At the risk of sounding sanctimonious,' Korda said, 'it might also be the break those poor kids are waiting for, not to mention their parents.'

'You don't need to tell me that,' Ford rebuked him right back.

Korda lifted one of the phones on his desk.

'I'll tell the others,' he said.

Chapter 68

He was going to let them play their first *real* game tonight.

He knew it was too soon for Dakota, who hadn't had time to settle down, to get properly accustomed to the environment or VR controls. She wouldn't be ready, psychologically or physically, which would make it harder for her. On the other hand, the others had all had too *much* time to build up, and look what had happened to them. So he'd decided to throw Dakota in at the deep end, while Steel was still in such good shape.

Anyway, he didn't want to wait any longer for the real thing. He needed to see them play *together*.

Tonight. Just a few hours away.

Finally.

Rianna couldn't decide which was worst. Darkness. Silence. Isolation. Or not knowing what was going to happen.

All of the above.

The *Limbo* stuff the abductor had been showing her was just a crock. She'd been telling herself that ever since she'd first realized that the goggles and other stuff were part of a fantastic VR simulator – *like some of the rides at Disneyland* – to make her feel as if she was *inside* the game. Just a crock. Make-believe. All of it. The tunnels that weren't tunnels, the sewer, the whole underneath-Manhattan 'experience'.

Not real.

Except . . .

Except *she* was real, wasn't she? This was still her, Rianna

Woods, wearing Dakota's dumb non-PC get-up. Playing a part, apparently, the way it seemed Robbie Johanssen was playing Steel.

The big, big question was *why*? It helped, just a little, to think about that, to fool around with it, to occupy her mind. Trouble was, the answer that kept coming back at her was that the man who had taken her and Robbie and Michael and the others (that was something else she wouldn't let herself think about, the reason she hadn't seen any of *them*) was just a major league psycho who happened to be into *Limbo*.

Rianna wished now, passionately, that she hadn't seen so many movies about crazies, that she had listened to her father when he'd told her not to because they'd give her nightmares.

'I don't get nightmares,' she'd told him.

Boy, was she having one now.

One thing, one semi-consolation, was that she – *they*, presumably – were being fed. The food and drink came in cartons and cups with lids, like junk food, and it arrived when she was in the dark, trying to sleep. She heard it coming in – *real* sounds, not like the VR effects. The first time she'd heard it, she'd been sure he was coming to get her, and she had lain as still as she could, trying to pretend she was sleeping. But he hadn't touched her, had just left the food and drink and gone away again.

It had taken a while for her to summon up the courage to taste that first meal in case he'd poisoned it, but she'd been hungry by then, had known she *had* to eat, or die. And it hadn't tasted too bad, a chicken sandwich, though halfway through she'd thought about poison again, and it had been hard keeping it down after that, but she'd managed it and it hadn't made her ill, so *that* was the semi-consolation. He wanted her to eat, which meant that he didn't want her to die.

Not yet, anyway.

Chapter 69

Another night of waiting. Weighted down with all the same terrors, but underpinned, at least a little, by the hope that the arrest might lead us to Rianna, Robbie and Michael.

Baum had gotten me a crumb: the suspect was being interviewed in Philadelphia.

Philadelphia, Pennsylvania.

Was *that* where my baby was?

It had taken all my strength not to get on the first plane out there, but commonsense had told me there was no point; that even if I got close, no one would let me see the scumbag, nor would they tell me a damned thing if they didn't choose to.

If they were going to tell me anything, they'd call me.

So I'd stayed home, so they'd know where to find me.

Lydia had called late that evening, after Ella had gone to bed.

'I won't ask how you're doing,' she'd said.

'Me neither,' I'd responded.

'I'm here if you need to talk,' Lydia had told me.

'I'm glad about that,' I'd said.

Simple talk, yet it had helped a little. Things had shifted again between us since I'd called her about the suspect. We felt close again, despite the physical distance. Like lovers who'd had a fight and had tentatively made up. Though, of course, we weren't really lovers, despite what had happened that night; we were kindred spirits being thrown about in the same, scary ocean, hanging onto each other for dear life.

The guilt was still there in Lydia's voice, though. I think she felt that if, God *forbid*, something bad were to happen to Rianna, I would hate her, blame her.

Maybe she's right, I don't know. I don't *want* to know.

I'd tried to play *Limbo* again, on my own. I'd sent Kim home to Tom hours ago, and the game was driving me nuts, mostly because I couldn't begin to get the hang of it.

I had the overall picture yet again, though, of what it was about.

Vulnerable young people at the mercy of evil.

If there was a message in the game designed to help me, I couldn't find it.

One thing: the kids in the game survived – or rather, if they got wiped out, they came back to life next time you played. *Survival*. That was one message I was glad to believe in.

But in the game, Dakota and Steel never went home again.

Because in the game, New York's been wiped out, so there is no home.

Some comfort.

Ella came looking for me at two in the morning, found me in the living room, slumped in an armchair, feet up on the sofa.

'Sweetheart, you should be asleep.'

'Can't.'

I looked at her. She was wearing a baggy T-shirt, and her cheeks were flushed because it was a warm night. Her eyes weren't pink, so I figured she hadn't been crying. But she looked so *sad*. I hadn't seen Ella look so sad for a very long time.

'You too old to sit on my knee, honeybun?'

She didn't speak, just came over. I lowered my feet from the sofa and made a little space for her on my chair. She sat down and leaned against me. I held her gently. Lord knew I wanted to hug her much tighter, but I was afraid I might alarm her with my own neediness.

She needed me to be strong. I was sure of that.

231

'Daddy?' Very soft, muffled by our closeness.

'What, sweetheart?'

'Is Rianna dead?'

If anyone else had asked that, I think I might have hit them. But it was Ella who had asked. *The* question. Rianna's little sister, mine and Simone's second child. And if that was what was tormenting her most, she needed to feel free to ask me. And hear the answer. The answer I was sure of. Truly, deep in my heart and soul.

'No,' I answered, and pulled away a little so she could see my face, read the truth in my eyes. 'Rianna is *not* dead, sweetheart. She's alive, and she's going to come home to us.'

'When?' Ella asked.

'I don't know, baby,' I said. 'I wish I did.'

Chapter 70

Rianna woke. Feeling bad. Worse.

Her ankle felt strange. She tried to flex it, met cold resistance, moved her head to look down, and realized she was wearing the headset.

She'd gone to sleep without it. She was sure of that.

Her head was muzzy. She remembered, abruptly, that she'd felt that way soon after eating her last sandwich. Tuna salad on rye. And then she'd fallen asleep.

He's been here. He did this.

She whimpered in fear, then forced herself to look around. She was 'in' the subway, in a semi-collapsed tunnel – which was, at least, better than being 'in' the sewer. She *hated* the sewer.

Rianna craned her head with difficulty, looked down at her ankle.

And saw the trap.

An animal trap, like a big steel cuff, attaching her to an old broken rail.

Cute trick. A virtual reality trap.

Except it wasn't. If she moved her leg, the steel edge dug into her ankle.

It was real.

He had woken Robbie, told him to put on his headset and junk.

Another goddamned exercise, he'd assumed, and sworn, but had put it on anyway, too tired, too fogged with sleep to think of arguing.

A tunnel in the subway, all busted up, roof caved in, the usual.

Not quite.

There was something on the ground, a way away, something on the track . . .

Robbie peered.

Dakota.

Something different about this exercise. Until now, it had been either him playing Steel on his own, or Dakota – old and new – going through some kind of faked-up crap on *her* own.

Something definitely felt different about this.

Rianna heard something.

A rumbling sound. Low and steady. Getting louder.

She felt it, too. A vibration. Growing stronger.

She knew what it was. Knew, too, that it couldn't be.

Can't be.

She jerked her ankle harder, but the trap held her.

The sound was getting louder. She yanked more powerfully, ignoring the pain, *real* pain, tried to sit up, bend forward, but she felt clumsy, hampered, and when she did reach for the steel cuff with her right hand, the glove was too unwieldy.

The rumbling was turning into a dull roar.

Rianna lifted her chin, looked towards the sound.

Saw the light, in the distance, but coming closer.

Robbie saw it too, knew what it meant, told himself it was more crap, that it was just the dumb old ghost train out of *Limbo*, but at the same time he could see the girl's face – the part that wasn't covered; he still hadn't seen her eyes, wished he could . . .

The roar was getting louder, the light brighter, closer.

It might not be real, but the girl's mounting terror was real enough.

He started towards her, realized, with a fresh shock, that he really *was* walking, that he wasn't on the walker thing, wasn't holding the VR handlebars. He'd been so dopey when he'd woken, and the game had begun as soon as he'd put on the headset, and suddenly he wasn't even sure he'd woken in the same room as he'd gone to sleep in . . .

Louder.

Christ.

Rianna saw him – Steel – coming to save her, just like in *Limbo* . . .

Robbie, not Steel.

He was calling to her.

'It's not real!'

But it was still coming, she could *see* it, could *hear* it, like hundreds, no, *thousands* of buffalo stampeding . . .

'Get me off the track!' she screamed over the noise. 'Robbie, *help* me!'

And he was there, flesh and blood, *real*, and if it weren't for the train coming closer by the second, she would have been so happy . . .

'Open the *trap*!'

'I'm trying.' Robbie yanked at the cuff with all his strength, but it didn't shift. 'I can't *move* it!'

'Try the knife,' Rianna shouted, reaching out, pointing at the knife in his waist band. That looked real enough, too, but she wasn't sure . . .

'It won't work!' Robbie yelled back at her, but he pulled the knife out anyway, then dropped it, and it wedged beneath one of the tracks – and how could that be, if this was VR? *No time to think, just pick it up*! He snatched it up, tried using it to snap the trap at the edge, but the knife wasn't any good, and he'd worked that out already, hadn't he; it was metal, but it was blunted – of *course* it was blunted. *Come on, Robbie, come on, Steel*!

They could both see the train now. It was coming closer, almost there.

And something else. Something *impossible*. The collapsed tunnel roof was restoring itself, folding back into shape, like a movie rewinding . . . The light from the train was brightening, dazzling them as it neared . . . The horn blared a warning . . .

Rianna understood first, a burst of clarity exploding through the fear.

'The headsets,' she screamed at Robbie. 'We have to take off the headsets!'

She fumbled at hers, couldn't manage it. Robbie was just standing there, bewildered, and then suddenly, realization hit him, too, and he swung around, dropped the knife, came to help her with her headset, but his gloved hands were too bulky . . .

'Okay!' He had it, saw her face, her *whole* face, saw that her eyes looked stunned, realized he'd plunged her into darkness, but her hands were already reaching out blindly towards him, and she was trying to get to *his* headset, and he put his hands up to help her, but they were running out of time, the train was almost on them, and he steeled himself for the impact . . .

The goggles came off, then the earphones.

Blackness. Ringing, deafening silence.

The train had gone.

Moments passed. They half sat, half lay, collapsed, exhausted, both slowly becoming aware that the silence was no longer absolute.

It was filled with the sounds of their breathing. Of survival.

They took off their gloves then, instinct driving them in the dark, and found each other's hands. Skin, warmth, *strength*. Rianna cried out, a wordless cry of relief, and Robbie savoured the sound.

They held each other.

Rianna spoke first.

'You're Robbie, aren't you?'

She felt his surprise.

'How'd you know my name?' he said.

'Long story.'

'We've got time,' Robbie said.

They were still holding each other, too scared to let go.

'Robbie?'

'Yes.'

'The train wasn't real, was it?'

'No.'

'Not the tunnel either.'

'Uh-uh.'

A small shudder, like an after-shock, went through Rianna.

'Then how come the trap's still around my ankle?'

He watched them for a while longer.

Too emotional to move. Or speak.

Too shaken. Drained.

Better than he'd hoped. Better than anything he'd ever seen or done.

He used to think that watching the game on the screen in the dark in the privacy of his own home was good enough. Making Steel and Dakota *his*, making them do what *he* wanted them to do, watching them meet danger head-on time and time again, seeing their handsome cyber-faces contort with fear, mouths tauten with determination, virtual thighs flex with strength.

He still remembered the first time, that accidental discovery, remembered the surprise of it, the half-embarrassment, half-shame. Most of all, though, the *surprise*.

And, of course, the sheer glory of the shock, that physical and emotional collision he'd sought in so many ways for so many years.

So simple. And absurd.

He'd known straightaway that he could never tell anyone about it; no one, not his shrink, not even his priest.

It was private. Harmless.

It had taken him a long while to work out how to make it better.

Perfect.

But he *had* worked it out.

And he was right, oh, so very right.

It *was* perfect.

And it was going to get even better.

*

237

Robbie and Rianna were both waiting for the other shoe to drop.

Still clinging together in the dark, waiting for something to happen, waiting for *him* to rip them apart again, or worse. Robbie had come to the conclusion that he too must have been drugged, that he'd almost certainly been moved from his own little room to one that felt, he thought, a little bigger, a little different.

For one thing, she was in it.

Moments ticked by.

'So tell me,' Robbie whispered. 'About you, and how you know about me.'

Rianna told him her name. 'Practically *everyone* knows about you – you're famous. But your mom—'

'What about my mom?' He jumped on that. 'Is she okay?'

'She's fine,' Rianna whispered. 'She has the whole FBI out looking for you, and my dad – who's a professor now, but used to be a cop – and your mom are looking out for each other, and now I've been taken too, I know they're going to find us, get us out of here.' She paused. 'What about the others?'

'Others?'

'Four other kids were taken before you – they know that much because they all got the game and the note.' Rianna stopped. 'Except me.'

'*Four* others?'

Rianna heard his shock. 'Haven't you seen anyone else down here?'

'Uh-huh,' Robbie said. 'But just one.'

'Boy or girl?' Rianna thought about Mikey.

'Girl,' Robbie said.

Rianna said nothing.

'*Are you having fun?*'

His voice.

They didn't answer, just held each other tightly.

And heard a sharp click in the dark.

'The trap,' Rianna whispered, feeling it release. 'He's opened it.' She wriggled her leg free, let go of Robbie for a moment, reached down to massage her ankle, then grabbed hold of him again.

'Better?' *he* asked.

Rianna didn't answer.

'You're afraid I'm going to separate you again, aren't you?' They could hardly breathe.

'You can relax,' he said. 'After all, Steel and Dakota belong together, don't they?' He paused. 'Don't you?'

Chapter 71

I called Kline's office again in the morning, knowing he wouldn't be there, assuming he was in Philadelphia. It was Tuesday, July 25, and Rianna had been missing for two and a half days.

He called back two hours later, just as I was about to leave another message.

'Okay,' he said, 'I can give you some baseline information and no more.'

'I'd be grateful for that much.' True enough for a starving man.

'Guy we're talking to is a registered paedophile and sex offender whose name showed up on the *Limbo* "masters" index. Don't get too excited, Professor, we're just asking him some questions.'

'Guy have a name?'

'You know better than that,' Kline said.

I guess I did.

'No charges yet – perhaps never – and we're still looking at other suspects and avenues, so please don't get your hopes up.'

Hopes.

I thanked him, knowing that was all the information I was going to get, knowing he'd been doing me a genuine favour.

Three of his words were percolating in my brain.

Paedophile. Sex offender.

I was in my study. Rianna looked at me from out of a photograph.

Smiling her sweet smile.

Right into my eyes.

I only just made it to the bathroom in time.

Baum called again that afternoon. Kim had managed to persuade Ella over to her place, though Ella had refused to go anywhere she'd be out of phone contact with me in case there was any news.

'I got a little more for you,' Baum said.

God bless Norman Baum. I told him what little Kline had shared with me.

'Ex-con's name is Eric Barnes,' Baum said. 'He claims he's never played *Limbo* or any other computer game, but a PlayStation and game were found in his apartment. Barnes swears they arrived through the mail a week ago, claims he never ordered them.'

'Do we believe him?' God help me, it sounded like it *might* be the damned truth, and who the hell was that going to help?

Baum sounded tired. 'Barnes says he knew soon as the package arrived what it might mean to him because he'd read about the case.'

'Did he call the cops when the stuff arrived?'

'Too scared,' Baum said.

'Does he have alibis?'

'Not one, though he claims that's because he never goes anywhere except his counselling sessions in case he gets tempted or falsely accused of something.'

I felt sick as a dog. '*Has* he been seeing his counsellor?'

'Off and on.' Baum paused. 'Could have mailed the package to himself.'

'Yeah.' I tried to focus. 'Does he have a job?'

'No,' Baum answered. 'No money either – lives in a one-room – clean as a Reverend Mother's jokes, probably obsessive-compulsive.'

'Could he be some kind of fucked-up idiot-genius?'

'Not so far as my pal's heard.'

'They're wasting their time, aren't they?' I said grimly.

'Maybe,' Baum said. 'Or maybe there's stuff we haven't heard about.'

Chapter 72

The elation had gone.

Shame in its place. Awful, *awful* shame.

He'd learned that at a young age.

About the evils of sex.

That it had to be scrubbed away.

Father had made him scrub till he bled. He'd called it a fine antidote to lust. And it was. Oh, Christ, it *was*. He'd tried to get past that, but he'd failed.

Because he'd known, deep down, that it was wrong.

Just as his father had told him it was.

And that knowledge had ruined everything.

Until that night – long, long after Father had gone – working alone in a dimly-lit office; alone, that was, except for Dakota and Steel, when he'd realized that he had a hard-on. It had been so long since he'd had one, but he could still recall the horror, the *mortification* of that moment, and then the amazing, *fabulous* moments that had followed, the incredible relief of release.

He'd gone home that night and scrubbed till he bled again, had prayed for forgiveness, vowed it had been the last time. But after that the need had never gone away, had just grown and grown. Taken over.

He knew now that he'd lied to himself at the start of this. Had lied when he'd told himself it was going to be just a game. It had always been something dirty, *bad*, he knew that. But he'd lied to himself, because that had been easier than admitting the truth.

It wasn't even night now, but the truths were starting to stab at him again. They were becoming more relentless, more merciless as time went on, giving him less and less peace.

What kind of a *thing* found ecstasy in the terrors of captive children? What kind of a *thing* screamed when he killed – and then did it all over again? And then went to work and pretended to be human.

Not for much longer.

None of it.

That much was clear.

Even to a monster.

Chapter 73

'So what does Baum feel about this man?' Lydia asked when I called her.

'That it's too soon to feel anything conclusive,' I answered.

'What do you feel?'

I wasn't going to tell her anything but the truth, such as it was. 'I think it's possible the poor bastard's been set up.'

Lydia took a moment. 'By the kidnapper, you mean?'

'It's one theory.'

'Is that what Kline thinks?'

'Who knows?' I said. 'They may have something on Barnes we don't know about.'

Lydia was mulling it over. 'You're suggesting that whoever has our children may have – what exactly? – hacked into the *Limbo* "masters" index?'

'Like I said, it's just a theory.'

'So he could have taken a name from the paedophile register in Pennsylvania and simply added it to the Eryx index?'

'Not *simply*,' I said. 'But then, I don't have the kind of computer know-how to tell you how easy or tough that would be to achieve.'

'Do you think the abductor could be a hacker?' Lydia was growing excited, jumping on the idea like a dog on a bone. 'Have you told Kline what you think?'

'I tried calling him again before I phoned you. Guess I've had my quota for today.' I shook my head, trying to clear it. 'Anyhow, if I've thought of it, the FBI's already on it.'

'You really still have that kind of faith?' Lydia asked quietly.

'I don't know,' I said. 'I don't think I know anything any more.'

I hadn't asked Kline for permission to share the information with either Lydia or the Coopers, but he hadn't asked for secrecy and I figured he wasn't a man to forget something like that. I think I would have shared it with Lydia in any event. And I had no compunction about calling Fran and Stu.

They'd already been told, by an agent in the Boston field office who'd been taking care of them for a while now.

'Do you think they have him?' Fran asked. 'Do you think this could be it?'

I heard the fragment of hope in her disintegrating voice, and knew I couldn't be the one to take that away from her. In any case, I told myself, I was in no position to tell her I thought he might just be a patsy.

'I don't know, Fran,' I said.

'I guess we just have to wait, don't we?'

Lord knew I'd felt for them from the moment I'd first heard about Mikey's disappearance. But now I found I could not bear to contemplate what any parent might feel when their child had been gone for as long as he had.

I phoned Lydia again, told her I had something to ask her.

'Anything,' she said.

'You have to feel free to turn me down, okay?'

'What are you asking, Jake?'

'Would you come back to New Haven?' I paused. 'You could stay here in the guest room or you could go to a hotel, as my guest – unless that would make you uncomfortable . . .'

'I think I'd be more comfortable in your guest room.' There was a hint of a smile in her voice. 'If you and Ella don't mind.'

'We don't mind.'

'Have you asked Ella?'

'Ella's out with Kim,' I said, 'so I can't ask her. But I know

246

she won't mind, Lydia. Since you got yourself arrested, she considers you pretty cool.'

Only the briefest silence attested to the fact that I seemed to have come to terms with the fact that the monster who'd pounced on Rianna would have done so whether I'd gone upstate or not.

'I'll take the first available train,' Lydia said. 'Be there this evening.'

Glad was not the word.

Glad didn't even *begin* to describe it.

Chapter 74

Robbie and Rianna were still together. They knew he had said he wasn't going to separate them, but they also knew they couldn't trust anything he said.

He had turned on the light a while back, and they had seen each other fully for the first time. Whole faces, eyes unmasked.

'You're gorgeous,' Robbie had told her straightaway, sounding amazed.

There was no way to see herself, and Rianna was sure she must look the *pits*, but hearing him say that had made her feel better, *really* better, which was probably pretty shallow in the circumstances, but true nevertheless. He looked thinner than he had in the photographs Rianna had seen, dark smudges beneath his eyes and a shadow of a beard, but when all was said and done he was still cute.

'I thought I was never going to see anyone again,' Robbie had said.

'So a frog would probably look gorgeous,' Rianna had managed to joke.

'Are you kidding?' He'd stared at her. 'And what you did, when the train was coming—'

'When we *thought* the train was coming,' Rianna corrected.

'But you figured that out so fast' – Robbie was frankly admiring – 'and you knew what to do.'

'You'd have figured it out a second later.'

'I don't think so.'

Rianna moved about the room, checking things out. It was

the same room she'd gone to sleep in, she was as sure about that as she could be, but now there were two mattresses instead of one, and there were two bars of soap and two towels.

'This is all so weird,' she said softly.

'Sure is.' Robbie was sitting on one of the mattresses, almost too tired to stand.

'You okay?'

'Just beat.' He looked up at her. 'Do you know how long I've been here?'

Rianna remembered the date he'd been taken from the newspaper. 'You disappeared on May 31.' She hesitated before going on. 'Do you remember anything about what happened?' She'd already told him about the gym and the false message and her own capture.

'I remember,' Robbie answered. 'Candice's birthday.'

'Candice?'

'A friend. A bunch of us were at a restaurant. I went to the bathroom and got – jumped, I guess.' He shook his head. 'But I don't know how long it was before I woke up down here.' He looked up at her again. 'You said "*down*" before, too. Do you know that, or do you just feel it?'

'I just feel it.' Rianna took a moment. 'I'm pretty sure, aren't you?'

'Yeah.' Robbie paused. 'So how long has it been? Do you know what date you were taken?'

Rianna sat down on the mattress beside him. 'It was Saturday.' She thought. 'Twenty-second of July.' She paused again. 'I don't know exactly how long I've been here either – hard to be sure. I *think* it's probably just a few days.'

Robbie didn't speak.

Rianna understood why. It had to be mind-blowing, *shattering*, for him.

'Fifty-two days,' he said finally, very softly. 'I've been here for more than *fifty-two* days.' He paused. 'Half the summer . . . Josh's birthday . . .'

'Josh?'

'My friend – best friend.'

They were both silent for several moments, and then Rianna moved close enough to put one arm around his shoulders. No point saying anything. There was nothing she could say that would comfort him. Or herself, for that matter.

'At least we have each other now,' she said, after a while.

He nodded.

'And we both know they won't give up before they find us.'

'Yeah,' he said. 'I guess.'

'I know,' she said.

She took her arm away but stayed close, reflecting on how utterly bizarre even *this* was. She might have known about Robbie Johanssen before she got here, but he was still really a stranger who knew next to nothing about her. Yet here and now, in this terrible place, Rianna thought she felt about as close to Robbie as anyone – family and the Ryans and Shannon apart – she'd ever met in her life.

'I guess we *are* almost like Steel and Dakota now,' Robbie murmured. 'The last two teenagers under New York, looking out for each other.'

Rianna shifted a little, looked at him. 'Is that where you think we are?'

He nodded. 'Uh-huh.' Then shrugged. 'I don't know.'

The light went out again. Rianna shuddered, and Robbie put his arm around her. His turn to give comfort.

'You'll get used to it,' he said.

'I don't think so,' she whispered.

'Me neither,' he admitted. 'But it's going to be easier for me now you're here.' That sounded lousy to him. 'Not that I'm glad he got you too.'

She didn't answer.

'Let's get some sleep,' Robbie said.

They lay down together, staying close, not caring if it was not what they'd have done outside, in *normality*, just needing to stay that way for as long as they could.

Robbie lay very still, listening to Rianna's breathing, heard it level out as she fell asleep. He was glad she could escape that way, at least for a while. And it gave him a little private thinking space.

Something was bugging him about this, and if the same thoughts hadn't occurred to Rianna, he didn't want to add to her fears. If they were supposed to be like Steel and Dakota – to actually *become* them, this crazy bastard's pieces of living software – then this was something he didn't recall ever happening in *Limbo*, the computer game. Thing was, Dakota and Steel were always getting together through their adventures, always saving each other, but they hardly ever got to be together for more than a little while, never got to *stay* together . . .

Maybe he was just being kind to them?

Not exactly this creep's style.

So Robbie was thinking maybe he wanted to watch them for a while, see how they got along together, listen to what they talked about, any plans they might be trying to hatch. *What* plans? He wished there *were* plans for him to eavesdrop on.

It made him sick to think about that dirt-bag spying on them, maybe watching through some peephole or filming them via some hidden camera while they talked or ate or took a pee or slept. Then again, he hated that other recurring thought even more – that maybe the sonofabitch would *stop* watching and go away, that one of these days-nights no food or drink would get pushed into their cell . . .

That the light would never come on again.

You want to stop thinking about that, man.

'Robbie?' Rianna's voice, so soft it seemed to float in the dark.

'Thought you were sleeping,' he said.

'What are you thinking about?' she asked.

He could hear the fear in her voice.

'Nothing.' He paused. 'Do you think we could get just a bit closer?'

'That would be good,' Rianna whispered.

It was.

Chapter 75

He was keeping his ear to the ground for news on Barnes, wondering how soon they'd let him walk, or how long they'd make him sweat, poor bastard.

Poor bastard, nothing.

He was a child molester, a paedophile.

Nothing more evil, nothing more cowardly in the world than that.

Except a thing-monster.

That was why he'd picked on Barnes. He'd had to find someone to act as temporary scapegoat, dupe, dope, and this had seemed an efficient enough way to go, in keeping with the rest.

When they had to let him go, he could always find them another.

Thing-monster needs more time.

Steel and Dakota had so many more games to play.

They'd hardly begun.

He'd enjoyed watching them, holding each other, huddling together.

More time.

Chapter 76

Not long after Lydia arrived, Baum called again. I told him she was here, said she was going to pick up the extension.

We heard the click as she picked up in the living room. I was in the kitchen.

'How are you holding up, Lydia?'

'Could be worse,' she said. 'How are you, Norman?'

'I'm good, thank you,' Baum told her.

'What've you got?' I ended the pleasantries.

'I'd say they'll have to let Barnes go soon,' Baum told us. 'Word is no one really believes he's a master of *Limbo* or anything much else.'

'So it was a set-up,' I said.

'Which could lead back to Eryx, surely?' Lydia said quickly.

'Could just as well lead to a hacker,' Baum told us both. 'Maybe the abductor, maybe just some sick mischief-maker.'

'Oh God,' Lydia said. 'You think someone would really do that?'

'They'd do it,' I said quietly. 'Some lamebrain computer genius taking a break from inventing viruses.'

'They haven't let Barnes go yet,' Baum reminded us.

Which meant they'd found cause to hold him longer than was usual.

'Why *are* they still holding him?' I asked. 'You said he has no money, so he couldn't have the resources to have taken kids from six states.'

'He wouldn't need great resources,' Baum said. 'Just a van,

I guess – and no, I don't know if Barnes has a driver's licence.'

'Does he have the know-how or guts to steal a New Haven cab and tamper with Coach Carlin's car in broad daylight, then dump the cab and know *exactly* how to clean it, leaving just one hair?'

'Doubtful,' Baum said.

'Because it isn't Barnes, is it?' I said loudly. 'Because all he is is your average sick screwed-up pervert.'

'Which is why he'll probably be released by morning,' Baum said.

'Why wait till morning? Maybe they do have something we don't know about.'

'I don't know, Jake.' Baum was patient as ever with me.

I could hear Lydia's soft breathing on the line. I'd almost forgotten she was listening. 'I'm sorry,' I said to them both. 'Thanks for calling, Norman.' I couldn't continue with the conversation any longer. Suddenly I just felt like weeping.

'Take it easy,' Baum said.

I put down the phone, took a couple of deep breaths, scrubbed the back of my left hand across my eyes, and walked into the living room.

Lydia was sitting on the sofa, staring down at her hands folded in her lap.

'You okay?' I asked.

She looked up at me, her eyes wet. 'Could still be someone at Eryx, couldn't it?'

I half nodded, half shrugged. I couldn't speak.

I sat down beside her.

We both felt the same way, no doubt about that. Our kids were still missing and no one seemed to be any further along.

How else *could* we feel?

Chapter 77

He had hoped for more than forty-eight lousy hours.

Lord, this was draining. Having to deal with too much at once. Look after the kids. Deal with life, work, *people*. Make sure the next suspect was ripe for picking.

Up and down, up and down.

Thank God for his intelligence and stamina.

Flagging a little just now, which maddened him.

They hadn't reached the best part yet. The kids weren't ready for that yet. They needed more groundwork, more games, which *he* had to provide. No wonder he got low, no wonder his morale sagged now and then. There really was no need to beat himself up the way he had lately, no need to bad-mouth himself.

'*Thing-monster.*' So ugly, so unkind.

When what he was, what he *really* was, was a genius.

Up and down, up and down.

More time. That was all he needed.

To make it perfect.

Chapter 78

Ella was at her friend Maggy Stewart's house over near Short Beach for the day. She'd said she didn't want to go, that she wanted to stay home with me, and in many ways I wanted that too, but at the same time, if there was a chance of a few hours of something *close* to normality for my little girl, I wanted her to have it.

'If you want to come back early, that's okay,' I told her before Mrs Stewart arrived to drive her over. 'All you have to do is call or tell Maggy's mom.'

She looked at me with her powerful eyes. 'Same deal for you.'

I guess I looked puzzled.

'If you need me to come home, Daddy,' she said. 'You can call and I'll make Maggy's mom bring me, okay?'

I smiled, bent down and gave her a big, fat cuddle. 'Okay, baby.'

'You promise?'

'Oh, yes,' I told her.

I never knew, until last Saturday, that Ella could be like this. Rianna had always been my helpmate, the stand-in for their mom, I guess, while Ella was almost always the more difficult, the more *testing*. Now, suddenly, she was showing a side I'd never realized was there.

Taking Rianna's place.

Soon as Mrs Stewart's car had pulled away, I ran back up to the apartment, passed Lydia in the hall without a word, went into the bathroom, closed the door, sat on the side of the tub and wept like a baby.

'You have to eat, Jake,' Lydia said a while later.

She was making omelettes. I didn't know how I was going to eat.

Baum's call saved me from that, at least. Not from much else.

'Barnes has walked,' he told me.

'Okay,' I said.

'My source tells me they're talking to someone else.'

Hope again, like a shock along my spine. 'Tell me.'

'Nothing to tell, except he's another offender.'

When Baum said *offender*, I knew what he meant.

Sex offender.

The words burned like white-hot pokers in my mind, sending flashpoints of pure rage through me, making even my fingers feel like they were sizzling.

Like they could kill.

Lydia was watching me from the table, the food just served. I looked at her. Dressed in jeans and a blue T-shirt, no make-up, hair brushed long, straight and simple. Looking so beautiful and scared and longing, and so *despairing* that I wanted to drop the phone, drop everything, take her in my arms and crush her pain – our pain – away.

Wouldn't work though.

You have to do *something, Jake*.

'Jake?' Baum's voice. 'You still there?'

'Still here.'

Photographs of Rianna seemed everywhere, even in the kitchen – I'd never noticed before these last few days how many there were. Watching me, too, like Lydia, grey eyes gazing at me with such trust. *Daddy, help me*.

Do something.

But *what*?

'If I get any more, I'll tell you right away,' Baum said. 'I do know that the investigation's just as open as it was.'

'Meaning this could be just another poor schmuck.' I forced myself to think logically. 'Resources,' I said. 'That's what keeps coming back to me. I know what you said about not needing much, but I don't buy that. Resources equal money, and that often goes hand-in-hand with arrogance, and the way this bastard dangles that damned game and his notes, and the way he left that single hair . . . A man who does things like that might believe he's not going to be touched by the FBI – maybe because he's influential, or maybe because he has a track record of being so *litigious* that—'

'Eryx again,' Baum interrupted. 'Yet everything you just said could apply to thousands of rich men all over this country.'

'So let's meet halfway,' I said. 'Is Kline looking for *Limbo* masters who happen to be wealthy, as well as paedophiles and other low-lives?'

'Kline's probably looking at everything,' Baum said, 'though I don't see rich, powerful types being keen to get on a games corporation's database; they're usually into heavy duty privacy.'

'Like Fitzgerald.' I thought some more. 'The *kids* of rich and powerful parents might like being known as masters.'

'Sounds more like it.'

'Can you pass that on?'

'I can try,' Baum said. 'Though they're probably already on it.' He paused, sensing my renewed gloom. 'There are a couple of new things, Jake.' He sounded reluctant.

'What?'

'Don't get excited – and don't get Lydia too worked up.'

I shifted my position slightly so she could no longer see my face. 'Okay.'

'One's just a rumour,' Baum said, 'that Korda's divorce may not have been as civilized as it seemed, may have covered up something nastier. Just a rumour, okay?'

'Okay.' My pulse was quickening, but I kept my tone down-beat.

'The second is something Thea, my partner, dug up on Fitzgerald.'

Something *real* was coming now, I could hear it in Baum's voice.

'This isn't confirmed either, but it seems that way back in high school – Catholic school not far from Stamford – when he was about fourteen or fifteen, our boy Bill was accused of assaulting a female teacher.'

Jesus.

'Nothing sexual,' Baum preempted, 'but definitely strange. The lady claimed he lay in wait for her one winter's afternoon, knocked her out and then locked her into a shed on the school campus. Could have been a prank, could have been more than one kid involved, but she only named Fitzgerald.'

'What happened to him?'

'The cops picked him up for questioning, but then the teacher withdrew the charges and the case was dropped.'

Which was why we hadn't found this out before, I thought.

'Maybe mom and pop had some local influence,' Baum said. 'There's no more than that, Jake. No one seems to have any idea why young Bill might have done such a thing.' He paused. 'Thea thinks maybe we should try checking out the accident that killed his wife.'

My heart went into overdrive.

'Do I take it you want to keep this from Lydia?'

'For now,' I said.

'Your call, I guess.' Baum paused again. 'This could all be nothing, Jake.'

'Anything's possible,' I said.

If I'd asked myself ten minutes earlier if I would choose to lie to Lydia or keep information from her when it so patently might affect her every bit as much as me, I'd have said no way.

Yet when I put down the phone and turned to face her, still sitting silently at my kitchen table, I knew I was about to lie through my teeth.

'Tell me,' she said.

I told her about the new suspect, told her the guy had priors and that was all we knew, but that Baum would give us more soon as he had it.

'What was the last part of the call about?' she asked. 'After you talked about rich people's kids.'

I took my time, sat down facing my by-now cold omelette, saw that Lydia's plate was just as untouched, gave a small shrug. 'Just Norman telling me he feels Kline's people are on the right track now, and that he thinks I have to stop regarding Eryx as the enemy.'

'That's all?' she asked. 'Seemed like more than that.'

'No.' I shook my head. 'Just a lecture on knowing when to move on.'

'So he really does think Eryx is just another victim?'

'Commercially speaking, I guess.'

I thought she was buying my story. I hadn't realized I could lie so well. I wasn't proud of it. 'He said he'll pass on the idea about rich kids.'

'Not kids,' Lydia said. 'I can't believe that. It's too terrible.'

'Young people sometimes do terrible things,' I reminded her. 'Think of the Menendez brothers.'

'That was very different,' Lydia said.

'I could give you a list of other cases.'

'Please don't,' she said.

I left her with the washing up – she wanted to do it, and I was seldom so glad to escape. From my deception, not from Lydia.

No real alternative now, I told myself. If she knew the truth, knew what I'd just made up my mind I was going to do – and I *had* made up my mind because Baum's words were burning holes in my brain – she'd insist on coming with me, and I couldn't let her do that . . .

I went into my bedroom, shut the door, called Baum back and told him.

'What are you, *nuts*?' was his instant reaction.

'Maybe, maybe not,' I said, 'but I can't sit here for one more night doing nothing if there's even a tiny chance I might be able to find out who has our kids.' It was a major effort keeping my voice down.

'Don't you think Kline's found out the same things Thea has?'

'Kline doesn't share with me, Norman. I can't waste any more time waiting for his crumbs.' I was talking fast, wanting to get it said before Lydia came looking for me. 'I know this is what Lydia tried to do that day, but I'm going to do it a lot more carefully and I'm going to do my damndest not to get caught.' I paused. 'And I suppose what I'm hoping is that you might agree to go with me.'

'Hope is free,' Baum said.

'Someone kidnapped my daughter, Norman. Maybe one of those men, maybe not. But I know I stand a better chance if a guy like you—'

'A guy *like* me,' Baum cut in ironically.

'A guy who knows a thing or two about poking around places he's not allowed.' I was sitting on the edge of my bed, rubbing the back of my neck with my left hand, praying he was going to say yes, praying I hadn't been wrong to ask him, and Jesus, I was wound so *tight*. 'I'll understand if you refuse, but—'

'But you'll go anyway,' Baum said.

'Of course I'll go. I've never really let go of the feeling that one of them has the kids – has *my* child now.' I was shaking with the strain of speaking softly. 'I'm sure Rianna was taken at least partly to punish me for trying to keep the heat on Eryx. And look at it this way, Norman: if I'm wrong, then at least I won't be wasting FBI time or manpower. Let them look where they want, and I'll do the same.'

I stopped. I had no more to say, and I wanted to conserve my strength.

'You're not going to share any of this with Lydia?' Baum asked.

'Not yet.' I waited for him to bawl me out.

'Not right,' he said. 'But maybe for the best.'

'That's a surprise,' I told him.

'I don't want to go with you, Jake.'

'Okay.' I was disappointed, but not surprised.

'But you're definitely still going?'

'I already answered that.'

'Then I guess I must be as crazy as you.'

'You're going to come?'

'Only because I know if I were in your shoes, I might do the same thing.'

Gratitude blew away my ability to speak.

'But what I'm going to do first,' Baum went on, 'is gee up another pal I already persuaded to hack into planning records for architectural drawings of any of the Eryx men's houses – looking for cellars, that kind of thing.' He was thinking as he went. 'Not that it would make much sense for any of them to keep the kids at home. You're the one who talked about resources, and these men have plenty.'

'Except—' I thought I heard footsteps, then went on again. 'Except if it is one of them, then he's probably crazy, and we've all agreed that crazy people don't always follow logic.'

'I guess not,' Baum said dryly. 'Judging by this conversation.'

Chapter 79

Just after five p.m., I told Lydia that I'd just talked to Stu Cooper, who'd said that Fran was almost climbing the walls, *really* losing it, and that Stu had asked me to drive to Brookline to see her.

'Has he called their doctor?' Lydia asked, reasonably.

'The doc isn't happy about prescribing stuff for Fran right now.' More lies.

'Poor Fran.'

'Stu seems to think talking to me might help a little.'

'You have to go,' Lydia said with certainty.

I hesitated. 'I was supposed to go fetch Ella, but her friend's mom says she's happy to bring her home.'

'Do you think she'll mind being alone with me?'

I shook my head. 'Not one bit.'

'Then there's no problem, is there?' Lydia said. 'I'll be here for Ella. You go visit with the Coopers. Sounds like they could both use a piece of you right now.' She saw something in my face and misinterpreted guilt as worry. 'Jake, if there's any news, I can call you there.'

I could hardly look her in the eye.

I picked Baum up outside the Omni, and we got out of New Haven as fast as traffic allowed.

'What if Lydia calls the Coopers?'

'Taken care of,' I told him. 'Stu's agreed to cover for me.'

'You didn't tell him where you're going, I hope?'

I shook my head, keeping my eyes on the road. 'I just said I had to go somewhere alone, but didn't want to offend Lydia.'

She had looked at me when I was leaving, a strangely penetrating look, as if she knew perfectly well that I wasn't going anywhere near the Coopers, but knew, too, that there was no point challenging me. I'd felt like a heel then, felt no better now.

'How about a little forward planning?' Baum relieved me of my thoughts.

'Sure,' I said. 'I figure we should start at Fitzgerald's, then, if we get nowhere, drive up to Korda's house, and if things stay fast and smooth and negative, I'd like to hit the horse farm.'

'What about Hawthorne's place?' Baum asked. 'After all, if he's our man, what better place to move the kids to after the FBI search?' He shrugged. 'I mean, if we're aiming to cover three-quarters of Connecticut, what's a side trip to Chester?'

I threw him a wry glance. 'Think I don't know how nuts I sound?'

'I guess you do,' Baum allowed.

'I know we have to wait till after dark before we go near anyone's house, and I know we'll be lucky to get to first base, and I *know* this is a job for at least five skilled men, not one five-minute cop and an ageing PI – no offence.'

'None taken.'

'And maybe I *have* let myself get fixated by Eryx.'

'But you still have to do this,' Baum said.

I was grateful enough to want to hug him. 'And if there's time, maybe we will take another peek at Hawthorne's house on the way home.' I grinned. 'Though I guess the New York winery may have to wait for another night.'

'Yeah, Jake,' Baum said, 'I guess it will.'

Korda heard from Ford that Woods and Baum were on their way upstate while he was in Hal Hawthorne's office with Ellen Zito and Dave Kaminski.

Korda put Ford on the speaker phone so Hawthorne could hear too.

'My operative says they could be going anyplace,' Ford said.

'But you feel they're coming this way?' Korda asked.

'It's a possibility.' Ford paused. 'I need to give my guy instructions.'

'I'll get back to you.'

Kaminski looked startled. 'You have a tail on Jake Woods?'

'That's a little over-dramatic, Dave,' Korda turned to smile at him, 'though the professor and Mrs Johanssen *have* been obsessing about Eryx to anyone who'll listen to them, so Nick felt it wise to keep an eye on them.'

'You heard what happened over at Bill's house last week,' Hawthorne said.

'Sure,' Zito said. 'Poor woman must be losing it big-time.' She shook her head. 'And the professor, too, now.'

'Absolutely,' Korda agreed. 'Which is one reason we need to make sure they don't do something foolish and give themselves even more grief – and at this time of day, without an appointment, I doubt they're coming to the office.' He looked at her and Kaminski. 'I guess that's it for now.' He paused. 'Ellen, do you think you could find Bill, ask him to step in?'

'No problem.'

Zito and Kaminski headed out of the room, aware they'd been dismissed.

Fitzgerald came within two minutes, looking sour. 'What the hell are we going to do with these people, Scott?'

'Nothing, yet,' Korda said. 'We don't know where they're going.'

'Ellen said Ford thinks they're heading our way.'

'Possibly.' Korda paused. 'I'm going to have Nick pull his guy.'

'Why?' Hawthorne asked.

'I can't see much point tailing them now,' Korda answered. 'Either they're coming here or to one of our houses or they're not – and if not, it's none of our business where they go.'

'And if they are?' Fitzgerald said.

'Then we handle it.'

'How? By calling the cops?' Fitzgerald was scathing. 'So they can give them a warning pat on their heads and send them on their way?'

'I'm not telling either of you what to do if they show up at your places,' Korda said. 'That's your decision. I'm going to go home to wait and see.'

'Maybe they just want to talk,' Hawthorne said.

'Without calling ahead?' Fitzgerald was sceptical.

'I don't think we should overreact.' Korda picked up a folder he'd brought with him and started towards the door. 'I'd prefer to avoid trouble, if possible.'

'I agree,' Hawthorne said.

'I think we should talk to Tillman,' Fitzgerald said.

'Be my guest,' Korda said.

Chapter 80

Maggy Stewart's mother had brought Ella home a while ago, and though she knew her father had only gone on a visit to the Coopers, Ella had been clearly upset by his absence.

'Are you all right with just me for company?' Lydia had asked her right away. 'Because if you'd rather, we can call Kim, see if she's free.'

She'd hoped, as she spoke, that Ella wouldn't suggest calling the Coopers, because she was almost certain – though she wasn't quite certain why – that Jake was not in Brookline this evening, and that wherever he *had* gone, the trip had been sparked by something Baum had said during their phone conversation. Something Jake had chosen not to share with her. So the last thing she wanted now was to create a situation where Ella might be alarmed at not being able to locate her daddy.

'I don't need a babysitter.' Ella's nine-year-old tough-guy chin had quivered.

'I know that.' Lydia had resisted the urge to put her arms around the child. 'But I also know that I could certainly use your company this evening.'

'You don't really know me.' Straight from the hip.

'I think I'm getting to,' Lydia had said. 'Which is why I said I'd like your company. If you don't mind too much, that is.'

'Not too much, I guess,' Ella had answered.

The phone rang a little after seven-thirty. Ella ran to pick it up, spoke for a moment, then brought the cordless phone to

Lydia, who was just adding tomato sauce to Ella's bowl of spaghetti.

'It's for Daddy, but she wants to talk to you.'

Lydia took the phone and motioned for Ella to start eating.

'Lydia Johanssen speaking,' she said.

Ella stayed where she was, watching her carefully, as if she didn't quite trust Lydia to share grown-up stuff with her.

It was Thea Lomax, Baum's partner.

'Nothing big, Mrs Johanssen,' the PI said swiftly, aware that every call had to send the parents' heart rates sky high. 'Just that I think Norman told Professor Woods another suspect was being questioned.'

'Yes, he did.'

'I'm afraid he wasn't our man either.' Lomax was gentle. 'They let him go.'

'Oh.' Lydia didn't know what else to say.

'Seems to have been another cross match, not with the masters index this time, but this guy was a games nut as well as a creep.' Lomax paused. 'Our contact in the Bureau reckons there are a few jokers out there planting these hook-ups.'

'Jake said he thought it might be a hacker playing games.' Lydia saw Ella's eyes spark as she spoke, knew it was the mention of hackers.

'Could be.'

'Or it could be the man himself – he's into games, after all, isn't he?' Lydia paused. 'Mightn't that be a way for Kline's team to trap him? It seems to work in the movies,' she added wryly.

Ella had given up all pretence of eating her spaghetti.

'In movies, they do seem able to trace people thousands of miles away in a millisecond,' Lomax agreed. 'Truthfully, Lydia, I don't know. I do know the FBI has amazing resources, and I'm sure Kline's pulling out all the stops to get your kids back home – but I don't know if or how they're using the hacker idea.'

'No,' Lydia said. 'I appreciate your honesty.'

'Just thought you and the professor should know about the suspect.'

268

It occurred to Lydia, abruptly, that Lomax might know Jake's whereabouts. 'If you wanted to speak to Jake personally,' she said, a touch slyly, 'he's gone to see Michael Cooper's parents. Maybe they should know this too?'

'Norman told me he's trying not to load the Coopers with too many negatives. I know they're just about at the end of their rope. As you must be too,' she added. 'But people cope differently, don't they?'

'I guess so.' Lydia paused. 'Is Norman off duty this evening? Only he usually calls Jake himself.'

'Even Norman Baum needs time off sometimes,' Lomax said.

Lydia couldn't tell if the other woman was fobbing her off or not. She still wanted to believe Jake, had been more than a little upset by the notion of his lying to her. Then again, she was almost certain that if he *had* done that, it had probably been out of some mistaken belief that he'd be protecting her, or maybe even Ella – but *that* might mean he was contemplating taking some kind of risk. That was why she hoped Thea Lomax was lying to her too, because then maybe wherever Jake had gone, Baum might be with him, looking out for him.

'What did she say?' Ella asked as Lydia returned to the table and sat down.

'That was Mr Baum's partner—'

'I know who it was.' Ella wasn't being rude, just impatient.

'It was nothing to worry about,' Lydia said, knowing, as she spoke, that it wasn't anywhere near a good enough answer for this sharp child. 'The FBI were talking to a man—'

'A suspect?' Ella said.

Lydia nodded. 'He *was* a suspect, but they let him go because they realized he had nothing to do with taking Rianna or Robbie.'

'Or the others,' Ella said.

'That's right.'

'Does she think they can catch the man if he's the hacker?'

Sharp was not the word. 'She doesn't know. She said, more or less, that if anyone can do that, the FBI can, but she can't say more because they won't talk to just anyone about it.'

'Would they talk to Daddy?' Ella asked.

'Probably not,' Lydia answered.

'Only I don't think Daddy went to the Coopers.'

Lydia's stomach knotted. 'Why do you say that, Ella?'

'Because he'd have called home by now to make sure I was okay.'

'He's probably just not there yet.' *Careful*. What was she going to tell Ella in an hour from now?

'I think he's gone to see the FBI.'

'Do you?' Lydia's surprise was genuine. 'Why would you think that?'

'Because he knew I didn't want to go to Maggy's, but he told me I should, and I knew that wasn't right because he doesn't really like me being away from him right now, except when I'm with Kim and Tom.'

'But your daddy knows Maggy and her family, doesn't he?'

'That's different,' Ella said. She looked into Lydia's face with one of those searching looks of hers. 'I thought, at first, it was because he wanted to be alone with you, but then he wouldn't have gone out, would he?'

Lydia smiled. 'Maybe you should be a detective when you grow up.'

'Maybe.' Ella paused. 'Daddy used to be a policeman, you know.'

'Yes, I do,' Lydia said. 'And then he was an investigator.'

'A general investigator for the State Attorney,' Ella expanded proudly. 'But he likes teaching better. I don't know why. I think being a detective's much cooler.'

'I don't know,' Lydia said. 'I think being a university professor's pretty cool.'

'Do you?'

'Yes.'

There was that look again, longer this time.

'Do you love my daddy?'

Lydia took just a moment.

'Yes, Ella, I do.' She paused. 'Do you mind that, do you think?'

270

'I'm not sure.' Ella's head tilted to one side. 'I don't *think* so.'

'That's good,' Lydia said.

'Lydia—' The child hesitated. 'Is it okay if I call you that?'

'It's fine.'

'Do you think Daddy's all right?'

A time to lie, at least a little.

'I'm sure he is, Ella.'

Chapter 81

Okay . . . *okay* . . .

Getting ready for them. For *him*.

The *father*.

On his way again, to mess with things he didn't understand.

Mess with *him*.

He was getting angry now, he had to admit that. He'd been so cool with the kids, with everyone else, managing to hold it together even though the nights had been getting worse and worse; but still he had stayed cool for the most part, hadn't he? *Hadn't* he? But now he was starting to get really mad.

His plans were being spoiled. His latest dupe-dope had already been released, and it wasn't *fair* – he'd planned that so well, had found a child-rapist nuts about all computer games except *Limbo*, which had made it even better because that in itself was deserving of some punishment . . .

But they'd let him go so damned quickly, which meant that time was running out faster than ever – and there'd been little enough before.

He had responsibilities, after all. To take care of the kids, feed them – oh God, oh *God*, how long was it since he'd last fed them? He couldn't remember, was losing track, starting to lose his sharpness, getting confused . . .

Except about one thing.

He was angry now.

And he was ready for them.

For *him*.

Chapter 82

According to the architectural plans, Fitzgerald's house had a substantial cellar beneath it. Fitzgerald, the only one of the three Eryx partners with a known arrest to his name – and an ugly one at that. Fitzgerald, whose pregnant wife had died in an accident that just *might* not have been as accidental as they'd thought.

William Fitzgerald, work-obsessed, Olympics-crazy, highly protective of his privacy – as had been proven when Lydia had been picked up for doing little more than ringing his front door bell.

She had told me, on the drive back to New Haven last Saturday (how could that be just last Saturday? How could what felt like a lifetime in purgatory be just a matter of days?) that the Fitzgerald place had hardly seemed to merit being referred to as an estate. She'd described it as attractive, a family-style house, though Baum had previously told us that Fitzgerald had bought the place *after* the death of his wife.

A house with a big cellar.

Nearly there now.

Chapter 83

Rianna and Robbie were still in the dark.

Nothing had happened for what seemed a very long time. No games or exercises. No light. No food, either.

If they hadn't had one another to talk to, be close to . . .

'Maybe,' Rianna said tentatively, trying to keep the tremor out of her voice, 'he's never coming back. Maybe he's leaving us to starve to death.'

There. She'd said it. God knew she'd thought it at least a hundred times already, but she hadn't said it out loud until now.

'Of course he's coming back,' Robbie said.

'Maybe he's dead.' Might as well express them all now she'd started, all her fears – at least those she'd dared face up to even in the privacy of her own mind.

'Why should he be dead?' Robbie sounded a lot more logical than he felt.

'He could be. People die.' Equally logical. 'He could have had a heart attack or been run over in the street, or maybe he's had a stroke and can't speak.' She paused. 'At least there's water in the basin for us to drink.'

'He isn't dead.' Robbie was very firm. 'It probably hasn't been anywhere near as long as it seems to you. He's stayed away for longer than this before.' Not true, as a matter of fact, but she didn't have to know that. 'He's always come back before, and he will now.'

Rianna's thoughts turned a corner. 'Maybe he's been

arrested? Maybe they're questioning him right now, making him tell them where we are?'

'In that case,' Robbie said, 'it won't be *him* who comes back, it'll be the FBI.'

'Or maybe he won't tell them,' Rianna said.

Chapter 84

We'd arrived at Fitzgerald's place. I stopped the Cherokee not far from the gateway, could see the start of the long, tree-lined driveway leading to the house.

'Yellow birches,' Baum said unexpectedly.

'How can you tell in the dark?'

'I like trees,' the PI said simply. 'I guess I recognize shapes.' He craned his head, peered further. 'Oaks closer to the house, giant hemlocks, too.' He paused. 'Lot of them in Devils Hopyard.'

I glanced at him. 'You looked this up.'

'Uh-huh.' Baum grinned. 'But I do like trees.'

The moment of lightness, of normality, passed.

Grimness in its place.

'I'm going to do this alone,' I said, suddenly, decisively. 'I've been thinking about it along the way, and I don't want you risking your licence.'

'Forget it,' Baum said.

'I'm not going to argue about this.'

'No argument.' My good-natured friend was resolute. 'Like you said yourself when you were asking me to come along, you're just a five-minute cop, and *that* was a good while back.'

'You're not exactly Bruce Willis,' I pointed out.

'Maybe not, but I've learned a thing or two about locks and alarm systems.'

He had me there.

Though it implied we might be on the brink of breaking and entering.

First time for everything.

'Pull right off the road, Jake.'

I steered the Cherokee as close as I could to the bank of earth at the side of the road, leaving room for Baum to get out and back in. I'd already turned out the headlights and adjusted the interior light so it wouldn't come on when the doors opened.

'We should wait a few more minutes,' Baum said. 'Even on the public highway there could be cameras picking us up.'

I glanced around, saw nothing, knew that didn't mean much. 'They can't arrest us for sitting in our car out here.'

'You never heard of loitering, Jake?'

'I'm not interested in loitering tonight, Norman.' I was already itching to go. 'Taking a real good look around and finding a way into Fitzgerald's cellar, *that's* what I'm interested in.'

Baum laid his left hand briefly on my arm. 'Take it easy. The more we rush, the more likely we'll screw up.' He paused. 'This is probably just our first call tonight, remember?'

'Which is why we should make a start.' My door opened quietly. 'Coming?'

Baum's door opened with the faintest of creaks. 'Don't close your door,' he warned me, 'just lean it to.'

We left the vehicle, walked towards the gateway.

'Hold on,' Baum murmured. 'Why's the gate open?'

'Lydia said it was open when she came. Maybe it's never shut.'

We both looked at the big gate over to our right. I slid the flashlight – smallest I'd been able to find in the apartment – out of the pocket of my sports jacket. I'd have worn the dark blue tracksuit I have in my wardrobe, but I never wear clothes like that and it occurred to me that Lydia might have found it strange attire for me to choose to visit the Coopers.

The gate looked a little askew, one corner jammed down in the dirt.

'Okay,' I said. Baum nodded.

We moved through the gateway and veered off to the left so we could stay under cover of the trees for as long as possible.

A dog began to bark.

'Shit,' Baum said. 'Lydia didn't mention dogs, did she?'

I shook my head. 'Might have got one since.'

The barking was the kind of sound, I realized, that all but the most hellbent of housebreakers would probably turn away from. Deep and pretty loud – though it did seem to be coming from *inside* the house, not out on the land, which was something, I guessed. I started forward.

'Hold on.' Baum put a hand on my arm, halted me. 'You know what I said about liking trees?' His voice was low but clear. 'If you could see my face properly right now, Jake, you'd know there's one thing in this world I'm really scared of – I mean, *really* scared, you know?'

'Shit,' I said.

'*Especially* big guard dogs.'

The barking *was* weighty sounding.

'And that sounds like one *big* sucker,' Baum said. 'Maybe more than one.'

We stayed motionless for a few more minutes, waiting and watching.

'With that noise,' I said, 'alarm or no alarm, if anyone's home, and *if* they're law-abiding, sane citizens, they're bound to come out and take a look.'

'Or call the cops,' Baum added.

We went on waiting.

No cops.

No one coming out of the house.

'Maybe no one's home.' I knew that might be wishful thinking, but Rianna was uppermost in my mind, and though I'd never been particularly brave or foolhardy, if there was even a chance my daughter was in the cellar of that house, no dogs or alarms or even Fitzgerald himself with a goddamned *shotgun* was going to stop me doing my absolute one hundred per cent damnedest to find out.

'You'll have to stay put,' I told Baum softly.

'No way, Jake.'

'Shut up for one minute and listen to me.'

Baum shut up. The dog – or dogs – did not.

'I'm going to need back-up,' I said. 'Like you said, we don't want to screw up this early in the night, so I'm going to head towards the house on my own, and you're going to stay here, be my look-out *and* back-up. Okay?'

'I don't know about this.'

'I *do* know,' I told him. 'My little girl could be in there, and *I* don't have a problem with dogs—'

'If Fitzgerald lets them loose, you'll have a problem,' Baum said.

'If that happens, I'll run.' I gripped his arm for a moment. 'We'll *both* run like hell, okay? *Okay*, Norman?'

The dogs won. 'You're the boss,' Baum said.

'No,' I said. 'I'm just the father.'

'If something happens, I'll—'

'If something happens to me,' I interrupted, 'you have to go get help, call the cops, okay? *Okay*?'

'Okay.' Baum paused. 'Just do me one favour, though, will you?'

'Name it.'

'Don't *let* anything happen.'

'I'll do my best.'

I began to move away, heard him take a couple of steps back into the trees. I didn't need the flashlight now my eyes had grown accustomed to the darkness.

On your own now, Professor.

Baum watched Jake move away, shifted a little, felt something touch his back, and froze.

It was a tree trunk, just a damned tree trunk.

Settle down, Norman, he told himself, *do your job*.

Easier said.

Jake was disappearing fast into the darkness.

Baum remembered his hip flask.

He wasn't a big drinker, but he always brought a little

279

something on night-time stake-outs. He'd brought a bigger flask of coffee, too, of course, but he'd left that in the Cherokee.

And a nip of whiskey was just what he needed right now . . .

Jake was out of sight.

Baum felt for the small hip flask, found it, unscrewed the top, took a swallow.

Good stuff.

He started to screw the top back on when he heard the sound behind him.

Shuffling.

He began to turn too late, felt the arm grab him from behind, a hand clamping over his mouth, an arm snaking around his throat, choking off his windpipe.

Pressure on his neck, at the side.

Pain.

And then he was gone.

The barking was getting louder, fiercer, but no one seemed to be paying the dogs any heed, and I'd come too far to back out now. If Rianna and Robbie and Michael weren't here, and if I got caught, I was absolutely willing to take the consequences, go to jail, whatever . . .

So long as I found Rianna first.

Please let me find my little girl before they lock me up, and then I won't care about anything else . . .

Something moved.

Behind me.

I began to spin around.

Too slow.

I felt the blow to my temple.

Nothing more.

FIVE

FIVE

Chapter 85

Ella was finally in bed and – last time Lydia had checked – sound asleep.

The apartment was silent now, wretchedly so.

She wandered into the kitchen, thinking she might make some tea, then, not really wanting it, she wandered back out into the hall – and found herself entering Rianna's bedroom.

So normal it was painful.

Lydia was about to turn away when the game caught her eye. The box was tucked in with a bunch of CDs on a shelf, yet it might as well have been flashing neon at her. *Limbo*. Probably the copy Jake had asked Kim to buy in case it yielded anything useful. It hadn't helped him one bit, but maybe . . .

She found Rianna's PlayStation, was debating how to turn it on—

'Need some help?'

Lydia turned around, saw right away that Ella was wide awake and that there was absolutely no point sending her back to bed. She was less certain, though, about letting her play the game.

'It's okay.' Ella read her doubts. 'Daddy lets me play.'

'Does he?'

'Don't you believe me?' A clear-eyed challenge.

'Why wouldn't I?'

Ella didn't answer that one, but Lydia let her take over, set things up, knew it was probably just as well, because she could recall almost nothing about the lesson she and Jake had sat through at Eryx – besides which, that equipment had seemed quite different.

'Actually,' Ella confessed a few moments later as they sat side by side at Rianna's desk, Lydia in the chair, Ella on a stool, 'Daddy doesn't let me play this kind of game.'

'Does he not?' Lydia said without reproach.

Ella shook her head. 'I learned at a friend's house.'

'Maggy's?' Lydia asked.

The girl didn't answer that either, clearly above snitching.

'Rianna never does stuff like that,' Ella said after another moment. 'Like cheating on Daddy's rules.'

'Oh, I don't know,' Lydia said lightly. 'She's probably broken a few.'

'Rianna's a much better person than I am.'

'I'm sure you're a very good person too.' Lydia wondered where this was heading, could see a clear glint of misery behind the bravado.

'I get so *mad* about things sometimes,' Ella said. 'I upset people, even Daddy.' She paused. 'Rianna, too.'

Guilt again, Lydia thought. Damnable guilt. Even in a child.

'Everyone does that, Ella.' *Handle with care*.

'But you shouldn't make people you love unhappy, should you?'

'Not deliberately,' Lydia told her. 'Not at all, if you can help it.'

'That's the thing,' Ella said. 'I can't always seem to help it.'

'Me neither.'

'Really?' The eyes were checking for untruths.

'Absolutely,' Lydia said.

Ella turned back to the machine. 'Want me to show you how to play?'

'I don't think so,' Lydia said, 'but thank you.'

'Is it because I told you Daddy doesn't let me?'

'I suppose so. It doesn't seem quite right for us to play just because he's out.'

'Okay.' Ella gave way easily.

'Could I ask you a couple of questions, though, about the game?'

'Sure.' Ella switched off the PlayStation and moved across to sit on Rianna's bed. 'What kind of questions?'

Lydia swivelled around in the chair to face her. 'Some people tried to teach me about *Limbo* a while back, but I guess I wasn't paying as much attention as I should have been because I can't seem to remember much about it.'

Ella grinned. 'Like me at school.'

Lydia smiled back at her. 'Remind me what Steel and Dakota are trying to do. Just survive?'

'They're trying to get out,' Ella said.

'But if New York City's been destroyed, what's the point of that?' Lydia wasn't sure if Jake would approve of this either, talking about the destruction of a major city practically next door, but since the child knew all about the game already, she couldn't see *too* much harm.

'The point,' Ella answered, 'is there's a helicopter waiting for them.'

'I didn't know that.' She did remember it, vaguely.

'Sure.' Ella was in her element now. 'The last chopper in the city – like Dakota and Steel are the last two teenagers, you know? Only it's in a booby-trapped helipad.'

'And where's the helipad?'

'On top of 34th Street Station,' Ella said with exaggerated patience. 'But there's no way out of the station because all the exits were wiped out when the city was nuked, so everything's sealed up, and there aren't any tanks or machines for Steel and Dakota to use.'

'Okay.' So much for nine-year-old sensibilities. 'So in a way, all the adventures they face are really stepping stones to get them out? So every time they get past one problem, there's another, until they reach 34th Street. Is that about right?'

'I guess.'

'Have you ever got that far?'

'No way, but I know some kids who have.'

'And have any of them ever reached the helicopter?'

285

'No *way*,' Ella said again.

'But if they did' – Lydia was remembering the lesson at Eryx now – 'then they'd be *Limbo* masters, wouldn't they?'

'I guess,' Ella said again.

The child was too hyper to go to bed, but after some warm milk Lydia managed to persuade Ella to let her tuck her up under a blanket on the sofa with a cartoon channel for company. Now, finally, she did seem to be dozing off again, freeing Lydia to go into Jake's study to browse through his bookshelves.

Not that she knew exactly what she was looking for. All she did know was that a new and awful idea was taking shape in her mind – though no more appalling than most that had come and gone since Robbie had been taken.

Not here. Why would it be?

'There are more books in the living room.'

Still not asleep.

'Ella, honey, you really do need to get some rest.'

'I'm okay,' she said. 'If you want to look something up, why don't you try on the Net?' *Millennium child*. 'You could use Daddy's PC – he wouldn't mind.'

'Good idea.'

Ella, of course, wanted to switch it on for her, show off a little with talk about booting up and logging on and search engines. Here at least Lydia knew enough to get by on her own, but she also knew that helping a grown-up might make the disturbed youngster feel a little better.

'Thank you, Ella,' she said, after a while. 'I think I can take it from here, and you really have to go to bed.'

'I will, in a minute,' Ella said. 'What are you searching for, Lydia?'

Lydia hesitated. 'I guess our conversation got me interested in finding out a little more about the New York subway system,' she said carefully. 'Maybe transport systems in general.' Surely dull enough sounding, she figured, to send any child fleeing to bed.

'Log onto *Ask Jeeves*,' Ella suggested, and showed her how

to pull it down from her father's list of favourite sites. 'Now type it in. Just *New York Subway System* – that's right. And wait.'

'Won't you please go to bed, Ella.'

'In a minute,' she said again.

'Your father will be mad at me if he finds out I had you helping me all night.'

'There.' Ella pointed to the screen. 'Now you choose from those, or ask another question.'

Lydia looked at the choices, could scarcely believe her eyes.

Third option down was *exactly* what she'd been looking for.

Where can I find abandoned subway stations in New York City?

She clicked on the *Ask* icon.

Seventeen pages worth. Swiftly, she scanned through – nothing, so far as she could tell, relating to 34th Street . . .

'Is that where you think Rianna is?'

Lydia froze, then turned and saw Ella's scared eyes, and realized with a flood of shame how selfish, how unpardonably *careless* she had been.

'No, sweetheart,' she said, 'of course I don't think that.'

Quickly, she turned back to the computer, logged off, switched off.

'I hate subways,' Ella said, and shivered.

Lydia got up and put out her hand. Ella took it.

'You're cold,' Lydia said, and guided her out of Jake's study.

You've done the damage, now deal with it.

'I don't think Rianna's anywhere like that,' she told Ella, leading her towards her bedroom. 'It's just that silly game making me think about the real subway.' She paused. 'That's all *Limbo* is, you do know that, don't you, Ella? A really dumb game, which is exactly why your daddy doesn't want you playing it.'

Ella's door was open, the light out. Lydia turned on the bedside light, a big rose pink balloon bulb that filled the room with soft light.

'I need to use the bathroom,' Ella said.

'Okay. I'll wait here.'

She was steeling herself for Ella's next question, but when she came back and got into bed, there *were* no more questions, and that seemed almost worse to Lydia, indicating that the child knew how terrible this situation was; too terrible to dare voice real fears.

'How sleepy are you, sweetheart?'

'Not very.'

'How about a story? Or are you too old?'

Ella shrugged. 'I guess not.'

Lydia went across to her bookshelves, saw two Harry Potters, decided against them, then picked out *Charlotte's Web* and walked over to the bed. 'How about this? I know you probably read it a long time ago.' She willed the child to agree.

'Okay.' Ella lay back against her pillow. 'Good old Wilbur.'

Lydia offered up swift, silent thanks, sat on the edge of the bed and began to read the tale of a pig in peril and the spider who saved him. She hadn't read aloud since Robbie's childhood, and she was pretty sure that this young girl hadn't had or needed story-reading at bedtime for a long time either.

'Will you stay till I fall asleep, please?' Ella's voice interrupted just once.

'Definitely,' Lydia said.

The peace, when it came at last, brought tears to her eyes.

She waited a little longer, wanting to be certain this time, then stood up, dimmed the light to a faint glow, and left the room.

And went to the guest room.

There was one question she hadn't liked to ask Ella, had almost been afraid to ask, and that was whether Rianna shared her fear of subways.

Robbie had always liked the New York subway, had never had any problems with tunnels or enclosed spaces or darkness.

Lydia hoped – as she had so many times since Jake's daughter had been taken – that wherever their children were, they were together.

Chapter 86

I came to, flailing like a drowning man, my recall fogged but terrifyingly instant.

Someone behind me. A hand coming at me, that hammer blow to my temple, searing, blinding . . . then nothing, until . . . *until* . . . A half-remembered moment of waking to pain, nausea, trying to see, to talk, then more pain, but different, slower, sending me down again into thick, sickening darkness . . .

Until now.

Something around my head, over my eyes. *Blindfold*? I reached up to pull it off, but my hands were thickly gloved . . .

Can't see. Oh Jesus.

I tried getting up, but my legs were weak.

'Hey.' My voice was weak, too. 'Hey!' What had I done? How in hell was I going to help Rianna now?

Get the gloves off.

I put my right hand up to my mouth, used my teeth to try dragging the glove off, but it was fastened too securely over my wrist. I lost patience, put both hands up to my head, tried to pull at the *thing* . . .

The sudden blue light made me jump with shock, made me slam my hands back down on the ground to keep me from toppling over. I blinked, trying to clear my vision, but the light was coming through the things – *glasses? goggles?* – over my eyes, and, oh God, this was so *freaky* . . .

Get them off!

I ripped at them, hard as I could.

'Leave them.'

A voice, male, out of nowhere. *Him.*

'Don't touch anything till I tell you to, Professor.'

I waited a second, then started yanking at the damned thing again.

'Don't you want to see her again, Professor?'

My hands fell back down, trembling fists.

'Are you going to behave?'

Rage took away my power of speech, while some inner resource told me to stay as calm as I could and listen carefully to the voice, see if I could identify it, but it was too distorted. *Fitzgerald*? One of the others?

'I asked if you're going to behave, Professor?'

I took a breath, brought myself under some kind of control. 'Yes.'

Sonofabitch-dirt-bag, I said in my mind. So long as I didn't say it out loud, the shit-bag couldn't read my fucking *mind*.

The blue light went out.

Fade to black.

'*Hey!*' I yelled, couldn't help myself, wanted to *scream*, not just yell.

And then, suddenly, there they were.

There *she* was.

Thank God, thank God, thank God.

'Rianna!'

She didn't answer, didn't hear me, didn't see me, maybe *couldn't* see me. There was something covering her eyes, ears, half her face. My hands reached up quickly to my own face, identifying what I now saw on hers – goggles, headphones, all one piece, fastened at the back of my head.

Covering Rianna's beautiful eyes. *Oh Christ.*

'Rianna, it's Daddy!' I yelled.

Nothing.

Rage consumed me utterly. She was wearing a tunic made of leather, cut real short, exposing her arms and long legs, and her feet were bare. Like the girl in the game.

Like Dakota.

I felt suddenly violently sick, but forced myself to focus on the young man sitting beside my daughter, close to her, almost huddled up.

Robbie. Face only half visible, but Robbie.

Together and *alive*, thank Christ, that was the main thing.

I wished I could have told Lydia that much.

Get them both home, Jake. That's the only thing that counts now.

The only thing.

Chapter 87

It was starting again.

Rianna and Robbie both saw it, heard it, simultaneously.

The sewer again.

'No,' Rianna whispered.

Her skin began to crawl; she wanted to climb *inside* herself, run away, make herself invisible, go to sleep, *escape*. She'd disliked the sewer games since the first time she'd seen Shannon and another kid at school playing them, had *hated* the rats and the disgusting gunk that flowed around Dakota's ankles when she was down there. She could almost feel that now, slushing over her bare feet . . .

Just a game, Ree. Shannon had said that – oh God, she missed her friend so much, was so scared she'd never see her again.

'It's okay,' Robbie told her now, softly, then, hearing something, he clutched involuntarily at her arm.

It was going to be the rats again, goddamned hateful bastard *rats*.

He waited for the squealing, the screeching.

'It's okay,' he said again, lying. 'We know we'll be okay.'

'I know,' Rianna said, lying too.

'We just need to remember none of it's real, okay?' His voice was shaking. *Jesus, man, stop it.* 'None of this is *real*.'

Not rats.

Something new.

Oh *God*!

A smell. A *real* smell.

'What *is* that?' Rianna asked, then covered her nose and mouth with one hand.

Robbie did the same. The stench was awful, the absolute worst, and how the hell could that be, if it was all VR, all pretend?

'Oh my God, Robbie, *listen.*'

They both scrambled to their feet, holding hands tightly.

The sound was growing louder.

Water.

Rushing water.

They both stared till their eyes burned, stared through their goggles, waiting for it, staring through the dark sewer tunnel, and oh, dear God, it was coming, *really* coming, and if it weren't real there wouldn't be that *stink*, would there? And it was getting louder, roaring . . .

A wave, a great big tidal wave of sewage . . .

Rianna screamed.

Robbie put both his arms around her, clasped her tightly to him.

'Close your eyes,' he yelled over the noise. 'Hold on tight and close your eyes!' He did the same, blotting it out. 'It's not real, remember!'

Not real.

I know terror when I see it.

I was seeing it now, in my own beloved child . . .

She stood locked in a kind of petrified embrace with Robbie Johanssen, her open mouth almost certainly screaming at some unseen horror – unseen by *me*, at least. But while I might not be able to see what was terrifying Rianna and Robbie, whatever they were seeing through those terrible goggles, I was feeling it along with them, and it was almost enough to unhinge me – more than enough to make me want to *kill* the man behind the voice. Thank God, at least, for Robbie, for Lydia's son, hideously scared too, that was plain enough, but doing his best to protect Rianna; shielding her, it seemed, from something

293

very real to them, something only *I* couldn't see – and Robbie's arms were wrapped so tight around my little girl, and I'd never felt such intense gratitude to anyone in my whole life . . .

It went black again.

They *disappeared*.

'No!' I yelled, outraged, terrified again, desperate. 'No, you *bastard*!'

'Wasn't that wonderful?'

The voice again.

'Did you see them, Professor?' The words came breathlessly, tight with something, *something*.

Enthrallment.

I felt so damned sick I could hardly breathe, let alone speak.

'Don't they make a *perfect* couple?'

Chapter 88

He had enjoyed that.

So much.

Not quite the way he'd planned, the way it would have been if it had just been the three of them. Steel, Dakota and *him*. But immensely exciting all the same.

Fun, too.

He'd been watching on two monitors: kids on one, father on the other. His fear, the *father's* fear, had been the fun part, but it hadn't been a turn-on. A different kind of entertainment.

Inspirational enough to have brought him back, just for a short while, to the game, the new version, *his* version; it had brought with it a new twist, and maybe, if there was time, he would get around to writing that in. He'd begun to think there wouldn't be time even to get his game written, let alone drawn or created – robbing him of time was one of the reasons he'd been getting so angry at the professor. But now, mad as he still was, maybe he *would* manage to get the game down, even in rough form, just enough for someone to see, later, after he'd gone, to see how brilliant he had been . . .

And maybe having the professor here might buy him a little extra time. After all, no one knew where Woods was, any more than they knew where Steel or Dakota were.

He wondered, for a few moments, about the other man. Baum.

He'd hit him pretty hard. Maybe hard enough to kill, though he doubted it. It hadn't *felt* like killing, hadn't made him sick to his stomach, hadn't made him scream, so maybe the guy had woken up again. But even if he had, it wouldn't make any difference, not for a while, at least, because Baum hadn't seen him, had he?

Even if someone found him, he hadn't *seen* anything.

Which meant he did have just a little more time.

Chapter 89

Kim came in the morning, got Ella occupied as swiftly and completely as she could, and Lydia could see how great she was with the child, why Jake had come to depend on her so much.

He hadn't called.

'He did call,' Lydia had lied to Ella first thing. 'Very late last night.'

'No he didn't,' Ella had said. 'I'd have heard the phone.'

'It was a while after you finally went to sleep.' *White lies*. 'I picked up the phone very quickly so you wouldn't wake up.'

'But I wanted to talk to him.'

'I know, but you'd been up so late, and your daddy said I should let you sleep and tell you this morning that he won't be able to call till much later, but that he loves you very much.'

She had been prepared to swear to that, cross her heart and hope to die, but Ella had set about eating her breakfast, and Lydia had been unsure if she'd really bought it or just pretended to, either for Lydia's sake or, in some self-protective way, for her own.

But Jake had *not* called, neither during the night nor this morning.

And Kim had just gone out with Ella to do some shopping.

Enough.

Lydia found the Coopers' phone number in an address book in Jake's study, sat down at his desk and made the call.

Stu Cooper lied for about a minute and a half, then caved in.

Lydia's next call was to Thea Lomax.

'I know Jake never went to the Coopers.' *Begin as you mean to go on.* 'And I'm actually hoping you were lying to me too when you said that Norman had the night off. I'm *hoping* that wherever Jake went, Norman went with him.' She paused. 'Please tell me the truth this time, Thea.'

Lomax barely hesitated. 'They did go together.'

'Where?'

'I don't know.' The PI paused. 'That's the truth. I only talked with Norman briefly before they went, and all he said was that Jake wanted to continue what you'd started before Rianna was taken.'

Lydia's stomach knotted tightly. 'And you've heard nothing since?'

'Not yet.' Lomax accelerated before Lydia could say anything. 'I *strongly* recommend that you stay put, Lydia. Believe me, if I knew exactly where they'd gone, I'd be on my way right now and glad for you to come along. But frankly, without a shred of proof that they went anyplace near Eryx, if we try bulldozing our way into either the offices or any of their homes, we'll do more harm than good.'

'Shouldn't we tell the FBI they're missing?'

'Two grown men out for one night doesn't constitute missing, Lydia. Besides which, we'd just piss Kline off.'

The subway idea was still on Lydia's mind, had been festering all night, so she told Thea about it, expecting the PI to tell her it was a crazy notion.

'No crazier than most,' Lomax said. 'Call Kline's office, put it to them.'

'You think I should?' Lydia was startled. 'Don't humour me, Thea.'

'I don't do humouring,' Lomax said.

Kline wasn't there, but Angela Moran took Lydia's call.

'As a matter of fact, Mrs Johanssen,' the agent told her, 'we came up with the subway hypothesis very early on, but ruled it out.'

'Why?'

'Many reasons,' Moran said gently. 'Just one of them being that Manhattan's underside is like a rabbit warren – though that wouldn't have kept us from following up on the idea if it had been the right one.'

'You're certain it wasn't?' Lydia asked quietly.

'So far as I know,' Moran said.

Lydia put down the phone.

Lomax had said last night that the Coopers were nearing the end of their rope.

She had a feeling she was fast getting there herself.

Chapter 90

Nights were proving better in this place than at home for *him*. No tossing and turning and fretting about hell and damnation and *truths*. Night and day, day and night, all one, and up to him if the light stayed on or went out.

This night, he'd been working on the game.

The new twist. The father. The new character. Dakota's dad, believed lost in the apocalypse above, but who'd survived, after all, and come down into the bowels of the city to find his little girl. And once Dakota knew he was here, she was going to want to find him, be with him, but nothing, of course, could be *that* easy, could it?

He'd always meant the game to have the usual ingredients. Violence, horrors and other dangers, the *usual* . . . It was the relationship between the kids that he'd intended to be different. In the first two psychologically one-dimensional *Limbo* games, Steel would save Dakota, then she'd save him, the ultimate target for them both to escape. Love, of course, of a kind – another ingredient – for how could those two beautiful young people *not* fall in love? But no sex, and Lord knew he approved of that, didn't he? Knew all about sins of the flesh and hell.

Love went hand in hand with other things, too, in the real world.

Like *abuse* of love, for instance.

He knew all about that, if anyone did. The cold, cruel side of love. That was why he'd planned to teach Dakota and Steel –

his kids – how to fight properly, and he wasn't just talking the Tae Kwon Do stuff that Dakota had used against the tasteless Ghoulo. He was talking about *Dim Mak* – the art he'd learned so well from his master, the small, slender teacher who'd shown him what really mattered.

How not to be afraid any more.

Too late to help with Father, of course.

But not for *his* children.

He'd planned to teach them many important things. That love never lasted, for instance; that people either died or abused you or just went away.

Most important, though, the end to fear. Through *Dim Mak*. Death touch, the basis of so many martial arts. Dangerous. Lethal. Exciting beyond belief.

He knew how afraid they were, and, God help his immortal evil soul, that excited him almost as much as their beauty and the knowledge that they were *his*. But he truly had intended, if he'd been granted the time, to put an end to their fear.

Bullcrap.

Truth, that evil worm, wriggled back into his head.

He could *choose* to think the game was about helping them, about teaching them strength and the end of fear, but really it was still *sex* he was thinking about, the way it had always been, because he was a filthy, perverted, murdering *thing-monster*, the only kind of person who'd think up a game like this . . .

All the professor's fault.

That shoved at the worm, sent it on its wriggling way, cleared his mind.

He blamed him – the *father* – for everything. He'd taken the man's child, and surely that ought to have been enough of a warning. But the professor couldn't stay out, could he? He and the woman.

Lovers, probably, by now.

Even while their children were missing, in danger.

Forni-fuckin'-cation (to paraphrase that old Bobby Darin song), that's the name of the game.

301

Except for him.
Except for *him*.
All he'd asked for was a little more time.
But that had been too much, hadn't it?

302

Chapter 91

So *dark*.

I'd ripped the damned goggles and earphones off some time back, and the gloves, but the uncompromising black silence had pushed me into a series of panic surges, pitching up to something huge enough on the Richter panic scale to pulp New Haven. So I'd put all the stuff back on again, because what counted down here was seeing Rianna and Robbie, and it seemed that wearing these was, for the moment, the only way I was going to be able to do that.

Nothing.

I yelled for a while, for the bastard, for the kids, told Rianna, just in case she could hear me, that I was here now.

'I'm *here*, baby,' I'd shouted as loud as I could, 'so it's just a matter of time till I get you and Robbie out of here. And everyone's fine – your mother's okay, Robbie, and Ella's great, sweetheart, and all they want is to have you both back home where you belong. And it's going to *happen*.'

Nothing.

Was this it? Was this *all*? Did we die now? Was that the plan?

Of course it's not all. Of course we don't die now.

This was some kind of a game, after all. To *him*. To the abductor.

Games had endings. *Limbo* had an ending, so far as I remembered from that lesson at Eryx. Something about escaping in a chopper . . .

I recalled that session, our two young teachers, the guy with the apple cheeks. Lars. A Scandinavian name, though he hadn't looked my idea of Scandinavian, whatever that was . . .

Could Lars be the one? That possibility had never occurred to me. He'd been so youthful, so enthusiastic about the game, about his work. Not a sicko type. Whatever *that* was.

Kaminski. The one whose role at Eryx we'd never worked out.

Doesn't matter now.

Now that he had *me*.

Only one thing mattered now.

Focus on escape.

Rianna had cried for a while, and then she'd felt ashamed because Robbie, who'd been through so much more, had been so kind, so supportive.

'Don't you ever feel like doing that?' she'd asked him afterwards.

'Sure I do,' Robbie had told her, 'but I felt like that a whole lot more often before you got here.' He'd paused. 'You okay now?'

'Better,' Rianna had said.

Still no food or drink.

Yet *he'd* been there, they knew that.

Unless he worked the game by remote.

That was a possibility.

One they didn't choose to dwell on for too long.

For the usual reasons.

Chapter 92

Kim and Ella had come back from shopping not long after Lydia had finished speaking to Moran, and Kim had taken a swift look at her face and asked if it would be okay for Ella to spend the rest of the day with her and Tom, who had a free day and was longing to see *A Bug's Life*.

'I saw that already,' Ella had told her grouchily. 'You know I did.'

'I know,' Kim had said breezily. 'But you did say you wanted to see it again, and Tom really wants to see it with you.'

Ella had looked at Lydia then, had clearly seen a woman she'd sooner *not* spend the day with when there was a great movie to be seen, albeit for the second time, and said okay, she didn't mind doing Tom a favour.

God bless Kim Ryan.

She'd waited for them to leave, having quietly ascertained that Kim could stay with Ella later if, by chance, neither she nor Jake had come home, and then Lydia had taken a cab to the train station and caught a train back to New York City.

And now here she was, having walked from Penn Station to 34th Street, having taken the subway steps down at Herald Square, right at the corner of Macy's.

And here was that *feeling* again. The one she'd experienced in Korda's office – that cold sense of malevolence. And the weather this afternoon was really warm; even down here at the

305

foot of the steps, she could see from other people's flushed faces that the cold was in her mind, no place else.

Imagination.

She wasn't quite sure she believed that, though.

She bought a token and went further down, into the depths.

Hopeless was the word that came to mind.

What on earth was she doing here, wandering around aimlessly amongst all these people – there were always crowds of people, she guessed, at 34th Street – gazing at the different signs, suddenly seeming impossibly complicated: **Local/Express/ Shuttle/Nassau St Local** . . .? So many lines and tunnels, *open*, functioning tunnels, let alone defunct ones leading nowhere, those in which a monster might be hiding six missing teenagers . . .

A maze. A labyrinth.

Agent Moran had been right.

She climbed back up to the surface, to the hectic street, terribly weary now, yet still oppressed by that awful, ugly feeling. She stood, half leaning against one of Macy's windows, for a few moments, tried to pull herself together, remembering her conversation with Ella last night. She looked around Herald Square, jammed as usual with vehicles and pedestrians, shoppers flowing in and out of the department store, in and out of the station – and wondered where the creators of *Limbo* had thought they could stash a helicopter here.

After the apocalypse, there wouldn't be any cars or people.

Plenty of space then, assuming you were a 'master' and managed to get out of wherever the hell you were.

Ludicrous, wicked, *stupid* game.

Ludicrous woman for taking that maniac's note seriously and looking at the game for help. Though Jake had tried that too, hadn't he, and according to Angela Moran, even some of the sharpest minds at the FBI had made their own infinitely more sophisticated attempts at penetrating *Limbo* for answers – and had come up empty. People who *knew* about such things, unlike her.

A frantic, desperate mother.

The feeling was still there.

Lydia moved away from the store window and peered back down the steps that led to the subway, saw the people moving up and down, all going somewhere normal, she thought jealously, home to families or back to work or nowhere in particular, but safe and sound.

Not losing their minds.

Robbie, where are *you?*

Chapter 93

He was getting more frustrated by the minute. He couldn't concentrate on his work. He really wanted to do this, *needed* to do it, but he just could not seem to get to grips with this latest version. There were just too many pressures on him. People just couldn't begin to imagine the burden of commitment on a man – *kidnapper* – who wanted to, *really* wanted to take good care of his captives.

The young ones, anyway.

It was, he realized now, an aspect of his plan that he hadn't paid enough attention to in advance. *Before* he became a kidnapper.

Don't use that word, I don't like it!

Kidnapper. Pervert.

Stop it.

Killer. Multiple killer.

That wasn't my fault.

Sure it was. You liked it.

I hated it. It made me sick to my stomach.

You always were a coward.

Shut up!

Thing-monster.

Shut the fuck up!

He couldn't concentrate. How could anyone concentrate with all that going on in his head?

All the professor's fault.

If you say so.
I do say so.
Sure you do, sonny.
Don't call me that!
What else should a father call his son, sonny?

The worm in his head was growing bigger. He could feel it, taking over, hardly wriggling any more, just swelling and swelling, fat with worm-children, and soon, if he didn't do something, if he didn't find a way to stop it, it would burst and his brain would be jammed with them, hundreds of them, worm rush hour . . .

Stop!
He screamed, just once. He had to.
No one could hear.
That stopped the fucking worm, at least for a moment.
He looked at the monitors.
Steel and Dakota were huddled together again.
Look at them. Clinging together like primitives in a dark world.
Making him feel so much more than he'd expected.
Moved. Sorry.
No! No more *shame* – he'd had a lifetime of that.
From now on he needed anger.
And he knew where to direct it. Who deserved it most. Who'd stolen time from him, who'd made it impossible for him to go on with his *perfect* plan as he'd intended to. Who'd made him resort to knocking him senseless and bringing him here, where he was, even now, still intent on destroying his private little Happy Valley . . .
The *father*.

Chapter 94

'How are you doing, Professor?'

It had been a long while since I'd heard his scumbag voice, and I hated him so much that the sound of it made my flesh crawl, made my hands clench and unclench. Yet it was what I'd been waiting for, too, because *he* was my route to Rianna, and so long as I sat there in that unrelenting silent darkness, she and Robbie were getting no help from me, were they?

'Never better,' I answered.

I wasn't too bad, considering. My headache had long since taken a back seat to rage and frustration, and I'd used some of the damned waiting time to try and work out, as well as I could, if he'd left me anything I could use. Unlike the kids, I was at least wearing my own clothes, that is, my jeans and shirt – the jacket had gone, and the shoes and belt, and the Swatch watch the Ryans had given me last birthday. My wallet was still in the back pocket of my jeans, complete, so far as I could tell in the dark, with a fifty dollar bill, two tens, a five, my driver's licence, and two credit cards, which might just come in useful if I came across a door with a cheap lock . . .

In your dreams.

'That's good,' he said. 'I'm glad you've had a little rest time.'

'Who *are* you?' It was the first time I'd asked him that.

'You know who I am.'

'No, I don't,' I said. 'Why don't you tell me?' I paused. 'It's not as if I can walk out and tell the cops, after all.'

310

'Or Agent Kline,' he said.

'So who are you?' I was playing them all off one at a time inside my head: Korda, Hawthorne, Fitzgerald – then, at a lower level, Kaminski, Hendrick or the other two men at Eryx I'd scarcely thought about since the first few days after our visit: ponytailed Anton Gluckman and anorexic-looking Jazz Brown.

'Don't you even want to guess?' he asked me now.

'I'm not in the mood for guessing games.'

'You'd better *get* in the mood for games,' he told me, almost genially. 'There's another one ready to roll soon as you've got this one.'

'Who *are* you?' One more time. Indulge him.

'I'm their father,' he said.

My stomach heaved.

'Or good as,' he added, as an afterthought. 'Their *adoptive* father might be a better answer, I guess. You *were* Dakota's father—'

'Her name is *Rianna*.' I was up on my feet in the dark, eyes wide and staring.

'And your friend Lydia *was* young Steel's mother.'

If I'd seen so much as a moving *shadow*, I'd have been on him, ready to squeeze the life out of his invisible neck.

No shadows. Just his goddamned distorted voice.

'Put on your headset, Professor.' Hard suddenly.

'Go fuck yourself,' I said.

'Put it on *now*.'

Robbie and Rianna both jolted when they heard *his* voice.

They'd been dozing, almost forgetting.

He brought them back.

'New game,' he said. 'Different kind of game.'

Robbie reached for Rianna's hand, found it, held on tight.

'Dakota, honey,' *he* said, 'your dad is here.'

Rianna felt her heart stop, then flutter, then start thumping wildly. Robbie found her arm, gripped that too, listening, disbelieving.

311

'You thought he was dead, along with everyone else up there,' *he* was declaiming suddenly, like a kind of upbeat quiz show host, 'but he's *not* dead. He's come down here and he's trying to find you.' Pitch and mood changed again; now he was lower, dramatic, like a TV announcer talking up next week's soap. 'But he's not *going* to find you, not yet anyway . . . And Dakota, honey, here's the thing.'

Rianna couldn't help herself, it burst out of her in a great yell: '*Daddy*!'

'That's right, Dakota, he's here,' he went on, 'but listen now. You too, Steel, listen carefully, because this concerns you both.'

Robbie had not known it was possible to feel so much tension, would never have believed it was possible to have every centimetre of flesh, nerve, muscle, pulled so tight.

'Here's the thing,' *he* said again.

What? Rianna screamed silently inside her head.

'You've become very close to each other, haven't you?' he said. 'Just the way Steel and Dakota have always been. Inevitable, I guess – all those adventures, all those dangers, always looking out for each other, would have to make you close.'

Robbie realized he was gripping Rianna's arm too tightly, but he couldn't seem to help it, certainly wasn't going to let go. He could hear her breathing, such *scared* breathing, could only imagine her heart rate, could feel his own, pumping crazily in his chest. *What now? What* now!

'So I don't suppose you're going to like this next game too much.' He paused. 'We were going to have a lot more time together, you know. That was the plan. Time enough for me to teach you things, the way all good fathers teach their kids.' Another pause. 'I don't suppose either of you ever heard of *Dim Mak*?'

Neither Rianna nor Robbie answered.

'No, I figured not. Not martial arts types. Well, kids, *Dim Mak* isn't just any martial art, it's *the* one, and that's what I'd planned to teach you. Only that would have taken time, and now, thanks to your father, Dakota – your *biological* father, as they say, though *I'm* your daddy now, you see, and yours, too, Steel.' He swept right on. 'I went through so much to adopt you, bring you here, to our special place, where I could watch you play our games, watch you get close. And if we'd had time, I would have taught you to fight well, beautifully, intelligently, but there isn't any time now because of *him*, so we're all going to have to suffer because of him – and that's why you're suffering, Dakota, don't forget that, will you? Because he let you down – because if he'd been a *good* father, I wouldn't have been able to come and get you, would I?'

'He *is* a good father!' Rianna shouted into the dark. 'He's the *best*.'

'Attagirl, Dakota.'

'I'm *not* Dakota, I'm Rianna Woods, and my father's Jake Woods, and you can just go to *hell*! I'm not going to listen to you any more!'

'Oh, you'd better listen, Dakota, and you'd better not get too upset, because we have a game to play. It's the biggest of all, and you're going to need your strength. It's a game we may have to take in stages, because I think you may try to hold out on me to begin with—'

'*Why*?' Robbie thought he was going to burst. 'What is it? Which one?'

'Not one you've ever seen before, Steel, my boy, because it's new, hot off my sketchpad – so new it hasn't even made it into production yet. But it's a *hot* one.'

'If it's so hot,' Robbie said, 'why don't we just get *on* with it? It's all bullshit anyway, we know that, we've worked that out. None of it's real, which is why we're not afraid of it any more.'

'None of it's real, Steel,' he said, 'except you and Dakota. You're real.'

Robbie said nothing. Not afraid? He'd never, *never* felt so afraid.

'That's what makes this game so special. Because its only components *are* you two.'

313

Oh-my-God, went through Rianna's brain, all one word, one thought, like a bicycle out of control racing down a hill. *Oh-my-God, oh-my-God, oh-my-God.* She couldn't stop it, couldn't *stop* it.

'Because you're going to fight each other,' he said.

'No,' Robbie said. 'We're not.'

'Yes, you are,' he said. 'Because you're about to reach 34th Street again, for the last time, and we all know that *Limbo* ends when Steel and Dakota get to the helicopter over the station and fly away.'

They were both listening now. Sweet Jesus, were they ever listening.

'The thing is,' he said 'in this new and improved version, the chopper only has space for *one*. Understand, children?'

'No,' Rianna said.

'Oh, I think you do, Dakota, you do understand.'

'We're not going to fight for the space,' she told him, her voice almost, but not quite, failing. 'We'll stay, we'll find another way out.'

'There isn't another way out, Dakota. You have to fight.'

'We're not going to fight, you bastard,' Robbie said. 'You lousy *bastard*.'

'I *love* your courage,' he said. 'You know that? That's what I really love the most about both of you. You're so *brave*.'

Neither spoke.

'The thing is,' he said again, 'what happens if you *don't* fight.'

'What happens?' Rianna's voice shook as she asked the question. She didn't want it to shake, but she couldn't help it; she didn't know how much more she could bear, didn't think she *could* bear any more.

'You really want to know, Dakota?'

'Yes.' *No.* 'Yes!'

'If you don't fight,' he told her, 'your daddy, the professor, will *die*.'

I heard him.

Heard that filth telling my daughter and Lydia's son to fight.

Telling them what would happen if they didn't.

The words filled me, *all* of me, filled even the dark space around me, jangling unbearably, the way clanging bells did when you got too close, the kind of noise that more than hurt, the kind of sound that could almost *kill* you because it burst your eardrums and sent you insane . . .

If you don't fight, that monster had told my baby, *your daddy will die.*

I ripped the crap off my head again, goggles, earphones, the whole damned thing, gloves too, started moving, roaming around in the dark like big cats do in a cage, I guess, when they've had just about all they can take, when they're ready to break out or kill.

No fear in me any more, not one single ounce; the rage – the *craziness* – had driven it right out of me . . .

Getting out of here. Now.

That was all that mattered, getting Rianna and Robbie out of this hellhole. I didn't know how, didn't *care* how, didn't care if it killed me – I hoped, oh Christ, I really did hope and pray that it killed that filthy sonofabitch *devil* – but I was going to get those children out of this place, and I was going to do it *now*!

My left shoulder struck a wall.

The voice spoke again.

'Put your headset back on, Professor.'

You talking to me?

Big fucking deal.

I felt the wall with my bare hands and followed it, trying to find a door, I guess. There *had* to be a door, but I couldn't find it; in the dark it all felt the same to me, no joins, no cracks, *nothing*, but I went on anyway, moving around the room, trying to get the wall's measure, its *feel*, seeking weak spots, tapping on it . . .

'There's no point to what you're doing, Professor,' he said. 'You have to watch, that's part of the game. You have to watch them fight, because in a way, it's in your honour now, isn't it?'

I ignored him, went on with what I was doing, tried to block him out of my head. *Has to be a door.*

'And because if you *don't* watch,' he said, 'then *they* die.'

I stopped.

'That's the thing, you see, Professor,' he said. 'That's the deal.'

I heard a sound, a weird sound, a low kind of growling.

I was making it.

I started moving again, went on feeling those walls, and the part of me that was still rational, still registering reality of a sort, was becoming aware that the wall was not concrete – at least *this* side of it wasn't, the side I was touching. So maybe it wasn't a supporting wall, *maybe* it was just a partition wall, and if it was just a partition, then it could be knocked down more easily, and I'd felt something like this before . . .

In Lydia's apartment, in the music room, the *soundproofed* room.

Which made sense, of course, here, in this prison.

Okay, you bastard.

'I don't *want* to kill them, Professor.' The voice sounded almost reasonable. 'I really, honestly don't. I hate killing more than you can imagine, you should know that . . .'

I stopped listening, honest to God, I cut him right out of my head.

I was seeing Rianna's open, terrified mouth again, hearing her shaking voice.

Remembering what the *filth* wanted her and Robbie to do.

Letting the rage fill me again, *consume* me, take away reason.

I needed every ounce of rage now. The kind that helps mothers lift motor cars off their children after accidents.

The kind that helps fathers knock down walls.

I stepped back from the wall, went on moving backwards, away from it.

Far as I could go.

Burning with it.

Felt the other wall behind me.

Took one deep breath—

And launched myself forward at it.

The collision was so damned hard it knocked the wind out of me and cracked the right side of my head.

Pain. Pain was good.

The voice was still talking to me, *at* me, but I was almost oblivious to it.

I felt the wall where I'd impacted, found a small indentation, nothing more.

A solid wall wouldn't have indented at all.

It'll come. I'll do better next time.

Soon as I got my breath back, I'd go again.

He knew now what was going to happen.

In a startling flash of sweetest clarity.

He had thought he would hate this moment, that it would enrage him.

Make him afraid.

But there was no fear, not now.

That was *good*. That was *right*. Suddenly, he saw that.

Maybe this was what he'd planned all along, deep down.

Father to the rescue.

Best for the game.

Bringing them all closer to the end.

Good for everyone.

Especially thing-monster.

I was at the other wall again, getting back to full strength.

Pumping up. Psyching.

All I had to do was think of Rianna, what *he'd* said to her.

Jesus Christ Almighty.

If it was just an acoustic wall, it *ought* to go down if I hit it hard enough.

If it wasn't . . .

The voice was talking to me again, penetrating again.

'They're going to do it, Professor. They're going to fight each other to the death, and I'm going to watch them, and it's going to be the best ever – the saddest, too, of course, but the very, *very* best.'

The words tore into me, ripped at me – lit the final fuse.
'Thank you, you piece of *garbage*!' I screamed.
And went for it like a goddamned human bulldozer.

It happened in a kind of slow motion.
　　Cracking sounds. Groaning. Deafening.
　　It was caving in, and I was going with it.
　　No control now, just a *part* of the wall, moulded into it.
　　Ripping. Tearing.
　　Rumbling like thunder. Crashing.
　　Down.

He watched it happen.
　　One ending, he thought. One ending, at least.
　　Time to leave now.
　　Leave it all behind. Steel, Dakota, all of this.
　　Thank Christ.
　　He thought he really meant that.
　　Leave it to Father.

Chapter 95

Rianna and Robbie were waiting.

For the game to start.

Nothing.

'I don't get this.' Rianna's voice was hushed and terrified. 'I don't understand what's going on.'

'You and me both,' Robbie whispered back.

'Is my father really here? Does he really have him too?' She clung to Robbie, crying now, unable to help herself. 'Oh God, if he does have him, then that's *it*, isn't it? There's no hope.'

'Sure there is,' Robbie soothed her, *tried* to soothe her, though Lord knew he was every bit as freaked out, every bit as confused, and it made no sense at all, though nothing had ever made sense down here, had it?

'He said he wants us to *fight*, Robbie.'

'And we told him, didn't we?'

'But he said . . .' She couldn't finish the sentence, couldn't bear to think about that last threat to her father . . .

'It's okay, Rianna.' Robbie stroked her hair.

Not okay. About eighty zillion miles from okay. He knew it, and she knew it, and there wasn't anything, not one damned *thing* either of them could do about it.

Except wait.

I was too stunned to get up.

The sounds were still ringing in my ears, dust clogging my

eyes, nose and mouth, choking me, and any second now I knew my enemy was going to be there, jump me, whack me again, and I needed to be ready to fight with everything I could muster . . .

Oh God, it was hard just to move, but I had to get up, get ready.

Find the kids.

I tried to blink the dust clear, tried to wipe away some of the grit without making it worse, but my eyes were tearing now and the moisture was helping.

Still dark.

One room to another? Was that all I'd achieved? Oh, Christ . . .

Except . . .

Air.

A tiny whisper of breeze, from somewhere to my left.

And *sound*. Not any particular sound, just not the absolute, thick blanket of silence that had filled that room whenever *he* wasn't speaking and I wasn't yelling.

I was up, finally, back on my feet. I knew I was cut and bruised, and my whole body hurt like hell, but I didn't give a damn about any of that. I was on the move again, out of that room, at least, and moving towards the breeze, carefully, tentatively, hands stretched out ahead of me in the dark because I'd already hit one wall too many today.

I was listening, too, for him – or the kids – mostly, right now, for *him*, still remembering how quiet he'd been out at Fitzgerald's place before he'd hit me.

Was that where we were? Still on Fitzgerald's property? Maybe in the cellar that Baum had located on the plans?

Where *was* Baum? I couldn't believe I hadn't thought about him, about my good new friend, till now. *Shame on you.* Was he down here too, I wondered suddenly? Were *all* the missing kids here, not just Rianna and Robbie?

The sound was not, as I had first thought, nothing in particular.

It was a low hum, coming from someplace to my right. An

electronic kind of sound. The kind you'd expect to hear from a computer room, maybe.

From the hub of an operation like *his*.

Shit.

Go towards the sound, or towards the breeze?

The absolute $64,000 question. Or in that new millionaire programme everyone was so nuts about, the fifty-fifty split, A or B?

Except that if *breeze* equalled *exit*, I wasn't going that way without the kids.

No real contest.

Slowly, carefully, I turned towards the hum, hands outstretched again.

My right hand touched something hard, solid. Wall. *Right a little more.* Sound growing louder. *Louder.* My fingertips – both hands – grazed something.

Another wall?

A door.

A goddamned door, with a goddamned handle.

I stood very still.

No real choices now. If *he* was in there, I'd fight. If he had a gun, I'd probably die, and maybe, just maybe, my death might satisfy the piece of dirt, and maybe, *maybe*, he'd allow it to end there and let the kids go free.

Or not.

Don't think about that, Jake.

He'd said he didn't like killing, had said he hated it more than I could imagine.

Please, God.

I opened the door, hard, fast, slammed it all the way back like I *thought* I remembered being taught a long, long time ago . . .

No one.

The room was dimly lit, but it was *light*, thank Christ.

No one. Just a bank of monitors, some kind of computer, a bunch of switches and no place to hide. If *he'd* been in here, he was gone now.

I was shaking, hadn't realized I was shaking till then, but suddenly my legs were so weak they wouldn't support me any more, and I only just got to the single chair in time, sank onto it.

Looked up at the monitors. Blank. Turned off. I looked harder, searching for an on-switch. *There*. I used it. The screen flickered.

Nothing.

Damn.

I turned on a second monitor. More flickering.

Oh God. Oh, dear, dear God.

Rianna. And Robbie. Ugly contraptions off their faces.

Clinging to each other. Oh sweet Jesus.

How to talk to them? There had to be a way. Same way *he* talked to me.

Another switch over to my right. Talk-back. Simple.

I pushed it down. A green light beside the switch illuminated.

'Rianna?' I was nervous of talking too loud, in case he heard. I saw her head tilt a little – she looked so tired, so *scared*.

'Rianna' – a little louder this time – 'it's Daddy.'

I watched her fear turn first to sweet confusion and then, swiftly, to joy, and my own heart turned over. 'I'm here, baby, I'm here, and I'm coming to find you.'

Same kind of look on Robbie's face. *Ah, Lydia, if you only knew*.

'It's just a question now of finding exactly where you are, okay?'

Rianna was trying to tell me something, but I couldn't hear.

'I don't know how to have a two-way conversation, sweetheart,' I told her, 'but it's not important, because I'm coming to find you right now, and then I'm going to get you and Robbie out of here, okay?'

She was still trying, urgently, to ask me something, and Robbie was trying too.

Suddenly I understood.

'He's not here,' I told them both, fighting to stay cool and clear. 'I don't know if he's gone or not, okay? But he hasn't tried to stop me yet.'

Be careful, Daddy. I think that's what Rianna was trying to tell me.

'I'll be careful, baby, don't worry about me.'

Nah. Sure. What's to worry about?

I looked around for something I could use as a tool, or maybe as a weapon if I needed one. Something weighty.

Nothing.

The chair.

It took a few minutes, too many minutes, but my hands were still shaky and I wasn't exactly at my best, but finally I got there, got the damned steel legs unscrewed, and they weren't much, but they were pretty solid, so . . .

No flashlight anyplace.

Hey, how about *that*! A lift-up lid covering a panel of switches on the wall closest to the door.

I flicked them all then and opened the door to check.

Let there be *light*.

Robbie was having trouble believing.

He could feel from Rianna's taut, trembling body, hear from the hugely heightened level of excitement in her voice – almost ecstasy – that she most certainly *did* believe; that so far as she was concerned her dad was here, had come to save her, *them*, and that was great, that was amazing, and he thought he could believe that, he sure as hell *wanted* to believe it.

What he did *not* believe, no way, was that *he* had gone, just like that, leaving the way clear for Rianna's father.

Letting them go.

'You don't think he can do it, do you?' she said suddenly, in the dark.

'It's not him I'm thinking about,' Robbie said, hating to ruin these moments of hope for her, just so damned afraid they might be all they had.

'I know,' Rianna said.

'You think *he*'s going to let this happen?'

'I don't know,' she answered simply. 'But I know my father. He said he's here. He said he's coming to find us and get us out.'

'I know he did,' Robbie said, still gently, 'but—'

'But nothing.' Rianna was adamant. 'That's what he said, and that's what's going to happen.'

I was out of the computer room, going back the way I thought I'd come.

The lighting was pretty dim in the narrow hallway, but it was eight thousand times better than the dark. Not that there was much to see.

Mind, I wasn't looking for the goddamned Eiffel Tower. I was looking for doors. The first one to take me to Rianna and Robbie, the second to take us all *out*.

I turned a right-hand corner, wielding one chair leg in each hand, just in case.

And saw the remains of my wall.

Wow. I had some trouble believing I'd done that. If time hadn't been so precious, I'd have taken a photo.

Not that I had a camera.

Another corner. I turned this one police academy-style, wishing like hell I had one automatic instead of two damned chair legs. *Better than nothing, Jake.*

No one.

He really might be gone. I felt he was, thought I could feel that, couldn't imagine somehow that I wouldn't have sensed his presence if he were still here.

You didn't sense his presence at Fitzgerald's place.

A door. Complete with handle.

Heart racing, I turned it.

Nothing. *Nothing*. Damned thing wouldn't open, and there was no lock.

That was when I noticed what I'd missed – how the hell had I missed *that*? A digital pad on the wall over to the left, the kind I'd seen in modern offices to keep strangers out without employing a bunch of security people. The kind where you usually had to key in a four-number combination and the door would open.

Damn.

I'd refrained from knocking till now in case the kids weren't inside, in case . . .

The hell with it.

No response.

Of course, if this room was sound-proofed too, no response didn't mean much.

Limbo.

I remembered, abruptly, a scrap from the lesson at Eryx.

Go back, talk to the kids again.

I went fast, running now, scared suddenly that there might be a time limit on this bid for freedom, maybe some kind of booby-trap that might wreck everything if I took too long, all part of the damned game, *his* game.

Back in the computer room (and why was there no digital lock on *that* door? No need if only he was using it) I put down the chair legs, pushed down the talk-back switch again, spoke fast, watching the monitor as I talked.

'Kids, listen – Robbie especially, I guess.' I saw him nodding. 'In *Limbo*, in the *real* game, is there a special code, say, of four numbers, or any combination, that lets Steel and Dakota in or out of locked rooms?'

Robbie was nodding again, saying *something*.

'Remember I can't hear you,' I said urgently. 'If it's numbers, use your fingers.'

Another nod, then Robbie put up three fingers.

'That's three, right?' I said.

Rianna was nodding too now. Robbie put up his whole right hand and the four fingers of his left.

'Nine.'

Now just four fingers.

'Four.'

Two fingers.

'Two,' I said. 'Three-nine-four-two, okay?'

Robbie wasn't done. I could see him working something out,

325

could see Rianna laughing, actually *laughing*, but Robbie looked deadly serious, and I was glad of that.

Six fingers went up.

Finally I had the code. Five digits, not four: 39426.

'Sure?' I repeated the numbers, saw them both nod.

I picked up the chair legs, my weaponry, kept those numbers in my head and started back fast, *too* fast, almost forgetting the risk of ambush.

No ambush.

Back at the panel, I keyed in the numbers and prayed.

I heard a click, turned the handle, and the door opened.

The room was empty.

Christ. I wanted to weep, to *scream.*

Find another room, Jake.

One more corner, another bare corridor, same dim lighting. Another door. Another control panel.

I entered the code, made a mistake, tried again, but it wasn't registering. I started panicking – then calmed myself down, pressed ERROR, then CLEAR.

39426.

Click.

The door opened.

My daughter was there, on the other side.

Lydia's son beside her.

Both alive and, almost unbelievably, well.

None of us said a word. I put the chair legs down on the floor, carefully, quietly, and then I held out my arms.

And Rianna came into them.

Chapter 96

Lydia had gone home, to her *own* home.

She'd worried about that for a while, because, after all, Jake had expected her to stay with Ella. And if Kim hadn't shown up that morning – though, face it, Kim Ryan was a much better, certainly infinitely more *familiar*, person for the nine-year-old to be with in the absence of her daddy, definitely better for her than a messed-up woman who'd felt compelled to go wandering around a New York City subway station – but if Kim had *not* been available, Lydia would, of course, still have been there in the Woods apartment.

Waiting for a man who'd lied to her about where he'd been going, when it had been her absolute right to know the truth.

Why wasn't she angrier about that? Why was she still feeling guilty about leaving New Haven? Especially since she'd talked to Kim a while back, and she'd told her there was absolutely no need for her to come back right now because she was happy to stay with Ella.

So here she was, all alone again, growing more demented by the hour.

Not really angry with Jake at all. Just afraid for him. *Terrified* for him, and about the possible implications for Robbie and Rianna of whatever might have befallen him and Baum.

She called Thea Lomax, told her how she felt.

'I'm getting pretty anxious myself,' the PI admitted.

'I know it's not twenty-four hours yet,' Lydia said, 'and I

know you'll probably say no one's going to accept that the abductor may have taken two grown men when we all know he's into teenagers, but—'

'But you think the FBI should know.' Lomax cut her short.

'I do, yes.'

'I already talked to Agent Moran.'

'You did?'

'I figured they might regard me as less of a basket case than you – no offence intended.'

'None taken, are you *kidding*?' Gratitude flowed through Lydia. 'What did Moran say?'

'As much as she could, in the circumstances,' Lomax said. 'That she'd pass on the information that the guys were heading in the general direction of Eryx. The problem remains, Lydia, that we can't be more specific than that, so until there's more to go on—'

'They won't do anything,' Lydia cut in flatly.

'I'm not sure that's true,' Lomax said.

'But they won't tell us what, if anything, they *are* going to do.'

'That's a definite.' The investigator paused. 'I'm sorry.'

'Nothing for you to be sorry about,' Lydia said. 'You tried.'

She came away from the telephone, drained, frustrated, more afraid than ever, went to pour herself a glass of wine, thought about running a bath, thought about maybe calling the Franklins, or maybe seeing if Melanie Steinman was home and free to come up for a visit – something, *anything*, to try to relax, or at least compose herself for yet more waiting.

Pointless exercises.

How else could she feel *but* out of her mind with fear? How else was a woman whose son had been missing for *ever*, and whose new *maybe* lover, definitely new dear friend, had gone off like some gung-ho fool with a private investigator old enough to know better, and disappeared off the face of the earth – how else was a woman in that position supposed to feel?

328

She knew that Jake and Baum were in danger.
Like both their children.
So no wine. No warm bath. No friends.
Just coffee, and plenty of it.
And some prayers, perhaps, to go with it.

Chapter 97

We'd started looking for the way out.

Still no sign of *him*.

We'd done a lot of hugging, had checked each other out, Rianna making a big deal of my cuts and bruises and the remains of the wall still clinging to me. We hadn't done a lot of talking, except for trying to figure out where we were.

Underground, we all agreed – still felt that even though we were no longer in the dark. Probably in Connecticut, *possibly* under Fitzgerald's place – or maybe somewhere entirely different, someplace no one even knew existed.

What we needed, of course, was another door, one leading *out*. The layout of the whole place didn't appear that complex, kind of squared off, but just confusing enough to stop me getting a real handle on its exact shape. Every way we turned we hit another stark corridor, one or two doors off it, but no apparent exit, which might mean, I thought, that it was an area within something else. Maybe. *Maybe* all kinds of things – maybe we were on the goddamned *moon*.

We'd opened a door to another bleak little cell-room using the same series of numbers which, Robbie had swiftly explained, was just an alpha/numeric idiot code made up using the letters of *Limbo*. Thank God it was that simple, I'd told him.

'And thank God you remembered it.'

'I didn't,' Rianna said.

I couldn't help but notice the way she looked at Robbie. It was the way I'd sometimes seen her look at me at those great moments (from my standpoint) when she'd thought me particularly smart. Admiration, I guess, created by love. Most daughters, I believe, with halfway decent fathers, feel that way about them sometimes. But I'd never seen Rianna look at another male that way.

I guess I didn't blame her one bit.

Another corner. I was getting confused, sure we were going back and forth over the same small stretch.

Another door. No digital pad beside it, but locked anyway.

'We could knock it down,' Robbie suggested.

Rianna took hold of my arm abruptly. 'Let's not bother.'

I saw new fear in her eyes, knew she was afraid *he* might be behind it.

'We'll leave it,' I said, 'for now.'

And then I remembered the breeze.

'For heaven's sake,' I said out loud.

'What?' Robbie was staring at me – they were both staring at me.

'I felt air, like a tiny breeze,' I explained, 'before I found you.' I closed my eyes for a moment, trying to get my bearings. 'Just after I got out of my room.'

'Let's go back there,' Rianna said, wanting to get away from here.

We tracked back and I shut my eyes again for another moment, then went from there as I thought I had before, feeling the whisper of air again, and heading straight for it.

A darker stretch of corridor.

I don't know how we'd missed it before – too busy searching for doors, or maybe subconsciously avoiding dark places?

'Hey,' Robbie said, 'we're used to this, aren't we?'

I couldn't believe the guts of this young man, couldn't wait to tell Lydia about him, about the depths of her son that even she had probably never known existed. *Please, God.*

'Okay,' Rianna said.

Her, too, of course, but that was another matter. I couldn't seem to bear to contemplate my daughter's courage, couldn't stand to think about what she'd been through.

Now was no time for contemplation of any kind.

'Come on, guys,' I said.

I went first, clutching one chair leg, Rianna right behind me, holding on to my shirt, Robbie bringing up the rear, holding the second piece of steel.

Steps, at the end of the corridor.

'*Yes!*' I heard Robbie hiss, like he was punching the air.

I was more tentative. 'You guys stay here. I'll go up, take a look.'

'No way,' Rianna said. 'We're coming too.'

No time to argue. I started up ahead of them, feeling my way, though it wasn't as dark as my room had been. The stairs were circular, and I counted twenty-two before I reached the top.

A landing.

Another door.

Locked too. No digital pad.

I looked back at Robbie, behind Rianna on the small landing. 'I'm going to need a hand here.' I raised my steel chair leg, held it like a crowbar. 'We can try levering it off its hinges.'

'Okay.' Robbie pushed gently past Rianna, coming to help me.

Men at work with iron bars.

It wouldn't budge.

'I think it opens outwards.' I grinned back at Rianna. 'Your dad the DIY man.'

'If you want a shelf putting up,' she explained to Robbie, 'for one night only.'

'Such faith.'

'Oh, she has faith in you,' Robbie said. 'Believe me.'

I looked at his face, much gaunter than in his photographs, and I was so damned touched by him. 'I do believe you, Robbie.'

'What now?' Rianna asked.

I looked back at the door. 'Time for my human bulldozer routine again.' My body and head ached at the very thought of it.

'Let me try,' Robbie said, picking up on my feelings.

332

I regarded him again, doubted that the teenager, in his present shape, could shift this door, but the last thing I wanted to do right now was humiliate him.

'We could try it together,' I suggested.

'I want to help,' Rianna said.

'No way.' I didn't care about humiliating *her*, didn't care either, right that minute, if I was being sexist.

Robbie and I paced back and forth a couple of times, flexed shoulders and arms, psyching ourselves up more than anything, I guess.

'Ready?' I checked with Robbie.

'Sure.'

'On three, okay?'

I counted it down – and then we *went* for it.

Got nowhere.

'Not enough power,' I said.

'We need a longer run,' Robbie pointed out.

'I mean, come *on*' – I was trying to pump myself up again – 'I knocked down a whole goddamned wall! I'm not going to let one little door beat me, right?'

'Right.' Rianna sounded doubtful.

'You need to move out the way,' Robbie told her.

'Why don't you let me help?' she said.

'Because you're too small,' Robbie said. 'You'll get hurt.'

'I'm a gymnast,' she told him. 'I'm stronger than I look.'

'You've been locked up for nearly a week, sweetheart,' I said.

'Robbie's been locked up for two *months*.'

Robbie grinned at her. 'What can I tell you?'

I called a halt, not happy about wasting time, great as it was to hear the kids fooling around.

Rianna got out of the way and I counted down again.

We went a second time.

It gave some this time, but not all the way.

'One more go,' I said, soon as I could breathe.

'Yeah,' Robbie panted.

'Be careful,' Rianna counselled us.

I wondered, suddenly, what was going to be waiting for us.

Or *who*?

I had a sudden image of Fitzgerald, waiting out there, playing with us, maybe holding a shotgun – or wasn't that hi-tech enough for him?

'Okay?' Robbie asked.

I nodded. No point telling him – no point, either, telling Rianna to maybe go further down the steps, get ready to hide. I knew she wouldn't do it.

'This is going to be it, guys, all right?' I made my voice strong, positive.

'All *right*,' Robbie said.

'Sure,' Rianna said, backing off again to give us more space.

Robbie and I moved back as far as we could.

'One,' I counted. 'Two.' I took a breath. '*Three*.'

We went for it like bulls, perfectly synchronized, hard as hell . . .

The door gave with a great screech of splintering.

And we went right on out with it.

Light blinding us as we went, yelling with exuberant triumph, skidding with the busted door, hanging onto it like a pair of surfers.

'*Let go*!' Rianna screamed—

And hurled herself forward in a tackle, grabbing at my jeans, missing, crashing down hard on the concrete ground, still screaming, 'Let *go*!'

I let go first. Robbie took a half-second longer. I was still too dazzled to see properly, but I managed to grab hold of the kid's leather tunic.

The door went on without us, we heard a loud cracking noise, were just in time to watch it vanish from sight.

Rianna was still screaming, wordlessly now, holding on to my left leg with all her might, her hands feeling like claws.

Suddenly I saw why she was screaming.

Why Robbie's breath sounded like sobbing.

We were not in Connecticut.

We hadn't just climbed up out of some underground cellar.

We were on the *top*, at the very goddamned *edge*, of the roof of a *skyscraper*.

More skyscrapers, many of them much, much higher, all around us.

And a shatteringly familiar sight far below.

Herald Square.

New York City.

The door was still spinning down, spiralling.

Heading straight for the street below.

Chapter 98

'More than twenty-four hours now,' Lydia told Thea Lomax on the phone.

'I know it,' Lomax said.

'So are you going to call Kline or Moran again, or am I?'

'I guess I am.'

'Maybe we should both call,' Lydia suggested.

'Overkill,' Lomax said. 'We'll just piss them off.'

'I don't care.'

'You'll care if they're already working on finding Jake and Norman and we just waste their time.' Lomax paused. 'So let me make this call, and then, if we need to, you can take the next one, okay?'

'Okay,' Lydia said. 'But you'll be tough on them, right?'

'I'm going to kick up stink if they're not already on this, believe me.' Lomax paused. 'And I'm going to call the State Police, too, make sure the local guys know all about it.'

'What can I do meantime?'

'Nothing. I hate to say that,' Lomax added quickly. 'Believe me, I do know that's the hardest thing for you right now. But there is nothing else you can do.'

'Please stay in touch, Thea.'

'You bet.' Lomax paused again. 'And I don't have to tell you that if you hear from Jake or Norman I want to know about it right away.'

'You don't have to tell me.'

Chapter 99

Oh Jesus.

Oh *Jesus*.

I had told – *ordered* – Robbie right back away from the edge, and even I'd waited a few minutes before going close again. I'd *had* to wait, because the world had been spinning like a top, and I was still shaking like Jello.

But now I had no choice.

I had to take another look over the side.

'Be careful, Daddy.' The sound of my older daughter, lying belly down on the flat roof, in pain because of her tackle of a few minutes back, but calling out in fear for me. Damned right I was going to be careful.

The rooftop was smaller than most, which meant that the door we'd busted through had been located closer to the parapet than most, which was why, with our combined power, said door had skidded and smashed right through the guardrail.

And nearly taken us with it.

I crawled back to the edge and peered over.

Until this second, I'd been conscious of the general cacophony of the city, added to the kids' voices and my own pounding heartbeat. Now, suddenly, as I stared down, trying to focus, trying to ignore, *lose* the dizziness, I was starting to hear more – much more – than I wanted to.

Horns. A siren.

People screaming.

'Oh dear God,' I said, out loud.

'*What*?' Both kids yelling the same word from behind me.

'Stay back,' I ordered again.

I did not want them to see this till they had to.

The door – *our* door – was almost invisible now, from here. *Almost*.

It had gone through the roof of a bus, embedding itself.

Traffic in and around Herald Square was at a standstill, cars, yellow cabs, trucks at all kinds of crazy angles, people running around all over the place yelling, shrieking, crying.

And a bunch of them, the group growing by the second, looking up.

Pointing right at me.

338

Chapter 100

Lydia was asleep on the couch when she heard the buzzing.

Asleep! How could she have fallen *asleep*?

'I'm coming,' she said, knowing no one could hear her from there.

She walked, muzzy-headed, out into the hall, over to the intercom.

'Yes?'

'It's Joseph, ma'am.' One of the part-time doormen. 'You have a visitor.'

'Who is it, Joseph?' Lydia was tentative. Her new anti-social streak was getting to be a bad habit, but she couldn't seem to help it, didn't really care what people thought of her, could neither bear to sit and make small talk, nor share her real feelings with anyone except . . .

'It's Professor Woods,' Joseph told her.

The name seemed to take a second or two to travel from Lydia's ears to her brain. And then it was like a rocket going off. *Thank God*!

'Send him up,' she told the doorman. 'Send him *up*.'

She started running around crazily – first to the mirror there in the hall, grimacing at what she saw, then to her bedroom in search of her hairbrush and some perfume for an instant fix, then back to the front door, wanting it to be open and welcoming when Jake got here – *oh, thank you, God*! Then a dash to the bathroom to splash her face with cold water and rinse her mouth.

Slow down, Lydia.

She stopped, took a deep breath, then walked, rather than ran, back into the entrance hall.

Someone was standing just inside the front door, the door closed behind them.

Someone she had met before. Only then, he'd looked relaxed and confident. And now he looked . . .

Strange.

Not Jake.

Another man.

Wearing chinos and loafers and a white T-shirt that looked as if its wearer had been perspiring heavily.

In his right hand, a gun.

Chapter 101

'I can't put much weight on it, Daddy. It hurts pretty badly.'

'I don't want you to put any weight on it, sweetheart.' I'd finished doing what little I could in the way of examining Rianna's ankle. 'I think it could be sprained – I'm almost certain it isn't broken.'

'Sprains can be pretty bad,' Robbie said.

'Which is why I want you to stay still,' I told my daughter, then managed a kind of a smile. 'One thing, at least: we don't have to worry about how we get down from here, because the cops are going to be coming up here to get us.'

'Will we be in trouble?' Rianna asked.

She had crawled quite close to the edge a few minutes ago, with me holding on to her – while she took a look through the section of guardrail still intact. I'd seen her face, and Robbie's too, as they'd both stared down, had observed that they were both torn for just an instant or two, as only young people could be, I think, between excitement and dismay ... And then horror had taken over as their imaginations had begun to consider what might have happened to the bus passengers.

'I don't think we'll be in trouble for one minute,' I told her, 'though there's bound to be one heck of a lot of questions to answer.' I didn't want them to start worrying again until they had to, either about the bus, or about where *he* might be hiding. They'd been through too much – I still couldn't begin to imagine, still didn't *want* to imagine – how much.

'We're okay, you know, Daddy,' Rianna told me, as softly

as she could above the Manhattan background noise. 'Thanks to you.' She looked over at Robbie, sitting on the roof a few feet away. 'And you, too. You were incredible.'

'Thanks,' Robbie said.

He was very quiet, I noticed, had been ever since we'd all started getting over the shock of finding out where we were, not to mention of almost getting killed.

'Tell me about my mom,' he said now, suddenly, still quietly. 'Is she really okay? I mean, I know you said she was when we were still inside, but . . .'

'She's fine,' I told him, smiling. 'Though not nearly as fine as she will be when she hears your voice – when she actually *sees* you.'

I got down between the two of them, closer to Rianna, put one arm around her shoulders, and extended the other towards Robbie, an invitation, if he wanted it.

He did.

I can't begin to describe how great that felt, that big armful of kids, almost grown as they were. Rianna was weeping now, softly, steadily, leaning against my chest, and Robbie, too, was roughly wiping away some tears of his own with the back of one hand.

I didn't bother wiping mine away.

We stayed very still. Waiting.

Chapter 102

Lydia didn't care what happened next. She had to ask the question, gun or no gun.

'What have you done with my son?'

'Your son's okay,' he told her quietly. 'And the professor's girl, too.' He paused. 'And the professor, come to that.'

'Where are they?' She didn't move, stood absolutely still, face freshly washed – *for Jake* – determined to ask the questions that had to be asked before anything else, before real fear set in, or . . . 'What have you done with them?'

'I guess they're probably free by now,' he said, then shrugged. 'If not, it's just a matter of time. You can stop worrying.' He raised the gun a little, not threatening her with it exactly, just gesturing. 'I'd like to sit down now, if you don't mind, Mrs Johanssen. I'm very tired.'

Without another word, Lydia turned and walked ahead of him into her living room, towards the couch, its cushions still dented from where she'd been sleeping on them, just minutes before.

The phone rang.

She looked back at him. He shook his head.

The machine picked up, but it was in her study, and all Lydia could hear was a man's voice speaking, words indecipherable, then the sound of the machine resetting.

He waited a moment, as if expecting her to sit first, but then, as she remained standing, he shrugged again and sat down in one of the armchairs.

'I'm sorry,' he said, still quietly. 'I didn't want to hurt anyone.'

Lydia said nothing. He was holding that gun, yet she didn't seem to feel any immediate danger. And then she thought of something else she wanted to ask.

'Why are you here?' she said. 'Why come to me?'

'Good question,' he said, as if he needed to think about that.

Which was about as much good news as she could expect at this particular moment, Lydia decided.

He wanted to think or maybe even talk, rather than kill her outright.

Chapter 103

We heard noise from below, inside the building.

The cops, I guessed, breaking in.

Robbie started to get to his feet.

'No,' I told him. 'Stay here. Stay close.'

'Daddy,' Rianna said, uncertainly.

'It's okay, honey. It's all going to be okay.'

It took some time before we heard them coming up the steps.

Four uniformed NYPD officers, hands on holsters, unsure what to expect.

'Take it easy,' I told them, staying still, seeing them register us as a group with no hostility either between ourselves or towards them. I saw them visibly relax a little, knew I'd been right to greet them this way.

'What the hell happened up here?' a sergeant asked.

'Long story,' I told him.

'Better make a start then,' the cop said.

'Anyone hurt down there?' I asked.

'What do *you* think?' another officer asked me, nastily.

Rianna began weeping again. I held her tightly for one more moment, murmured to her, speaking close against her ear, telling her that it was going to be fine, and then I got carefully, *painfully*, to my feet.

'Stay back, sir.' The sergeant again, African-American, aged about thirty, his hand back over his holster, taking no chances with someone as suspicious-looking as I guess I was, covered with building dust and fragments and with cuts and

345

fresh bruises on my head and arms. Not to mention the two scared-looking kids I might just have been holding against their will.

'For Pete's sake,' Robbie flared suddenly, 'he just finished saving our lives! We've been locked up in this place for Christ knows how long.'

'We were *kidnapped*,' Rianna added for good measure.

The sergeant looked startled, *more* than startled, and then he stooped to take a closer look at the kids, and light dawned.

'You're Robbie Johanssen.'

'Yes, sir.' Polite now.

'And you are?' Still a little hostility, a lot of suspicion, towards me.

'He's my father,' Rianna said, and made an attempt to stand, but her ankle wouldn't hold and she sank down again. '*He* was taken prisoner, too,' she told the sergeant, 'and he knocked down a wall all by himself so he could rescue us, but then we couldn't find the way out, and that's why he and Robbie had to force that door open.' She paused, glanced towards the edge, swallowed down tears and went on even more fiercely. 'And they *had* to throw themselves at it so hard because it wouldn't open any other way, but when it did give, it just went skidding, like the roof was *ice*, and we didn't know there was a roof out here, we thought we were underground, and Robbie and my dad almost went over the side with the door.'

'Wow.' One of the other officers, a young guy with dark, amazed eyes, said it for everyone.

'Wow indeed,' the sergeant echoed, wryly.

I couldn't help smiling. With a spokesperson like Rianna, no one against me stood a chance.

I put out my hand to the sergeant, told him my name, showed him my driver's licence. He shook my hand, identified himself as Sergeant John Thurlow, directed two of the other officers to check on Robbie and see to Rianna's ankle, and then I told him, as quickly and quietly as I could, that they needed to contact a whole bunch of people, starting with Special Agent Roger Kline of the FBI, and Lydia Johanssen. And then they needed to start looking for the sonofabitch who'd done all this and more.

Thurlow drew me a few feet away. 'What about the other missing kids?'

I shook my head. 'No sign.'

'Looks like a pretty weird set-up down there,' one of the other men remarked.

'You don't know the half of it,' Robbie told him.

Chapter 104

'Would you like a cup of coffee?' Lydia offered.

'If it's not too much trouble.' Courteous as a well-schooled boy. Which, of course, he had once been.

He followed her into the kitchen, sat at her table and rested the gun on the surface, right in front of him. Lydia doubted if she could steal it away from him, doubted if he would allow her to keep it even if she could manage it. Doubted if she could shoot him, if push came to shove.

Different if he were still wherever Robbie was, threatening him. She could shoot him in those circumstances, no question.

No one at risk right now, except maybe herself.

She set about making the coffee, taking her time.

Chapter 105

More noise from below, and then, minutes later, another uniform came up through the smashed doorframe, face white as a ghost, gesturing to Sergeant Thurlow for a word away from me and the kids.

In another instant or two, John Thurlow, too, was looking shocked and grim. He took a moment, then motioned to me to come across.

I knew he meant alone.

'We need to talk,' he told me, closer to the doorway. 'Better sit down.'

'I'm fine,' I said. 'What we really need is to get the kids away from here. They've had about all they can take, and then some.'

'We know that, sir,' Thurlow said, 'but we're still clearing a safe route for them. We're going to have to carry your daughter out, and the last thing any of us wants is for someone else to get hurt.'

'You still haven't told us what happened to the people on that bus,' I said.

'We've had a few other things on our minds,' the man told me.

I looked at him. His deep brown eyes were still unmistakably shocked. I suddenly wasn't one bit sure I wanted to know what had done that to him.

'Have you talked to Kline?' I asked.

Thurlow nodded. 'Yes, sir.'

'So you've checked out my story?'

Another nod. 'We weren't in much doubt, after your daughter's – statement, I guess would be the word.'

I smiled, glanced across at her, saw she was calm enough for now, but that Robbie looked as if he was getting uptight, itching to get up and come across. And then Rianna reached for his hand and he seemed to settle down.

Quite a team.

'Sir.' Thurlow wanted my full attention. 'Professor Woods.'

I gave it to him, knew I wasn't going to escape from whatever new darkness he wanted to share with me. 'Tell me.'

'We found some bodies.' The man spoke as quietly as he could, anxious that his words not carry on the wind. 'In one of those locked rooms – one I guess you didn't, or couldn't, get into.'

I remembered Rianna's reaction to that one door, the one Robbie had suggested we tried to knock down, the one she'd seemed agitated by, keen to get away from.

I felt sicker than sick, and cold, intensely cold.

'Maybe you should sit down,' Thurlow suggested.

I didn't move, just leaned against the wall nearest me.

'I take it you knew nothing about them,' he said softly.

I looked at him, saw there was nothing remotely accusatory there, shook my head.

'*Them*,' I echoed, careful not to turn around now, to try to keep my reaction from the kids. 'The missing children?' Mikey Cooper's face flashed into my mind.

The sergeant needed a moment before he could answer. 'We can't tell that yet – haven't been able to take a proper look.' He paused. 'They're all wrapped up, Professor – some kind of *shrink*-wrapping, for Christ's sake.' His face worked. 'But there are seven bodies down there, all lined up in that room.' He swallowed hard, met my eyes. 'It's a *cold* room, refrigerated, you know?'

'God almighty,' I murmured, then paused to try and clear my head. 'You said seven. There were only six teenagers missing, Sergeant, and that figure included my daughter and Robbie.'

'I know,' Thurlow said. 'I know that, sir. We're waiting on a bunch of people to get here – homicide team, the ME.' He paused. 'I guess you'd know all about that.'

'Some,' I said.

'You were with the department once, is that right?'

'Right.'

I left it there, not bothering to put him straight about the brevity of my NYPD career, hoping he wouldn't ask. Frankly, if there was any chance of that tenuous kinship buying us a slightly easier ride out of this hellhole, I was grabbing it, for the kids' sake.

Thurlow didn't ask, was still too shaken up.

'You know,' I took the opportunity, 'I really do want to get Rianna and Robbie out soon, get them to a hospital, have them checked out.'

'You look like you could use some checking out too,' Thurlow told me. 'And after that, there are going to be a lot of questions for you and for them. The FBI and our people are going to need every ounce of information they can get.'

I wanted to ask about *him*, but I had one more question to put first.

'Has anyone talked to Lydia Johanssen yet? Told her that Robbie's safe?'

'So far as I know, we haven't been able to reach her yet,' Thurlow said. 'She wasn't home, last I heard.'

'That's because she's at my place,' I told him. 'She's been staying there with my other daughter.'

Thurlow shook his head. 'No, sir, she's not there either.'

My instant panic must have lit me up like a flare.

'Ella's just fine.' Thurlow sought to reassure me. 'The woman with her . . .' He checked his notebook. 'Mrs Ryan?'

'Kim Ryan, yes.' *Relief.*

'She told the New Haven police she's staying with Ella until further notice. She said Mrs Johanssen had to go somewhere.'

The wildfire panic was gone, but my stomach was still clenched tight. I took a quick look over my shoulder at Rianna and Robbie, saw they were hanging in, turned back to the sergeant. 'You haven't found the sonofabitch, have you? I mean, we don't have a clue where he is? Fitzgerald – if it *is* Fitzgerald?'

'Not yet.' His face told me he wasn't sure who Fitzgerald was.

'Okay.' I could feel my jaw clenching. 'Then I want someone at my home to stand guard over Ella, okay?'

'Professor—'

'This bastard is crazy, Sergeant, totally *nuts*. We know now what he's capable of, don't we? He might go after Ella, same way he did Rianna. He might do just about *anything*.'

'I'll see what I can do,' Thurlow said.

My mind did another spin. 'Do you know what happened to Baum?'

The other man's face was blank.

'Norman Baum,' I told him. 'He's a PI who was helping me out when I got whacked at Fitzgerald's place.' I scrubbed wildly at my hair, realizing how much there was that I didn't know, that maybe these cops, maybe even the FBI, didn't know about yet. 'You need to tell Kline to get out there, to Fitzgerald's house. I mean, there's a chance that's where the creep's gone, though I doubt it. But someone needs to look for Baum – maybe he's still *there*.'

Thurlow put out a steadying hand, gripped hold of my right arm. 'Take it easy, sir. We're dealing with everything fast as we can.'

I knew it had to sound as if I was rambling, but there wasn't anything I could do about that. 'One priority, please, Sergeant – my daughter.' I managed to keep my voice low. 'My *other* daughter. You have to tell the New Haven PD to get right over there, keep Ella safe, *please*.'

'I'll radio that in,' Thurlow said, 'right away.'

'It isn't *over*.' I knew I was beginning to sound borderline hysterical, but *Jesus*. 'I thought it was over when we got out, but it isn't, it won't be over till you find that *filth*.' I shook off the NYPD man's hand. 'And I really need to get those two kids out of here.'

'Soon as it's safe,' Thurlow said.

'*Safe*? What do you mean, *safe*?' I didn't understand. 'Do you think the bastard's still down there? Is that what you're trying to tell me?'

'No, that's not what I'm saying at all,' the sergeant assured me. 'The place has been gone over too well for that, Professor.' He paused. 'Like I said, it's a matter of clearing a route for them.' Another beat. 'We really don't want your daughter or her friend seeing those remains, do we?'

Oh Jesus.

Seven.

Chapter 106

She'd ground coffee beans and boiled water, and now it was filtering slowly through paper into a glass pot, and she kept expecting him to hurry her up, maybe become aggressive, but he was still just sitting there quietly at her kitchen table, looking tired, like an ordinary man after several bad days at the office. Tired and preoccupied. And strange. *Strange* was the word that kept coming back.

Of course he's strange.

He'd told her that Robbie was okay, but she didn't know what that really *meant*, realized that whatever he said, she couldn't believe a single word that came out of his mouth. They'd probably be free by now, he'd said, but she didn't know what that meant, either. *Free* could mean . . .

She wanted to grab him scream at him to tell her the truth, tell her exactly where Robbie and Rianna and Jake were (*and the others, don't forget about the others*); but for all Lydia knew, he might still be holding the power of life and death over them all.

And anyway, he had the gun.

So instead, she set a tray and brought it to the table, poured coffee for him, left him to help himself or ask her for cream and sugar, and then sat at the opposite end – not too close, not too threatening for either of them. He didn't ask for sugar or cream, and now a dozen debates were wrangling in her mind about how best to proceed, if she had the choice.

Ignore the gun, and maybe he'll forget it's there.

354

'You must be angry,' she said quietly.

Start a dialogue. Wasn't that what hostages were advised to do?

He shook his head.

'Upset then,' Lydia said.

He didn't respond.

'If you've let them go,' she said. 'If it's all over, you must be upset.' She picked up her cup, wasn't sure how she managed to. 'I thought you might have come here because you were angry with me.'

'Why would I be angry with you, Mrs Johanssen?'

At last, an answer.

'Because I got involved. Got Jake Woods involved.' Lydia paused. 'Told the FBI I was suspicious of Eryx.'

A small, almost sad kind of a smile played on his lips.

'I was angry,' he admitted, 'with you and the professor.' He paused. 'Not any more, though. I feel much calmer now.'

He was so well-mannered.

Don't let that fool you. They say Ted Bundy had great manners.

He didn't touch his coffee cup, though.

Chapter 107

We were *out*.

Down on the street, bewildered again, dazed by New York City and by events, being guided by the good sergeant and two officers through the cleared area outside the building. Rianna and Robbie both covered up with blankets, not that that was stopping the rubberneckers, and I caught myself wondering what they'd think if they could see the skimpy outfits the bastard had made them wear – as it was, our bare feet must have been intriguing.

I paused to look around, trying to use the familiarity of the location to maybe anchor myself. It was so crowded, so incredibly noisy – after rush hour, I saw, glancing up at a clock on a building, but still wild just the same. There was Macy's, diagonally across the square from us, early evening customers flowing steadily in and out. Other stores, flashing their booty at us, a big toy shop, Florsheim, GAP, the usual. The little patch of square in the centre with its bronze memorial to James Gordon Bennett, founder of the *New York Herald*. Entrances all over to 34th Street Station.

'Do you believe that?' Robbie said, on my left, staring at the station.

'No helicopter,' Rianna said.

I got what they were saying. I'd almost forgotten the *Limbo* connection. Age, I guess, or maybe an intense urge *to* forget.

'Come on, my friends.' Sergeant Thurlow nudged me.

The bus was there, at the Thirty-fourth Street intersection, and we could see that the door, *our* door, had sliced through its roof, right through the interior. No passengers, not any more. No clues as to what had happened to them. No blood, thank God, at least not on the outside.

I gripped the kids' arms, Rianna one side, Robbie the other, as we passed the bus on the way to the waiting ambulance, wishing I could have shielded them from that sight. *One too many*? Who knew?

'Was anyone killed?' Robbie asked.

'Not so far as we know,' one of the officers moving with them answered, trying to propel us all a little faster.

'You *must* know,' Robbie insisted, getting upset.

Rianna wasn't crying now, had stopped a while back, up on the roof, but she was very quiet, too quiet, I thought.

'I need to know,' Robbie persisted. 'I let go the door, *I* let it go through the rail over the side. I need to *know*.'

'Why don't you get in the ambulance,' Thurlow suggested to him gently, 'wait in there while I find someone who can tell me what happened? Okay?'

'Good idea,' I said, and nodded gratefully at the sergeant, hoping he'd catch my thought waves and make sure that if the news was bad, he'd keep it from Robbie at least a while longer.

We reached the ambulance, got inside.

'Where's my mother?' Robbie asked suddenly, getting more agitated by the second.

'It's okay,' Rianna said to him. 'It's all going to be okay now, Robbie.'

She got up from where she'd been told to sit, moved so she was right beside him, put her arm around his shoulders, and again I could see that she was calming him down, at least a little. Watching them, I wondered at the closeness between them, tried for a second to imagine what they must have endured together, then stopped myself from imagining. Too cowardly, I guess. Or maybe just too soon.

Thurlow came back, smiling. 'Good news,' he told us all, from outside on the sidewalk. 'No one killed, thank God.'

'But injured?' Robbie again.

'One woman broke her arm,' the sergeant told him, straight. 'A young guy fractured his ankle, some general cuts and bruises and a few cases of shock, which is hardly surprising, considering . . .' He looked up at Robbie, looked him in the eye. 'No one killed, okay? No major injuries.' He paused. 'You believe me?'

Robbie nodded.

'*Say* you believe me, Robbie,' Thurlow pressed. 'Make me feel better.'

Robbie almost smiled. 'I believe you.'

Thurlow stepped back, and the doors were closed.

The ambulance began to move. I realized, suddenly, that I hadn't taken a real look at the building we'd been held in, but it was too late; I couldn't see from inside the vehicle, which made it seem all the more unreal. Hard, almost impossible, to believe. I made up my mind to come back, when all this was over, when they had Fitzgerald – if it *was* him – when we were *sure* it was over, to take a proper look, maybe help lay a few ghosts.

'You two okay?' I asked.

They both nodded. Very pale now. Drained. Survivors.

My mind was jammed with wall-to-wall questions, all unanswered, all apparently unanswerable for the time being. Where had Lydia gone? Where was Baum? And still, the number one question: who was *he*? Was it William Fitzgerald, my *numero uno* candidate? And right or wrong, where was *he* now?

And tangling through all that brain wreckage, an image, only *imagined*, thank Christ, of the bodies.

The cops had done all they could, had hung up sheeting over the broken doorframe so the kids couldn't see inside the room, but as we'd passed by, the unnatural cold had hit us all, and I'd heard Rianna cry out with surprise and Robbie mutter something under his breath. No one else had said a word, but I knew it was something we were going to have to deal with along with everything else, especially . . .

Oh God. The Coopers.

Seven bodies. And no sign of Michael.

Oh, dear *God*. Poor, poor Fran and Stu and all the other parents.

Another thing to tear my mind away from as we jiggered about in the back of the ambulance. *Focus on what you* can *do, Jake*.

First, make sure that Rianna and Robbie were safe and sound at the hospital.

Second, find a phone, talk to Ella, then Kim, then the New Haven police to convince myself that my little one was safe and protected.

And then, last but by no means least, I was going to find Lydia. See her face when I told her that Robbie was fine.

Hold her.

Chapter 108

'It's true,' he said suddenly, 'that it's all gone wrong.' He shrugged. 'What's another screw-up?'

Lydia waited for more, but that seemed to be it.

'Most people,' she ventured, 'would call you a very successful man.'

'Why?' His mouth quirked. 'Because I helped create a game that earns millions of dollars?' His blue eyes seemed almost amused for a moment. 'A game that keeps too many kids glued to electronic boxes when they could be outside, breathing fresh air?' He paused. 'My father wouldn't have called that successful.'

Lydia's brain flicked back wildly, trying to remember Baum's report on this man's family, but her mind wasn't working properly.

'Your father?' she prompted him, carefully.

He blinked, seemed to go blank.

Wrong question, Lydia.

'I'm hungry,' he said, suddenly. 'What I'd really like is something to eat. If you don't mind, that is.'

Polite again, as he had been about the coffee, not like a hostage-taker making demands.

Which he is, Lydia reminded herself − not that she *needed* reminding, but what she was thinking about now, just at this minute − namely what was in her refrigerator and what would be the best thing to give him − was just so commonplace, so *ludicrous*, under the circumstances . . . *Nothing spicy*. She'd read in a magazine at the hairdressers' a few months ago – in another lifetime – that some people's stress levels rose when they ate certain things, and she'd scoffed at it then, but now she wished she could remember which foods they'd said were soothing . . .

Which foods, ideally, could send a gunman into a *coma*.

She walked across to open the door and peer inside. She hadn't been cooking, of course, but Josh's mother, still the proverbial good neighbour, had brought her up some kind of covered casserole several days ago which she'd never even looked at. She took a look now, saw it was a good old-fashioned pot roast. *Comfort food*, she thought, took out the dish and walked back to the table to show him.

'Pot roast?' she asked.

'Fine,' he said. *Less polite*.

Lydia sent blessings to Melanie Steinman and carried it away again, placed it on the worktop, then bent to switch on her oven.

'The microwave would be faster,' said her dinner guest.

'Not as good,' Lydia said.

'Good enough,' he said. 'I want to make sure I have enough time to eat.'

That scared her again.

Enough time before what?

Chapter 109

We were at Bellevue; *not* the place I'd have chosen to take those kids, recalling a visit with a friend some years back, remembering their ER as a major zoo, but Thurlow had reminded me, somewhat sternly, that it was a damned good hospital and more than equipped to take care of Rianna and Robbie for now. Yet again, the sergeant had been right. Those people knew only a fraction of what the kids had been through, yet all I'd seen thus far was gentleness, protectiveness, and a heaven-sent touch of normality.

A doctor named Lundquist, attractive blonde woman of about thirty, came out to tell me that both kids seemed in pretty good physical shape, which was, she felt, kind of amazing, especially in Robbie's case.

'We're going to X-ray your daughter's ankle,' she said, 'though we're almost certain it's just a sprain, as you thought.'

'Did she tell you she's a gymnast?' I hadn't even thought of that till now – it hadn't seemed remotely important in the grander scheme of things – but suddenly, life, blessedly *ordinary* life, lay ahead, and Rianna's love of gymnastics mattered again.

'She told me,' Lundquist said, 'and I'm ninety-nine and a half per cent sure there won't be a problem.' She paused to take a long look at me. 'You look like you could use a check over, too.'

'Not necessary.' One of the cops had taken my torn, stained shirt and found me a clean, white T-shirt and some sneakers, and already I felt better.

She reached for my left arm and raised it for inspection. 'Those lacerations need cleaning up, maybe a stitch or two.' She let go of the arm and took another look up at my face. 'I hear you knocked down a wall and a door today, Professor Woods.'

I shrugged. *Macho man, but modest with it.*

'Maybe a couple of X-rays for you, too.' Lundquist smiled. 'Better safe.'

'Not before I find a phone.' I smiled back at her. 'I'm sure you'll find someone more worthwhile to take care of in the meantime.'

The lady was already gone.

I called home, fingers trembling a little.

Ella picked up.

Joy. The pure, unadulterated kind.

'Daddy, are you okay? Is Rianna with you? Is she really okay? Kim says she's fine, but is she *really*? What *happened* to you?'

'We're both fine, baby.' The damned tears started up again.

'Daddy, why are you crying? Daddy, what's *wrong*?'

'Nothing's wrong, sweetheart.' Now I was laughing. 'Everything's absolutely wonderful. Rianna hurt her ankle a little – nothing major, I swear it. I'm only crying because I'm just so happy to hear your voice.'

We went back and forth like that for a few minutes. Ella had somehow gleaned the information – I guessed from eavesdropping on the phone, since I knew Kim would never have told her – that I'd been nabbed by the abductor, and so once she'd established that Rianna and I were alive and well, she wanted chapter and verse on what *exactly* had happened. And maybe later, *much* later, I would find sufficient carefully chosen words to satisfy Ella's thirst for detail, without pouring too much more darkness into her nine-year-old brain. I remembered someone telling me once that too *little* information could be as damaging as too much when it came to kids and their all-too-vivid imaginations . . .

Not now though.

'I have to talk to Kim, honey.' It was the third time I'd tried to persuade Ella to relinquish the phone. 'Now, please. It's important.'

At last, she gave it up.

'Are the cops there?' I asked Kim without preamble.

'Right outside the street door. Two good guys, big and tough-looking, and *not* the kind to drop their guard.'

I blessed her for those details.

'Are you both really okay, Jake?'

'We really are, incredibly enough.' I paused. 'They told me Lydia's not home. Have you any idea where she might be? Do you know if she said anything to Ella before she left?'

'We were out when she left.' Kim paused. 'Though Ella did mention that Lydia had been getting hung up about the subway.'

'Subway?' I echoed, stupidly. New Haven has no subway system.

'Ella said Lydia was looking up stuff about the New York subway on the Internet,' Kim explained. 'A website that had to do with abandoned tunnels. Ella said she asked her if that was where she thought Rianna was, and Lydia said definitely not, but I know it got Ella thinking.'

'So do you think Lydia came back to New York?'

'I assumed she'd gone home,' Kim said.

I hung up a moment later and tried Lydia's apartment. The machine picked up, and I started to leave a message – the kind I really wanted to leave – but some of what I wanted to say wasn't the stuff you left on a machine, so I kept it simple, told her the single thing that was going to matter most to her:

'It's Jake. Robbie's safe, Lydia. He's *really* safe, and so's Rianna, and we're all at Bellevue, *not* because anything's wrong, just because they want to check the kids over. But Robbie's safe and fine, and where *are* you?' I paused. 'I'll try you again soon.'

Out of the corner of one eye I saw Dr Lundquist looking my way, turned my face away, made my next call, to FBI headquarters, and was almost instantly patched through to Special Agent Kline in Connecticut.

'Good to hear your voice, Professor.' He sounded genuinely glad. 'Great news about your daughter and the Johanssen boy.'

'Doesn't look good for the others,' I said.

'We have no ID yet on those bodies,' Kline cautioned.

'I'm not going to talk to anyone,' I told him swiftly, then got on with what I wanted to know. 'Have you found Fitzgerald?'

'Not yet,' Kline said. 'We're out at his place right now.'

'What about Norman Baum? You know he was with me when I got whacked outside Fitzgerald's house?'

'No sign yet,' Kline said, 'but his partner is here with us, so you can rest assured people are looking for your pal as we speak.' The agent paused. 'There's a PERT team – that's Physical Evidence Response—'

'I know about PERT.' It was good they were already on the scene.

'We're not taking it as given that Fitzgerald's our man, even if you *did* get taken on his land – though we are looking for him and the other Eryx partners *big* time, so you can relax.'

Relax. I couldn't remember the last time. I knew that by *big* time, Kline meant agents at every conceivable airport, train and bus station, at car rental companies, probably checking on helicopter and small plane arrivals and departures. But right now there was something else I wanted to ask the man about, but it was dancing around on the edge of my brain, which seemed to have turned to goddamned useless mud. What the hell had happened to all my own training, for heaven's sake? My responses were *shot*.

It came back to me.

'Do we know yet,' I asked, 'who leases the top storeys of the building we were being held in?'

'We're way ahead of you, Professor,' Kline said. 'Details still coming in.'

'Korda's the biggest property collector of the bunch, isn't he? Apartments and houses all over the place – maybe a floor or two on top of Herald Square?'

'Maybe.' Kline reverted to brisk. 'You going to let us do our jobs now, Professor? We're rounding up all three men fast as we can.'

I managed not to say *about time*. 'Let me know when you find Baum.'

'Speaking of finding,' Kline said, 'have you talked to Mrs Johanssen?'

'She's not answering her phone,' I told him.

'We've talked to her doorman, and he buzzed her, but no answer,' Kline said. 'Seems a damned shame for her not to know her son's safe.'

'Tell me about it,' I said.

Chapter 110

It was dark outside.

The food was on the table. Lydia had put down two plates, Melanie Steinman's casserole dish on a heat-proof board between them. It was serving to block out the view of the gun, but even so, Lydia couldn't imagine she was going to be able to eat. She supposed he wanted her to share this meal since he'd clearly chosen her to share . . .

Share *what*? She still didn't know why he was here.

He laid his napkin on his lap, picked up his fork, took a bite, shut his blue eyes, swallowed, opened them again.

'Very good,' he said. 'I don't think I've had pot roast since I was a boy.'

'Did your mother make it for you?' Lydia asked.

He laughed. A hollow kind of laugh. 'As I recall, I don't think my mother ever cooked anything.'

Lydia took a small forkful, managed to swallow it, not really tasting it, could hardly comprehend what was happening, how she was managing to sit at her family table, eating supper with the man who had abducted Robbie and Rianna and at least four other children.

For a moment, she experienced a surge of panic, and then it subsided, submerged immediately by something almost worse; an awful, frightening sense of detachment from herself and her surroundings, from the man sitting opposite her with the gun. It felt like being trapped in cotton wool and she *hated* it, and it seemed to take a supreme effort for her to punch a hole in the blanketing cloud, but she managed it. *Fall apart later, Lydia.*

She picked up her fork for the second time, looked across at him, saw that he really was eating, really did seem to be hungry, as he'd said, wondered again what exactly she was doing here now, feeding him, sharing pot roast with him.

Waiting, she answered herself. Waiting to be saved.

Surviving. For Robbie. And Jake.

Chapter 111

Thea Lomax was only fifty yards away when a deputy from the Middlesex County Sheriff's office, carrying a flashlight and gun, found Norman Baum.

In a thicket of trees, some way back from William Fitzgerald's driveway.

Hands and feet tied with cord, handkerchief stuffed in his mouth, semi-conscious and hypothermic.

But alive.

Chapter 112

Dr Lundquist had told me that she thought both Robbie and Rianna should stay in for one night's observation, and her suggestion to me was that I do the same, but the fact was, I wasn't prepared even to *contemplate* that with both Fitzgerald and Lydia still unaccounted for.

Lomax had called a little while back with her news about Baum, and to tell me that, upon reflection, she thought *she* might have been one of the last people to talk to Lydia.

'In fact,' she'd told me, 'I figured out that we last spoke at around the time you and the kids were ramming your way out onto that roof. I know what time that was because the door hitting the bus in Herald Square made the news, and they said it happened at around six p.m., still rush hour, and that was when Lydia and I agreed it was time to report you officially missing.'

'And you're sure she was home then?' I asked.

'She called me. I have caller ID.'

Hanging up, I had a bad, *bad* feeling.

The question was whether or not I was going to tell Kline about it.

Answer: I was not. Because just supposing there was some substance to this new feeling – and I was hoping to hell and back that I was wrong, just imagining things . . . But supposing I was *right* and Lydia was in some kind of trouble right there inside her apartment, and I passed on that information to the FBI . . . then a whole damned SWAT team would head over to

West Seventy-third Street, which would almost certainly plant Lydia smack in the middle of a siege situation.

Whereas maybe – just *maybe* – I could find a way of going in quietly.

I did have one advantage. I had talked to him, the man behind the distorted voice. I knew some things about him. I knew that while he had murdered seven people that we knew of, he claimed to have hated killing. More significantly, I decided, he hadn't *wanted* to kill any more, because if he had wanted that, he would have killed Rianna or Robbie or me, or all three of us. And he had not done that.

I knew he was a deeply sick, deeply disturbed and, by now, *deranged* man. Which meant that if he was Fitzgerald, for example, then he surely had to have taken a massive nose dive into the psychological pit since anyone else had last seen him.

I have never hoped so intently to be wrong in all my life.

I hoped – prayed – that the bastard had crawled under a stone someplace and killed *himself*.

But I made one more phone call.

To the doorman on duty at Lydia's building.

'I already told the FBI—'

'I know you did,' I said, 'but I need you to buzz her one more time.'

'No problem.' The man sounded amenable.

The wait was endless.

As I heard the clatter of his phone being picked up again, my nails were gouging tiny crescents into my palms.

'No answer. Would you like me to go upstairs, sir? Ring her bell, maybe? I'm due to go off duty in just a little while. Soon as Joseph gets here to relieve me, I could take a ride up to the fifteenth . . .'

I hesitated for just an instant.

Then told him no.

Kline had just received word that Korda had been seen by his ex-wife in New York City about ten hours earlier.

Pamela Korda had told an agent from the field office that

371

he'd come to see his children and then left, and she didn't know where he'd gone after that. Unless he was actually taking their kids or going overseas, she said their father was not in the habit of reporting his schedule to her.

The lawyer for Eryx, Alan Tillman, had talked to Agent Phil Rubik, informing him that he had suggested to Korda that he hole up for a few days because he was so sick at heart about the abductions. Tillman told Rubik that he was personally appalled by the news of the deaths, though relieved by the news of the rescue, and said he was certain that Korda, Fitzgerald and Hawthorne would all feel the same way as soon as they heard.

The search of Fitzgerald's property was still underway. If the owner showed his face there, a substantial armed presence would be ready and waiting for him.

Kline, in the meantime, was boarding a chopper.

Heading for New York City.

Rianna was safely settled in her room for the night, Robbie next door. Plenty of hospital personnel taking care of them, and one of John Thurlow's officers sticking around too, though Robbie had forcefully made the point that if he wasn't going to be allowed to walk about the hospital corridors, get himself a drink, a little *freedom*, then he wasn't going to stay. He knew as well as I did that he didn't have too much choice in the matter, but we all got the message. The poor kid had been a prisoner for more than two months.

And if truth be told, I was no longer nearly as anxious as I had been that either he or Rianna might still be at immediate risk from the abductor.

Killer.

I was, by now, too damned scared that our man had gradu-ated to adults.

Which was why I'd cleaned myself up some more, given Rianna a big hug, told her I was going out for a while, and then left Bellevue and caught a cab uptown.

*

Joseph, the doorman now on duty, a tall, reedy-looking man with a small head topped with frizzy red hair, was helpful and friendly, without the air of suspicion some Manhattan doormen bestow on strangers asking questions. Right now, I wasn't sure if that was good or bad news.

'Mrs Johanssen was home a few hours ago,' he told me. 'But Anthony, the guy who just went off duty, told me there's no one answering now.'

'How do you know she was home earlier?' I asked him. 'Did you see her?'

Joseph shook his small head. 'I sent up a visitor.'

'Who?' My antennae were up and prickling.

'I can't tell you that.' Suspicion, finally. 'Do you want me to try the apartment again?'

'Is there a spare key to 15C?'

Joseph's hazel eyes were growing beady. 'I can't use a spare key without Mrs Johanssen's permission.'

'I'm not asking you to use it.' *Stay calm.* 'I'm asking you to give it to me so *I* can use it.'

'Impossible.'

'I understand your position, Joseph.' I looked quickly around the lobby, saw it was still empty, leaned a little closer across his desk. 'The problem is, I think it's possible Mrs Johanssen might be up there with a dangerous man.'

Joseph's eyebrows lifted a little, then his eyes narrowed further. 'That's not what the FBI said when they phoned and talked to Anthony.'

'That's because they didn't know.'

'And you do?' The doorman's scepticism was growing.

'I'm not one hundred per cent sure, which is why I just want to let myself in quietly, without a fuss.' I looked him in the eye. 'You're welcome to wait outside in the hall, make sure I don't burglarize the apartment.'

'If you think there's something bad going on, you should call the cops.' Joseph shook his head again. 'I mean, I don't know you from Adam. What did you say your name is?'

I hadn't said. I did now.

The other man's face grew more distrustful.

'What?' I asked. '*What*?'

The doorman bent his head, frowning at the book on his desk, then looked back up at me. 'You're Mr Woods?'

This was the kind of thing that made people with short fuses grab others by their scrawny *necks*. 'What is your problem now, Joseph?'

'My problem,' he told me, 'is that someone else came by today using the same name.'

'To see Mrs Johanssen?' The bad feeling was growing more powerful.

'Except he was a professor.' Joseph checked the book again and nodded. 'Professor Woods. 15C. 6.03 p.m.'

Bad gave way to full-blown panic, but just then a middle-aged woman with heavy-looking shopping bags came in off the street and Joseph, on automatic, turned to greet her, offering to help.

I bit down on the panic. If I wanted to help Lydia now, I had to stay *calm*.

The woman headed for the elevators just as a young man with tinted spectacles and purplish hair emerged from one, waved hi to Joseph and disappeared through a door into what I guessed was the mail room.

'Okay,' I got the doorman's attention again, 'you *have* to listen to me now, Joseph. Are you saying that the man calling himself Professor Woods was allowed to go up to 15C? Is *that* what you're saying?'

'I buzzed the apartment.' Suddenly Joseph was on the defensive. 'I talked to Mrs Johanssen, told her Woods was down here and she told me to send him up.'

'Listen to me, Joseph.' Starting to look and sound threatening, the only way now. 'The man you let go up to 15C was *not* Professor Jake Woods. *I* am. That man is almost certainly a kidnapper and a murderer. Are you with me?'

Poor guy was with me okay, little eyes almost popping out of his skull.

'If you give me that spare key, right now' – fast and hard –

'then maybe, just maybe, this whole mess can be cleared up and no one may ever need to find out that you were the one who let him in.'

'How the hell was I supposed to know?' Starting to bluster. 'We don't get told to ask for ID. Guy gave his name, I called it up, that's all I'm meant to do.'

'Fine,' I said. 'Give me the key.'

'How do I know *you're* telling the truth?'

'You don't yet, but you will.' I remembered the wallet in my back pocket, the driver's licence and the fifty still in there, remembered the power of greed. I pulled it out, snapped the licence and the money under his nose. 'These help you believe me?'

Joseph glanced around nervously.

'Just between ourselves,' I told him.

He opened a drawer in the desk, started fishing around in it, then stopped. 'What if I give you the key and it makes things worse? I should call the cops first.'

I leaned in closer, getting ready to grab all the keys if he left me no choice. 'If the cops come in now,' I told him through gritted teeth, 'they're going to turn this thing into a siege. And if something happens to Mrs Johanssen, it'll be the fault of the fucking *moron* who let a killer into the building in the first place. Do you get my drift, Joseph? *Do* you?' I thrust out the money again.

Joseph found the key, held it up, looked at the fifty. 'If I don't hear from you in fifteen minutes, I'm calling 911.'

I grabbed the key. 'Make it an hour' – I was running to the elevators, pushing the call buttons – 'then call the cops *and* the FBI. Ask for Special Agent Roger Kline.'

'Half an hour,' Joseph haggled as the kid with purple hair came out of the mail room and shot him a quizzical look.

The elevator arrived.

I got in and pushed the button.

Chapter 113

The man at Lydia's kitchen table was ready to start talking again.

He had eaten most of his pot roast in near silence, and now he laid down his fork and looked straight at her.

'We were talking about my father,' he said.

As if the intervening half-hour or so had not happened.

'We had the same name,' he said. 'He was Hal Hawthorne, too. No one called me Junior, thank God for small mercies, but they did call me "young Hal".'

Lydia suddenly remembered Baum's report on his father. *War hero*. That was it. Disabled war hero and benefactor. Died young.

She waited.

'My father was an amazing man,' Hawthorne said. 'Everyone said so. A hero. Vietnam. Not rejected, like so many – too much money, I guess. He used his disability afterwards, as well as his wealth, made it work for him. My mother told me once that sport was never a big deal to him before 'Nam, but afterwards he made out it was his unattainable Holy Grail. If *he* couldn't have it, Father said he wanted to help as many others as possible to have the good fortune he'd missed out on.'

He paused for breath. He'd been talking rapidly, his receding hairline damp with perspiration.

'He funded other things, too,' he went on. 'Hospitals, schools, but when he could, he focused on sports: tennis farms, swimming pools, gyms all over.' He nodded. 'Gymnastics was the ultimate from his perspective, the toughest, he thought, maybe just the one most out of reach for a man in a wheelchair. Though he liked anything that required courage. *Guts* was my father's favourite word.'

Hawthorne stopped again, looked across the table into Lydia's eyes. 'I'm sorry,' he said, and his glance veered away, down to the gun on the table. 'Truth is, I think perhaps I need to talk now, while I can.'

Lydia said nothing, had no wish to stop him, knew that what she needed most was time. Time for people – Jake, the FBI, Thea Lomax, Baum, *whoever* – to come find her, extricate her from this.

Where are they all?

'I'm not feeling so great,' Hawthorne said. 'I'm not exactly sure why I came here, Lydia, but I think – though my mind's been getting a little mixed up these past few days . . . I *think* I figured that being a mother, you might be the one to talk to.' He shook his head. 'Not that I expect you to really *understand*. Not after the things I've done.' He paused. 'But women, so I've been told, are better listeners, more understanding than men.'

377

Chapter 114

The phone rang in Robbie's hospital room while he was dozing.

'Hey, man,' Josh said, 'how's it going?'

Robbie had called him earlier, had been cautioned by the FBI not to talk to anyone but family about his release, but had claimed Josh as a close cousin, partly because he'd wanted to hear his voice, but mostly because he'd hoped Josh or his mom might know where his mother was.

'Anything?' Robbie asked now, sitting up.

'I'm not sure,' Josh said, keeping his voice low. 'But I just heard something down in our lobby and figured you'd want to know.' He hesitated.

'What?'

'A guy – I think it was this guy, Woods, your professor, okay? Anyway, he was down there telling Joseph the doorman he thought something bad might be going down in your apartment.' Josh paused. 'And then Joseph gave him a key, and Woods said if he didn't hear from him in an hour, he could call the cops, but Joseph said a *half*-hour, and Woods got on the elevator—'

'Okay.' Robbie's voice was sharp. 'Here's what you have to do, Josh. Josh, are you *listening*?'

'Sure I'm listening.'

'I need some clothes – and sneakers.'

'My clothes?' Realization was already hitting Josh, too late, that maybe his friend was the very *last* person he ought to have told about this.

'Of course, *your* clothes, unless you feel like going up to 15C and asking a goddamn kidnapper if you can go into my bedroom and fetch—'

'Okay, okay.' Josh cut him short. 'You really think he's up there?'

'I don't know,' Robbie said, 'but if Jake was there and said that . . .' He focused again on what he needed. 'So I need clothes, and a weapon, like a knife – one of those mean-looking kitchen knives—'

'Hold on,' Josh said. 'Have you gone *nuts* or what?'

'Didn't your dad used to have an air rifle?'

'No, my dad never had an air rifle,' Josh said, 'but if he did, I sure as hell would not be stealing it to give it to you, so you can—'

'Keep your pants on,' Robbie said. 'Forget the rifle, but bring a knife or *something*, so I don't have to go in unarmed.'

'*Unarmed*? Jesus, man, I wish I hadn't told you now.'

'You told me because you're my best friend,' Robbie said. 'So are you going to help me or not? Because whether you do or not, Josh, there's no way I'm going to sit here one minute longer while my mom's in danger.'

'We don't know if she *is*,' Josh pointed out.

'Then if she isn't, I won't have a problem, will I?'

'You have to tell the FBI,' Josh said, 'let them handle it.'

'No way,' Robbie said. 'Chrissake, we *know* what happens when the cops come in too soon and things get out of control.'

'That's just in the movies.'

'It's on the news, man, all the time, you know it is.'

'So where's it different if *you* go in?' Josh asked.

'It's different because it's personal,' Robbie answered. 'I love my mother, the cops don't. *And* I care about Jake.' He paused. 'So are you going to come, bring the stuff, or what?' He waited. '*Josh*?'

'Yeah, okay,' Josh said.

'Then for Christ's sake, *hurry*.'

379

Chapter 115

Hawthorne and Lydia both heard a sound – like a dull thump from somewhere outside the apartment, but *in* the building nevertheless, close enough to stop him talking, close enough to make him reach for the gun, pick it up, get to his feet, go to the kitchen door and listen.

'It's just neighbours,' Lydia said, staying in her seat.

Hawthorne turned towards her and motioned with the gun for her to be silent, his face suddenly taut, veins standing out on both temples, his breathing rapid and shallow. For the first time, Lydia was *truly* afraid of what he might do; not so much for herself, but the thought of Robbie coming home, at long last, and finding tragedy was simply unthinkable.

And Jake. A flash of memory, of the warmth and strength and tenderness of the man, swept over her.

Another reason to get through this.

I'd taken the elevator to the thirteenth floor, so I could walk up to the fifteenth and approach as quietly as possible.

I knew what I was doing was foolhardy at *best*; knew that last time I'd gone off half-cocked I'd got Baum concussed and myself locked up; knew there was a good chance *he* might hear or even see me come through Lydia's front door, in which case I might end up increasing the danger for her, the *last* thing I wanted to do.

That was why I was treading softly along her corridor, praying no neighbour would emerge and ask what I was doing, and questioning my own motives as I went. Was this about playing the hero for Lydia? *If it is, stop right now.* But it wasn't that, was it? It was about a breakdown in trust, in the system, and maybe I was wrong, God help us all, but what I was doing here and now was trying for a last-chance end to the nightmare without recourse to a SWAT operation that would inevitably put Lydia in the line of fire.

No neighbours, thank Christ.

I put my ear to the front door of 15C, heard nothing, crouched low enough to listen at the narrow gap between door and floor.

Something. A voice. Male. Scarcely audible from here.

I'd tried, in the cab from Bellevue, to remember the exact layout of Lydia's apartment, and now I figured that *he* was either in the living room or kitchen – and I hoped it was the kitchen because that had two doors, one from the living room, the other from the corridor leading to the bedroom area.

Whichever, I was committed now.

I straightened up, held the key up to the lock. My hand was shaking. I took a breath, told myself to get a grip.

Slid the key into the lock.

Hawthorne was back at the table, the sound forgotten.

'The thing is,' he said, 'my guts-are-all-you-need dad had a coward for a son.'

Lydia watched the vigilance leave his face again as he got back into history, sent up a prayer of thanks for more time bought.

'The son didn't like it that way, would have given anything to be the courageous type of kid his father wanted, *needed*, but it just wasn't possible. My father decided from his wheelchair that his son was going to be the bold, physically remarkable specimen *he* could only dream about being. Young Hal was going to be a great athlete or a gymnast, he was going to play polo, ice hockey – you name it, so long as it was *tough*.'

'That must have been hard,' Lydia said.

'Some of it wasn't so bad,' Hawthorne said. 'I could wing it with some sports, just muddle through, play the games and never quite make it onto the team, you know? If they were school sports, Father couldn't always be there to watch – though he never did just *watch*, of course, he had to coach and heckle and bellow from the sidelines.' He paused. 'And then, out of school, he took young Hal to one of those damned great swimming pools he'd paid to have built, and tried to turn him into a diver.'

Lydia listened and watched, still afraid, of course, but a little fascinated, despite herself . . .

'Father didn't just want young Hal to dive off the side, though.' Hawthorne was speeding up as he talked, as if he knew he was running out of time and had a lot to tell. 'Father wanted him up on the boards, and not the bottom board, either, or even the intermediate – it had to be the *top* board, the kind that Olympic divers take their headers and back flips off – you know the kind?'

'I know,' Lydia said.

'The thing was,' Hawthorne said, 'the *problem* was, young Hal was scared to death of heights.'

Chapter 116

Josh was in a cab on the way to Bellevue.

He'd felt like a thief or some kind of spy, though all he'd done was take his own tracksuit and sneakers – and a kitchen knife – and tell his mom he was going out for a walk.

'Sure, honey, take care,' was all Melanie had said, and he'd been out of there. He'd seen Joseph down in the lobby, looking freaked out, checking his watch and staring at the phone on his desk, and Josh had snuck past him real fast. There'd been a cab right outside, letting out an old guy, and Josh had almost flown into it.

And here they were now, just pulling up outside the hospital, and though Robbie hadn't said anything about how they were going to get back to the building, Josh figured he'd want to make a quick getaway, so he asked the driver to wait.

'I'm picking up a patient,' he told the guy. 'And I'll give you a real good tip.'

He expected the driver to bitch about it or refuse, but maybe he'd picked up on Josh's agitation and thought he was upset about someone who was real sick, because he just said, 'Sure,' and kept the meter running.

Chapter 117

'Did I tell you about the hunting?' Hawthorne asked Lydia.

'No,' she said. 'You didn't.'

He was starting to lose the thread, snatching at memories as they flew past.

Lydia had thought she'd heard something a few seconds ago. A *real* something, just the tiniest sound, and one which *he* hadn't appeared to notice at all; a sound that probably seemed to him like nothing more remarkable than the dripping tap in the sink or the occasional creak of pipes in the walls, or the sound the vertical blinds at the living room window made when the breeze rippled them.

But Lydia knew her apartment very well. She knew the sound that a key inserted quietly, *deliberately* quietly, made, because she had a teenage son who sometimes came home later than agreed – and *that* was what she'd heard just now, unless she was much mistaken.

Hawthorne was telling her something about hunting.

'Father loved it, even in his wheelchair – I guess he thought it proved he was still a *man*. He had to take an entourage to assist, but he still held his gun the whole time, still did the shooting himself.'

Guns. Lydia wished he'd go back to talking about diving or gymnastics.

'One problem, I think, was that my mother was – *is* – a Catholic, and she taught me about hell and damnation, so that was something else to be scared of.' Hawthorne paused.

'Young Hal asked her once about hunting, and she said that *any* killing was evil, and young Hal was so glad to hear her say that, because he hated killing even so much as an insect.'

'Didn't she tell your father that?' Lydia had been trying to tread a fine line between not interrupting and appearing interested. But now she was almost certain that someone had opened her front door and was standing out in her hallway, and she was more determined than ever to keep this conversation in full flow.

'Mother wouldn't have told Father anything like that,' Hawthorne answered her question. 'She gave young Hal what she regarded as basic guidance, then left him to get on with life as well as he could. Mother had her *own* life.' His mouth quirked ironically. 'Heroic wife of heroic invalid, who ran a perfect household and lunched and shopped and raised funds for charities.' He looked across the table into Lydia's eyes. 'You're thinking she was a bad mother, but that's not really true.'

Lydia decided 'bad mothers' might be dangerous territory, kept silent.

'I think that's a good illustration of women being more understanding than men,' Hawthorne went on. 'Mother *understood* that bringing up young Hal was Father's job, and that Lord knew he'd been deprived of too many other things by his disability, so she wasn't going to ruin that for him, too.' He paused again. 'Besides, she probably didn't dare.'

I was in the hall.

My guess had been right – they were in the kitchen, which was not, on reflection, quite as good a thing as I'd first thought, since just about everything I could think of that I might use as a weapon was in that room.

For the first time in well over a decade, I really wished I were still a cop, because at least then I'd have a gun and some up-to-date training to go with it. I wondered what, if anything, *he* was armed with – though maybe he didn't need an actual weapon, not with those damned lethal hands of his . . .

Something . . . Anything . . .

I began a swift mental search through the potential arsenal of the average household . . . Bleach, cans of spray – in the kitchen, along with the knives and, most probably, screwdrivers and the like. Scissors – probably in Lydia's study or Robbie's bedroom – or maybe a letter opener. Hairspray, perfume – not the greatest, but something to spray in his eyes – better than nothing . . .

Floorboards. I couldn't recall any creaking the night I'd stayed here – but then again, I hadn't been creeping around, so I mightn't have noticed . . .

Shoes off.

Robbie's room first. I knew which was his, because Lydia had gone in there to fetch something once when I was here. Door hinges well-oiled, thank God . . . No obstacles to knock into . . . Maybe the kid had a Swiss army knife hidden in a drawer – I figured he'd have had to hide that from his mother . . .

No knife of any kind, nothing really useful at all. A pair of paper cutting scissors, better than nothing, again, if the angle of attack was just right, if I was *desperate* enough . . .

Hurry.

Out of Robbie's room, into the bathroom. *Open the cabinet carefully.* Anti-perspirant, cologne, antiseptic, nothing heavy duty, nothing *blinding*, and most stuff in here was pump action, environmentally friendly, good for the earth, no use for stopping fucking murderers . . .

Lydia's study. Letter opener spectacularly *un*lethal, made of blue plastic, scissors no better than Robbie's . . .

Wasting time . . .

Music room. Piano. Stool. Metronome. Music stand. *Nothing.*

Her bedroom. Sweet memories. *Not now.* Touch of guilt opening her bedside drawer . . . nothing . . . Over to the other side, more guilt – Aaron Johanssen's old drawer. Not his anymore . . . Letters, photographs, old spectacles . . .

Wait.

Last thing I'd expected to find.

A mace spray. Probably ancient, a relic from college, or maybe not.

Best I was going to find here, anyway, and no more time to browse.

Mace, paper scissors and – if the floorboards didn't let me down – the element of surprise.

Chapter 118

Rianna had just limped into Robbie's room when Josh arrived.

She was so restless, had grown bored with TV and trying to sleep, and she'd talked to Ella and Kim and Tom, and the FBI had asked her not to call anyone else, so she hadn't spoken to Shannon, and anyway, she didn't quite feel up to that kind of conversation yet. And she didn't know *where* her dad had disappeared to, and her ankle still hurt, but she couldn't see why she couldn't go home with just a sprained ankle. The only good thing about having to stay here was that Robbie was here too, and suddenly, her family aside, there was no one in the world she'd rather be with.

'Nice to meet you,' she said to Josh when they'd been introduced.

'You too,' Josh said, eyeing her with interest, trying to picture this cute girl in Dakota's leather get-up.

'What's going on?' Rianna asked, seeing Robbie taking a bundle of stuff from Josh's sports bag into the bathroom.

'Keep watch, Josh,' Robbie told his friend.

Josh rolled his eyes but went to the door, opened it a little way and peered up and down the corridor. 'All clear, man.'

'Robbie, what's going on?' Rianna asked again.

Robbie emerged from the bathroom wearing Josh's track-suit. 'Sneakers are a little tight.'

'Well, pardon me for having smaller feet than you, Rob.'

'Why are you wearing Josh's clothes?' Rianna asked.

'Because I'm getting out for a while,' Robbie told her.

Josh looked back towards Rianna. 'Because he's—'

'Because I'm going stir crazy,' Robbie cut in quickly. 'Because I'm going out of my *brain* being cooped up again, so I asked Josh to smuggle in some clothes so I can go outside and get some fresh air.'

He stopped, looked at her, trying to see if she was buying his story.

Hard to tell.

'So would you please cover for me if anyone asks where I am? Tell them I've gone to the cafeteria for something to eat.'

Rianna gave him a long, searching look, then looked at Josh, who didn't meet her eyes, let his gaze slide away, letting her know for *sure* that something else was going on. And then she looked back at Robbie.

She looked, he saw, a little hurt. And a lot worried.

But she didn't say a word.

God, she was terrific, Robbie thought, for about the hundredth time.

Chapter 119

'My father had a cruel streak,' Hawthorne told Lydia, 'but I
think a lot of it came from pure disappointment. I don't think he
could help despising timidity. I think he was trying to do his
son a favour by turning him into a *man*.'

'His idea of a man.' Lydia was being very careful, still a
little fascinated, particularly by Hawthorne's partial references
to himself in the third person.

'Young Hal's problem with killing irked him more than
anything,' he went on, 'turned him extra mean. Father took to
carrying a golf club across the armrests of his chair, used it if he
saw so much as a *bug* big enough to whack at in sight of the
kid.' Hawthorne's blue eyes were very distant. 'He'd ask the
stable hands to tell him when they saw rats, and then he'd make
young Hal watch while he battered the creatures to death before
his eyes.' He paused. 'The rats would squeal, and the boy
would cry, and Father would laugh.'

Chapter 120

Kline was in New York, working out of an MCP – mobile command post – a highly equipped camper van now parked outside the homicide scene on Herald Square.

Scott Korda had been located at his own Upper East Side apartment, where he had been spending the evening with a woman friend from London named Susan Bentinck. Kline had not yet seen him, but had been reliably informed by Moran that while the Eryx president *had* been close enough to the kidnapper's lair to be suspect, his alibis appeared to be holding.

William Fitzgerald had arrived back home fifty-three minutes ago – ostensibly from a visit to his late wife's parents who lived in Cambridge, Massachusetts – to find police and federal agents crawling over his property like roaches on a mission. Anger over the invasion of his property had given way to apparently genuine shock at the news that Baum and Woods had been attacked outside his house.

Zito and Kaminski, when questioned, had both stated that all three partners had been alerted by Nick Ford to the fact that the professor and the PI might be on their way to see them. Korda claimed to have waited for a while, then grown irritated and decided on impulse to go to New York. Fitzgerald's contention was that he'd chosen *not* to stand his ground and wait for Woods and Baum after all, because he'd feared he might be unable to control his anger, which was why he'd gone to Cambridge.

Both Korda and Fitzgerald were being held for questioning.

Susan Bentinck and Fitzgerald's late wife's parents were also still being interviewed.

There had, to date, been no sightings of Hal Hawthorne. Local police had checked the house outside Chester, his apartment in Boston and the New York winery, and had come up empty on all three.

Kline was still waiting on ownership information for the two top storeys of the Herald Square building. Latest, according to Moran, was that those floors were maintained for the 'personal use' of the landlord, and that the whole building was privately owned – though as yet, no one seemed capable of finding out the landlord's identity.

Right now, Kline wasn't letting that needle him.

Right now, the information appeared almost academic.

Prints lifted by PERT from scores of places at the crime scene had tallied perfectly with those lifted inside Hal Hawthorne's office at Eryx; from his desk, chair, telephones, calendar, from the flushing handle of his ensuite john, and any number of other places.

He was still missing.

As was Lydia Johanssen.

Robbie and Josh had made it out of the hospital and were in Josh's cab on their way back to Seventy-third Street.

'Smooth as silk,' Josh had said, relieved, at least for the moment, as he and his newly-nutso buddy sank back against the seats.

Robbie rested for a few minutes, then leaned forward to talk to the driver. 'Second thoughts,' he said, 'can you drop us on Amsterdam and Seventy-second?'

'No problem,' the driver told him, and Robbie sat back again.

'So the plan is we go in from next door, use the basement fire exit door.'

The building next to their own on Seventy-third, designed by the same architects, was almost identical, with a communal back garden and a linked basement with swimming pool, shared laundry room and caretaker's workshop. Robbie and Josh both remembered – from back when locked doors and hide-outs had been their speciality – that that particular door had always been easier to open from the outside than it ought to have been.

'That way,' Robbie went on, his voice low, 'if Joseph or anyone else has called in the cops since you left, we can still get into our own building without being seen.'

'Then what?' Josh's major misgivings were creeping back.

'We take the stairs all the way up to the top – *past* 15 – right up to the roof.'

'I don't want to ask why,' Josh said.

'You know why,' Robbie said.

Josh understood, stared at him. 'You don't mean the trap-door.' He saw from his friend's face that that was *exactly* what he meant. 'You can't be serious, man. You can't be crazy enough to think you could get in that way without the guy seeing or *hearing* you? Jesus Christ, the door *creaks* – even the door from the stairs creaks!'

'No one's going to hear the trapdoor unless they're in the guest room,' Robbie said, 'which they probably won't be.'

'They might be.' Josh raked his hair. 'This is really *nuts*, Rob. This is off the frigging *wall*, you know it is.' He shook his head wildly. 'Tell the cops about the trapdoor – they could use it.'

'Sure they could use it.' Robbie raised a finger to his lips to quieten his friend. 'And that bastard would definitely hear *them* climbing all over the roof and then *they'd* use it to go in all guns blazing.'

'They wouldn't do that,' Josh argued, 'with your mom and Jake inside.'

'They'd overreact,' Robbie insisted. 'They'd spook the sonofabitch.' He saw the growing dismay on his pal's face. 'All I want to do is take a quiet look, see what's going on. If he does have a gun or something heavy, I swear I'll call the cops.'

'I don't believe you,' Josh said again. 'Once we're in, that's it, and if we go in alone, something bad's going to happen.'

393

'Not *we*,' Robbie said quietly.

Josh was staring at him again.

'What?'

'You look different,' Josh said.

'I'm not different.'

Josh didn't say any more, was too unnerved to say more. There was something so unfamiliar about Robbie's face; that was what scared him most. His buddy had always been a laid-back kind of a guy, gutsy enough but gentle. Right now, he looked downright pugnacious – and *he'd* just brought him one of his mother's frigging *knives*.

And then, to top it off, Robbie looked at him and smiled.

'I'm not going to do anything Steel couldn't handle alone,' he said.

That *really* freaked Josh out.

Rianna was starting to climb the walls.

She hadn't felt so helpless since the first hours of her captivity. Now, just when she should have been feeling relaxed, safe, knowing that life, real, normal life could begin again, everyone had deserted her, left her in this void.

Worse, no one was telling her anything.

They were treating her like a *child*, and surely, after what she'd just been through and survived, she'd earned the right to be told the truth, however unpleasant or frightening.

She was angry now, at her father for going off on what she was increasingly certain had to have something to do with Lydia and – and this was the frightening part – the *man* who, after all, had not been caught, had he? And it was fine for her dad to want to help, up to a point, if Robbie's mom was in a jam of some kind, but he had no right to put himself back in danger without at least telling her about it.

If something happens to him . . .

Rianna bunched up her fists and dug them into her eyes, trying to blot out her thoughts, her damned *imagination*.

Her father wasn't the only one. Robbie had gone, too. And no *way* had he gone out for some fresh air – she hadn't bought that for a second. But he'd asked her to cover for him and, like an idiot, she hadn't refused.

Wherever her dad and Robbie were, whether they'd gone to the same place or not, Rianna knew that Lydia had to be the link.

What was the *matter* with men, for God's sake? Why couldn't they just act sanely and tell the police or FBI what they were frightened about? Even if they were too damned chauvinistic to think *she* could be trusted with bad news, what about the task force, or maybe Sergeant Thurlow who'd brought them down from the roof?

'I've had it.' She looked at the clock on her bedside table.

Nine-thirty-three. Robbie and his friend had been gone for more than twenty minutes. If she waited much longer, Rianna was starting to feel very certain she might have left it too late.

Whatever Robbie and her father were trying to do, she knew it had to be dangerous. Dumb. *Crazy.*

She was *not* crazy.

'Okay,' she said.

Call button or phone?

'Both,' she decided.

Kline was not a happy man.

News had just been patched through to him that not only had Jake Woods disappeared from Bellevue, but so too had the Johanssen boy.

Add to that the information, still coming in as he summoned a car to get him uptown fast, that there was some kind of trouble – not yet confirmed – at the Johanssens' apartment building up on Seventy-third Street . . .

He wasn't a betting man, but right now Kline would have bet the fucking *farm*, if he'd had one, that they were looking at a hostage situation, possibly an armed siege.

Goddamn *amateurs*.

Chapter 121

It had taken me several moments, listening from my new vantage point in the corridor midway between the bedrooms and the second kitchen door, to become certain who it was I was listening *to*.

Not Fitzgerald, the former Yalie.

Nor the Massachusetts tones of Korda, the collector.

Harvard, yes, but less clipped than Korda. Softer. A voice currently dwelling in the past, someplace in a childhood tainted by personal horror.

Hal Hawthorne.

Mr Oh-So-Helpful with the FBI. Mr Sure-you-can-come-in-and-search-my-home. And they could have gone on and searched his Boston apartment, too, *and* his goddamn winery, and found not a trace of a clue as to the kids' whereabouts.

He was talking about *hunting*.

Lydia had a strong sense that whoever had come in through her front door a while back had been moving around the apartment, and that any moment now, Hawthorne was going to stand up, wielding his gun, and turn from storyteller to killer . . .

But if he did hear anything, he didn't show it.

'Young Hal had a dog,' he said, 'which he truly loved. Not any kind of a special breed or anything, just a mutt he'd found and been allowed to keep.'

'What was its name?' Lydia asked, afraid that if he stopped talking, he might hear, so she was slipping in a question now and then, staying interested and understanding. '*Women are better listeners, more understanding than men.*' She pictured that in a dictionary of quotations – *Hal Hawthorne, 2000.*

'Scamp.' Hawthorne smiled. 'Father said it was a ridiculous name, and maybe it was, but Scamp liked it well enough. *Father* said I shouldn't talk to the dog like it was a person, said it was just an animal, born to do my bidding.' He paused. 'He used Scamp to make young Hal go hunting with him. Either young Hal went with him, or Father said he'd kill the dog. It was okay, Father said, young Hal wouldn't have to shoot anything himself, just assist him. It was torture for the boy having to witness all those killings – but far worse was his certainty that one day Father would make him use the gun himself.'

Lydia cringed, realized it was for young Hal, for the boy who'd become the man with the gun. *The man who kidnapped Robbie, don't forget that.*

'It was a deer.' Hawthorne's voice grew softer. 'So lovely that young Hal exclaimed with pleasure when he saw it, and Father jumped right on that, told him to load and *fire*, told him it was the deer or the dog. Young Hal fired off a shot and missed deliberately, then swore he'd done his best. But back home, when Scamp came running to greet young Hal, Father grabbed hold of his hand and tried to force him to grip the gun while *he* shot the animal.'

Tears in Hawthorne's blue eyes now, Lydia saw. And in her own.

'Young Hal screamed and yanked his hand away, and Father let off a bullet, whisker-close, just to torture the boy and the dog. Scamp was never the same again after that, always cowering in corners.' Hawthorne paused again. 'Not unlike young Hal, I suppose.'

Chapter 122

Down on the first floor, the building was being systematically sealed off, visitors and residents alike being refused entry, people being told to stay inside their apartments.

Roger Kline had a fine team: seventy per cent FBI, thirty per cent NYPD, all answering to *him* tonight; tactical agents, search and surveillance men and women, top-notch shooters, no one trigger-happy enough to make a mistake . . .

Seven bodies already.

The decision had been made that evacuating the other occupied apartment on the fifteenth floor might alert the killer to their presence. According to Albert Loomis, the super for the block, the family who resided in 15A were away until after Labor Day, and the Rubinsteins, in 15B, had already been spoken to by phone and ordered to remain inside, away from windows and doors.

Joseph, the doorman, had given a jittery but accurate description of Hawthorne, the first man he'd let up to 15C several hours earlier.

Whether or not Hawthorne was presently armed, Kline now knew that the people found dead at Herald Square had all been gunshot victims. Five teenagers, two adults. They were assuming Hawthorne had a gun now.

Hell, they were *assuming* he had a fucking *arsenal*.

Robbie had refused to let Josh go with him up to the roof.

'I've got the knife, if I need it, which I won't,' he'd said after

398

they'd gotten into the basement of the twin building and were on their way to the staircase. 'And if I go alone, there's only half the chance I'll be heard, and anyway, this is *my* fight—'

'It isn't anyone's fight,' Josh had said, knowing already that he had no chance of talking his friend out of this craziness.

'If my mom's up there with *him*,' Robbie had said, very quietly, 'it's because of me. That makes it my fight, don't you think?' He'd gone straight on. 'And I couldn't live with myself if you got hurt, okay?'

Josh had wanted to scream at him then, would have if they hadn't been trying to get up those stairs quietly at the time, but then, halfway between the fourth and fifth floors, Robbie had said the most sensible thing he'd said in the past hour.

'Anyway,' he'd said, 'if things don't go well and the cops *do* have to go in, you're the only person who can tell them about the old trapdoor not being nailed shut any more.'

So they'd parted company on the thirteenth floor, and Josh had gone back into Camp Sanity, the Steinman home, while Robbie had continued on his way up to Christ knew what . . .

'Josh, thank *God*!' His mom had greeted him with the kind of hug he ordinarily hated these days, but didn't mind so much tonight, and his dad was in the hallway too, but saying nothing, just looking at him.

'Where have you *been*?' Mercifully, Melanie hadn't given him time to answer. 'Did you see what's going on downstairs? The police have been telling us all to stay inside our apartments, and we were getting so worried because we didn't know where you were.'

'I was out with some of the guys.' Josh prayed she wouldn't ask who exactly, because he wasn't sure he was up to lying just yet.

'So how did you get back inside?' his mother asked. 'We heard they're not letting anyone into the building.'

He shrugged. 'No one stopped me.' He looked at his father, swiftly looked away again, uncomfortable under David

Steinman's scrutiny. 'Just lucky, I guess.' Full focus on Melanie. 'So what's it all about, Mom?'

'Zelma Rubin says she heard it's some kind of robbery,' Melanie said. 'But Sidney Khama said *he* heard there was a man with a bomb somewhere in the building, but your father said that can't be right, or they would have evacuated us.'

'Sounds right,' Josh said, then thought perhaps he should keep quiet.

'I'm just glad poor Lydia's still out of town,' Melanie said to her husband. 'Heaven knows she's going through more than enough without this kind of nonsense on her doorstep.'

Josh took the opportunity to slide away into his own room.

This was getting *way* too heavy.

A knock on the door.

Josh knew before it opened that it would be his dad.

David Steinman hadn't said a word out there in the hall, but Josh knew that his father was a quiet, observant man.

'Want to tell me where you've *really* been, Joshua?'

Chapter 123

'That was where young Hal first learned something about sex,' Hawthorne said. 'During those hunting trips with Father.'

He stopped, suddenly.

Lydia froze, tried desperately not to show it.

'You know, I'd *really* love some more coffee, if you don't mind.'

'Not at all.'

She stood up, legs a little numb, would have found it a relief to move around for a few minutes if she hadn't been so scared he might do the same and find whoever was out there in the corridor.

Hawthorne stayed put at the table.

I edged closer to the kitchen door.

It was ajar, but the opening was on the side away from me, so if I wanted to take a look through, I was going to have to pass the doorway.

Can't stay here like this forever.

Though maybe that might be safer. For Lydia.

But I needed to know if *he* was armed.

The telephone rang, was answered, in Lydia's study, by her machine.

I used the instant to make my move. Not *much* of a move, but enough to get me to the other side of the door, and there was Hal Hawthorne, in a rumpled-looking white T-shirt, sitting at

Lydia's table, and now I could see Lydia, too, putting dishes or something into her sink.

Hawthorne didn't look like much more of a psycho than he had when we'd first seen him at Eryx.

But he was. No question.

And he *did* have a gun.

Towards which his right hand was currently moving.

And now he was holding it. *Taking off the safety mechanism.*

My heart was banging like a drum.

Lydia, aware of what Hawthorne was doing, was turning around from the sink. Her face was pale, incredibly tense. Her eyes darted swiftly to the door – *my* door – and then, with what had to have been a superhuman effort, she turned back to the sink.

'Maybe you'd prefer decaf?' she asked Hawthorne.

To which Hawthorne replied:

'Why don't you come in and join us, Professor?'

SIX

Chapter 124

I slipped the mace spray into the pocket of my jeans. The jacket I'd put on a thousand years ago when I'd told Lydia I was going to visit the Coopers would have been useful for hiding the scissors, but all I could do was tuck them in the back of my waistband.

'Aren't you going to join us?' *So* polite.

I went in slowly.

Hawthorne trained the gun on me, then shifted it towards Lydia.

'Put the scissors on the table, Professor.'

I drew them out, moved closer, leaned forward, put them down.

'A little closer to me, please,' Hawthorne said.

I slid them closer. Glanced at Lydia. Tired, strained, but okay.

'Thank you. Step back again.'

I stepped back.

'Any other weapons? Cops give you a gun, maybe?'

'No.'

'Please roll up your trouser legs, one at a time.' Hawthorne kept the gun on Lydia. 'Nice and slowly. Good.'

I straightened up. 'No concealed weapons,' I said. 'You've been watching too many movies.'

'Maybe I have,' Hawthorne said.

'And for the record,' I added, 'no one knows I'm here.'

'Probably a bunch of cops and FBI outside by now,'

Hawthorne said. 'The phone's been ringing. Maybe a nego-tiator, wanting to talk to me.'

'I have friends,' Lydia said. 'They call me sometimes.' She paused. 'We were just going to have some coffee. Would you like a cup, Jake?'

I looked at her fully for the first time since entering the kitchen, smiled into her eyes. She smiled back. Her mouth did not even quiver.

'I'd love a cup,' I told her.

'Sit down, Professor,' Hawthorne said.

I chose the chair on my side of the table, from where I could still see Lydia, and where, when she returned to her chair, I'd be sitting between her and the killer.

She doesn't know he's a killer.

Hawthorne didn't object to my choice of seat.

'Robbie's fine,' I told Lydia, wanting to get it said, just in case. 'He's absolutely fine.'

Her back was to me, but I saw the shudder pass through her. I wished I could get up and go and hold her; I wished that like *hell*. But I stayed in my chair.

'Rianna?' she asked me softly.

'Fine, too.'

'So *that's* all very nice,' Hawthorne said, and rested his right hand on the table, still gripping the gun. 'Tell me, Professor, how much did you hear from out there? I was talking about my father.' He paused. 'You know, I hated you for a while, just because you were – are – a father. A good father.'

I didn't say anything. Lydia began making coffee.

'I was just telling Lydia something that might interest you too, Jake. Is it okay if I call you Jake now? Lydia and I are on first name terms, and she doesn't mind, do you, Lydia?'

'Not at all, Hal,' she answered, back still to us both.

'I was talking about sex,' Hawthorne said. 'About my first lessons on the subject, taught to me by my father, when he took me hunting. The old man used to brag, when we were alone together in the woods, that killing gave him an erection. A *hard-on*, he called it. He said it had been the same in the army.

406

He said that killing came naturally to men, as naturally as getting a hard-on and doing something about it. *He* had never had any problems in that department, he said. Even then, in his chair, he was still a *man*, could still satisfy young Hal's mother. Maybe, he said, if young Hal got over being such a wimp about killing things, he might grow up to be some kind of a man.'

Lydia was pouring boiled water over ground coffee now, getting down clean cups from a cupboard, opening a drawer to get spoons. I saw her look into the drawer for a second longer than necessary, knew she was probably looking at knives, maybe weighing up the risks.

She *almost* closed the drawer.

'I found a magazine once.' Hawthorne was talking rapidly again, locked back firmly in childhood, it seemed. 'One of those smutty rags, and I could hardly believe it when the pictures gave *me* a hard-on – I was so happy I wanted to run find my father and tell him.' His left hand was on the table too now, and once in a while its fingers would touch the barrel of the gun, just *brush* it, then rest on the table surface again . . . 'But something stopped me, because I knew all about Father's moods, so I couldn't be sure how he'd react – and anyway, looking at dirty magazines wasn't up there with *killing*, so I kept those pictures to myself, played with myself at night in bed, jerking off into a plastic bag so I wouldn't leave a mess for the maid to find and tell my mother.'

I stole a look at Lydia, who'd turned around now. She was holding the coffee pot in both hands, her face unreadable, and I thought maybe she was considering pouring the hot liquid over Hawthorne, or maybe smashing the whole pot over his head, but the man's right-handed grip on the gun looked tight, seemed to be growing stronger as he trod old, ugly paths . . .

'Bring over the coffee, why don't you?' Hawthorne broke off, disconcertingly. 'Forgive me, Lydia, mouthing off like that while you stand there, waiting.'

'That's okay.' Lydia came across and set down the fresh pot.

'No,' Hawthorne said. 'It's not okay, *I* know that, you think I don't know that? None of this is okay. But as I told you before, Lydia, we're running out of time, and there's still so much I want to tell you.'

The shooters were all in place, marksmen scattered around, poised on or inside surrounding buildings at every vantage point, each armed with differentials with regard to height and build of the two men believed to be in the apartment.

The MCP, driven over from Herald Square to catch up with Kline, was parked on the corner of Columbus, traffic being diverted to clear two blocks in all directions. Inside the stripped out, equipment-packed ex-camper van, Kline was currently working with Moran, Drew Frankenheimer (a young agent assigned to LIMBO because of his computer and surveillance skills) and Kline's favourite tactical expert, Joan Storm.

All frustrated as hell, their talents hog-tied by an infinite number of unknown quantities. Infrared sensors were not picking up activity in either the living room or any of the three bedrooms with windows, and something was interfering with the apparatus that ought by now to have been picking up sounds from inside the Johanssen apartment.

No sign of Hawthorne or Lydia Johanssen or Woods as yet. Nor of the trained negotiator who Kline had been told was on his way a goddamn *hour* ago. Nor of the psychologist also en route from somewhere in the city. Moran had just finished grilling Loomis, the super, about the exact shape and size of the rooms in the apartment, the areas with and without windows, and any items of furniture or equipment substantial enough to make a difference to the marksmen. Loomis was falling apart, daunted by the pressure, had told Moran that he hadn't had call to go into 15C too much, that the Johanssens were pretty good at taking care of small repairs themselves. He could tell them there was a room with a big piano and music stand, and that the TV in the living room was in a wall unit, so *that* wouldn't get in anyone's way, and there was a sofa and chairs, but that was about it, and he was sorrier than he could say. Moran had seen he was about to burst into tears and next to useless and had let him go.

Negotiator present or not, Kline had decided a while ago that he was more than ready to try to talk to Hawthorne, but the phone in the apartment was being picked up by machine, and though Kline had addressed the killer loudly and clearly, he had no way of knowing if the creep was even *hearing* him.

David Steinman was not listening to his wife.

Melanie wanted him to stay put, not to interfere. But he'd tried calling down to the lobby, asking to talk to the police or FBI, and all he'd been getting was the runaround by people who knew nothing, so now he'd decided to just go down there himself and *make* someone listen to him.

'*Please*, David.' Melanie was pleading now, actually clinging to the left sleeve of his shirt. 'If you go down there, *anything* could happen to you.'

'Nothing is going to happen to me.' David extricated his sleeve from her fingers as gently as he could. 'Our son has just told us he's helped put Robbie and Lydia in even greater danger than they were before.' He got to the front door and opened it. 'The FBI have to know about this *now*.'

Robbie was up on the roof. In the roof garden.

He peered through the darkness across at the twin building, half expecting to see a SWAT team crawling his way, maybe even swinging across on ropes strung from next door's roof to this.

Nothing.

If they were in place, he couldn't see them.

If they *were* in place, he would ignore them.

He stayed low, anyhow, heading towards the trapdoor.

There was a bench over it, had been for years, moss more or less hiding the old entry point. He knew he was going to have to move it very carefully so as not to make a noise. The door from the stairs had creaked, just as Josh had warned it would – it had goddamn *groaned* – but there'd been no sign of anyone hearing it, and after that he'd been silent as snow. He looked at the bench. In the past, he and Josh had always moved it together because it was heavy. Now he was on his own. But he was also stronger than he had been at age ten.

It was eerie up here this evening in the dark.

Way too reminiscent of other dark places.

He put his hands up to his face, almost expecting to feel the damned VR goggles . . .

Just skin. Eyes.

Josh had asked him, just before they split, about what he'd said about Steel.

'You're not getting too carried away by this Steel thing, are you, man?'

Robbie had laughed, had told him no, of course he wasn't.

He knew he wasn't Steel.

After all, he was wearing a tracksuit and he had sneakers on his feet.

And a real *knife at his waist.*

'I felt better for a while,' Hawthorne told Lydia, 'back when you were making our dinner, when you sat down with me to eat. Almost my old self.' He shook his head. 'That's not true. I never had an old self like that.' He shrugged. 'I guess I felt the way I might have *liked* things to be. Normal. Having pot roast served to me by a nice lady. *Normal.* Something I've never had the privilege of being.' He paused, grimaced. 'Though at least *before*, I wasn't a kidnapper.'

It was interesting, I supposed – if *interesting* was the word – how he seemed to be channelling his whole retrospective towards Lydia rather than to us both. Maybe because it was she he'd chosen to visit, which made me the uninvited guest. Or maybe he did still feel the hate for me, as a *father*, that he'd talked about a while back.

Lydia was amazing me more every minute. It was hard to guess how long she'd had to endure Hawthorne's presence before my arrival, yet she showed few signs of real fear. Once in a while, I noticed her moisten her lips with her tongue or a sip of coffee, but there was no tremor when she held her cup.

It was there, though, deep in her eyes – I could see that all right, when we looked at one another. A kind of imploring. *Make this be okay, but don't do anything crazy.*

I wasn't sure what my eyes were telling her.

'Isn't this nice?' Hawthorne said abruptly. 'This is the second pot of coffee she's made me, Jake.' Talking to me again now. 'And, of course, the pot roast – which, by the way, I'm not sure if I've ever had before, after all. And I have to be honest and say it wasn't my *favourite* thing, but killers can't be choosers, can they, and last suppers are last suppers, when all is said and done.'

That word, *killers*, hung in the air.

Lydia looked at me, pupils dilated with shock, terror renewed, despite what I'd told her about Robbie being safe. I shook my head, gave her a little smile of reassurance, and she got my message, nodded, but I could almost *see* the new and terrible thoughts goosestepping through her mind. *If not Robbie and Rianna, then Michael Cooper and the others.*

'A nice woman.' Hawthorne was back to *nice* again. 'She hasn't once tried to scald me with coffee or stab me with one of the knives in her drawers. And now here we are, having a chat, and I'll bet I'm one of your more *unusual* visitors, Lydia. A kidnapper.' His mouth twisted. 'A murderer. A *real* man, by Father's standards, a man who's learned how to kill with just a touch of his fingers. Or with a bullet, of course – *easier* when it's not hands-on, though it still makes me sick to my stomach. I told you that, Jake, didn't I?'

'You told me.' I was waiting, just *waiting*, for him to let go of the gun and give me a chance, but he hadn't let go of it for one damned second, had picked up his cup with his left hand, scratched his head with his left hand, gestured a couple of times – all with his left fucking hand.

The phone had rung again, several times, and we could hear – even the man with half his brain drowning in the past had to be hearing it, too – a male voice, talking loudly to the machine, though the words were still undistinguishable. Kline, I guessed, or maybe a negotiator, but Hawthorne showed not a *grain* of interest in responding.

'Father found young Hal doing *it* once.' Hawthorne slid all the way back again. 'He laughed at him for needing pictures to turn him on, for needing to be alone, shut up and shameful. He beat him for it, from his wheelchair, used both his hands, hitting young Hal over and over again. No woman, he said, would ever respect him or want him. Not a dirty, filthy, shameful coward like him. And then he made young Hal go take a shower, made him take a brush and scrub at himself down there till he bled, *watched* while he did it, *enjoyed* watching, too.'

Hawthorne stopped.

'I'm sorry,' Lydia said.

I think she meant it.

'Me too,' Hawthorne said.

Someone on the roof.

Frankenheimer's equipment had picked up what human eyes had not.

A figure crouched on the roof of the Johanssens' building, directly over apartment 15C. According to the architectural drawings and to Loomis – though no one was setting much store by the distraught super – there was no way from the roof into the apartment, but they all knew the variety of methods used by New York City thieves to lower themselves from rooftops to homes.

If it *was* the perp, and if they managed to get line of sight, neither Kline nor Storm nor any of the shooters poised was going to have so much as a millisecond's compunction about blowing him to kingdom come.

The problem was, no one knew if it *was* Hawthorne.

No one knew who the hell it was.

Chapter 125

In a room at Hartford Hospital, Thea Lomax was sitting beside Norman Baum, fresh out of the ICU, fully conscious, prognosis excellent so long as he rested, obeyed orders, and suffered no unforeseen complications. At Baum's insistence, Lomax had been filling him in as best she could, trying to stick to *good* news, but Baum knew her too well, was like a dog with a bone, and now that he finally accepted he'd gnawed all the way down to the marrow, he wanted to get up, find his clothes and go to New York City.

'I've hidden your clothes,' Lomax told him. 'And what exactly would you plan on doing when you got there, naked or not?'

'Whatever it took,' Baum said.

There was no humour in him right now, because among the other facts he'd dragged out of his partner had been the deaths of the five missing kids – *five*, not the four they'd known about – which meant tragedy for one more family, and which also, almost certainly, meant that the body count included Michael Cooper, the boy whose disappearance he'd originally been called in to investigate. And he vividly remembered those poor people, the raw, bleeding hole punched in both their hearts because their boy was missing. And Norman Baum had never been capable of detachment, and so, right now, he wanted to weep, wanted to yell, and, given the opportunity, he thought he might even be capable of killing.

'I'm sorry,' Lomax told him.

'I know you are,' he said, and let her hold his hand.

But sorry didn't help.

413

Chapter 126

The elevators were out of commission, so David Steinman had taken the stairs, but between the ninth and eighth floors he had encountered a uniformed police officer and another guy in plain clothes who both drew guns, demanded to see ID – which it so happened he'd had the foresight to slip into his back pocket before he'd left the apartment – and then ordered him back to 13B.

'Not before I talk to whoever's in charge.'

'You have to go back to your apartment, sir,' the plain-clothes man told him.

'You're not listening to me,' Steinman said.

'No, *you're* not listening.' The same guy had holstered his gun, but now his hand was hovering over the butt. 'You're impeding an FBI operation, so unless you want to be placed under arrest—'

'For God's *sake*,' Steinman yelled, then hastily lowered his voice, 'there's a *kid* up on the roof right this minute trying to get inside the Johanssen apartment – *that's* what I'm trying to tell you!'

'Father told young Hal once that there was nothing more painful for a father than to feel ashamed of his only son.'

Lydia and I listened in silence as Hawthorne sucked us down into his personal abyss. It occurred to me, for a moment, that any profiler would relish this opportunity, and that some psychologists might feel the same way. For another second or two, I think I actually felt *guilty* because I knew I was listening to the outpourings of a soul in true torment. And then I reminded myself that personal torments or not, Hal Hawthorne had become a child killer – and my guilt was gone.

'Father said the same things to young Hal's mother, who passed them on – together with the account of her son's sins of masturbation – to her priest, Father Kilkenny, and he came and talked to the boy, ever so *gently*, about his prospects of burning in hell.'

The apartment was unnaturally silent now, broken only by the regular drip from Lydia's tap hitting the edge of a cup in the sink.

'One day,' Hawthorne went on, 'Father asked the boy to accompany him on another hunting trip, and young Hal, defiant for once in his life, refused to go. And later that same day, Father *shot* himself through the forehead. Afterwards, just a few hours after she'd heard the news, Mother told young Hal that having a coward for a son had been the greatest sadness of Father's life, said that he had told her, more than once, that he'd sometimes wished himself dead because of that . . .'

The blue eyes were no longer hazy with memory, nor moist. Just blank.

'So after that, young Hal knew that whatever happened between then and his *own* death, it was really all decided, all written.' Hawthorne shrugged. 'All over but the burning.'

The shooters with weapons trained on the roof over 15C had been alerted to the probability that the shadowy figure up there was Robbie Johanssen, not the perp, and that there was also a possibility of an entry point from there into the apartment. And now Kline, Moran and Storm had arrived in 13B, intent on draining every last drop of information the three Steinmans could give them.

Josh was in the kitchen with Moran, spilling all he knew about the trapdoor, while Moran called the details simultaneously through to Kline in the next room and Frankenheimer in the MCP. Because 15C had originally been part of the owner's private penthouse, Josh said, he had wanted personal access to the roof garden and had installed a trapdoor with a ladder and handrail. Aaron Johanssen had considered it a hazard and nailed it shut when Robbie was a little kid, and it had so remained until he and Josh had prised it open about six years back for their own secret use.

In the living room, Melanie and David Steinman were responding to Joan Storm's crisp questions, and Melanie, surprising herself with her own sudden calm, was describing, eyes shut, the three main windowless areas in 15C: kitchen, music room, hallway.

'And there are two bathrooms,' she added, 'but they'd be too small.' She paused, eyes open again, round with fresh alarm. 'Unless he's locked them in and taken over—'

'Furniture,' Storm interrupted, pushing her on. 'Picture the *whole* apartment, Melanie. Picture it dark, picture our guys trying to get through without knocking into things.'

'I can give you some of that,' David told the agent.

'Go,' Storm said.

Kline listened, to the Steinmans and to Moran, and talked to Frankenheimer, and checked positions, and did everything in his power to reach a state of preparedness for action. With their other listening equipment still not functioning satisfactorily, he and Storm had decided to risk moving the Rubinsteins out of 15B and placing visual and eavesdropping probes in the adjoining walls, dialling the Johanssens' phone number every few minutes so that the ringing would cover any sounds of installation. So far, however, their tiny cameras were only showing an empty hall and living room, and the only sounds being picked up were phones ringing, a machine answering in another room, the ticking of a couple of clocks and the hum of an air-conditioner.

And the faint, indecipherable voices of two males and one female.

Presumably Hawthorne, Woods and Lydia Johanssen.

Probably, they all felt, in the kitchen, one of the windowless rooms.

Goddamned architects.

Which meant, at least, that Hawthorne had not yet killed his hostages. Partly, they supposed, because had he done so, he would have lost the captive audience that they – and the psychologist now sitting with Frankenheimer in the MCP – felt sure he needed at this stage.

All the voices of experience concurred that a man who had killed at least seven people, and who now – rather than trying to escape – had chosen to place himself where he had to know he'd be located, was aiming for some kind of endgame. One that would give him the opportunity to unburden himself or to boast about his deeds, or both. One he also surely had to expect would culminate in his own apprehension or death.

The question no one could answer was what he intended *before* that for Lydia Johanssen and Jake Woods, possibly the two people Hawthorne might regard as the true agents of his downfall. And for Robbie Johanssen, if he blundered right back into Hawthorne's clutches.

Hal Hawthorne was a man with nothing to lose.

A man they had to take out, given one clear and safe opportunity.

One shot or fifty, Kline didn't give a damn.

A squad of shooters was now in position near the top of the stairs leading to the roof, ready and waiting for a command to move onto the roof garden and enter from there. Joan Storm herself, the lightest and fleetest of foot of the team, was about to head up there to see if maybe she could retrieve the teenager before he went inside.

As things stood right now, *that* was their number one priority.

Any chance that presented itself – so long as it didn't increase the jeopardy to the innocent parties already inside 15C – they were to try to *stop* Robbie Johanssen from opening that trapdoor. If they could not stop that happening, none of their options was good.

It was, they pretty much agreed, too late for talking – with or without the missing negotiator. If Hawthorne had wanted to talk, he'd have picked up the phone long ago, and if they used a loudhailer they risked freaking him out and destroying any good that Woods or Robbie's mother might have achieved.

And if they went in behind the kid, however quietly, they would block his best way back out and thereby place him in even greater peril.

Whichever way they went in – trapdoor, front door or through the goddamned *windows* – Hawthorne would have time to kill his hostages before they reached the kitchen.

No win – no win.

Chapter 127

Robbie hadn't got inside yet.

He'd only just finished moving the bench out of the way. It was so damned hard to see up there, and the first time he'd moved the thing he'd misjudged, and so he'd had to move it back the other way, and he'd almost dropped it, which had freaked him out. It was heavier than he'd remembered, or maybe he was weaker than he'd thought, which was probably why they'd wanted him to stay in the hospital, and he was starting to wish he hadn't sent Josh away . . .

Though the person he *really* needed beside him now, of course, was Dakota.

That thought stopped him in his tracks.

Cut that out, Johanssen.

Last thing he needed was to start believing he was Steel, for God's sake.

We already got all the crazies we need, man.

He was unaware of any movement or sound from the roof of the neighbouring building. He was totally and absolutely focused again on getting the trapdoor open. On getting *through* it and rescuing his mom and Rianna's dad.

Nothing else mattered.

'The week my father killed himself, I went to a pool and made myself take a dive off the highest board.'

First person again, suddenly, I noted, and glanced at Lydia,

419

saw she was pretty deep in Hawthorne's tale, her eyes bleak, faraway.

'I was so scared, I thought I was going to die, too, really believed that dive was going to *kill* me – and then, when it didn't, I looked around for Father, was so sure I'd see him there at the side in his chair, punching the air with triumph. But of course he wasn't there. No one was there who gave a damn about whether I made a lousy stinking dive or not.' Hawthorne paused. 'A younger boy was there, though, being taught to dive off the side, only he was too scared to do it, and I watched him and his teacher and some of his pals for a few minutes. There was such *scorn* in their faces, and for the first time in my life, *I* felt scorn, too. Finally, when it was too late, I understood how Father must have felt about me.'

He stopped, looked first at Lydia, then at me.

'Pretty screwed-up, right?' He shrugged. 'That's how I grew up, I suppose, screwed-up. On the physical front, too – *that* front, you know? No sex with women, because Father had said they wouldn't want me, and he was right. No masturbation either, not ever again after that time . . .' He paused. 'And then there was hell to consider – heaven and hell used to make sense to me. Nothing much makes sense any more. Not for a long while now.'

Rianna was meant to be sleeping.

She had slept for a while, earlier, out of a mix of pure exhaustion and a need to escape, but in her sleep she had dreamed she was Dakota again, chained to a subway rail with rats running over her legs, squealing, and she had screamed for Steel to come and save her . . . But then she'd turned her head to the left and had seen that her father was chained to another track, and a train was coming through the tunnel towards him, horn blaring, coming closer and closer, and Steel was nowhere to be seen . . .

She'd decided against more sleep after that.

A nurse had offered her a pill to help her relax, but Rianna had told her she was fine, and the nurse had gone away.

She'd thought about calling Kim, knew that, if asked, Kim would leave Tom with Ella and come to New York to be with her. But it was late now, and she didn't like the idea of Kim driving in the dark, maybe too fast out of anxiety for her, and that was how her mom had died, wasn't it – though Simone hadn't even been worrying about *them*, she'd just been late getting someone's dinner delivered on time . . .

Soon, Rianna thought, lying on her side in the uncomfortable hospital bed, staring out of the window, if someone didn't come and tell her the *real* truth about what was going on with her father and Robbie and Lydia, she might stop behaving well, the way Rianna Woods almost always did behave. Soon, she thought she might start *screaming* – except she doubted if that would bring any answers. All that would probably bring was someone with a hypodermic to knock her out.

Rianna wasn't crazy about needles, but right now, a little bout of enforced unconsciousness was quite a tempting idea.

Except, of course, for the dreams.

Joan Storm had decided that going out to get Robbie was way too dangerous for *him*.

In the first place, the door had groaned like hell when she'd touched it, and just because the teenager had gotten through it apparently without attracting the killer's attention, didn't mean *she* could do the same.

In the second place, peering at the young man through the crack in the slightly open door, it was plain from his body language that he was hell-bent on getting that damned trapdoor open, and Storm knew that if Robbie had wanted their help he'd have come to them – and who knew what kind of psycho-logical shape he was in after all he'd been through?

The last thing they needed was a struggle between agent and victim.

'It wasn't easy, after my father had died that way. Growing up, getting on with my life, the way I was expected to.'

Still talking, talking, like a fucking verbal waterfall.

I didn't know what was inside Lydia's head, but every fragment of anything even approaching pity in me for 'young Hal' had disintegrated, and I was about ready to blow. Too much more of his damned voice, filling that kitchen with his self-indulgent *crap*, and I wasn't sure how I was going to stop myself launching right at the sonofabitch . . .

But he was still holding the gun.

'Easy in some ways, obviously,' Hawthorne rambled on. 'I couldn't complain of being deprived of material things. I just never felt I was like anyone else, never felt *normal*.' Another shrug. 'But I did go on, went to Harvard, did pretty well, even found something I really liked and was good at. Nothing Father would have approved of, needless to say.' He paused. 'Though I did find my *Dim Mak* master, I did do that, and maybe the old man mightn't have thought that too bad.'

The phone was ringing again, machine picking up again.

Hawthorne ignoring it again.

Though suddenly he was looking at us, *really* looking at us.

'Don't you have any questions for me? Before the end?'

'A bunch,' I said. My voice was a little husky, my throat dry.

'Better ask them then,' Hawthorne said.

'Would you like some water, Jake?' Lydia asked me.

'No time wasting.' Not too sharp, but Hawthorne's grip on the gun seemed to tighten.

'Why don't you answer the phone next time?' Lydia asked him.

'No one I care to speak to,' he answered. 'Except the two of you.' He smiled. 'And Steel and Dakota, of course; I'd *really* like to talk to them again, but I know that's impossible.'

I saw the startled, confused look on Lydia's face, realized she still had no idea what had gone on in Herald Square. 'Hawthorne's names,' I told her quickly, 'for Robbie and Rianna.'

'They were really terrific, you know, Lydia,' Hawthorne said. 'You should know that, especially about your boy – though Dakota was excellent too, would have been remarkable, I think, given more time. Better than any of the others.'

'*Why*?'

The tone in Lydia's voice, its sudden change to pure anger, put me on red alert.

'Why what?' Hawthorne asked her. 'Better be specific now. With so little time left.'

'Why did you *do* this? *Any* of it. Why did you take those *children*?'

'They were not children,' Hawthorne said. 'They were young men and women.' He paused. 'You'd understand better if you'd been there.'

'No,' I said, hard and clear. 'She would not.'

'I don't get it.' David Steinman was exasperated. 'If you think it's too late to get Robbie off the roof, why don't your people simply follow him and get in the same way?'

'Same reason we haven't stormed through the front door.' The young agent from the Manhattan field office, designated by Kline to remain with the Steinmans, used the 'we' with pride. 'We don't want to get innocent people killed.'

'So you're just letting that *boy* go in alone?' Melanie was equally dismayed, relieved that Josh had gone to his bedroom and was now playing loud music in a vain attempt, she felt certain, to block out his own fears.

'Chances are,' the agent said, 'he's already in.' Truth to tell, he didn't know that, didn't know much about *anything*, except it was his job to keep this family in their apartment and out of trouble until the operation was over.

'So what *are* you doing?' David demanded.

'Everything we can, I'm sure.'

'It was like a movie, in a way,' Hawthorne said, 'a *live* movie.' He moved back again, into his past. 'That was something I did try, long after Father was gone, when the needs were coming back, *those* needs. I rented movies, but they reminded me of what happened after Father found me with the magazines, and I told myself I had a decent enough life without that. I had Eryx by then, partners who respected me.'

He stood up, abruptly, for the first time since I'd come into the kitchen. He didn't *go* anywhere, just stretched his legs on the spot, then transferred the gun from his right hand to his left, flexed the fingers of his right, moved the hand around from the wrist to get the blood circulating, then put the gun back where it belonged.

Whole exercise no more than seven, eight seconds, tops.

No time to *do* anything. Certainly no time to get to that half-open drawer and try to find a knife.

'Then, one night, while I was working late, all alone in my office with just Dakota and Steel – my little cyber-pals – for company, it happened.' Hawthorne shook his head. 'It just *happened*.' He sat down again, heavily. 'It appalled me. I thought about Father, went home to Chester, stood under my shower and scrubbed myself till I bled again, told myself I was evil, swore it would never happen again.' Another smaller shake of the head. 'Only I couldn't stop thinking about it – and of course, I *did* need it. Everyone does, don't they? And after that, the need just grew, and I realized what I'd been missing – and it wasn't *hurting* anyone, and hell and damnation still seemed a long way off.' There was a little trace of a smile in those blue eyes now. 'And the thing was, the more I did it, the more I found myself falling in love with—'

I *snorted*, derision and revulsion getting the better of me.

'I know how it sounds, Jake, but it *did* feel like a kind of love to me. Those gorgeous, perfect bodies, their *courage*—'

'They weren't *real*.' I had to interrupt. 'They were like cartoons!'

Hawthorne ignored me. 'The more I loved them, the better I became at work, the more creative, the more imaginative.'

'*Imaginative*?!' I knew Lydia was tensing, but now I'd begun, cut into that man's vast psychological junkyard, I couldn't stop. 'Abducting *kids*, locking them up, terrorizing them, abusing them—'

'I *never* abused them!' His pitch heightened with indignation. 'I took care of them. I fed them, I—'

'You *killed* them!' I exploded. 'You murdered seven people!'

'And I *hated* it!' Hawthorne almost spat the words at me. 'You can't imagine how much I hated it, either of you. I've already *told* you how I felt about killing, how I could hardly bring myself to stamp on an insect—'

'You killed seven *people*,' I yelled at him, half out of my chair, only staying there because the hand with the gun was off the table top again and clenching hard. 'And that's all the cops *know* about – you could have killed *twenty*-seven for all we know!'

'*No!*' Hawthorne was distraught. 'Just those people.'

'*Just?*' Lydia echoed.

'If it isn't you,' Fitzgerald said to Korda, 'and it isn't me, and if no one's telling us one damned thing about Hal, then . . .'

Released by the FBI some time ago, the two partners had agreed to return to Eryx rather than go home. Better to come in tonight than in the harsher light of morning, with a full complement of personnel to answer to.

Korda's office *looked* the same. Yet both men felt borderline defiled. Sick at heart. Shocked.

'I can't believe it,' Korda said. 'I *don't* believe it.'

'Me neither.'

'Maybe they've got it wrong.'

'I'm not so sure,' a female voice said.

Korda and Fitzgerald looked at the doorway, saw Ellen Zito standing there, leaning against the frame.

'I've often wondered about Hal,' she said.

'Have you?' Korda was startled.

Zito came into the office a little way, as if checking the temperature. 'Didn't either of you find him a little weird sometimes?'

'No more than most,' Fitzgerald said, deadpan.

'Come and have a drink, Ellen,' Korda said.

Zito stepped in a little further, watched her boss pour a brandy for her. 'What's it going to mean for us? For the company? If it does turn out to be Hal?'

425

'I don't know,' Korda said, and handed her the glass.

'All those kids,' Fitzgerald murmured.

'I *still* don't believe it,' Korda said.

'They weren't all young,' Hawthorne said, 'the ones I had to kill.' He licked his lips, breathing more rapidly. 'The man who helped with the VR set-up – I *had* to shoot him because he kept asking questions.'

I was back in my seat, mute again. Lydia, too, was very still, looking dazed.

'Most people didn't really ask questions,' the killer was going on. 'They just did their jobs and took the money. The soundproofing was easy enough – no fuss from the electronics guy, either – and I didn't need anyone's permission for the works, because Father had left that building to me, rather than Mother – tax breaks, I guess – so it seemed the perfect place. And I'd always kept the penthouse and next floor down for my own use, so no one had any right to second-guess me. But the VR man did, and then the guy who installed the cold room got too curious – and, *oh Christ*, I hated that, too.'

'Did you?' Lydia sounded sick.

'Of course I did.' He shook his head. 'I never meant to kill anyone.'

'You're a liar,' I said softly. 'A filthy, murdering *liar*.'

'I know,' Hawthorne said. 'I know that now. I know what I am, *now*. I call myself names. *Thing-monster*. That's what I call myself.'

Lydia stared at me, helplessly.

'But in the beginning,' Hawthorne said, 'it was just meant to be a *game*.'

426

Chapter 128

Robbie was still struggling to prise open the trapdoor without making any noise, but it had rusted up some since they'd last used it, and Josh had been right about this one too – it *did* creak as it opened – oh, shit, shit, *shit*.

Looking around, trying not to drop the goddamn door, Robbie thought he saw something move in the darkness over on the neighbouring roof.

SWAT team, his best guess. He saw a light flash a couple of times, realized they were trying to communicate with him, then saw another flicker, just a little chink of light over by the door he'd come through from the stairs . . .

Any minute now, some gun-toting cop was going to come and try to haul him off the roof. Except maybe they didn't dare, in case *he* – if he was down there – heard them.

Tempting, suddenly. To give it up, leave it to the experts.

If they're here, man. A little tear gas, a little nifty shooting.

Probably no one killed but the bad guy.

Probably.

Not good enough.

He folded the door all the way back.

The hinges squeaked.

Robbie hardly dared breathe.

The room below – the guest room – was pitch dark.

You're used to the dark, Steel.

The old ladder was concertinaed up beneath the opening, but

if the *door* had made a noise, he didn't like to imagine what *that* might sound like if he tried pushing it down.

But if he jumped, that might be even louder.

Everyone was standing by, green-lighted to kill Hawthorne, given a clear shot.

The kid going in would be the detonator, they were all sure of that.

The negotiator had finally called in to say he'd only just been freed from a jammed elevator downtown in which his damned cell phone had refused to work.

'No one would make *that* up,' Moran said.

'Hope you told him not to bother,' Kline said grimly.

'Too late for a gabfest now,' Storm said.

This whole operation was a nightmare. It had been more than tough enough without this messed-up sixteen-year-old *donating* himself to the fiasco. Kline wasn't about to admit it to anyone, not even Storm or Moran, but in his opinion, unless luck decided to swing their way at the last minute, they were royally fucked, whichever way they looked at it.

'Don't you think I know what I've done?' Hawthorne said. 'Don't you think I've wanted to *die*, thinking about it? But I couldn't just abandon my kids. I'd looked after them so *well* – you can *ask* them, they'll tell you. I fed them well, made sure they had juice and milk.'

'Kept them locked up and terrified in the dark,' I added.

Hawthorne ignored me, looked right at Lydia.

'Ask Steel sometime,' he said. 'He'll tell you.'

Robbie had taken off Josh's sneakers and clambered over the side, and now he was hanging onto the edge of the opening with both hands, knowing that this was the way Steel would do it, and it *wasn't* that he thought he *was* Steel, he knew exactly who he was, but *thinking* like Steel was helping him do this thing right.

And if he dropped to the floor, let himself fall sideways,

like a paratrooper, maybe he wouldn't make *too* much noise.

So he dropped.

Hawthorne heard the sound.

We *all* heard it.

I watched his right hand tighten on the handle of the gun, knuckles whitening.

He started to get up.

'What about' – I said loudly – 'telling Lydia what you wanted the kids to do?'

Hawthorne wasn't listening to me.

'After you got *me* into your hideout, your faked-up virtual reality *Limbo*,' I said. 'Are you going to tell Steel's mother what you wanted the kids you'd looked after so well to *do*?'

'What did you want them to do?' Lydia understood me. '*What*, Hal?'

Hawthorne was on his feet, but the questions had penetrated, were distracting him just enough. He looked down into Lydia's accusing eyes.

'I wasn't really going to make them do it.'

'Do *what*?' The eyes widened, no act now.

'I wasn't going to let it go too far—'

'Let *what* go too far?' Lydia's hands clenched around the edge of the table. 'What did you want them to *do*, you *bastard*?'

Another sound. A real *thud* this time, from the rear of the apartment.

Hawthorne motioned to us both to stay where we were.

My mind flew back into the rule book, seeking guidelines for times like this.

If agents were inside the apartment, there was going to be shooting.

Wait for the moment, then grab her, get her down, under the table.

Hawthorne was insane and had never read a police manual, but he was no fool.

He stepped away from the table, moved smartly around to Lydia's chair, and positioned the barrel of his gun to the back of her head.

Just as Robbie appeared in the doorway.

He's in.

The word sped back and forth, lightning streaks alerting the troops.

More messages.

Movement from north-facing room.

Then gone again.

Into the invisible heart of the apartment.

Storm issuing short, sharp, FBI-speak orders.

All meaning: *Wait*.

Hardest command of all to comply with.

Even Kline, back in the MCP with Frankenheimer, always so trim, so honed, was sweating, feeling almost physical pain. He *hated* when things were out of his hands. Yet he knew he had a fine team, knew they were all at the peak of readiness . . .

Wait.

Robbie stared at Hal Hawthorne.

He'd never seen *him* before.

Lydia, at the kitchen table, began to rise, reflexively, but Hawthorne pushed her back down, left hand on her left shoulder.

Robbie stared at the gun trained on, actually *touching*, the back of his mother's head, and boiling, *scalding* rage rose in him.

His hand moved to the knife at his waist.

'I wouldn't, Steel,' Hawthorne said.

'Take it easy,' I told him, softly.

'I'm okay, Robbie,' Lydia said. 'He's not going to hurt me.'

'Your mother's right, Steel,' Hawthorne said. 'So just do what I tell you, nice and slow.' He smiled suddenly, an incongruously boyish smile. 'Like in the movies – nice and

430

slow.' The smile was gone again. 'Put that knife on the floor, Steel, and kick it towards me.'

Robbie glanced at me. I nodded. The gun at his mother's head made him obedient. He took the knife from his waistband, bent and placed it on the floor, kicked it with his bare right foot.

The knife came to rest between Hawthorne's feet and my own.

'Thank you, Steel,' Hawthorne said. 'You're a good boy.' He paused. 'Okay, Jake, now you bend down, pick it up, and put it in my left hand.' The blue eyes narrowed a little. 'Cut me, even *scratch* me, and I'll pull this trigger.'

I did what he said. Nothing else I could do.

Hawthorne kept the gun on Lydia, tucked the knife into his own belt.

I was finding it hard – *too* hard – to make this bastard out. One minute – most of the time while I'd been here – he was the most out-to-lunch maniac I'd ever heard about, let alone encountered. Yet now he was cool as ice and, to all intents and purposes, sane.

'I'm okay, Robbie,' Lydia told her son again, softly. 'How about you?'

'I'm fine, Mom.' Robbie swallowed hard. 'I love you.'

'I love you too.' Her eyes filled with tears.

'We're all okay.' I took my opening, so long as Hawthorne was letting us have our little reunion. 'All we have to do is take it easy.' I paused. 'We've been talking about things, Robbie.'

'Who's with you, Steel?' Hawthorne wanted to know.

Reunion over.

'No one,' Robbie answered.

'Who came *with* you?'

'If someone had come with him,' I said, 'they'd be in this room now. Cops don't send teenagers into battle ahead of themselves.'

'*They're* not cowards, you mean,' Hawthorne said.

I didn't say a word.

'This bastard's the biggest coward in the world,' Robbie told his mother.

'Don't be mean, Steel,' Hawthorne told him. 'It doesn't become you. Anyway, we all know it's not the police I'm asking about.'

'Not the FBI either,' Robbie said.

'You know better than anyone who I'm talking about.'

I realized first. 'He means Dakota.'

'Of course I mean Dakota,' Hawthorne said. 'Where's she hiding?'

Crazy again. As the proverbial March hare.

Not crazy enough to forgive, though. Nowhere *near* enough for that.

'Nowhere,' Robbie answered him. 'Nowhere, you crazy sonofabitch.'

I saw Lydia blink, knew she had to be registering how much her son had grown up since she'd last seen him. Rites of passage. Poor kid. Poor Lydia.

'Careful, Steel,' Hawthorne said.

I watched his right hand shift a little, but the barrel of that gun was still touching Lydia, and if I let myself really think about that, really *absorb* that, I thought I might go a little crazy, too. My eyes went to Lydia's face, saw that hers were fixed on Robbie's face, and there was an amazing kind of look in them that seemed to say that if he was the last thing she ever saw, it was okay with her.

Not with me.

I remembered the mace in my back pocket, remembered, too, that it was probably too old to function, and anyway, while the gun was positioned that way . . .

'You hurt my mother,' Robbie told Hawthorne, 'and you'll die too.'

'Maybe I don't *care* if I die.'

'If that's true,' Robbie said, 'why not move the gun away from her and shoot yourself instead?'

'Because maybe that's not the way I care to die.'

'Maybe *I* didn't care to be kidnapped and locked up and scared half to death,' Robbie said. 'Maybe Rianna didn't care for that either, or any of the others.'

'Dakota,' Hawthorne corrected. 'Okay, yes, I can see your point, Steel.'

'I'm not Steel.'

Another smile. 'Oh yes you are, and it's good to see you, even in these circumstances.' Hawthorne paused. 'How exactly did you get in, Steel? There's no back entrance.' He thought. 'No balconies either, so it must be the roof.'

Robbie didn't answer.

'Good,' Hawthorne said. 'Fresh air. Just what the doctor ordered.'

He took a step back, moved the gun swiftly from the back of Lydia's head to her right temple. 'Come on, everyone. Stand up, Lydia.' He nodded at me. 'You too, Jake.'

I stood, keeping my eyes on the gun and Lydia's face.

'Steel, you lead the way. Then the professor, and Lydia and I will bring up the rear.' Hawthorne paused again. 'Any tricks from anyone, I *will* shoot. Understood?'

'Yes,' I said.

Robbie went to the door, looked around at his mother.

'I'm okay,' she told him again.

He looked at me, and there was a real flash of *boy* again, uncertain, scared, which was good, I felt, safer than too brave right now.

'I wouldn't *like* shooting,' Hawthorne said as he moved us on out of the kitchen and into the corridor after Robbie. 'God knows I wouldn't like it – that's why I want to go up to the roof, get some good fresh New York City air.'

Robbie was heading to the back, to the guest room – the room I'd slept in that one night – *part* of one night . . . He hesitated, glanced back, then moved on again.

'I really do need to get out now,' Hawthorne said from behind me, from behind Lydia and the gun, 'otherwise I really might shoot this nice lady, and I truly don't want to do that. I came to you, Lydia, because I knew you were smart and brave, and because I figured I owed you an explanation.' His voice sounded suddenly like a piece of elastic stretching too thin. 'It makes *thing-monster* sick when he has to shoot people, I told

433

you that, I *told* you. It makes him scream, too, but he still does it when he has to. Like *Father* taught him.'

Movement again, in that same north-facing room, still in the dark.

Three – no, four people.

Moving. Not close enough to the windows to tell . . . Bunched up together, too close to risk a shot . . .

Kline, still in the MCP, felt his skin crawl.

Another report.

Looked like they were going up to the roof.

Kline got the hell up and *ran*.

'It'd be easier with the light on,' Robbie said.

'Anyone touches a switch,' Hawthorne said, still in that close-to-snapping elastic band voice, 'I shoot Lydia.' He took a tight, harsh breath. 'Pull down that ladder, Steel.'

I watched Robbie try to reach it, saw, even in the half-dark, how thin he was, how little strength he had left in his shoulders and arms.

'Let me help him,' I said.

'Steel can do it,' the scumbag insisted.

'I'm trying.' Robbie yanked at it, but it wouldn't give. 'It's *stuck*.'

'Let Jake *help* him,' Lydia said, her own voice sounding close to the limit.

'Okay,' Hawthorne agreed. 'Steel doesn't seem quite himself. Maybe he could use a little help.'

I walked up to Robbie, stood beside him. We locked eyes.

'I told you to get the fucking ladder *down*.'

We both pulled at it, pushed, then wrenched at it again.

'We need more help,' I said.

'Forget it,' Hawthorne told me. 'I'm not stupid, Professor. Messed-up, *wicked*, perhaps, but not stupid.'

'What are you hoping to achieve?' Lydia asked, despite the gun.

I prayed, suddenly, for her to say no more – I wanted nothing more than for Hawthorne to get up on the roof and turn himself into a target.

'Fresh air,' Hawthorne answered her. 'And an ending.'

Amen.

The ladder flew down suddenly with a loud crash, startling us all.

Lydia seized the instant, wrenched away from Hawthorne, ran back into the darkness of the corridor. I put my head down, cannoned into him, struck him in the chest, sent him reeling, off-balance but still holding the gun.

The mace.

I pulled it out of my pocket, got the top off, pointed it at Hawthorne's face and sprayed, long and hard.

Useless.

But enough to trigger a shock reflex.

The sound of the gun going off reverberated around the room, rattled the windows.

Robbie cried out.

Fell.

'*No!*' Lydia screamed. '*Robbie!*'

'Lydia, run!' I got down, trying to find the boy's wound. '*Run!*'

'You *bastard!*' She threw herself at Hawthorne, careless of the gun now, wild, almost insane herself, hitting him, punching him in the face, on his chest, *anywhere*, and he let her, seemed too stunned to fight back, but the gun was still in his right hand.

'Lydia, *stop!*'

I got up again, my movement jolting Hawthorne back to life. He gave a kind of bellow, then grabbed hold of her, strong left arm gripping her around her waist, dragged her towards the ladder, started to climb, pulling her with him.

'Go *after* them!'

Robbie's voice, from the floor.

I stared down at him.

'Jake, I'm okay – just *go!*'

I got to the ladder, started up—

Saw lights suddenly blazing up there—

435

Got myself through the trapdoor, blinking, dazzled . . .

Hawthorne and Lydia, ahead of me, in silhouette, too close together – and he was *moving*, the lousy, stinking piece of garbage, moving back and forth with her, twisting and turning so no one on the roof next door, where some of the light was coming from, could get off a clear shot . . .

'Drop the gun, Hawthorne.' A voice, female, resonant, commanding, rang out from the other direction, somewhere to my left, echoed across the roof and over the black abyss between the two buildings. 'Let the lady go, place the gun on the ground, and no one's going to shoot.'

'No one's going to shoot so long as I'm *holding* her,' Hawthorne yelled back, and turned again, pulling Lydia over to the perimeter wall, kept on *turning*, blurring their target.

'I thought you hated people thinking you a coward,' I called out. 'Can't think of a greater act of cowardice than hiding behind a woman.'

'Just figuring out what's next,' Hawthorne said, still turning.

'Give it up,' I told him. 'That's all that's next.'

'I was thinking' – another twist – 'more along the lines of getting back on the high board for one last dive.'

My stomach heaved. 'Great idea,' I said, 'but let her go first.'

'Let Mrs Johanssen go, Hawthorne!' the other voice commanded.

Hawthorne kept on turning, almost spinning, had to be getting dizzy, and Lydia's face as he twirled her back and forth was ashen.

'How good a diver *is* Lydia, do you know, Jake?'

'*No*!' Robbie's voice screamed from the top of the ladder at the open trap.

A sudden dark streak of movement, fast, then frozen, to my left.

A crash from below.

Both Robbie and I turned, instinctively, to look down towards the noise, could both hear – could *all* hear – the sounds of people moving, *running*, through the apartment underneath us.

436

Another sound. Lydia crying out.

I whirled around.

Hawthorne was up on the wall, the gun still in his right hand but hanging from his fingers, dangling.

'*Lydia!*' I screamed, looking for her – then found her. *Thank Christ.*

Still on the roof, hunched over against the wall, staring up at Hawthorne.

Only a second, but *infinite*.

The marksmen on the other roof taking aim.

'*Watch me, Father!*'

Hawthorne's voice seemed a little higher, almost boy-like.

As he took his final dive.

Though even that was ruined as the storm of bullets smashed into him, pounding him, ripping him apart, and sending him flailing, spiralling, crashing down into the dark.

Chapter 129

The day Lydia brought Robbie home from the hospital, Rianna, Ella, Josh and I were there, in the Johanssen apartment, waiting for them, as we'd all agreed.

We had something important to do.

Another visit to the roof garden – from the staircase this time. I'd redone Aaron Johanssen's work, nailed up that trapdoor again, made quite a decent job of it, if I say so myself.

Didn't think he'd mind.

I'd brought up a big old metal container loaned to me by Albert Loomis; the kind gardeners use to burn leaves and weeds.

We started a fire, a nice little controlled blaze.

And then Robbie and Rianna and Josh and Ella threw all our copies of *Limbo* into it.

One of those symbolic things, you know?

The fire smoked a lot, stank surprisingly little, considering.

It felt good to me. And looking at Lydia, and then at our children's faces, Josh's too, I could see it felt the same way to them.

Thank God.

The psychologist who had visited Robbie in the hospital and Rianna back in New Haven, had expressed concern to us that our kids might suffer long-term effects after the horrifically abnormal nature of the whole ordeal. Lydia and I had talked later about the kinds of things we both needed to look out for, and she said that the psychologist had told her, more specifically, that she feared Robbie might have grown to have some degree of belief in his *Steel* persona.

I admit that had been one of so many things that had alarmed me that long night, seeing Robbie standing in the doorway, feet bare, knife at his waist; and I knew Josh had expressed similar fears about his buddy's insistence on going it alone onto the roof.

No recurrences since then, we're all immensely grateful to say.

Lydia's watching him, though. We all are.

Watching our children every moment we can. *Too* closely, I guess, at least for them. Damaged goods, all of us, to varying degrees. Healing slowly and gently, and *together*.

The shrink also suggested that if, and *only* if, the kids wanted to attend any of the funerals of the teenagers murdered by Hawthorne, it might do them more good than harm. Some people, she said, suffered irrational guilt over surviving traumas in which others had died, and joining in the grief process might just help them with that.

Rianna and Robbie joined in the grief at Michael Cooper's funeral.

And found it very hard to bear.

Mostly, I knew, they found it hard to bear seeing the expressions on Fran's and Stu's faces. I knew, because I couldn't bear it either.

So they didn't go to any of the other services.

Lydia and I attended all of them. Offering condolences and help. Knowing there was no help to give. Fearing that those other parents surely had to resent us because we had our children back.

We know how lucky we are.

Lucky doesn't *begin* to describe it.

We're lucky in other ways too.

Finding each other. No matter how it happened.

Korda and Fitzgerald, and Ellen Zito, were at all the services too, looking deeply, genuinely shocked.

439

Limbo and its sequel had been withdrawn from sale, we heard, all warehouse copies destroyed, and Korda and Fitzgerald had announced plans for a major project aimed at helping troubled teenagers, to be funded by Eryx Software, in the names of the victims. Not before lawyer Tillman had issued a statement stressing that neither his clients nor the corporation bore any responsibility for the actions of their former business partner, Hal Hawthorne.

'Probably got a new game ready to roll,' I remarked to Lydia, after we heard about the project. 'All that self-sacrifice should whip up enough positive spin to make up for the bad PR.'

'I don't know,' she said. 'They looked very bleak at the funerals.'

'I should *hope*,' I said.

Rianna and Robbie have been seeing each other as often as possible.

Lydia and I are happy for them to be good friends, though anything more than that, we fear, could become complicated. Especially if their relationship were to lead to a parting of the ways, as most teenage involvements inevitably do.

Complicated, I mean, in view of our *own* growing relationship.

Maybe that makes us selfish. I just hate the thought of unhappiness creeping in, getting between us, spoiling what we have. What I hope we're *going* to have, in time. Family.

One family.

As it is, as much as I love Robbie, I sometimes fret about Rianna spending so much time with the person with whom she shared the greatest terrors of her young life. I wonder if it might be healthier for her to cut off from the memories.

Norman Baum says I worry unnecessarily. We still live in different cities, he says. It'll work itself out, he says.

Wise words, I guess.

Rianna tells me I'm *totally* wrong, tells me that Robbie's the best person in the world for her to spend time with. The only one who really understands.

But I'm the one who runs into her room at night when she wakes up screaming.

She admitted to me a while ago that she dreams about being Dakota almost every night, and that most times the dreams are nightmares.

Sometimes, though, she says, she wakes up smiling.

Because she's been dreaming about Steel coming to save her.

Ella's changed through it all, too. The childish tantrums seem gone forever, but so has that prematurely grown-up phase. She clings to me more now, and to her big sister and Kim – claims not to care, but doesn't like letting any of us out of her sight for too long.

I know how she feels.

I don't have nightmares too often, but that's mostly because I don't get much sleep. I'm thirty-eight years old, and I never had problems like this when I was five. But these nights, I'm almost afraid to put out the light.

Except for those nights I get to spend with Lydia.

Those nights when we're all together, under one roof.

Those nights, I think we all feel safer.

A SELECTION OF NOVELS AVAILABLE
FROM JUDY PIATKUS (PUBLISHERS) LIMITED

THE PRICES BELOW WERE CORRECT AT THE TIME OF GOING TO PRESS.
HOWEVER JUDY PIATKUS (PUBLISHERS) LIMITED RESERVE THE RIGHT TO
SHOW NEW RETAIL PRICES ON COVERS WHICH MAY DIFFER FROM THOSE
PREVIOUSLY ADVERTISED IN THE TEXT OR ELSEWHERE.

0 7499 3214 7	**Blind Fear**	*Hilary Norman*	£5.99
0 7499 3167 1	**Lip Service**	*M. J. Rose*	£6.99
0 7499 3267 8	**In Fidelity**	*M. J. Rose*	£6.99
0 7499 3118 3	**The Angels of Russia**	*Patricia le Roy*	£6.99
0 7499 3112 4	**One Hundred and One Ways**	*Mako Yoshikawa*	£6.99
0 7499 3116 7	**Stigmata**	*Phyllis Perry*	£6.99

All Piatkus titles are available from:

www.piatkus.co.uk

or by contacting our sales department on

0800 454816

Free postage and packing in the UK

(on orders of two books or more)